MW01128476

WOLF'S BANE

Book One: The Empire's Corps
Book Two: No Worse Enemy
Book Three: When The Bough Breaks
Book Four: Semper Fi
Book Five: The Outcast
Book Six: To The Shores
Book Seven: Reality Check
Book Eight: Retreat Hell
Book Nine: The Thin Blue Line
Book Ten: Never Surrender
Book Eleven: First To Fight
Book Twelve: They Shall Not Pass
Book Thirteen: Culture Shock
Book Fourteen: Wolf's Bane

WOLF'S BANE

CHRISTOPHER G. NUTTALL

The characters and events portrayed in this book are fictitious. Any similarity to real persons, living or dead, is coincidental and not intended by the author.

Text copyright © 2018 Christopher G. Nuttall
All rights reserved.
No part of this book may be reproduced, or stored in a retrieval system, or transmitted in any form or by any means, electronic, mechanical, photocopying, recording, or otherwise, without express written permission of the publisher.

ISBN-13: 9781983509889
ISBN-10: 1983509884

http://www.chrishanger.net
http://chrishanger.wordpress.com/
http://www.facebook.com/ChristopherGNuttall

Cover by Alexander Chau
(www.alexanderchau.co.uk)

All Comments Welcome!

A NOTE FROM THE AUTHOR

As always, I would be grateful for any spelling corrections, grammar suggestions, nitpicking and suchlike. Please send reports directly to my email address or through Amazon.

Thanks for reading! If you liked the book, please write a review. They help to boost sales.

CGN

PROLOGUE

From: *The Day After: The Post-Empire Universe and its Wars.* Professor Leo Caesius. Avalon University Press. 46PE.

Materially speaking, the Battle of Corinthian - technically, the Corinthian Campaign - was not a decisive encounter. Wolfbane did not lose enough men and materiel to ensure its defeat, nor did the Commonwealth gain enough of an advantage to reasonably claim to have the upper hand. The loss of hundreds of thousands of soldiers, spacers and civilians did not affect the balance of power. In many ways, the battle was as meaningless as the skirmishes over Cantor, a stage-one colony that swapped hands a dozen times during the course of the war.

But, politically, the Commonwealth won the Battle of Corinthian.

For the first time, the Commonwealth lured the Wolves into fighting on terrain of its own choosing, using its technological advantages to offset the enemy advantages in men, machinery and firepower. Admiral Singh, now unquestioned ruler of the Wolfbane Consortium, bore the sole blame for a campaign that cost hundreds of thousands of lives and destroyed many of Wolfbane's most powerful military formations. And while her position was - on the surface - secure - she knew as well as anyone else that her defeat might lead to her fall from grace. Resuming the offensive, therefore, was simply impossible.

It must have been frustrating to Singh to know - as she did - that the Wolves still held a considerable advantage in military tonnage. A direct strike at Avalon itself might have ended the war in their favour, despite the growing array of firepower the Commonwealth had assembled to defend its capital. A noted military theorist like her - like most admirals of the late Empire, Singh's experience in extensive naval combat was purely theoretical - could hardly have failed to note the possibilities, all the more so as uncovering Wolfbane would not have weakened her position notably. And yet, launching such an offensive was politically impossible.

And so the war paused, while the universe held its breath.

The Commonwealth, too, was aware of the weakness of its position. Technologically, it held a considerable advantage; materially, it was outnumbered and outmatched. The Wolves could afford to lose more than the Commonwealth in any major battle - indeed, the loss ratio in almost all major encounters was two-to-one in the Commonwealth's favour - and production of the new weapons and technology was hardly keeping up with demand. Given time, Singh and her allies would rebalance themselves, purge the naysayers, and resume the offensive.

Worse, there were rumours that the Wolves were developing their own advanced weapons and technologies. While Singh had been badly worried by her first - and bruising - encounters with Commonwealth weapons, she was too experienced a naval officer to allow herself to panic. The Commonwealth had surprised her, true, but it had not produced a single workable silver bullet, a weapon that would render the entire pre-collapse Imperial Navy obsolete at a stroke. Given time, she told her allies, the Commonwealth's advantages could be negated and their weapons duplicated. And she was right. It was ruefully acknowledged by the Commonwealth - during and after the war - that the new weapons were never as advantageous in the field as their designers proclaimed.

The window of opportunity for taking the offensive, for knocking the Wolves back on their heels, was therefore closing rapidly. For all its advantages, the Commonwealth might still lose the war - and with it, all hopes of replacing the fallen Empire with something better, something that would weather any future collapses with ease. The fate of the war - and humanity itself - hung in the balance.

Fortunately, Edward Stalker had a plan.

CHAPTER ONE

Admiral Rani Singh had never been one to despair. She'd worked her way up the ranks through ability alone, even though jealous and amorous superiors had done their best to put her down. She still smiled whenever she remembered Admiral Bainbridge, the randy old goat who'd done his level best to destroy her career after she'd declined his advances. The old man had transferred her to System Command, never realising the power he'd put into her hands until it was far too late. She'd never given up, even when she'd lost Corinthian to the Commonwealth and had to flee to Wolfbane. She was mistress of a hundred stars, unchallenged ruler of a small empire of her own…and weaker, perhaps, than she dared admit, even to herself.

She stood at the window, staring out over the city. Tryon blazed with light, towering skyscrapers reaching up to touch the very edge of the atmosphere. Governor Brown, whatever one could say about him, had done an excellent job of putting Wolfbane's economy back on a sound footing. The corporations were happy, the network of industrial nodes were humming along, producing an endless supply of everything she needed to extend her empire still further. And if someone didn't want to acknowledge Wolfbane as the new mistress of the universe, she had more than enough firepower to crack any defences. Opening up hundreds of colonies for her corporations had been easy.

And yet, the war with the Commonwealth had taken a dark turn.

She gritted her teeth in frustration. She'd talked Governor Brown into starting the war, pointing out that the Commonwealth's growing technical superiority would eventually turn it into a major competitor, perhaps even a threat. And she'd been right. If anything, she'd underestimated the Commonwealth's advantages. But Governor Brown had been assassinated, she'd taken command…and made a serious mistake.

Rani admitted that, in the privacy of her own mind. She'd allowed herself to be duped, believe - because she'd *wanted* to believe - what her intelligence agents were saying. And, perhaps, because she wanted to return to Corinthian, to recover the world she'd lost so many years ago. But it had been a mistake. Hundreds of thousands of lives had been lost, dozens of formations had been smashed…

She lifted her head, staring at the towers. They seemed to look back at her, mockingly. She had no illusions about the industrialists who ruled the planet, who bowed to her only because they feared her. Governor Brown had known how to talk to them, how to balance the dozens of competing factions in order to keep them happy and himself on top, but Rani didn't have that advantage. Diplomacy had never been *her* strong suit. The industrialists respected her military might, appreciated her willingness to use force in defence of their interests, but they didn't *like* her. And now they thought she was weak, she knew all too well, they would be plotting against her.

And I can't strike first without losing the war, she thought, grimly. She drew herself upright, centring herself. *They'll rip the industrial base to shreds if I try to purge them.*

She lowered her gaze, peering down into the darkness below the glowing towers. Wolfbane had a large and growing population, a population that was only kept in line through liberal applications of the carrot and the stick. Governor Brown hadn't helped by conscripting every technical expert for a hundred light years and transporting them to Wolfbane, forcing them to work to maintain and expand the planet's industrial base. There *had* been a shortage of trained technicians, Rani recalled, but in the long run it had been a mistake. Countless workers now had good reason to be angry at the regime, the skills to turn their anger into action…

…*And* they were too valuable for her to purge. She'd started training programs, of course, handing out rewards like candy to anyone who passed, but the demand for trained manpower was endless. Rani couldn't afford a crackdown, even on men and women her security officers *knew* to be subversives. She could only hope that she could keep the lid on long enough to win the war, which would allow her more freedom of movement. And yet, she knew that wasn't going to be easy. Resuming the offensive, after Corinthian, would probably provoke open rebellion.

She looked up, her eyes seeking out the starships and orbital battlestations protecting the planet. The corporations had demanded that she protect their homeworld - despite the risk of a major attack being almost nil - and she hadn't been able to refuse them. But it tied down hundreds of starships she could have taken to Avalon, if she'd had a completely free hand. It wasn't as if the orbital stations *couldn't* protect the planet...

And I'm down here in the fortress, she thought. *I can't even go back to orbit without looking weak.*

Her lips twitched in amusement. Governor Brown - or one of his predecessors - had created the fortress, apparently under the delusion that it represented an effective defence. Rani supposed it would be, against unarmed civilian rioters or even enemy soldiers, but it would be worse than useless against an enemy who gained control of the high orbitals. Hell, it was just a big target, one that would attract KEWs like flies to rotting meat. Unless, of course, Wolfbane managed to duplicate the Commonwealth's force field generator. Now *that* would give whoever had ordered the fortress the last laugh...

...And Governor Brown hadn't even been *in* the fortress when he'd been assassinated.

She turned, composing herself, as she heard the door open behind her. Only a handful of people had access to her private apartments, although she was honest enough with herself to admit that even the most *extreme* precautions wouldn't keep out a truly determined assassin or stop someone transporting a nuke into firing position. The fortress was designed to take a nuclear strike - the designer had layered the building with starship-grade hullmetal - but she had her doubts. Civilians, in her experience, rarely understood the realities of combat.

"Admiral," Paula Bartholomew said. "I have an intelligence update."

Rani nodded, tiredly. Paula was loyal, she *had* to be loyal. She'd betrayed General James Stubbins, then the Commonwealth...there was a good chance that, if someone found out the truth, that they'd charge Paula with betraying Governor Brown, too. Rani disliked using someone with such flexible loyalties, someone who might desert her at once if she were offered something better, but she had no choice. Besides, Paula was smart enough to understand the weakness of her own position. *No one* would defend her if Rani decided to have her killed.

They made an odd couple, Rani had to admit. She was tall, dark-skinned and dark-eyed; she held herself with a military bearing that was an unspoken challenge to every man in the room. She'd learnt, back at the Naval Academy, that the key to earning respect was to do nothing that might *dampen* that respect. Admiral Bainbridge's promised rewards would have been worthless, if her subordinates had believed - correctly - that she'd prostituted herself to earn them. And Paula was short, blonde and pretty in a way that owed everything to the body-shops. Her shirt was unbuttoned just enough to reveal a hint of cleavage, drawing the male gaze and short-circuiting the male mind. Rani was less impressed with that than Paula might have hoped - power was more interesting than sex, in her opinion - but she had to admit that it worked. Anyone who underestimated Paula would regret it.

She met Paula's eyes. "Spit it out."

Paula looked back at her, evenly. "Mouganthu and Hernandez had a meeting this afternoon," she said. "We couldn't get a bug into the meeting chamber itself, but we do know it lasted for at least three hours before Hernandez returned to his aircar and flew home."

Rani lifted her eyebrows. "And you're only telling me about this now?"

"Mouganthu had his security staff put the tower in lockdown," Paula replied. "Our agent didn't have a chance to send a message until 1900."

"I see," Rani said. "Were they alone?"

"Apparently," Paula said. "Our agent wasn't in a good position to be certain."

Rani nodded, turning back to the window. Mouganthu Tower was clearly visible in the distance, glowing with light against the dark sky. Hernandez Tower was on the other side of the fortress, out of sight. Mouganthu and Hernandez…two of the most powerful men on the planet, perhaps in the sector. Their meeting - and a secret meeting, one without aides or secretaries - boded ill for her. And yet, she could do nothing. She couldn't *insist* they opened their doors to her spies, could she?

She looked back at Paula. "And the others?"

"Nothing out of the ordinary, as far as we can tell," Paula said. "Tallyman may have been invited to the meeting - there was some encrypted traffic between the towers - but we don't know for sure."

"Of course not," Rani said.

She shook her head in annoyance. The Wolfbane Consortium was *built* on genteel - and sometimes not so genteel - competition between corporations. Governor Brown had *encouraged* it, insisting that it kept them sharp and himself on top. But he'd created one hell of a problem for his successor. She knew her intelligence staff would decrypt the messages eventually - she was sure of it - but by then it might be too late.

Or the messages will look innocuous, on the surface, she thought. *We won't understand the hidden meanings.*

"Keep an eye on the three of them," she ordered. "And see if you can find an incentive for Straphang or Wu to cooperate with us."

"Wu is bidding to get the next set of naval contracts," Paula said. "Straphang is facing financial troubles and probably trying to reduce her exposure. We could probably make them both decent offers."

She hesitated. "But we can't offer anything that would be *completely* convincing."

Rani nodded, irked. The corporate leaderships were practically an aristocracy in their own right, just like the never-to-be-sufficiently damned Grand Senate. She was surprised Governor Brown hadn't created a peerage system for them. But, whatever their titles, the leaderships kept one eye on the future at all times. They'd make preparations for all eventualities, including one where she fell from power or was brutally overthrown. And they certainly wouldn't commit themselves to her…

"Do it," she ordered. Keeping as many directors as possible on her side was important, at least until the war was won. "And then…"

Her wristcom bleeped. "Admiral, this is Tobias," a voice said. "I have an update for you. I think you'll like it."

"I hope you're right," Rani said. She glanced at Paula, who shrugged. "I'll meet you in my office, half an hour from now."

Professor Tobias Jameson was a young man who looked older, thanks to the abuse he'd suffered during his short career at Mouganthu Industries and then at the University of Wolfbane. He'd been very lucky, according to his file, to even get a place in the university, after he'd upset his corporate sponsors. Insisting that there was a better way to do things - that modern tech hadn't reached its limits - had won him no friends. Ironically, it had also won him a job after Governor Brown had realised that the Empire was gone.

"Professor," Rani said. She liked and trusted him, insofar as she liked and trusted anyone these days. It hadn't saved Jameson from an extensive security check before he was allowed into her office. "I trust that you have good news for me?"

"I do," Jameson said.

He took control of the projector and displayed a set of holographic images. "As you know, we have concentrated a great deal of effort on finding ways to either counter or duplicate the Commonwealth's force field generator," he said. "This has not proven easy, Admiral. Some of our researchers are still in deep denial about the whole thing."

Rani snorted, rudely. She'd been in denial too, but it hadn't lasted. *Theory* might insist that force field generators were as plausible as alien invaders bent on fighting their way to Earth and crushing humanity; *practice* told her that force field generators were a reality. Her sensors hadn't had flights of fancy when they'd reported missiles striking the force fields and detonating harmlessly. If the Commonwealth ever ironed out the bugs - if they ever managed to produce a force field that wrapped the entire starship in a bubble - the war would come to a very quick and unpleasant end.

And our researchers refuse to believe that it is even real, she thought, tiredly. *They don't have the right mindset to keep pushing the limits of the possible.*

"Thankfully, we do have *some* researchers who dug deep into the theory behind starship drives and suchlike," Jameson continued. "Their conclusion, after working through a number of computer models, was that the force field is *actually* a manipulation of the starship's *drive* field. In a sense, they have converted the standard drive field into a rocket - and diverted the rest of the output into a forward-facing force shield."

Paula leaned forward. "Wouldn't that slow the ship? I mean…the drive is pointing forwards. Right?"

"According to our computer models, probably not," Jameson said. "The missile - or whatever hits the force field - does not hit a solid barrier. Instead, it is torn apart by a series of tiny, but intense gravimetric fluctuations. The same is largely true of energy weapons, we think. An energy beam would be scattered long before it reached the hull."

He paused. "This wouldn't necessarily be true of the large-scale force shield they used on Corinthian," he added. "They'd have fewer concerns about shooting back in that case."

Rani nodded in irritation. "However it works," she asked, "can you duplicate the system?"

Jameson hesitated. "Yes and no," he admitted. "We…we don't have the technical skill yet to…to make the system actually work."

"But you know how it works," Paula protested.

"The Commonwealth Navy has effectively designed its own real-space drive," Jameson said, flatly. "Their drive units are considerably more flexible - more *innovative* - than anything the Imperial Navy ever designed, let alone put into production. I do not believe that we can rebuild a standard drive unit to project a force field, not without tearing the whole thing apart and rebuilding it from scratch. We are working on designing our own drive system, but it will take months to work out the bugs and put it into production."

Rani ground her teeth, but she couldn't say she was surprised. The Imperial Navy had simplified everything over the last three hundred years, ever since technological advancement had come to a halt. Most starship engineers *really* did nothing more than removing a broken component and replacing it with something new, if - of course - there happened to be one in stock. And God help the crew if the automated diagnostic system happened to fail. The components *were* over-engineered - they had to be - but they couldn't be repaired. A starship that ran out of spare parts was doomed.

And training up better engineers would take more time than we have, she thought. *They'd have to be taught how to think first.*

She pushed her frustration aside. Taking it out on Jameson would feel good, but it would be cruel and ultimately worthless. It certainly wouldn't get her anywhere. She'd learnt - the hard way - just how much damage a single yes-man could do. If the Grand Senators had learned that lesson, she suspected, the Empire might not have collapsed.

"However, we did come up with something else," Jameson added. "Actually, *two* other technological surprises. Both of them are built on missile drive systems."

He altered the display, showing a pair of modified missiles. "It's actually easier to fiddle with a missile drive unit," he explained. "The drives are cruder and considerably overpowered, if only because they're not expected to last very long. Their additional power reserves gives them a chance to reformat their drive fields before burn-out."

Rani nodded, impatiently. "And you believe we can use this?"

"We can," Jameson confirmed. He held out a datapad. "They may not be enough to give us a decisive advantage, Admiral, but they *will* give the Commonwealth a fright."

"I hope so," Rani said.

She sighed, inwardly, as she scanned the datapad. Technological development proceeded in fits and starts, it seemed. There was nothing to be gained by threatening the researchers with dire punishments if they failed to produce. Hell, they couldn't be blamed for their problems. The Empire had abandoned research and development centuries ago. Rediscovering the scientific method alone had taken longer than she cared to think about.

And each research project costs, even if it fails, she thought, sourly. *They're drains we cannot afford.*

She looked up at him, feeling a flicker of hope. If he was right, if the technology actually worked, she might just have a chance.

"These weapons," she said. It was hard to keep the excitement out of her voice. "How quickly can they be produced?"

"We can modify existing stockpiles of missiles within a couple of weeks," Jameson said. "I believe the *finalised* version, once we start churning them out of the industrial nodes, will be a great deal neater, but..."

Rani forced herself to calm down. They hadn't discovered a silver bullet, even if the missiles worked as advertised. And they might not. She had to keep that in mind, no matter how excited she was. But...

"Start adapting a number of missiles," she ordered, shortly. She didn't have time to be *too* careful. "And then prepare briefing notes for my officers."

"Of course, Admiral," Jameson said.

And if these weapons do turn the tide, Rani thought, *I can deal with my enemies here at leisure.*

CHAPTER TWO

"Edward," Gaby Cracker said. She sounded tired, very tired. "This is your son."

Ed could hardly breathe as she held out a bundle of cloth. A tiny face peered out, blue eyes flickering from side to side. He took it, as gingerly as he would hold a live hand grenade, and stared down at the wisp of dark hair. Douglas Bainbridge Stalker was small, so small that it seemed impossible he would grow into a young man. The baby was tiny, yet perfect. He was the most beautiful thing Ed had ever seen.

He held the baby in one hand and gently pressed his finger against the baby's palm. A moment later, the baby's fingers curved around his. Ed felt a...a *protectiveness* he'd never felt before, even back when he'd been trapped in the Undercity. He knew, at that moment, that he would do anything for the child, anything at all. He'd be a better father than *his* father had ever been.

You won't lack for anything, he promised the tiny newborn. The baby smiled back at him, turning his head very slightly. *And you will be protected from the world.*

He passed the baby back to Gaby, who put it to her breast. "The doctors say he's a healthy child," she said. "No genetic problems or birth defects."

Ed nodded, slumping in relief. Birth defects were alarmingly common on Earth, a result of the polluted environment and short-term genetic manipulation. He'd seen children who'd died before they reached their first birthday, just because they needed medical support to survive; he'd seen older children who'd been mocked, beaten or killed just for being different. He'd feared the worst for his son, even though Douglas had been born on Avalon with the very best of medical care. A time bomb lurking in his genetic code might have exploded when his son was born.

"That's good," he said. He met her eyes. "I'm sorry I wasn't there..."

"We knew it was a possibility," Gaby said. She'd grown up amongst insurgents. She knew the demands war could put on a person's time. "I don't blame you."

"I blame myself," Ed admitted. A father *should* watch the birth. "I should have been there."

Gaby reached out and squeezed his hand. "It wasn't your fault," she said. Her lips curved into a smile. "And you came home victorious."

Ed sighed. "At a steep price," he said. "Too many people will never come home at all."

He sobered. Avalon was celebrating - he'd passed a dozen parties on his way to the hospital - but the funerals would start soon enough. Thousands of young men would never come home, never even be buried on their native soil. Too many bodies had simply been dumped into mass graves, following the final battle and surrender on Corinthian. Maybe they'd be exhumed, once the war was over; their remains logged and identified, then transported back to their homeworlds. Or maybe their families would never have closure, never know for *sure* what had happened to their young men. War always came with a steep cost. Too many politicians had forgotten that, over the last three thousand years.

They won't forget again, he promised himself. *Military experience is practically an unspoken requirement for political office here.*

He forced himself to look at the child. "Did you...did you name him properly?"

"As we agreed," Gaby said.

Ed allowed himself a moment of relief. It was traditional, on Avalon, to name children after dead parents and grandparents. She'd been a little surprised when Ed had asked to name their son after his first Drill Instructor instead of his biological father, but she'd gone along with it. Ed had been relieved. His *real* father was a mystery, one of several possible names. His mother had never cared which of her affairs had resulted in pregnancy. Ed didn't know who had fathered him and didn't really care.

The asshole certainly hadn't stuck around after the deed to bring up his young son.

"Thank you," he said, quietly.

Gaby laughed. "Just remember you're changing him for the next few weeks," she said. She sounded tired, again. "He needs to be changed at least ten times a day."

Ed gave her a long look. Gaby had always been beautiful to him; a redheaded woman who'd been raised on a farm and then in a series of insurgent camps, strong enough to fight and smart enough to understand reality. And diplomatic too, diplomatic enough to convince the Crackers not to continue the war when they were getting most of what they wanted, then to convince a number of other worlds to join the Commonwealth...

And yet, she looked tired and worn.

"I will," he promised. "Are you all right?"

"I'm fine," Gaby said. She shot him a mischievous glance. "You do realise that women have been giving birth for hundreds of thousands of years?"

Her tired smile widened. "The doctors say that everything went as well as could be expected," she added. "I'm tired, but...otherwise, everything is fine. I should be fit to return to work by the end of the week."

Ed's eyes narrowed. "Are you going to?"

"I promised I would see out my term," Gaby said. "And oversee the next set of elections. A couple of peace parties have been gaining ground over the last few months, mainly on the grounds that we can come to terms with Wolfbane. I don't want to let them get too entrenched."

She sighed. "We might be able to come to terms with a decent government, but there's no reason to believe that Wolfbane will give us good terms," she added. "They'll be more likely to use the peace as a chance to prepare for the next war."

Ed nodded in grim agreement. Neither Governor Brown's corporate state nor Admiral Singh's military dictatorship could co-exist with the Commonwealth. The Commonwealth's technological advances, if nothing else, would practically guarantee a renewed war sooner rather than later. Governor Brown's backing, according to the debriefings, had depended on keeping the corporations happy, which meant keeping down the competition. Advanced technology would undermine their dominance quicker than open war.

And Admiral Singh has the same problem, he thought. *This is not a dispute that can be solved through peace talks and minor concessions.*

"Peace," he said. Douglas Bainbridge - the original Douglas Bainbridge - had been fond of pointing out the absurdity of any number of peace agreements that rarely lasted long enough to matter. "A period of cheating between periods of fighting."

"A saying that dates all the way back to pre-space days," Gaby said. She'd read a great deal of political theory since the end of the insurgency, although she'd complained at the time that none of it seemed to be written by anyone with genuine experience. "We have to end the war on decent terms."

"I have an idea for that," Ed said. He looked down at Douglas. The baby had gone to sleep, nestled against Gaby's breast. "But we can discuss it later."

"We will," Gaby agreed. She adjusted her position, slightly. "I *am* looking forward to walking around without a pregnant belly, even if I do keep threatening to topple over."

"Once the doctors release you, you can go straight home," Ed said. "But not until then."

Gaby stuck out her tongue. "This from the person who sneaked out of a hospital bed and climbed out the window to escape the doctors."

"Said person was also deafened by his CO and then ordered back to bed," Ed said. He'd been injured before, more times than he cared to think about, but he'd never *liked* staying in hospital. The doctors had always struck him as being absurdly careful. He'd known he was fine, damn it! "You're a little more fragile."

"Just you wait," Gaby said, rudely. "I'll show you just how fragile I am."

Ed sighed as he sat down on the bed. He wanted - he *needed* - to keep her safe. She was his lover, the mother of his child…he didn't want her to come to any harm. He wanted to protect her from everything, even herself. And yet, he knew Gaby would hate him if he tried to wrap her in cotton wool. She'd been fighting in an insurgency since she'd turned twelve, while Ed himself had still been trapped in the Undercity until he reached sixteen. The young Gaby would have laughed at the young Ed…

Or regarded him as a brutal barbarian, Ed thought. He'd grown up in the Undercity…and he'd never realised, not until he went through Boot Camp, just how many of its attitudes he'd imbibed. The distance between him and the thugs he'd thrashed, during his sole visit to the Undercity after Boot Camp, wasn't as big as he liked to think. *Gaby did far more with her childhood than I ever did with mine.*

He looked at the baby and felt another surge of protectiveness. Douglas would have every advantage Ed could get for him, whatever it took. He'd grow up on a farm, where he would learn to work from a very early age; he'd be taught to fight, to defend himself and others…he'd be taught to read and write and think for himself. He'd have all the advantages that Ed had been denied, thirty-seven years ago. And he would never have to look into the darkness and make the choice between becoming victim or victimiser.

"You can't start dressing him in BDUs yet," Gaby said, wryly. "He's barely a week old."

Ed smiled back at her. "Am I that transparent?"

"Just a little," Gaby said. "What father *doesn't* want his son to follow in his footsteps?"

Mine, Ed thought. *The bastard might not even know he had a son.*

He looked away, feeling oddly lost. His father was a mystery. There was no way to know, particularly now Earth was dead, who his father had been, let alone if he had survived long enough to watch the planet die. Ed was sure - fairly sure - that he had never followed in his father's footsteps. The Marine Corps - Douglas Bainbridge and his fellow Drill Instructors - had been his *real* parents. He'd followed in *their* footsteps, not those left by his biological father. In the end, God alone knew who his father had been.

"I'll be happy, as long as he is a honourable man," he said, finally. Honour - and trust - had been in short supply in the Undercity. It still surprised him, somehow, at just how strongly trust pervaded the marines. But then, anyone who *broke* trust would be lucky if they *merely* got dishonourably discharged and kicked out. "And you won't let him be anything else."

"I'll be setting the best example possible by resigning at the end of my term," Gaby agreed, sardonically. "And I'll be glad to retire."

"Not for long," Ed predicted. "You'll want to go back to work soon enough."

"My father's farm is practically dead," Gaby said. "I want to restore it to life."

Ed nodded in agreement. The farm had been seized after the end of the first Cracker Rebellion, but its new owners had never done anything with it. They'd feared, probably correctly, that their neighbours would turn on them. Gaby had taken him there once, after the end of the insurgency. The farm had been an overgrown ruin - the farmhouse had been damaged by the elements - but it still looked better than the Undercity. But then, the *Slaughterhouse* had looked better than the Undercity.

Of course it did, he thought. *The bar wasn't set very high.*

"I'm sure Douglas will like it," he said. "A farm will be a very good place to grow up."

"That's because you've never grown up on one," Gaby said. "It has its advantages and disadvantages."

She met his eyes. "Are you going to join me?"

Ed hesitated. He'd never really anticipated leaving the Marine Corps. The Corps had given him a life, one he didn't intend to waste. He'd always expected that he would eventually be retired from active duty and reassigned to the Slaughterhouse, where he would spend the rest of his days teaching new recruits how to avoid *his* mistakes. Assuming, of course, that he survived. The risk of a violent death had overshadowed his life from the moment his mother had brought him into the world.

And yet...he had a son now. He couldn't just leave his son, could he? How many boys in the Undercity might have been saved, if they'd had a strong male figure to guide them as they grew into adulthood? How many little barbarians would have been kept from turning into monsters, if they'd had someone to look up to? Douglas was his son, not a random child...Ed had a duty to him, even if his own father had forsaken it. He couldn't go off on a deployment that might last months, if not years...

But other families had the same problem, he thought. *They coped, didn't they?*

"I should," he said.

Gaby touched his hand. "Make your choice," she said. "But stick to it, whatever it is."

Ed nodded. He *loved* the corps. It was his family. And yet, he had another family now.

Gaby can't restore the farm on her own, he thought. *She'll need help.*

He'd never really imagined living on a farm, even though marines joked all the time about buying farms. Hell, retired marines often took land packages from colonial development consortiums, using their military experience to support their new homeworlds. But this was different. He was more than just a simple rifleman. He was the uniformed commander of the Commonwealth's armed forces. He was…

And we need to know if they can survive without me, he thought. He'd worked hard to avoid the problems that had bedevilled the Empire in its final years, but the only way to *know* if he'd succeeded was to take a step back and see what happened. *And if it doesn't work, we'll have time to fix it.*

He swallowed. "When the war is over," he said, unable to escape the sense that he was about to jump into the unknown, "I'll go on detached duty."

Gaby leaned forward. "Be very sure," she said. "I don't want you to resent it."

"We'll see," Ed said. He *liked* the military life. But…he had a son to raise. "I can always reapply when Douglas reaches adulthood."

"Yeah," Gaby said. She tapped her belly. "By then, he may have some brothers and sisters too."

Ed nodded, ruefully. He'd had four siblings and a single mother, all crammed together in an apartment barely large enough for two grown men. The sheer lack of privacy, of *space*, had threatened to drive him mad. He'd certainly never considered having more than one child, particularly when there were no benefits for growing families. But Avalon had plenty of room. A farmhouse large enough to house ten kids - to give each kid a room larger than his apartment on Earth - wouldn't cost *that* much. And the kids would be safe…

This isn't Earth, he thought. *Dangerous criminals are not coddled here.*

"After the war," he said. He took a breath. "If we win, of course."

"If we lose, we'll just have to launch another insurgency," Gaby said.

Her voice was casual. But Ed knew it wouldn't be easy. Admiral Singh would be a more dangerous opponent than the Civil Guard or someone who wanted to keep the planet reasonably intact. She might just decide to scorch Avalon clean of life as a drastic example to everyone else. Why not? Obliterating all the advanced technology - and all the workers who produced it - might just work in her favour. She'd certainly be in a position to control how the new technology flowed into galactic society.

And if she wins the war, there will be no one left to extract revenge, Ed thought. The Empire had shied away from mass planetary bombardment, while Wolfbane knew that the Commonwealth would retaliate in kind for any such attack. But if the Commonwealth lost the war, Admiral Singh would have a free hand. *Everyone will be too cowed to fight back.*

There was a knock at the door. "Come!"

He looked up as Command Sergeant Gwendolyn Patterson entered the room. "Colonel," she said. "The remaining troops have been off-loaded and given liberty for the next two days."

Ed nodded. The troops - *the survivors,* his thoughts mocked him - would have a good time of it. None of them, even the ones who hadn't seen direct action, would have to pay for a drink for the next few days. They'd certainly have no trouble getting laid. But then, they'd had very little to celebrate over the last year or so. Corinthian was the first unambiguous victory the Commonwealth had enjoyed since the war had begun.

"Thank you, Sergeant," he said.

Gwendolyn looked at the baby. "He has your eyes, sir."

Ed eyed her, suspiciously. In anyone else, he would have suspected flattery. Douglas's baby eyes didn't look anything like his. And yet, Gwendolyn was not one to flatter anyone. She had never hesitated to tell him when he was on the verge of doing something stupid, particularly after they'd been cut off from the Empire. He'd learned to value it as he'd grown into his role.

"Thank you," he said, resisting the urge to suggest that *she* have her eyes checked. "Did the Council have anything to say?"

"You're expected to give a preliminary briefing in two days," Gwendolyn said. "They wanted to summon you earlier, but I pointed out that you were meeting your baby for the first time."

"Very good," Ed said.

He grinned at Gaby. "Order the Strategic Planning Cell to be ready for a meeting in three days," he added. "We have an operation to plan."

CHAPTER THREE

"It's hard to imagine the colonel having a baby," Brigadier Jasmine Yamane said, as she walked towards the command complex. "He...he never seemed to have any life outside the military."

Emmanuel Alves gave her a sidelong look. "I imagine he would have needed some pretty odd modifications to carry and bear a child," he said. "Inserting a womb into his body would be tricky..."

Jasmine elbowed him. "You know what I mean," she said. "It's a change in his life."

"It happens all the time," Emmanuel countered. "People have babies; the babies grow into children and then adults and then the whole cycle repeats itself. And then people grow old and die."

"And end up as worm food," Jasmine said. She'd noted, in her will, that she wanted to be buried on her homeworld, but she knew that might not be possible. Her homeworld was lost somewhere in the darkness that had fallen over the Empire. "I still can't quite get my head round it."

Emmanuel looked at her. "Do you want children of your own?"

Jasmine hesitated. In truth, she'd never really given it much thought. She'd had eggs removed and preserved when she'd entered the Slaughterhouse, just in case something happened to render her sterile, even though she'd assumed that her sisters would bring the next generation into the world. And yet...the Slaughterhouse was gone, if reports were to be believed. Her frozen eggs might have been destroyed or lost forever.

And my sisters might be gone too, she thought. *I might be the last of my family*.

"I don't know," she said. She made a mental note to have more eggs removed, if it was still possible. Some of the enhancement treatments she'd had over the years might have damaged her reproductive system. "Pregnancy *does* tend to put an end to a female marine's career."

"I suppose," Emmanuel agreed. "But you could always hire a surrogate or use an artificial womb."

"I could," Jasmine agreed. Artificial wombs were rare, outside High Society. Or at least they had *been* rare. Now, she supposed the Commonwealth could put them into mass production if it wished. "Or I could give up on the idea altogether."

"Adopt a few orphans," Emmanuel teased. "You'd have the children without doing the work."

"Prat," Jasmine said.

It wasn't a pleasant thought. The insurgency had created hundreds - perhaps thousands - of orphans, some of which had never found homes. God knew the former government hadn't had any real interest in *helping* the poor children, although some of the oldest had been sent out to various farms as indentured labour. They'd deserted after the end of the war, claiming all kinds of abuse. Far too many cases were still working their way through the courts.

She kept her face expressionless as they reached the guards on the door, who scanned and searched them before allowing them to step into the entrance. The guards looked professional enough, she decided, although they'd be foolish to show any signs of unprofessional behaviour on Castle Rock. Jasmine and most of the other guests had a duty to report careless or unprofessional guards, particularly when they were posted outside the most sensitive buildings on the island. No one, absolutely no one, had a right to enter without permission. The guards would have arrested her at once if she hadn't been on the guest list.

The inner door opened, revealing a long corridor leading to a small briefing room. Jasmine took a breath, tasting the faint scent of oily *newness* in the air, then led the way down to the entrance. Colonel Stalker, Command Sergeant Gwendolyn Patterson, General Crichton Mathis,

Colonel Kitty Stevenson, Commodore Mandy Caesius and a handful of others she didn't recognise were seated around a table, chatting quietly as they waited for the other guests. Jasmine cursed herself under her breath as she took her seat. Avalon wasn't as ultra-formal as Earth, thankfully, but being the last to arrive rarely looked good. People would notice, even though the meeting wasn't due to start for another five minutes.

She nodded to Mandy, who smiled back at her. The young redheaded girl had advanced by leaps and bounds since they'd first met, moving into space and climbing into command rank with nary a bump. It was the sort of advancement that would have been flat-out impossible in the Empire - unless one had excellent connections - but now, merit played a far greater role in determining who was promoted. Jasmine couldn't help hoping that it stayed that way, particularly as memories of the Empire faded. The younger generation might not understand just how easy it would be to fall into the trap that had doomed the Empire.

"Seal the room," Colonel Stalker ordered. He cleared his throat. "It is my duty to remind you that this meeting is classified *top secret*. Security protocols are now in effect. You may *not* discuss it with anyone without prior permission from myself. If anyone has any objection to invoking the security protocols" - his gaze lingered on Emmanuel for a long moment - "please leave the room now."

There was a long pause. Jasmine kept her expression under tight control. Emmanuel had proved himself, time and time again, but she knew that old habits die hard. Reporters were the natural enemy, as far as the military was concerned. The Empire's reporters had been more interested in scoops than anything else, sometimes even putting troops in danger or accepting enemy propaganda without question just to make sure they were the first to publish. Emmanuel was only tolerated because he *had* proved himself. Even then…

The Colonel will want full disclosure, eventually, she thought. *And Emmanuel will be the one who'll write the story.*

"Very good," Colonel Stalker said. He glanced at Colonel Kitty Stevenson. "Kitty?"

Kitty tapped a switch, displaying a familiar starchart. Jasmine stared at it, comparing to the one she'd seen two days ago. Nothing seemed to have changed, as far as she could tell; the enemy's advance seemed to have been stalled. But she knew, better than any civilian, that the map could easily mislead the unwary eye. Anything could have happened out amongst the stars and no one would know, until the courier boat arrived. The green stars along the front might have been invaded and occupied by now. There was no way to be entirely sure.

"The current state of play," Kitty said. She'd lost most of her accent, Jasmine noted, but traces of Earth still shone through her speech. "As of the last set of reports, Wolfbane has stopped all offensive operations beyond a handful of raids directed at our industrial nodes and convoys along the front line. Our own raiders have reported that the enemy appears to have assumed a defensive pose, although - naturally - we're not sure how long this will last."

"And it could have finished by now," General Crichton Mathis inserted.

"Yes, sir," Kitty agreed.

"Intelligence has been doing its best to assess what we've been told by defectors and POWs since the Battle of Corinthian," she continued. "Our current conclusion is that Admiral Singh's position has been weakened by the defeat, although we have no way to know how this particular crisis will be resolved. Obviously, our *ideal* solution would be an enemy civil war that weakens them badly, but we cannot be sure that this will happen. Given the ideological threat we represent to Wolfbane, it is quite possible that the corporations will rally behind Admiral Singh. They may feel that she is a lesser threat in the long term."

Jasmine nodded, curtly. She'd never met Admiral Singh, not face to face, but she had a certain admiration for her opponent. The woman had built an empire of her own and, when she'd lost it, had somehow managed to get control of another. Her record was sparse, but Jasmine had enough practice at reading between the lines to suspect that Admiral Singh had made powerful enemies. They hadn't been powerful enough to keep her down.

"Our overall assessment is that Wolfbane will be unable or unwilling to resume the offensive for at least six months," Kitty concluded. "They will, if nothing else, have to come to terms with the scale of the defeat. It will not be easy for them, particularly as we've been slipping our own propaganda into their planetary computer networks. They will not be able to conceal upwards of a hundred thousand soldiers dead or captured on Corinthian."

"There's never been anything to suggest that Singh worries about casualties," Mandy said, quietly.

"Her subordinates will," Kitty countered. "They'll certainly have to rebuild the shattered or destroyed military units before they can resume the offensive."

"Unless they decide to bypass planetary targets and resume their drive on Avalon," Mathis put in. "They don't *have* to crush resistance to the last man."

Jasmine was inclined to agree, but she suspected that Admiral Singh *wouldn't*. Resistance, even a low-level insurgency, looked bad, even when it was strategically valueless. Someone like Colonel Stalker - an experienced military officer - might ignore it, but someone without such experience might insist that all resistance be smashed flat. Admiral Singh couldn't afford to give up an occupied world, even when it was militarily useless, for fear of appearing weak. Her enemies wouldn't hesitate to take advantage of it.

"Perhaps," Colonel Stalker said. "Kitty, if you will continue...?"

Kitty nodded. "We believe that we will have a brief window of opportunity to take the offensive ourselves," she said. "Despite our recent victory - and technological development - they still have a fairly major advantage. However, if we take the offensive now, we will rock them back on their heels and hopefully crack their foundations."

"Risky," Mathis observed.

"Correct," Colonel Stalker said. "This one is for all the marbles."

Kitty sat down. Colonel Stalker rose, adjusting the display. Jasmine leaned forward, despite herself. Normally, a junior officer would make the presentation. A senior officer doing the legwork meant that matters had already been decided. And that meant...

"Our window of opportunity is narrower than it seems," Colonel Stalker said. "They do, as Kitty said, still have a fairly major military advantage. And, on the other hand, they will have time to duplicate our new weapons and put them into mass production. We've certainly given them enough incentive to try!"

"Each of our ships is worth two of theirs," Mandy protested.

"Yes, but they have *three* ships for every one of ours," Colonel Stalker pointed out. He sounded oddly amused. "At the same time, however, they do have weaknesses. Their society is held together by force. Wolfbane grabbed every star within a hundred light years as soon as Governor Brown died and just kept expanding. If the defectors are to be believed, most of those worlds are either rebellious or a drain on their resources."

"Meridian certainly was," Jasmine agreed. The Wolves had put a POW camp on the first-stage colony world, but little else. There hadn't been much point. Meridian simply hadn't had anything worth looting. They'd conscripted a handful of people with technical skills, but otherwise they'd simply left the planet alone. "Do you think we could convince the other worlds to rise in revolt?"

"They would if Wolfbane itself took a blow," Colonel Stalker said.

He adjusted the display, focusing on two stars. "According to our last intelligence analysis, the Wolves have been running military reinforcements and supply convoys through Titlark," he said. "They built the system up pretty heavily before the start of the war, then used it as the launching point for their first major offenses. Five worlds were invaded directly from Titlark during the opening hours of the war."

"I remember," Jasmine muttered. She'd been on Thule, in command of the CEF, when it had fallen. The Wolves hadn't treated their POWs *that* badly - she'd been taught to expect worse from terrorists and insurgents - but it had still been humiliating. "Do you think we can take the system?"

"I believe we can devastate the orbital defences and smash their supply depots," Colonel Stalker said. "If nothing else, that will force them to rethink their deployments and concentrate on protecting their rear areas. We might even have a chance to take a shot at a number of convoys when they come into the system, all fat and happy. However, this is merely the first step in my plan."

He altered the display again, focusing on a second star. Jasmine caught her breath as she realised he was pointing at Wolfbane itself.

"We have a brief window of opportunity," Colonel Stalker said. "I mean to strike directly at Wolfbane before they can react."

General Mathis coughed. "I was under the impression that such deep-strike operations were inherently dangerous."

"They are," Mandy confirmed. "However, if we were careful, we would be able to withdraw without being trapped and destroyed."

"We might also spark off an uprising," Colonel Stalker said. "If Admiral Singh is an unpopular ruler, she might be unseated if we offer reasonable peace terms. Even if she wasn't removed from office, we could do a great deal of damage to the system's industrial base and cripple the Wolves. They might drive us out of the system and still lose the war."

Jasmine considered it for a long moment. She was no expert on naval warfare, but she understood the basics. The sheer audacity of the operation would work in its favour - Admiral Singh, a classically-trained naval officer, wouldn't expect Colonel Stalker to gamble everything on one roll of the dice. And yet, they *would* be gambling everything. There was no way to avoid the simple fact that losing so many ships would be disastrous, particularly if the Wolves retained most of their mobile forces. Admiral Singh would have no choice, but to launch an immediate counterattack. It might win them the war.

"It would be risky," Kitty said. "But it would also bring home to the corporations just how dangerous the universe has become."

"Perhaps," Jasmine said. She saw the logic. The giant corporations were disconnected from the real world. Governor Brown had slanted the odds in their favour. Hell, the *Grand Senate* had slanted the odds in their favour. Giving their leaders a shock - enemy warships materialising in their system - might bring them to the discussion table. "It might also convince them that they have to fight to the death."

"Not if it was unprofitable," Kitty countered.

"We will plan two separate operations," Colonel Stalker said. "Operation Counter Punch will be *officially* aimed at Thule. If anything leaks out…well, Thule is a logical target. We did promise to return, after all. Unofficially, we'll be bypassing Thule and heading straight for Titlark. We'll punch out the defences, then - officially - fade back into the Commonwealth.

"Operation Home Run will take us all the way to Wolfbane," he added. "If…if we lose too many ships during Counter Punch, we'll cancel that part of the operation and raid a number of smaller enemy targets instead. If not…then we'll go all the way.

"I shouldn't have to remind you that it is of the utmost importance that our true targets remain classified. The enemy must *not* have any warning of our intended destinations. We will be using our double-agents to try to convince them of our planned targets, but after Corinthian they may not believe our agents are actually on their side."

Jasmine had to smile, despite her concerns. She disliked intelligence operations, although she'd handled them a couple of times. It was a shadowy world, where treachery and betrayal was as commonplace as hot air. No one would believe a double-agent who'd misled them, even if it *was* an accident. The Wolves would be wise to assume that their agents had been compromised from the beginning. Admiral Singh would certainly refuse to listen to anyone who told her the truth.

And our plans are chancy, she thought, grimly. She was no stranger to the torrent of information that flowed into listening ears, ranging from certain truths to absurd rumours and utter nonsense. *Admiral Singh might dismiss any reports on those grounds alone.*

Mathis coughed. "Am I to assume that the decision has already been taken?"

"It has," Colonel Stalker said. His voice was very calm. "The War Cabinet met last night."

Jasmine glanced at Emmanuel. He looked as surprised as she felt. The War Cabinet normally took longer, much longer, to come to a decision. Avalon and the Commonwealth was generally better at keeping secrets than the Grand Senate - it helped that most of the representatives had seen war themselves - but there *had* been leaks. She wondered, suddenly, if the colonel had told them the full story. The representatives might not have been told about Home Run.

And if the colonel didn't tell them, she thought, *do they have a right to know?*

"We will plan the operation over the next few days," Colonel Stalker said. "Tomorrow, we'll break into planning teams to focus on individual sections of the offensive. In particular, we'll be looking for ways to maximise our advantages and offset the enemy's superior numbers."

"Like an operation on the ground," Jasmine said. "Something designed to give them more than one threat at a time."

"Correct," Colonel Stalker said. He smiled, humourlessly. "We'll be discussing that afterwards."

He looked around the room. "We cannot afford to go into this half-cocked," he said. "This operation - both operations - are risky. We could lose everything."

His voice hardened. "But we are still on the verge of losing the war. We have to take the offensive now, before it's too late. Singh will not make the same mistakes twice. She will rebuild her forces, then use her superiority to steamroll us into the ground. And that will be the end."

Jasmine nodded. The colonel was right.

"Grab some coffee," Colonel Stalker added. "It's going to be a long day."

CHAPTER FOUR

It was a nice prison, General Mark Haverford considered. But it was a prison all the same.

The Commonwealth hadn't treated him badly. He had a small apartment to himself and a reasonable semblance of privacy, something he hadn't expected when he'd surrendered and offered to defect. The Empire had rarely rewarded defectors, even when they had saved thousands of lives. But he'd also been questioned extensively by trained interrogators, men and women who had gone over every last detail of his testimony in the hopes of catching him in a lie. It was unpleasant and painful and - even though he knew it needed to be done - humiliating.

But it could be worse, he thought. *I could be in a camp.*

He snorted at the thought. Most of the POWs would have gone into camps, either on Corinthian or somewhere deeper into the Commonwealth. The former would have an uncomfortable time of it, after the planet had been devastated by the fighting. He had no doubt the locals would do everything in their power to make the POWs miserable. The Commonwealth might have promised to treat the POWs well, but Corinthian hadn't made any such promises. Mark doubted the Commonwealth could make them see reason.

And if they get liberated, they won't be blamed for being captured, he reminded himself. *I won't be so lucky if Admiral Singh catches me after I defected.*

He looked up from his chair as the door opened, revealing Colonel Stalker and Brigadier Jasmine Yamane. He vaguely recalled meeting

Jasmine once, after the Fall of Thule; she'd never made any attempt to defect, even though she'd had the chance. Instead, she'd gone straight into a POW camp and escaped through grit, determination and a certain amount of luck. She was impressive, Mark had to admit. Just looking at her made him think of a tiger on the prowl.

"General," Colonel Stalker said. "We need to talk to you."

"Of course," Mark said, welcomingly. It wasn't as if he was in any position to avoid the conversation. He'd been warned, more than once, that his position depended on being completely open with his interrogators. "Please, take a seat. Tea or coffee?"

"Neither, please," Colonel Stalker said. "I trust that the accommodations are to your liking?"

"They could be worse," Mark said. He watched them sit, noting the way they moved. Their training shone through, no matter how much they might try to hide it. There wasn't a single wasted movement. "They could be better too, but..."

He shrugged. "You're not the usual interrogators," he said, as he leaned back into his comfortable chair. "Am I to assume that certain decisions about the future have been made?"

Colonel Stalker met his eyes. "The last time we met, you told me that Admiral Singh had to be stopped," he said. "You've repeated that statement again and again, every time you were interrogated. Is that still true?"

"Yes," Mark said, flatly.

"I see," Colonel Stalker said. "You also told me that there was a very good chance of a civil war breaking out on Wolfbane."

"I did," Mark confirmed. There was no point in trying to hide it. The interrogators had wrung him dry, asking question after question until they had a fairly solid grip on everything he knew. "Has one broken out?"

"If it has, we don't know about it," Colonel Stalker said.

Mark nodded. It would take two months, at least, for a starship to travel from Wolfbane to Avalon. Longer, perhaps, if the starship didn't follow a direct course. The Commonwealth's awareness of what was happening on Wolfbane was painfully out of date. Admiral Singh might have fought and won - or lost - a civil war by now. Mark had no way to know. None of them did.

"I believe that it is only a matter of time," Mark said. "There are factions who will fight against her, now that she has suffered a defeat."

"So you said," Colonel Stalker reminded him. "I read your debriefing notes very carefully, General. You talked about industrialists and corporate leaders who might turn on her, as well as military officers. Do you believe they might have already moved against her?"

Mark took a moment to formulate his thoughts. "Governor Brown convinced them to back his government," he said. "Admiral Singh merely took over a structure he'd created. But…the prospect of losing everything will certainly concentrate a few minds. They may consider that there is more to be gained by turning on her."

"I see," Colonel Stalker said. "And how might we convince them of that?"

"You offer to respect their current positions," Mark told him. He allowed himself a tight smile. "If they believe, rightly or wrongly, that you are going to break the corporations apart, they'll remain united behind Admiral Singh. Better the devil you know and all that jazz, Colonel. They would sooner put up with kissing her ass than being brutally slaughtered."

Jasmine leaned forward. "You think they'd switch sides?"

"I think they'll do whatever they consider to be in their own best interests," Mark said. He wondered, absently, why Jasmine was there. Good cop, bad cop? Or was something else going on here? "On one hand, Admiral Singh has promised to back them - and she controls much of the military. On the other hand, if Admiral Singh looks like a loser, they'll switch sides just to preserve what they've built."

"Which won't be easy, because Admiral Singh still controls most of the military," Colonel Stalker commented. "Or do you believe that has changed?"

"I believe that most of the bigger corporations will have their own agents in place, within the military and planetary defences," Mark said. His lips thinned. "Promoting officers because of powerful connections rather than competence was a problem even before Governor Brown met an untimely end. I imagine Admiral Singh is currently doing everything in her power to limit their influence before it is too late."

He leaned back in his chair. "I don't think you came here to tell me this personally," he said, flatly. "Everything I just told you could have been taken from the interrogation reports. Why did you come here, now?"

Colonel Stalker studied him for a long moment, his eyes cold and hard. Mark tried to look back at him, reminding himself - sharply - that Colonel Stalker had a long and distinguished record even before the Empire had collapsed. He was no fool, nor was he inclined to tolerate someone playing games. There were limits to how far Colonel Stalker could be pushed, Mark knew, before he decided to push back.

"We are dispatching a team to Wolfbane," Colonel Stalker said, finally. "Do you have any contacts who might be of service?"

Mark felt his heart leap. "Some," he said, carefully. He didn't want to overplay his hand. "I believe, however, that it would be better if I came along."

Colonel Stalker sounded oddly amused. "You *are* aware of the risks?"

"Yes," Mark said, flatly. Admiral Singh might not *know* he had defected - he rather hoped she thought he was trapped in a POW camp somewhere - but she would not be pleased if her forces caught him on Wolfbane. Merely passing through a basic checkpoint might turn into a nightmare if his DNA set off alarms. "I understand the dangers."

"And you're prepared to help make contact with potential rebels?" Jasmine asked. "To betray your former leader?"

"Admiral Singh is mad," Mark reminded her. "She has to be removed."

"And you'd be in position to carve out a place for yourself," Colonel Stalker said. "Do you think we would trust you with it?"

Mark looked back at him. "I have never made any secret of my ambitions," he reminded them. "I will always regret never having risen to the highest ranks. But I would settle for a peaceful life, one that doesn't include the risk of being executed for treason or any other charges that can be ginned up against me."

It was true enough, he knew. There was no chance he'd be allowed to build up a power base of his own, not on Wolfbane. The industrialists might work with him - and the Commonwealth - but they wouldn't want to take the chance of creating another military dictator. And the

Commonwealth would certainly not allow it either. He'd be happy enough if he had a place to live, somewhere where no one knew who he was. Or who he had been.

Jasmine cocked her head. "You think you could convince the factions to support you?"

"You'd have to make them a good offer," Mark said. "But yeah…it could be done."

"Perhaps," Jasmine said. "How would you advise us to *get* to Wolfbane?"

Mark considered it for a long moment. Wolfbane was nowhere nearly as overpopulated as Earth had been, but there were still enough people within the system for constant monitoring to be almost impossible. A skilled team could move around for quite some time without being detected. And yet, passing through any of the bottlenecks - if they wanted to get down to the surface - would not be easy. DNA recombination techniques had their limits.

"Freighter crews are closely monitored, when they hit the surface," he said, after a long moment. "We'd probably want to pose as immigrants, men who have technical skills the corporations can use. Anyone with a certified qualification would be worth their weight in gold. Once you get down to the surface, you'd just need to find someone who could hack the computers and get you an ID chip and everything else you need."

He paused. "Ideally, you'd want a paper trail they could follow, just in case," he added. "If you appeared to have come out of nowhere, you'd definitely raise a few eyebrows."

It wasn't entirely true, he admitted privately. A skilled technician - one with formal training and genuine experience - would be snapped up quickly, once he entered the job market. The corporations were so desperate for trained manpower that they probably wouldn't look twice at anyone they *needed*. But it should remind them - again - that they *needed* him. His black market contacts were probably still there, unless they'd been picked up by the security forces and arrested. But he was fairly sure they'd simply bribed their way out of trouble.

"So we might be dropped off on one world and take passage to Wolfbane from there," Jasmine mused. "We'll be going over that in great detail."

"Calomel, perhaps," Mark said. "They have quite a collection of freighters coming and going - and they're not particularly supervised."

"A curious oversight," Colonel Stalker commented.

"It's the old problem," Mark said. "At what point do you start killing the goose that lays the golden eggs?"

He smiled, inwardly. Governor Brown had grappled with the problem for years, long before he'd taken control of an entire sector. Cracking down on unregistered freighters - and smugglers - was good for the corporations, but not always good for the economy. People wanted what they wanted - and what they wanted, most of the time, was low prices. The corporations might howl, but the independent freighters couldn't be stopped without crippling the economy. Admiral Singh *might* want to drive them out of her territory, yet how could she do it without cutting her own throat?

"They'll be very careful when we reach Wolfbane," Jasmine said.

"I imagine they will," Mark agreed. "But we can probably get papers at Calomel that will get us through the gates."

He looked at Colonel Stalker. "When do we go?"

"When the time is right," Colonel Stalker said. "You will be informed."

It was a non-answer. Mark bit down on his annoyance. Prisoner, defector or whatever, the Commonwealth wouldn't trust him with sensitive details. He would have done the same himself, although that didn't stop him finding the whole thing irritating. If they wanted him to go...he shook his head, silently telling himself not to be silly. He wasn't really in a position to bargain.

Colonel Stalker rose. "Thank you for your time," he said. Jasmine rose too. "We'll follow up on this later."

"Of course," Mark said. He stood. "And thank you for coming."

He watched them go, then sat back down, schooling his face into an unreadable mask. He wasn't fool enough to assume the apartment wasn't monitored. Going back to Wolfbane was a risk, a risk he didn't want to assume. He had no illusions about Admiral Singh - or about how he'd be treated, if he were caught. His contacts might easily sell him out, if they'd decided to stick with Admiral Singh to the bitter end. They couldn't be blind to the threat the Commonwealth posed to their long-term health, no matter how worrying they found their current military dictator. It was quite possible that Mark would lead the Commonwealth team into a deadly trap.

And I wouldn't survive, he thought. The Commonwealth would see him as a traitor - and Wolfbane, of course, would feel pretty much the same way. *Everyone would want me dead.*

He closed his eyes for a long moment, feeling a pang of bitter regret. Everything had seemed so simple, once upon a time. Governor Brown had made him - and the rest of the planetary militia - feel as though they were finally doing something more useful than standing around looking pretty. And then the war had started. And then countless thousands of young men had walked to their deaths on Corinthian. And then…

Admiral Singh has to be stopped, he told himself, firmly. *Whatever happens afterwards doesn't matter. She has to be stopped.*

"An interesting man," Colonel Stalker observed, once the door was shut. "Do you trust him?"

Jasmine shook her head. In her experience, the only people who could be trusted completely were marines. Everyone else - soldiers, spacers, civilians - had a breaking point, a point beyond which they could not go. Mark Haverford *might* be sincere when he talked about overthrowing Admiral Singh, but she didn't trust him. He'd collapsed the moment she'd shoved her gun in his face and ordered him to surrender.

"He might make the difference between getting a team to Wolfbane and being intercepted in transit," Colonel Stalker said. "Can you work with him?"

"You want me to go," Jasmine said. It wasn't a question. "It will be a challenge."

"Yes, it will," Colonel Stalker agreed. "Do you want to go?"

Jasmine frowned. She was the best-qualified officer for the job. She'd been the one who had sneaked down to Corinthian and started an underground revolution that had eventually forced Admiral Singh to flee. And she'd commanded military operations on Thule, escaped a POW camp and struck at Wolfbane itself, *and* carried out behind-the-lines operations on Corinthian that had weakened the invading forces as they advanced on the capital city. By any reasonable standard, she was the only person who *could* be sent. And yet…

"I'm the best choice," she said, ducking the question. In truth, she wasn't sure she *wanted* to go at all. She knew just how lucky she'd been to escape Corinthian, the first time. And she knew just what decisions she'd had to make to win her victory. She felt, even though no one else seemed to agree, that she'd gone too far. "I am the most experienced officer at your disposal."

She sighed, inwardly. She'd signed on the dotted line, once when she'd entered Boot Camp and again when she'd graduated from the Slaughterhouse. She didn't have a choice about where she was sent, not after she'd been given her Rifleman's Tab. She'd given up her freedoms when she'd joined the corps. Even now…a wise commander might hesitate to send her somewhere she really didn't want to go, but she *was* the best-qualified officer. She was needed.

Colonel Stalker gave her a long look, then nodded. "You can select your own team," he said, seriously. "Make sure they can back up whatever claims you put on the official paperwork - they'll be tested."

Jasmine nodded. The Empire's certification program had been a waste of time - insisting that hairdressers had an expensive piece of paperwork just made the bureaucrats look silly - but her team *would* need engineering and mechanical qualifications. They would definitely be tested when they reached Wolfbane. Luckily, there was no shortage of trained mechanics within the marines and their auxiliaries. She might be better off focusing on the auxiliaries, if she thought she could trust them to handle it. These days, with everyone doing everything in their power to make the Commonwealth work, the lines had blurred more than she cared to admit.

And we are running out of marines, she thought, grimly. *What will we do when we're all dead?*

Go to heaven or hell, her thoughts answered her.

"I'll see to it," she said, pushing the mocking thought aside. She'd have to chat with Emmanuel, too. There was no way *he* could come with her, not into the heart of enemy territory. It wouldn't be their first separation, but they hadn't had much time together since they'd returned to Avalon. "Colonel…when do we leave?"

"As soon as possible," Colonel Stalker said. "That's why I didn't disband the task force when we returned. We're going to need it."

"Mandy will need more ships," Jasmine said. She'd have to talk to Mandy too, if they had time. "And a *lot* more firepower."

"It's on the way," Colonel Stalker assured her. He nodded back towards the closed door. "You'll have complete access to our friend in there. Ask him anything, anything at all, that you think might be germane to the mission. I'll make sure intelligence knows to keep you in the loop too."

And hope he isn't planning to betray us, Jasmine thought. She disliked depending on anyone she didn't trust. *If we're wrong, he'll be in an excellent place to do us harm.*

CHAPTER FIVE

"You do realise that this is politically risky?"

Ed nodded, looking down at his baby son. "How bad is it going to be?"

Gaby shrugged as she leaned back on the sofa. "It depends on the exact terms," she said, dryly. "Anything that smacks of letting Wolfbane get away with...well, *anything*...isn't going to go down well with the council, or the electorate at large. On the other hand, an agreement that allows us and them to compete on even terms will probably be accepted."

"We need to end the war," Ed said. He rocked his son from side to side, very gently. "We could still lose."

"Unless we come up with something new," Gaby said. She smiled, tiredly. "I understand the logic, Ed. The man in the street might not."

Ed nodded. The Commonwealth had never been designed for a war. Its political structure was staggering, perhaps failing, under the strain of having to fight a long war. The politicians, thankfully, had plenty of common sense - having to deal with reality had seen to that - but the stresses of the war were pulling them in different directions. They just hadn't had the time to put the Commonwealth on a secure footing.

"If we have access to their markets, if we break their control over the worlds they've occupied, our long-term victory is assured," Ed said. "If they try to adapt to match us, they'll have to make political changes; if they don't, we will have a permanent advantage and their populations will grow restive."

"But it will take time," Gaby pointed out. "Years, perhaps."

Ed nodded. There was no way to predict a technological improvement, let alone a breakthrough. Researchers were looking at every idea that had been proposed and trying to determine what could be turned into useful hardware, but most of their concepts had turned into damp squibs. It was possible that they'd find something tomorrow that would render the entire navy obsolete at a stroke...and equally possible that they wouldn't manage to push the limits any further. All he could do was keep throwing money into research programs and hope for the best.

Not that it has been that *much of a failure*, he thought. *We wouldn't have the force fields or the advanced missiles without it.*

"I think we're going to have to get used to the idea of things taking time," he said. It was a bitter thought. "We're operating on a greater scale now."

He shook his head in annoyance. He'd seen too many problems prolonged by political incompetence, too many insurgences and wars that could have been halted with an effective combination of the carrot and the stick. The Cracker War had ended - quickly - because the marines had had the freedom to capitalise on their battlefield victory. But Wolfbane was simply too large a target to be taken down by a single engagement, no matter how savage and costly. The days when problems could be contained by the Imperial Navy were long gone.

"Then it's time we got used to it," Gaby said.

She picked up the datapad. "I'm pretty sure we can agree on a truce, followed by free trade and migration," she said. "As long as Admiral Singh's successors don't want to continue the war, I dare say everything else is negotiable."

Ed hoped she was right. Admiral Singh *needed* a victory, if the intelligence analysts were right. She *had* to cement her position before some kindly soul decided to assassinate her and rid the universe of a dangerous menace. But the corporations might not be much more inclined to be peaceful. He'd met enough corporate officers to know they could be just as cold and heartless as the Grand Senate, more concerned with meeting their stockholders' demands than ending wars on favourable terms. God alone knew how many insurgencies had kept going because the locals refused to be exploited by interstellar corporations.

But this is on a bigger scale, he thought, sourly. *They will see us as dangerous competition.*

"We won't seek to occupy Wolfbane," Ed said. "We'll just seek guarantees that the war will not resume in a hurry."

Gaby looked up at him. "And you're sure you can keep them from rearming?"

Ed shrugged. "There's no way to be sure of anything," he said. "Yes, we can beat them in their own system; yes, we can do a great deal of damage to their infrastructure; no, we cannot *guarantee* that we can keep them from rebuilding their military. But if we offer them a fairly decent short-term peace, they shouldn't want to resume the war until it's too late."

He allowed himself a cold smile. The corporations wouldn't want to encourage their military to think for itself, not when they'd already had one military dictator. Hell, they probably wouldn't even want to throw resources into an *unproductive* military. Given five years, perhaps ten, the Commonwealth would have a decisive advantage if the war broke out again.

And they probably won't seek to restart the war unless they're sure they can win, he thought, grimly. *They would lose everything if they restarted the war and lost.*

"True enough," Gaby said.

Douglas opened his mouth and started to cry. Gaby took him and pressed the baby to her breast. Ed watched, feeling an odd kind of helplessness. *He* hadn't been able to make the baby fall quiet, no matter what he did. Douglas was utterly dependent on his mother. It seemed impossible to believe, somehow, that Douglas would grow into a little boy, then into a strong man. The infant was *tiny*.

You were that size once, his thoughts pointed out. *And you grew up big and strong.*

Sure, he answered, silently. *And how many babies never grew up on Earth.*

He shuddered. Earth had been a nightmare. He'd known children who hadn't lived past their first decade, children he barely remembered amidst the horror of his life…he couldn't even remember their names. He felt a surge of protectiveness, mingled with guilt, as he saw the tiny form. Part of him felt as though he'd brought a helpless child into a horrific world, even though he knew better. Douglas would never have to grow up in a CityBlock, never have to fight for his life against older boys and predatory adults…never have to compete with his parents and siblings for food. Douglas would have a good life, Ed vowed. Ed would do whatever it took to make *sure* Douglas had a good life.

Teach him how to defend himself, he thought, grimly. *And teach him honour.*

He looked away, feeling another pang of guilt. He'd thought those emotions were buried, locked away at the back of his mind. He knew what *he'd* done to survive the Undercity, to try to stay alive long enough to escape. The world had been divided into victims and victimisers and he'd preferred the latter to the former. Maybe he hadn't been as bad as the drug lords or gangsters…

Douglas will never have to make those choices, he told himself. *And he will never have to fight to survive.*

Gaby cleared her throat. "The next council meeting is going to be interesting."

Ed glanced at her. "Are you going to take Douglas with you?"

"I may have to," Gaby said. She looked down at her son. "It'll have to be done."

"You *could* use a bottle," Ed said, slowly.

"Breast-feeding is better," Gaby said. "And women have been doing it for thousands of years."

Not on Earth, Ed thought.

He sighed. Women had been advised *not* to breast-feed on Earth, although he wasn't sure why. Perhaps it was dangerous - traces of dangerous elements were very common on Earth - or perhaps it was just a cunning plan to force everyone to buy baby formula. Or perhaps it was just a grim recognition that the two-legged predators infesting the Undercity would see a bare breast as an invitation. But then, those bastards would see an unprotected *woman* as an invitation, whatever she was wearing. Gaby had grown up with guns, she'd learned to shoot almost as soon as she could walk and talk. His sisters in the Undercity had been disarmed and helpless.

"I know," he said, slowly.

It bothered him. And he didn't really know *why* it bothered him.

"Good," Gaby said, sharply. She met his eyes. "I have to see out the rest of my term, whatever else happens. And then I can retire gracefully."

She smiled. "Don't your fellow marines have this problem?"

"No," Ed said. Female marines had birth control implants. It was unheard of for one of them to get pregnant on active duty. If they wanted children, they had to go on detached duty. It was a harsh rule, but necessary. The Imperial Army and Navy had had a long-standing problem with crewwomen - even officers - getting pregnant on active duty. "They don't."

Gaby's lips twitched. "Poor them."

Ed raised his eyebrows. "What?"

"They won't know the feeling of being pregnant," Gaby said. "They won't feel the baby kicking inside them. And they won't get to hold their child after they finally give birth."

"They can," Ed said. "They just have to go on detached duty first."

Gaby looked down at her sleeping son, then carefully detached him from her breast. "Maybe we should have timed it better," she said. "But..."

Ed nodded. They'd agreed to let chance determine when - if - they had a child. He'd been nervous for a while, wondering if he was even *capable* of siring a child. The Undercity was so badly contaminated that it might well have done permanent damage, even though his medical scan - when he'd reported to Boot Camp - hadn't revealed anything too far out of the ordinary. He'd even promised himself that he'd get checked properly, if they failed to conceive a child in five years.

But we had a child, he thought, as Gaby placed Douglas in his bassinet. *A perfect baby boy.*

Gaby yawned. "I need some rest," she said, lying back on the sofa. "Are you going to stay here?"

"I can't fit on the sofa," Ed pointed out. She gave him a nasty look. "But I'll be here until I get called away."

"Just be quiet when you go," Gaby said. "I don't get enough sleep these days."

She closed her eyes. Ed felt a hot flush of affection, mingled with guilt. He was going to go away and leave her alone...he was going to risk his life once again, running the risk of leaving her alone. He'd never understood why so many married marines went on detached duty, not until he'd had a child himself. Now…now, part of his mind refused to take the chance of leaving Gaby a widow. He didn't want to leave her alone.

And yet, I have no choice, he told himself. *I have to be in command.*

He looked down at his hands, silently. Did *he* need to be in command? Joe Buckley could handle the ground force, Mandy Caesius could handle the naval squadron…there was no reason, logically, for him to be in command. And yet, the whole concept was *his* idea. He *had* to be the one charged with turning the idea into reality. Thousands of years of marine history *insisted* that the planner who'd come up with the plan had to be the one who made it work.

Or realised, when he came face to face with reality, that the clever plan wouldn't actually work, Ed thought. Marines tended to learn better before they went through OCS, but he'd met a few Imperial Army and Navy officers who'd reached high rank without actually going on duty and seeing the elephant. They'd come up with some plans that would have made excellent flicks, when the scriptwriter was on their side, but gotten a lot of people killed if they'd been tried in real life. *And they did get a lot of people killed.*

He shook his head in annoyance. It was easy to lose touch with what was actually going on, even though he *knew* the dangers. God knew he'd faced the temptation to micromanage from a distance, despite knowing that micromanaging across light-years had helped bring the Empire to its knees. The Grand Senate had never learnt that matters didn't wait for their input before proceeding. Ed liked to tell himself that it would be different, that *he* would be different, but he knew better than to take it for granted. Losing touch with reality was all too easy.

Gwen will keep me from becoming too complacent, he told himself. *But we'll still need frequent reality checks.*

He reached for his datapad and flicked through the series of updates. General George Grosskopf's proposal for recreating the Slaughterhouse was waiting for him, silently reminding him that the *original* Slaughterhouse was gone. Ed had been resisting the temptation to recreate what they'd lost, even though he *knew* that they were running out of trained marines. Half of his original company had been killed in action or transferred to places where they could put their skills to work rebuilding the local economy. And yet…

Recreating the Slaughterhouse would be an admission that the universe has changed, he thought, as he rose to his feet and paced towards the window. *And that things will never be the same again.*

He reached the window and peered out over Camelot. Darkness was slowly falling, but Camelot was still glowing with light. It looked as though the city had somehow managed to expand again, doubling or even tripling its size and population since he and his men had taken ship for Corinthian. But that was no surprise, he told himself. Even now, even with the Commonwealth seeking to expand and diversify its industrial base, Camelot was still the centre of a growing interstellar power. Thousands of young men and women were flowing into the city, looking for jobs and training that would give them a fresh start on life. And many of them - perhaps all of them - were succeeding. Camelot thrummed with an energy he'd never seen on Earth.

High overhead, lights moved through the sky. Shuttles, climbing into orbit or descending to the nearest spaceport; aircars, flying from corporate headquarters to the mansions of the newly rich and powerful. Camelot never slept, these days. It was no surprise to *him*, at least, that the red light district had grown bigger, even though the streets were still remarkably safe. But then, the city council had a zero-tolerance policy for troublemakers. A few months on the work farms tended to convince even the nastiest drunk that he didn't want to pick fights in Camelot.

Earth might have been a better place to live, he thought, *if the Grand Senate had kicked out the troublemakers.*

He shook his head. Earth had had only one punishment for anyone foolish enough to be arrested, if they couldn't pay the bribe. They were deported, dispatched to stage-one and stage-two colony worlds as indentured labour. Hundreds of thousands - perhaps millions - of young men and women had been deported. And yet, it had only been a tiny fraction of Earth's immense population. Earth had been so heavily overpopulated that collapse - and disaster - had been inevitable for years. Policing had been impossible. Camelot, he hoped and prayed, would never become so overcrowded.

His eyes sought out the University, glowing against the skyline. Professor Leo Caesius was teaching there, trying to recreate the spirit of scientific enquiry. His seeds had taken root, Ed had heard, even though it meant that most of the students kept arguing with the teachers. But Professor Caesius had insisted that it was important. The students had to question, they had to reason things out for themselves, even if it meant irritating or embarrassing a handful of teachers. Ed doubted the professors enjoyed it, but they had no choice. Students had to learn to think for themselves.

And the technical colleges help, he thought, as he looked for the smaller buildings. *Our mechanics actually know what they're doing.*

It was a sobering thought. He'd never understood, not until he'd joined the marines, just how little he actually knew. He had been ignorant of so much that he'd actually been ignorant of his own ignorance. His command of thousands of pieces of trivia and thoroughly useless fragments of information had been worthless, back then. He'd been lucky - very lucky - that the marines hadn't cared about his academic achievements. He knew - now - that they'd been worthless.

The Commonwealth will not fall into the same trap as the Empire, he promised himself, silently. *We won't let ourselves be bogged down too.*

He looked up, again. The stars were clearly visible, twinkling brightly in the night sky. Sol was thousands of light-years away, so impossibly distant that he knew he couldn't hope to pick humanity's sun out against the others. There was no reliable data about the Core Worlds now, no way to know what was actually going on. Civil war…mass starvation and death…or a new empire, rising from the ashes. It would be a long time before he knew *anything* for sure.

And the Empire is gone, he thought. *We might be all that's left.*

He picked up his datapad, again. The plans were still there, mocking him. Approving them would feel like giving up, as if he'd surrendered; rejecting them would be a denial of reality itself. And he could not deny reality. It wouldn't go away when he closed his eyes.

We need more marines, he told himself. Shaking his head, he pressed his fingers against the scanner, approving the plans. *We need them and there's no other way to get them.*

But it still felt, somehow, as though he'd surrendered to the inevitable.

CHAPTER SIX

There was a moment - a long moment - of shuddering pleasure, then Emmanuel Alves collapsed on top of her. Jasmine shivered in delight as he flexed against her one last time, then wilted completely. She kissed the top of his sweaty forehead as he lay on top of her, his eyes bright and yet tired. She'd practically dragged him into bed as soon as he'd returned to the apartment. He hadn't put up much resistance.

"Thank you," she said. "I needed that."

Emmanuel managed a smile. "You're going to wear me out."

"Just take a few pills," Jasmine said, mischievously. "Or get one of those cock-enhancing implants."

"I don't want *anyone* operating on my cock," Emmanuel said. He rolled over, pulling out of her as he came to rest beside her. "I don't know how anyone can do it."

"I imagine having something to make up for their small egos helps," Jasmine commented, rubbing her breast. He'd bitten it during their love-making. "You'd think they'd just want to carry an Overcompensator around."

"I think that would be a little heavy," Emmanuel said, dryly.

Jasmine snorted as she sat up, looking down at him. Emmanuel looked exhausted, too exhausted to do anything, save for lying on the bed and waiting for his strength to return. She was tempted to join him, but she knew her duty. There were a whole series of meetings she was expected to attend, starting in less than two hours. She swung her legs over the side of the bed and stood, padding towards the bathroom. She wasn't too surprised when she heard him stand up and lumber after her.

"We don't have too much time," she warned, as she turned on the water. She'd never really appreciated showers until she'd gone to Boot Camp, where recruits were rarely allowed to spend more than two minutes scrubbing themselves clean. "And we have to talk."

"That sounds bad," Emmanuel said. He wrapped his arms around her, stroking her bare breasts. "Should I be worried?"

"Perhaps," Jasmine said. She turned, pressing against him. Tired or not, he was already growing hard. Perhaps he *was* taking something. "But we'll talk about it afterwards."

She kissed him, then allowed him to push her against the wall. Warm water cascaded over them as they made love, washing them clean afterwards. Jasmine luxuriated under the water for several minutes, reminding herself that she would have to go into lockdown and then a starship sooner rather than later, then hurried back into the living room. She dressed hurriedly, pulling on her regulation underwear as Emmanuel staggered out of the shower and grabbed for a towel. It still amused her that she could get dressed while he was looking for his clothes.

Good thing he's more organised on campaign, she thought, amused. *And that he's not foolish enough to risk lives for a scoop.*

"All right," Emmanuel said. He finished dressing and sat down on the chair, giving her a thoughtful look. "What do you want to talk to me about?"

Jasmine sat on the bed, glancing around the room. It was neater than the average bachelor pad, she had to admit, but it was messy enough to give her former Drill Instructor a heart attack. Even now, even given her rank, she would have hated to show the apartment to Command Sergeant Patterson. She didn't *know* if the Command Sergeant could give her additional push-ups or not, but she didn't want to find out the hard way.

"I'm going to have to go soon," she said. "You can't come with me."

Emmanuel winced. Jasmine felt a flicker of amusement, mingled with annoyance. They weren't going to Lakshmibai or Corinthian or some other world they could reasonably bring an embedded reporter. They were going to *Wolfbane*, the very heart of enemy territory. She was nervous enough about bringing auxiliaries, even though they'd been through intensive training and even combat. She couldn't bring a reporter.

"I understand," he said, finally. "But…"

He shook his head. Jasmine understood. Emmanuel was a good reporter - a *great* reporter, perhaps. But then, she *was* comparing him to the bottom-feeders she'd encountered on Han and Earth. The bar wasn't set very high. And yet…he understood the problem, he understood why he couldn't go, but he *wanted* to go. It would be the story of a lifetime.

"I'll see you again, afterwards," she promised. "You can have an exclusive interview."

Emmanuel smiled, wanly. "I don't *think* there's any market for marine romance stories."

Jasmine snickered. A handful of copies of *Marines In Bed* had been passed around the barracks, back in Boot Camp. They'd been greeted with howls of laughter, from the ridiculous dialogue to the ludicrously absurd sex scenes. Jasmine knew, without false modesty, that she'd been in the top percentile even *before* she'd gone to Boot Camp, but she couldn't have performed such acts without breaking something. Even a contortionist would have found it impossible. The recruits had generally agreed that whoever had written the book had never met a real girl, let alone a marine.

And was probably still a virgin at fifty, she thought, wryly.

"Maybe not," she said. "Although there *is* a market for trashy novels if you want a new job."

Emmanuel made a face. "I have my dignity, thank you."

"Not in bed," Jasmine said.

She sobered. "I'll be gone for at least four months," she said, grimly. She suspected Emmanuel would be allowed to embed with the colonel and his unit, but she didn't know for sure. "If…if you find someone else during that time, I'll understand."

"I waited for you when you were taken prisoner," Emmanuel said. "I can wait for you again."

Jasmine shrugged. She would have liked to believe it. She certainly *wanted* to believe it. But she'd seen too many relationships break up because of interstellar distances and long separations. It was harder for marines, perhaps, because they could be rushed right across the Empire at a moment's notice. She'd been warned, time and time again, not to get too attached to anyone. Better to have a brief affair, she'd been told, or even rely on self-stimulation. Getting attached...and breaking up...could mean the end of her career.

Which is why so few marines actually marry until they retire, she thought, sourly. Marriage almost always meant the end of a female marine's career. *And then they move to the Slaughterhouse, if they don't go find a nice stage-one colony...*

She shuddered. There had been *families* on the Slaughterhouse...what had happened to them? She'd had friends there, friends who'd taken her into their homes and helped her to learn their ways...what had happened to them? She knew, all too well, that she might never know.

Emmanuel leaned forward. "Jasmine?"

"It doesn't matter," Jasmine said, a little harshly.

She rubbed her scalp. She'd cut her hair short, but it was growing out again. "I don't know how long I will be away," she said. It *was* possible they'd meet again on Wolfbane, but she knew better than to count on it. No one, not even Colonel Stalker, could hope to direct a multi-pronged operation on an interstellar scale. "If you do find someone else, I don't mind."

Except that was a lie, and she knew it was a lie, and she suspected *he* knew it was a lie too.

Things have changed, she thought, ruefully. *And nothing is the same.*

"I'll wait for you," Emmanuel said. "I promise."

Jasmine snorted. "Thank you," she said, feeling an odd flicker of disquiet. Civilians! "And I will see you later, I hope."

She glanced at her appearance in the mirror, then walked out of the apartment and down the stairs to the ground. The guard on the gate glanced at her before standing aside, allowing her to head to the road. She hoped he wouldn't be *quite* so unwary when she wanted to go back in, if she didn't go straight into lockdown. Castle Rock was supposed to be secure, but there were too many people and aircraft coming and going for *total* security. No one, not even the military police, knew *everyone* who was meant to be on the island.

And it only takes one spy to ruin everything, she thought, as a pair of shuttlecraft roared overhead. There were other military spaceports now, but Castle Rock was still the largest on Avalon. *One word of warning to Singh and we're sunk*.

She schooled her temper and banished it as she walked down the road, passing a set of new barracks and training grounds. Castle Rock had just kept expanding, pushing the limits...she wondered, absently, just how long it would be until the older buildings were knocked down to make way for newer accommodations. She caught sight of a line of new recruits, chanting a rude cadence as they ran around the track; they looked so young, painfully young, that she couldn't help wondering why they weren't in school. It was hard to believe that the fresh-faced boys were old enough to bear arms and go to war.

They haven't gone to war, she told herself, stiffly. *Not yet*.

Her wristcom pinged as she reached the gates. She glanced at it. Mandy had messaged her, asking if she'd have time to meet for dinner. Jasmine keyed her wristcom, sending a non-committal reply, then walked through the first set of gates. The guards descended on her as soon as the gates had closed, scanning her and then patting her down before checking her name against the authorised list. Jasmine nodded in approval as they allowed her to enter the building itself. As irksome as the procedure was, it had to be done. The building had to remain secure.

She undid her wristcom and dropped it and her datapad into a secure box, then walked through a second set of doors and down the corridor. The air smelt vaguely of disinfectant, reminding her of days spent cleaning the barracks as a new recruit. She saw no one until she reached the office, where Rifleman Thomas Stewart and Rifleman Henry Parkinson were waiting for her. They both looked disgustingly cheerful. Jasmine made a mental bet with herself that they'd gone straight to the brothels, as soon as they'd disembarked from the shuttle, and not come out until she'd called them. She supposed it did have its advantages.

"Jasmine," Stewart said. "Or is it *Brigadier* right now?"

"It's Supreme Overlord," Jasmine said, sardonically. She was too tired to bandy words. "Or perhaps Your Supremacy."

"I don't think that either of them are recognised ranks," Parkinson said. "You could call yourself Mistress of the Knives, instead."

Jasmine smiled. She'd been the company champion at knife-throwing. She wondered, absently, if she still was. They hadn't had the time to get together and have a proper series of contests. How could they?

"I need volunteers for a mission," she said. "Can I assume that you two have volunteered?"

Stewart shrugged. "I knew I should have stayed drinking," he said. "Curse my low stomach volume."

"You'd be bitching more if you were fat enough to drink a trough," Parkinson pointed out, rudely. He looked at Jasmine. "Should I assume we've been volunteered?"

"Probably," Jasmine said. She smiled. "Risk of being caught, tortured and killed - high."

"I knew it," Stewart said. "I suppose you have a pair of volunteers. Now, what do you actually want us to do?"

"We're going to Wolfbane," Jasmine said. She didn't insult them by asking if they wanted to back out. "It should be fun."

"I suppose," Parkinson said. He elbowed Stewart. "You really *should* have stayed drinking."

"Yeah," Stewart agreed. He stood. "When are we going?"

"There's some briefing papers on the datanet," Jasmine said. "You can read them in the next room." She sat down behind the desk. "I have to interview a couple of others, then we can go through the planning stages. Hopefully, we'll have a full team in a day or two."

"Understood," Parkinson said. "We'll be ready for you."

Jasmine shook her head, inwardly, as she watched them go. She knew she was a little bitchy, but…she sighed, tiredly. Going to Wolfbane would be a challenge, a challenge she knew could end badly. Admiral Singh had every reason to hate her, personally. If she got caught - again - she knew getting out would not be easy. Admiral Singh would probably blow Jasmine's brains out before she had a chance to recover.

There was a knock at the door. "Come!"

The door opened, revealing a muscular young woman with short red hair. She would have been pretty, Jasmine considered, if she hadn't had a nasty scar on her face. No one would have blamed her for removing it, but she wore it like a badge of honour. The auxiliary uniform she wore was a warning not to take her too lightly.

"Meade Hazelstone," the newcomer said. "I understand you're looking for volunteers…?"

Jasmine nodded, motioning for Meade to take a seat. She'd never crossed paths with Meade before, if she recalled correctly. The young woman's file stated that she'd joined the company shortly before it left Earth, going into stasis without meeting the majority of the company's personnel. It would have bothered Jasmine, she admitted, if Meade hadn't enjoyed recommendations from people Jasmine trusted. She'd made quite a career for herself since Avalon had been cut off from the Empire.

"I am," Jasmine said. "Did you read the briefing notes?"

"Such as they are," Meade said, briskly. Her voice was accented, although Jasmine couldn't place it. "I believe I meet your requirements."

Jasmine lifted her eyebrows. "Certificates?"

"Grade Ten Mechanic, Five Star Shooter, Black Belt Semper Fu," Meade drawled. Jasmine had the impression that she was all too used to answering that question. "I failed the Slaughterhouse, not Boot Camp."

"Your file says you washed out," Jasmine said. "What *actually* happened?"

"I had a…personality conflict with the team leader during an exercise," Meade said. "It turned into a pretty bad argument. And so I got marked down."

Jasmine frowned. Marines *had* to be team players. She'd had to work with people she disliked in the past, no matter how she felt about them. For Meade to be *incapable* of hiding her true feelings, of burying them behind a veneer of professionalism…it wasn't good. She wouldn't have been given a second chance, either. Jasmine was mildly surprised she'd been allowed to go into the auxiliaries.

"You have excellent mechanical qualifications," she said, slowly. "How did you get those?"

"I grew up on a freighter," Meade said. "The family has always been engineers, always - my three brothers and I were taught the trade by my father. Problem was…the ship was too small for us when we grew up. My oldest brother got the ship; the rest of us scattered across the universe. I went to the marines."

Jasmine lifted her eyebrows. "Why didn't you stay an engineer? You have the qualifications, don't you?"

There was a flicker of pain on Meade's face. "These days - *those* days - it was unusual to find a female engineer who was genuinely qualified, let alone experienced," she said. "The only women who applied were silly idiots who'd been through the groundhog training centres, but couldn't do more than unhook a component and replace it with a spare. They had poor reputations. And it spilled onto me, even though I *could* fix a broken drive modulator with my eyes closed."

"Ouch," Jasmine said. "You didn't have good references?"

"Only from my family," Meade said. She sighed. "They did try, but it was a pain in the ass proving myself. I had a couple of unsatisfactory positions...well, let's just say I learned to hate being questioned all the time. I made it through Boot Camp, but I didn't do so well at the Slaughterhouse. Coming here, as a trained engineer, struck me as my last best chance."

"And it was," Jasmine said. She met the younger woman's eyes. "Are you sure you want to volunteer for this mission?"

"Yes," Meade said, flatly.

Jasmine studied her for a long moment. It wasn't unknown for auxiliaries to become resentful, over the years. They worked closely with marines, but - despite their technological qualifications - they would never *be* marines unless they returned to the Slaughterhouse. Meade had evidently had a chip on her shoulder long before she'd gone to Boot Camp, a chip that had eventually spoiled her chances of winning a Rifleman's Tab. Taking her could be dangerous...

...And yet, she *was* qualified. Perhaps a little *over*-qualified.

"We'll be going into lockdown soon," she said, meeting Meade's eyes. "If you don't get through the training, you'll stay in lockdown until the mission is over, one way or the other. I can't risk word getting out, even by accident. Do you understand?"

Meade looked back evenly. "Yes, Brigadier."

Jasmine nodded to herself. Meade *had* had plenty of training. She should understand the requirements, no matter how oppressive they seemed to civilians. And yet, Jasmine couldn't help feeling that Meade would be a two-edged sword. Her anger issues might turn into a serious problem.

So ride herd on her, Jasmine's thoughts mocked her. *She wouldn't be the first person you've had to supervise closely.*

"Take a break, take a walk," Jasmine said. She made a show of looking at her watch. "If you are determined to carry on with the mission, come back this evening at 1700. I'll make my final decision then. If you don't show up…well, I'll assume you decided to change your mind."

Meade's eyes glittered. "I understand," she said. "I'll see you at 1700."

"Very good," Jasmine said. "Dismissed."

She tapped the terminal as Meade left the room, bringing up the auxiliary's file. A string of commendations, matched with a line of disciplinary reports. Meade would have been busted out of the corps by now, if she hadn't been a *very* good engineer. No one doubted her bravery, it seemed, but they questioned her judgement.

I'll just have to keep an eye on her, Jasmine thought. *And hope.*

She keyed a switch. "Next!"

CHAPTER SEVEN

Commodore Mandy Caesius couldn't help wondering, as she waited outside the restaurant, if her sister had stood her up. Mindy had always been the sensible one of the family, but she *had* become a dirty groundpounder and fought - with honour - during the Battle of Corinthian. It was easy to believe that her sister, who'd been a mere *fourteen* when the family had been exiled to Avalon, had gone mad. She was still only twenty to Mandy's twenty-two.

Not that either of us have had an easy time of it, she thought, as a cold wind blew through the growing city. They were far too close to the docks for her comfort, even though she knew it was safe. She'd hated large bodies of water from the day she'd taken her first swimming lessons on Earth. *She went to the groundpounders and I…I went to space.*

She shivered, cursing the immature brat she'd been. She'd given her parents a hard time, whining and moaning and complaining because she hadn't had the latest of…well, everything. The older woman she'd become wished she could go back in time and slap her younger self, then point her at some genuine technical education. It hadn't been *entirely* impossible to get a decent education on Earth, but it had required a certain degree of self-study. The time she'd wasted in examining the latest dresses or chasing cute boys could have been spent studying science and engineering instead. By the time Jasmine had straightened her out, she'd almost wasted her life.

The wind seemed to blow colder, just for a second. She heard birds cawing in the distance as night fell over the city, reminding her that

Camelot was still an untamed environment. There were families who kept chickens, she knew; chickens that laid eggs and would eventually be slaughtered to provide a meal for their owners. She'd been sick, she recalled, when she'd finally grasped where her meat had come from. She'd never made the connection between the animals and her dinner.

I was a stupid bitch, she thought, with a flash of self-loathing. Everything she'd done - from sabotaging a pirate cruiser to becoming the youngest squadron commander in recent history - seemed to belong to someone else. It was almost as if she'd sprung into existence, fully grown. *And I should have died.*

She turned as she heard footsteps. A young woman was approaching, her hair cut close to her scalp…Mandy stepped aside automatically, then stared as she recognised her sister's eyes. Her body was so different - so muscular - that she couldn't help wondering if Mindy had actually transferred her mind into another body. But she knew that was absurd. She'd lost the rest of her baby fat during her captivity.

Fretting didn't help either, she thought. She'd done terrible things to survive. *I could have died out there…*

"Mandy," Mindy said. "You're looking good."

"You need your eyes checked," Mandy said. She looked down at herself. The shirt and trousers she wore covered everything below her neck. She just wasn't comfortable wearing revealing clothes, not now. "I look terrible."

"You look healthy," Mindy said. She struck a dramatic pose. "And how do *I* look?"

Mandy shook her head in disbelief. Mindy *definitely* looked different. Mandy couldn't help thinking of Jasmine, but there was an immaturity about Mindy - even now - that was nothing like the older marine. Mindy bobbed from side to side, as if she couldn't stand still even for a second. Her muscles were larger, her breasts were smaller…she looked… she looked strange. And yet, somehow, it suited her.

"You look older," she said, finally. She'd lorded her age over her younger sibling, once upon a time. She had a feeling that *that* wouldn't get her anywhere now. "Shall we go in?"

Mindy raised her eyebrows. "Shouldn't we wait for Jasmine?"

"She said she'd be here if she could make it," Mandy said. It was a disappointment - she'd hoped to meet her mentor - but military life had taught her that the military came first, always. At least she wasn't a wife staying at home, never knowing when her husband might come home on leave…or in a coffin. "I hope she'll come, but…"

She felt oddly out of place as they walked into the restaurant. It had been founded by a refugee family from Lakshmibai, one of the many people who'd helped the CEF as it battled its way to rescue the hostages. The refugees had done well for themselves, she decided, as a dark-skinned girl led them to their seats. She just hoped they managed to blend in as their children grew older. *Mandy* had learned, the hard way, that failing to blend in on Avalon could be disastrous.

"I'm going to NCO School," Mindy said, sitting down. The waitress passed them a pair of menus, then retreated. "I report to Castle Rock on Tuesday."

So she won't be going with us, Mandy thought. Mindy didn't know about Sucker Punch, of course. She'd certainly not been invited to the preliminary meeting. *Is that good or bad?*

"Congratulations," she said, instead. "I hope you do well."

"I hope so too," Mindy said. "Sergeant Rackham said I had potential, but I'd have to work hard."

"I think that's true of everything," Mandy said. She didn't *know* Sergeant Rackham, but she *did* know Command Sergeant Gwendolyn Patterson. The woman had scared her, when Mandy had first *met* her. Even now, the older woman was terrifying. "How long is the course?"

"Nine months, apparently," Mindy said. "If I pass, I get to do an apprenticeship before they give me a platoon of my own. And if I fail, I get sent back to my unit with a flea in my ear."

"Probably literally," Mandy said. "Have you thought about transferring to the navy?"

Mindy shook her head. "It isn't aggressive enough."

Mandy snorted. "It is."

"No, it isn't," Mindy said. "It's just lights on a screen."

Mandy rolled her eyes, although she took her sister's point. Mindy had always been the more physical of them. Even as a child, Mandy hadn't dared to push her sister around *too* much. Of course, she'd also been taught that violence never solved anything…she'd learnt, the hard way, that too many of her teachers were liars. When society collapsed, might made right.

Mindy would have been fine, if we'd stayed on Earth, she thought. *Wouldn't she?*

The waitress returned, carrying a bottle of wine. Mandy ordered quickly, then motioned for the waitress to wait as she saw Jasmine entering the restaurant. The marine looked tired, as if she'd walked for miles without a rest. Mandy couldn't help feeling a flicker of concern for the older woman, even though she knew Jasmine could beat both of them with one hand tied behind her back. Everyone had their breaking point.

"You have a terrible crush on her," Mindy whispered, as she poured three glasses of red wine. "Don't you?"

Mandy glowered at her. She'd had a couple of girlfriends, back on Earth, but they hadn't lasted. Boys had been more interesting, even when they'd turned demanding. Jasmine…was nothing like either of them. It was easier to think of her as an older sister, perhaps a cousin, than anything else. They were very different.

"Jasmine," she said, holding out the menu. "You're just in time."

Jasmine gave her a tired smile. "I wasn't sure I was going to make it," she said, as she took the menu. "Chicken Supreme, please."

The waitress looked alarmed. "That's the hottest thing on the menu," she said. "Would you not rather…"

"Chicken Supreme," Jasmine repeated. "I've eaten food prepared by Joe Buckley. I'll survive your curry."

Mindy giggled as the waitress scurried away. "Is he as bad as Private Baldrick?"

Jasmine pointed a finger at her. "It is a law of nature," she said, "that military cooking is always awful. Adding spicy sauce is often the only thing that makes it edible."

"Yuk," Mandy said.

"We shot a racoon back on Corinthian," Mindy said. "It tasted fine, once we got rid of the smell of buckshot."

Mandy glanced from one to the other, then shrugged. She'd eaten a few military rations herself, although the navy generally had better food. "You should probably have stuck with the ration bars," she said. "I thought they tasted like cardboard."

"That's why we slather them in sauce," Jasmine said. She leaned back in her chair. "How was *your* day?"

Mindy smiled. "I'm going to NCO school!"

"Lucky you," Jasmine said. "Remember to take an apple for the teacher."

"I don't *think* that would be a good idea," Mandy said.

"She'll need to be noticed," Jasmine said. She looked Mindy up and down. "Do you intend to return to the field or go into training?"

"The field," Mindy said. "I don't think I can shout for hours without losing my voice."

"There are augmentations for that," Jasmine said. "Just remember to look confident, even though you're panicking on the inside."

Mandy frowned. "Do *you* panic?"

"No," Jasmine said. She winked, showing a flicker of her old self. "Of course, I *could* be lying."

"I don't think you do," Mandy said.

Jasmine nodded. "I got over the panic reflex back home," she said, seriously. "And anyone who managed to *keep* it after a few months in Boot Camp probably wouldn't graduate."

Mandy nodded. She'd been through too much to panic at the slightest setback. "I can't imagine you panicking."

"Good," Jasmine said. "And what have *you* been doing?"

"Reloading the squadron," Mandy said. She kept her voice even with an effort. Mindy was the only person at the table who didn't know the truth. She'd be furious when she realised that Mandy had lied to her. "We're going to Thule in force, once we're ready to depart."

Mindy frowned. "There can't be much left there," she said. "Or am I wrong?"

"We might recover some of the industrial base," Mandy said, although she knew it was unlikely. She'd devastated every industrial platform within reach when she'd been forced to abandon the system. The

Wolves would make sure to devastate the rest when *they* were kicked out by superior force. "But it will also be a second blow to enemy morale. Thule was their first major victory, after all."

"And they're sending *you* back there," Mindy said. She sounded calculating. Mandy felt a shiver running down her spine. "I thought that wasn't allowed."

"I *am* a naval officer," Mandy reminded her, stiffly. "I *can* put my feelings aside for the greater good."

"And we're scraping the barrel," Jasmine put in. "Mandy is the only squadron commander without a current assignment."

"We *must* be desperate," Mindy teased.

Mandy kicked her under the table. "They're making you an NCO," she pointed out. "The end of the war is in sight!"

Jasmine coughed. "Remind me how old you two are meant to be again?"

"She started it," Mindy said.

Mandy flushed. It didn't matter how old she was - and it probably never would. Being with her sister meant becoming a teenager again. Or at least *acting* like a teenager. She shuddered, remembering some of the tantrums she'd thrown…she'd deserved to be slapped or worse, rather than her father's soft rebukes and her mother's screaming fits. But then, parents on Earth had had very little authority over their children. She'd certainly considered walking away more than once and going straight to a home for emancipated children…

And if the rumours from those homes are true, she thought grimly, *I dodged a bullet.*

"We're too old to be childish," she said, finally. They *weren't* children any longer, no matter how they felt. They were adults, with adult responsibilities. "Perhaps we should talk about something else."

The food arrived before Jasmine could reply; three bowls of curry, a large pan of rice and a piece of bread so large that it blocked the table. Jasmine picked up one of the bowls, removed a warning sign and dipped a piece of bread into the curry. Mandy caught sight of the waitress watching from the counter as Jasmine put the curry into her mouth and chewed it thoughtfully. The smell wasn't unpleasant, but it was *strong*.

"Not bad," Jasmine said. The waitress looked astonished. "Could do with a little extra spice, but otherwise..."

She held out the bowl. "Try some?"

"No, thank you," Mandy said, quickly. "I'll stick with something cooler."

"That's the navy way," Mindy needled. "You flee when the fire gets too hot."

Mandy scowled at her. "Poisoning myself isn't my idea of fun," she said, as she took some of her own curry. "I don't know how anyone can eat that...that...*stuff*."

"Modified taste buds," Mindy said. "Right?"

Jasmine shook her head. "My homeworld was pretty fond of spicy food," she said. "And Joe...well, *he* cooks by covering everything in spicy marinade and then adding extra sauce. No one can outdo him for food that tastes suspiciously like high explosive."

Mindy snorted. "Does cooking for the men bother you?"

"We take turns to cook," Jasmine said. Her face shadowed. "Or we used to, back when we were just a small platoon that was part of a larger company. The only people who didn't cook were the ones who volunteered to dig latrines instead. It wasn't much of an improvement."

"I would have thought not," Mindy agreed.

"Richard managed to give us all a bellyache, somehow," Jasmine added. "The entire platoon had the galloping shits for *days*. And then we threatened him with physical violence if he even *looked* at the cooking pots. I don't know *what* he put in his stew, but it probably violated a dozen laws on chemical weapons."

"Sounds a nice sort of bloke," Mindy said. "Have we met him?"

"He bought it on Han," Jasmine said. "The bad guys got lucky and potted him as he crawled along a rooftop. He..."

She shook her head. "He *was* a good bloke," she added. "But he *did* poison us all."

Mandy winced. "Can we talk about something else over dinner?"

"If you wish," Mindy said. "Have you found a new boyfriend yet?"

"No," Mandy said, swallowing a number of very nasty replies. "You?"

"It's a bit harder to find a boyfriend when you're going to the wars," Mindy said. "There was someone, but..."

"It didn't work out," Jasmine said. "It rarely does."

Mandy sighed. She hadn't *exactly* been raped, when she'd been trapped on a pirate ship, but she'd been pushed into surrendering herself. And if she hadn't been useful, if she hadn't had some engineering skills, she knew she wouldn't even have had *that* much choice. She could have been raped and murdered at any moment and no one would have given a damn. She'd broken up with her former boyfriend after returning to Avalon, then closed her heart. She couldn't bear the thought of letting someone else so close to her.

She met Jasmine's eyes. "And you?"

"Our relationship may not last," Jasmine said. "If we break up, we break up; if we stay together, we stay together."

"How very philosophical," Mindy said.

"Death can come at any moment," Jasmine pointed out, dryly. "There's no point in drawing up long-term plans when they might be completely useless - or worse."

"You want to wait until after the war," Mandy said.

"But there might be another war afterwards," Mindy countered. "The Wolves, the Trade Federation and ourselves can't be the only ones left."

Mandy nodded in agreement. The Empire was - had been - huge. There had been thousands of inhabited worlds, with rumours of hundreds more beyond the edge of explored space. The Core Worlds - Earth, in particular - might be gone, but that still left countless thousands of worlds that might start the return to space. Mindy was right. The three *known* interstellar powers *couldn't* be all that was left of the Empire.

Four, if you count Admiral Singh's little empire, she thought. *And five, if you count the RockRats.*

"We will see," Jasmine said. She lifted her wineglass and took a sip. "I'd like to know what happened to my family, but I may never get any answers."

Mandy felt a stab of bitter pity. She'd been exiled, sure, but she'd been exiled *with* her family. Jasmine's family were thousands of light-years away, if they were still alive. There was no way to know what had happened to them, save for going and looking. And while the navy *had* talked about dispatching missions corewards, the truth was that it would be a long time before they got off the ground. The Wolfbane War alone was consuming all of their resources.

We might never see the galaxy reunified in our lifetimes, she thought, morbidly. *And Jasmine may never see her family again.*

"You're part of our family now," she said, softly. "You're my older sister."

"A thankless job," Mindy teased.

Jasmine looked oddly amused. "I *am* an older sister," she reminded them, dryly. "It *was* a thankless task. I had nine siblings."

"Ouch," Mindy said. "Did you have an extended family?"

"One mother, one father, ten children," Jasmine said. "They were *busy*."

Mandy shook her head in amusement. She'd known families on Earth that had had dozens of children, but they'd all been extended families. The government benefits had been the only thing keeping some of them alive, too. Jasmine's parents had to have been mad…

"Very busy," she said, softly. "And now perhaps we can talk of happier things."

"And then go clubbing," Mindy added.

"Maybe not," Jasmine said. "Being recognised would be embarrassing."

Mandy laughed, regretfully. "Let us just talk of happier things," she said. "The war will wait a day or two."

"Unless Admiral Singh strikes first," Jasmine said. "That could be the end."

"You're not allowed to talk anymore," Mindy said.

CHAPTER EIGHT

If there was one advantage to having a relatively new intelligence service, Ed had decided long before the Battle of Corinthian, it was that the spooks hadn't had a chance to put down roots yet. The Empire's vast collection of intelligence and security services had been more interested in bureaucratic infighting and covering their collective asses than collecting, analysing and distributing intelligence to the military. He dreaded to think how many operations had gone spectacularly wrong because the intelligence staff had been ignorant, among other things, of their own ignorance. They'd cultivated an air of omniscience that had regularly bitten someone *else* on the behind.

The Commonwealth Intelligence Service hadn't had a chance to build a spectacular headquarters either, he reflected, as he walked into Kitty Stevenson's office. The spooks *wouldn't* have a fancy headquarters either, if he had his way. They would never have the chance to lose touch with the facts on the ground, or the men and women who depended on the intelligence officers for proper analysis. The building had an impermanent air, suggesting that the office could be closed down at a moment's notice. Everything, from the desks and chairs to the secure filing cabinets, was designed for hasty removal.

And a distributed service is harder to take out, he thought, wryly. The Empire had established three intelligence headquarters on Han, all of which had been obliterated in the opening moments of the war. *The CIS won't be crippled so easily.*

Colonel Kitty Stevenson rose to her feet as he entered, snapping out a salute. She was a tall, red-headed woman; her hair, very definitely not of regulation length, hanging down her back and brushing against her bottom. Her uniform was just tight enough to push the limits without infringing regulations, such as they were. Kitty had been in Naval Intelligence before being exiled to Avalon, but her staff were either drawn from civilian agencies or newly-recruited on Avalon. There was no real dress code for the CIS.

And she could just take off her uniform and blend into the civilian world, Ed thought. Kitty was tall and strong, but that hardly made her stand out on Avalon. *She wants people to look at her uniform, not at her face.*

"Colonel," Kitty said. "Thank you for coming."

Ed smiled, rather ruefully. He was used to getting by on very little sleep, yet a baby's cries - and demands to be fed - were alarmingly wearisome. He'd slept through incoming mortar rounds and shellfire - safe in the knowledge that the marines were hidden under a bunker - but his son demanded his immediate attention. He had the feeling he'd be going mad if he *hadn't* had plenty of experience in coping with little sleep. In truth, he had no idea how his mother - or Gaby - managed to cope.

"I meant to visit earlier," he said, taking the offered seat. "I trust that Operation Deception is proceeding as planned?"

"Yes, sir," Kitty said. She poured them both a mug of coffee, then passed one to him and sat back down behind her desk. "We've started spreading rumours about the squadron's planned targets in all the usual places. Everyone knows that Commodore Caesius and her fleet will hit Thule."

Ed nodded, sipping his coffee. "And the remainder of the squadrons?"

"Assigned to various reinforcement missions," Kitty said. "Their CO's have sealed orders, which will be opened once the ships are in phase space. The remainder of their crews have no reason to suspect that they're going somewhere else. I hear they're quite envious of Commodore Caesius's squadron."

"Good," Ed said. *That* spoke well for morale, even though the Commonwealth had taken a beating during the first year of the war. But then, his crews had been trained to think and plan for themselves, not follow orders slavishly. They *knew* they had the edge. "And our double agents?"

He took another sip of his coffee, smiling inwardly at the sour taste. The CIS received the same coffee blend as the rest of the military, a foul brew that banished sleep and damaged taste buds. He'd made sure of it, knowing just how easy it was for the spooks to obtain their own black market coffee. They couldn't be allowed to think of themselves as anything special, not when they had to keep their ear to the ground. Hell, he was pushing things by allowing Kitty Stevenson to remain in her office for over a year.

"They've picked up the message," Kitty said. "Hannalore *has* been cooperating."

Ed felt his expression darken. Governor Brent Roeder - the *former* Governor of Avalon - had accepted his demotion with good grace, but his wife had never been resigned to losing her position as queen bee. She'd slipped into treachery, selling out the Commonwealth in exchange for a promise that her husband would be allowed to rule Avalon after the war. And she'd been a hellishly effective spy. Ed had never really understood just how many people talked freely at Hannalore Roeder's parties, let alone how much could be coaxed out of them by a friendly ear. It had been sheer luck that Hannalore had been caught before she could do *real* damage.

She did quite enough, he thought, grimly. *And we can never forgive her*.

He scowled down into his mug. Hannalore had switched sides the moment she'd been caught, offering to send disinformation to Wolfbane in exchange for amnesty. Ed hadn't wanted to take the deal, even though he understood the necessity. The chance to mislead Wolfbane, to lure Admiral Singh into a trap, was one he couldn't afford to miss. But it still meant letting a known traitor get away with it. Hannalore would never be trusted again - she'd be exiled from Avalon once the war was over - but she'd be alive. She deserved to be put in front of a wall and shot.

"I'm glad to hear it," he lied. He would have been glad of an excuse to shoot the wretched bitch. She'd sold out the Commonwealth for a pipe dream. "Did she send the message?"

"Yes, she did," Kitty said. She cocked her head, thoughtfully. "However, sir, we must face up to the possibility that her position has been exposed."

Ed looked up. "What do you mean?"

"We used Hannalore - and the handful of other double agents - to convince Admiral Singh to launch her invasion of Corinthian," Kitty reminded him. "And *that* didn't end well for Admiral Singh. She may take everything she hears from Hannalore and her fellows with a grain of salt."

Ed made a face. If Hannalore was useless…he shook his head, angrily dismissing the thought. They'd made a deal. Perhaps it was a bad deal, perhaps it stuck in his craw…they'd made a deal. And they had to *keep* that deal. Hannalore couldn't be blamed - fairly - for Admiral Singh choosing not to believe her in future. She *had* sent the enemy some pretty damning misinformation, after all.

He took another sip of his coffee. "Do we have any reason to believe that Hannalore's cover *has* been blown?"

Kitty shrugged. "A smart intelligence officer would understand that Hannalore might have been misled herself," she said. "They don't have any easy way to touch base with her, not during wartime. We'd intercept any electronic message sent to her. But sir…in intelligence, there's always the risk that someone is playing games with you. I suspect they always took her intelligence with a pinch of salt. And now they have a good reason to discard it altogether."

"Ouch," Ed said.

"On the other hand, we *have* been seeding the idea of Thule pretty heavily," Kitty added, thoughtfully. "Any other intelligence operatives on Avalon will probably have caught wind of it by now. The message might already have gone out."

Ed shook his head. There were hundreds of thousands - perhaps millions - of newcomers on Avalon, with hundreds of interplanetary spacecraft and starships entering and leaving the system every day. There was no way the newcomers could *all* be vetted, any more than the ships could be searched without imposing impossible delays. And even a *good* search party might miss a microscopic datachip or encrypted files hidden within a commercial-grade datacore. A spy who landed on Avalon might find himself in a position to pick up a great deal of intelligence, as long as he was careful not to walk into one of the secure zones.

"As long as they believe it," he said, finally. "But we can't guarantee that, can we?"

"No, sir," Kitty said. "Admiral Singh may choose to disbelieve the intelligence."

"Or she may decide that Thule isn't worth defending any longer," Ed said. Intelligence was scarce, but it looked as though the insurgents who'd bedevilled the CEF were now bedevilling the Wolves instead. Thule's industrial base, the prize that had lured the Commonwealth into dispatching the CEF in the first place, no longer existed. "She might just withdraw her starships and abandon the system."

"Which we could spin into a major victory," Kitty pointed out.

Ed shook his head. The Empire's spin doctors had been experts at turning defeats or costly victories into one-sided engagements where the enemy had been exterminated on the cheap, but the population of Avalon wasn't so easily fooled. A good third of the population had *some* military experience, on one side or the other. They'd know that Thule was effectively worthless these days, that the other side had withdrawn rather than stand and fight...they'd know that the news reports were worthless. Putting out the truth, even when the truth reflected badly on the Commonwealth, was the only way to bolster confidence and trust in the long run. It would pay off, he told himself. Eventually.

And passing laws to make it clear that reporters can be held accountable for lies, libel and endangered lives will do the rest, he thought. *They're not considered little tin gods any longer*.

"We could certainly try to convince the *Wolves* that Thule was a major defeat," Kitty insisted, dryly. "It might push them to overthrow her."

"Too chancy," Ed said. Beaming propaganda into the enemy's datanets was easy enough, but it ran the same risk of overdoing it. Too many lies were easy to spot. "And besides, we're not *going* to Thule."

"We do have the system under observation," Kitty said. "They *might* just withdraw when they hear we're coming."

Ed shrugged. If *he'd* been in command of the opposing force, *he'd* have left a small force to hold the high orbitals and otherwise withdrawn from

Thule. The planet's short-term value was practically nil, now the industries were gone. He suspected the Wolves had already conscripted anyone with valuable technological skills and shipped them off to Wolfbane, leaving the rest of the system alone. In the long term, Thule would blossom again, but that would take years. Admiral Singh would no doubt prefer that it *didn't* blossom until she emerged victorious.

"It doesn't matter for the moment," he said. "How long until Admiral Singh hears the news?"

Kitty tapped a switch, displaying a holographic starchart over her desk. An expanding sphere, centred on Avalon, appeared in front of them. Ed leaned forward, silently assessing the situation. It looked unchanged, but he knew that looks could be deceiving. There was no way to track the war in real time.

"It's been two weeks since we started spreading the rumours," Kitty said. "Assuming they were picked up at once, and they should have been, word *might* be reaching the edge of enemy space by now. Hannalore's message was sent a few days later. I'd be fairly sure Admiral Singh will get the message in two to three weeks. They're using converted courier boats as spies."

Ed nodded in annoyance. Wolfbane had had a very definite advantage, although it had taken him some time to realise it. Governor Brown had had a small fleet of courier boats under his direct control, a fleet Admiral Singh had inherited. They were tiny ships, nothing more than phase drives with a cockpit attached, but they were fast, easily twice as fast in FTL as anything else. Admiral Singh could get word back from the front - and send out orders - faster than anyone else.

And she would know better than to rely on it, he thought, sourly. *She actually earned her rank. She'd understand the dangers of trying to micromanage from a distance.*

He ground his teeth. Long-distance micromanagement was always a disaster waiting to happen - the Grand Senate had proved that often enough - but Admiral Singh was *closer* to the war front than the Grand Senate had ever been. She could get her orders out to the front quicker than the Grand Senate, then hear their responses in time to do something about it…something that might actually be effective. She'd certainly have a much better idea of what was actually going on.

"And then she'll have to decide what to do," Ed mused. "A pity we can't push her directly."

"No, sir," Kitty agreed. "She would probably notice any manipulations, if we tried."

Ed leaned forward. "How solid *is* your intelligence on Wolfbane?"

Kitty frowned. "As solid as it can be," she said, waving her hand and dismissing the starchart. "We debriefed a number of defectors - we even debriefed a number of POWs who wanted to go into a POW camp, rather than defect. The Trade Federation has quite a few sources of its own on Wolfbane and they've shared what they know with us..."

She shrugged. "In truth, sir, we're not mind-readers. We can make guesses at what Admiral Singh is thinking, sir; we can make guesses about her likely opponents, but they're nothing more than guesswork. Too much depends on individual personalities, people who may know more or less than we *think* they know. People are generally rational in their own best interests, but we don't know what they *think* to be their best interests."

"They may decide that Admiral Singh is a safer bet for their futures than us," Ed said. "And they might be right."

"Yes, sir," Kitty said.

Ed silently gave her points for honesty. "And the prospects of a violent uprising?"

"Impossible to calculate," Kitty told him, bluntly. "We *do* know that life on Wolfbane is very restricted, but that was true before Governor Brown took control. The population might be discontented - it might be rebellious - yet it may be unable to translate that feeling into action. There's a shortage of guns, it seems."

"And without guns, revolution is impossible," Ed said.

"I imagine that the corporations would try to stave off a full-scale rebellion," Kitty said. "A long period of unrest would be very bad for business. But if the rebels got too aggressive..."

"They'd be squashed," Ed said.

"Yes, sir," Kitty said. "Admiral Singh holds the cards - and I don't think she's particularly squeamish."

Ed nodded, grimly. He'd read Admiral Singh's file carefully, time and time again. The Imperial Navy had always had a problem with personnel assessments - an assessment that didn't insist the officer could walk on water was damning - but, reading between the lines, it was clear that Admiral Singh had clawed her way up from almost nothing. Indeed, in many ways, she wasn't *that* different from Ed himself. It was quite possible that they shared an unspoken contempt for those who couldn't or *wouldn't* climb out of the gutter and reach for the stars. Admiral Singh might not hesitate to unleash armoured troopers on rioting mobs, with orders to kill as many as possible. She'd see it as teaching the survivors a valuable lesson.

"Then all we can do is hope," he said. "Jasmine and her team leave in a week, heading to Calomel. The remainder of the force will lift two weeks afterwards, spearheaded by all five platoons."

Kitty raised her eyebrows. "You intend to take *all* of the platoons?"

"Yes," Ed said. The CEF was good - and the Stormtroopers were coming along nicely - but the marines still had the advantage. "They're the best we have, even now."

"Risky," Kitty observed. "Can you even assemble them without setting off alarms?"

Ed smiled. "I think so," he said. Sneaking around Avalon galled him, but there was no alternative. The planet *was* under enemy observation. "Everyone *knows* the CEF is being redeployed, anyway."

"Unfortunately," Kitty said. "But at least it will add meat to the planned attack on Thule."

"Yes," Ed agreed.

He shook his head in cold annoyance. No one had fought a *real* interstellar war in centuries, not since the Unification Wars. The Empire's long string of military campaigns had been targeted on isolated worlds, not interstellar powers...even the Carpathian Revolt had involved only five star systems, none of which could muster a real challenge to the Imperial Navy. The high cost had been caused by naval incompetence, not enemy action. But the Commonwealth was learning as it went along...

Too many things could go wrong, he knew. Admiral Singh might not fall for their deception - she might not even *see* the deception. Or she might have her own plans...war was a democracy, after all. The enemy had a vote. She might be doing something, right now, that would undermine everything Ed had planned. Or someone might have assassinated her already. There was just no way to know.

"Make sure the word keeps going out," he said, rising. "And keep me informed."

"Of course, sir," Kitty said. "We *have* done this before."

"But the stakes have never been so high," Ed said. The Commonwealth had won a great victory, but it wasn't enough to put an end to the war. "We could still lose."

And having to play cloak and dagger games, he added silently, *only makes it harder to focus on what's truly important.*

CHAPTER NINE

"Transit complete, Captain."

Captain Christopher Brookes leaned back into his command chair as *Powerhouse* and her comrades crossed the Phase Limit, plunging into the Trieste System. It had been a long flight from Titlark, long enough for the unexpected additions to his crew to put a strain on morale, but it was over now. He watched the in-system display gradually start to fill up, revealing the presence of seven planets and a handful of radio sources deeper into the system. There were not, as he had expected, any starships within detection range.

He ran his hand through his brown hair, making a show of considering his next move. It wasn't as if there was any real point, but he had ambitions. And, to realise his ambitions, he had to *look* good as well as *be* good. The money he'd spent on his body - carving his face into a handsome mask - had not been wasted. People would be watching him. He could practically *feel* it.

"Take us deeper into the system," he ordered.

"Aye, Captain," the helmsman said.

Christopher nodded, curtly. Trieste wasn't particularly *important*, not in the grand scheme of things. Stage-two colonies were rarely able to do more than shake their fists impotently when enemy starships moved through their system or took control of their high orbitals. But Trieste *was* a Commonwealth world and so needed to be targeted. It never seemed to have occurred to the settlers that neutrality would have been a far better option when war started looming over the sector. They'd only been spared - so far - because they didn't have anything worth taking.

"Keep a sharp eye out for enemy ships," Commissioner Chad Carsten said. The pudgy man looked uncomfortable on the bridge, as if he knew he had no real right to be there. His ugly appearance suited his mind. "They might be trying to ambush us."

"Of course," Christopher said, blithely. The odds against being intercepted were staggeringly high. He was fairly confident that no one knew they were coming, but he'd made sure to come in on a random vector just to be certain. "If they want to catch us, Commissioner, they'll have to work at it."

He kept his face expressionless with an effort as the tiny force moved deeper into the enemy system. There were rumours - all sorts of wild rumours - about what had happened at Corinthian, ranging from a minor defeat to an enemy superweapon that had obliterated the entire navy. The latter was obviously untrue, but the sudden arrival of the commissioners - and armed internal security detachments - suggested that *something* had gone spectacularly wrong. Christopher was fairly sure the bastard didn't have the power to override him on his own bridge, yet he had no idea if that would hold up in a court-martial. The other captains seemed inclined to bow and scrape before the commissioners rather than challenge them.

And none of them know anything about naval operations, he thought, bitterly. It hadn't taken much questioning to prove to his own satisfaction that *his* commissioner had never been in the navy. *Some of them haven't been in space before.*

He pushed the thought aside and concentrated on the display. Squadron command at such a young age - even if it was a brevet command that could be cancelled at any moment - would definitely look good on his file. So *what* if he was raiding a largely defenceless system? So *what* if he was commanding five light cruisers and a courier boat? It was a chance to make a mark, to prove to Admiral Singh that he could handle something more than a single warship in a squadron. If he was lucky, it would get him promoted above his peers. Admiral Singh, unlike the Imperial Navy, knew talent when she saw it. God knew *she'd* had enough problems with backstabbing superiors in her life.

And then I can try to grasp a heavy cruiser or even a battleship, he thought. He'd heard rumours, too, of new battleships coming out of the shipyards. *Modern* battleships, rather than patched-up hulks. Command of one of *them* would practically guarantee him flag rank, within five years. *And then I might have a real chance at rising even higher.*

He smiled at the commissioner as the older man turned to look at him. The bastard didn't like him, but Christopher didn't care. He turned up the wattage of his smile, enjoying the faint displeasure on the commissioner's face. An enemy like that was a badge of honour. Let him sit on the bridge and scowl disapprovingly at the crew, if he wished. Admiral Singh would pay as little attention to him as she paid to supply bureaucrats who didn't seem to understand their true role in life. Christopher was a naval hero and the commissioner...was just a commissioner.

Better win the engagement first, he reminded himself, sharply. The hours were ticking by slowly, too slowly. *There's nothing to be gained by gloating too soon.*

"Captain," the sensor officer said. She was young, so young that she didn't remember the Imperial Navy, but she was good. The cynical side of Christopher's mind insisted that the two facts were connected. "Long-range scans are revealing the presence of two stations orbiting the planet. They both appear to be standard colony support units."

Christopher nodded, concealing his displeasure. It was *possible*, he supposed, that the Commonwealth had bolted missile tubes or energy weapons to the orbital stations, but even if they had they wouldn't pose any real threat. The stations could neither run nor hide. Their crews were probably hastily evacuating even now, launching lifepods before his ships entered missile range. He wouldn't blame them, either. Staying on their stations would mean certain death.

"Communications, transmit a warning message," he ordered. "Inform them that we will destroy their stations in" - he glanced at the display - "forty minutes. They have that long to evacuate."

"Aye, sir," the communications officer said.

The commissioner turned to face Christopher. "Are you warning them to evacuate?"

"Yes," Christopher said, resisting the urge to insult the idiot openly. He was on the damn bridge! Was there some confusion about his orders? "There's nothing to be gained by slaughtering the station crews."

"They might be technical experts," the commissioner pointed out. "We have standing orders to conscript all technical specialists wherever we find them."

"They'll have started to evacuate already," Christopher said. It was possible, he supposed, that the locals had missed his squadron, but he knew better than to count on it. The Commonwealth's sensors were alarmingly good. "And even if we did take them with us, could they be trusted?"

He ignored the commissioner's spluttering as he turned back to the display. The stations were launching lifepods, dropping them into the planet's atmosphere. Their crews would have a bumpy ride and a worse landing, but at least they'd be alive. Trieste wouldn't be too badly hurt by their visit, if only because they had nothing of any particular value. The colony world would probably be left alone afterwards.

"Entering missile range, sir," the tactical officer said.

"Take them out," Christopher ordered.

He watched, feeling a flicker of irritated frustration, as the two missiles lanced towards their targets. There was no counterbattery fire, nothing to slow them down; the warheads slammed home, detonating a moment later. Pieces of debris, none of them large enough to survive their passage through the atmosphere, rocketed in all directions. Trieste's government would have some work to do, clearing up the mess, once the war was over. Or maybe the Consortium would just divert a pair of warships to use the debris for target practice.

"Both targets destroyed, sir," the tactical officer reported.

"Good shooting," Christopher said, grudgingly. He had no doubt that the media would turn the raid into a staggering victory, but anyone who knew anything about naval affairs would not be fooled. Blowing up two stations wouldn't make a difference and he knew it. And there was nothing on Trieste worth the effort of bombing. "Helm, take us out on our planned vector."

"Aye, sir," the helmsman said.

Christopher scowled at the commissioner's back as the older man strode across the bridge, his gaze flickering over consoles as if he knew what the displays actually *meant*. They might as well have been glittering lights, Christopher suspected. He'd heard whispered stories of commissioners who'd pressed the wrong buttons and accidentally blown up entire starships, although he was sure they were exaggerated. Triggering the self-destruct device wasn't *that* easy. But...

The sensor console bleeped. "Captain, I'm picking up five ships heading to Trieste," the sensor officer said. "Two warships, three freighters."

Christopher rose and walked casually over to her console, burying the excitement beneath his professionalism. *This* was more like it. He'd always known he was lucky, but this time Lady Luck had outdone herself. If it was a simulation, he would have been suspected of hacking the computers to rig matters in his favour. The enemy ships would have to reverse course in order to escape, a difficult task with his squadron breathing down their necks.

"Two light cruisers," the sensor officer added. "They're both pre-Fall designs."

Christopher allowed himself an unpleasant smile. Five on two...he *liked* those odds. A Commonwealth ship would be a nasty customer - he was sure their sensors and weapons would have been updated, even if there *were* limits to what could be done with their hulls - but he had them outnumbered and outgunned. And while the *warships* might be able to turn and run, they'd have to abandon the freighters in order to escape. Either way, he won.

"Helm, take us on an intercept course," he ordered. *This* would be a better victory, worthy of his time. "Tactical, prepare to engage the enemy."

"Aye, Captain," the helmsman said.

The commissioner caught his eye. "Is it wise to intercept the enemy ships?"

"Yes," Christopher said, flatly.

"Our orders are to raid the planet and then get out," the commissioner said. "Captain, I urge you to reconsider."

"We have the advantage," Christopher insisted. "And a chance to obliterate two enemy ships - perhaps five - at minimal risk."

He returned to his command chair and sat down, studying the display. The enemy ships had noticed them, too late. They were taking evasive action, but they couldn't hope to alter course in time to escape. Their commanders would be put in front of a wall and shot for this, if they ever returned home. The Commonwealth might not even bother with the formality of a court-martial.

They probably expected the system to be safe, he thought. Trieste had a handful of asteroid settlements, but no major interstellar ships - or starships - of its own. *They weren't ready for trouble.*

"Enemy warships are assuming combat formation," the sensor officer reported. "The freighters are still altering course."

Christopher smiled, coldly. The *smart* move, given how badly they'd been mouse-trapped, would have been to abandon the freighters and run. No naval officer worth his salt would have *liked* the idea of fleeing, but there was no choice. The freighters *couldn't* escape, not now. There was no way they could build up the speed to reach the Phase Limit before Christopher's ships caught up with them. Their escorts were going to die for nothing.

"Launch two probes to keep an eye on them," he ordered. It was *just* possible that the freighters might go doggo, although it was unlikely to work. His sensors already had a pretty solid lock on their positions. "Tactical, inform the squadron. I want rapid fire as soon as we enter missile range."

"Aye, sir," the tactical officer said.

The commissioner looked displeased. "Wasting missiles…"

"Better the missiles than the starships," Christopher told him. "Think of this as a cheap victory."

He allowed his smile to widen as the squadron counted down the last few seconds to missile range. The enemy ships were holding position, neither trying to flee nor attempting to surrender. He saluted them, mentally, even though he knew they were wasting their lives and ships. The enemy

CO might deserve to be shot - his little fleet wasn't *that* far from the front - but his crews didn't deserve to die. And yet...

It's too late, he told himself. *They can't escape now.*

The display sparkled with glittering red icons. Christopher leaned forward instinctively - he heard a sharp intake of breath from the commissioner - and silently counted the enemy missiles. Fifty-seven... they hadn't enhanced their throw weight, it seemed. The light cruisers had probably been deemed too old for *real* service. He didn't blame the Commonwealth, either. The light cruisers would still be enough to deter pirates, even if the Wolves didn't see them as a threat. It would be cheaper to build a brand new ship than refit the older vessels to modern standards.

"Return fire," he ordered, quietly. "Point defence, prepare to engage."

"Point defence standing by," the tactical officer said. His voice was calm. "Datanet primed, ready to engage. Enemy missiles entering engagement range in ten...nine..."

Christopher braced himself as the missiles slipped into his engagement envelope. He'd drilled his crews relentlessly, pitting them against simulated missiles that were twice as fast and half the size of the latest enemy missiles. They'd done well, in simulations; now, it seemed they were doing well in the real world too. Dozens of enemy missiles flew into a tightly-coordinated web of fire and evaporated, blasted into dust before they had a chance to go active. They didn't even have any decoy missiles or penetration aids to help them to slip through the defences. The handful of missiles that reached their targets didn't do enough damage to matter.

He turned his attention to the missiles his ships had launched and felt his smile grow wider. The Commonwealth CO *had* drilled his crews too, he noted, but they just didn't have the firepower to make a significant difference. He'd fired too many missiles for them to take them *all* out before it was too late. Nuclear warheads slammed into their targets and detonated, laser beams tore into undefended hulls...

"Target One destroyed," the tactical officer reported. *Powerhouse* rocked as a missile got through her defences and slammed into her hull. "Target Two has taken heavy damage...she's launching lifepods."

"Invite her to surrender," Christopher ordered. It was unlikely they'd recover anything worth having from the hulk - the Commonwealth officers would make sure to destroy their datacores and any advanced technology before they surrendered - but it would look good in the media. The reporters would have a field day. "Tell her..."

Target Two vanished from the display. Christopher sighed, telling himself he shouldn't be too annoyed. He'd scored a tiny, but important victory. A few minutes either way and he might have lost the opportunity to intercept the enemy ships...

"Deploy shuttles to pick up the lifepods," he ordered. "And order the enemy freighters to surrender."

"Aye, Captain," the communications officer said.

Christopher wondered, briefly, just what the freighters were actually *carrying*. Trieste would need to import all sorts of machined products, but the Commonwealth *was* in the middle of a full-scale war. He couldn't imagine Avalon or Corinthian churning out farming equipment or mining tools or whatever else Trieste might need when there were more important matters on hand. Unless...perhaps they'd uncovered one of the Empire's old stockpiles. It was quite possible.

"The freighters are surrendering, Captain," the communications officer reported. "They're shutting down their drives and opening their hatches."

"Dispatch naval infantry to take possession," Christopher ordered. He considered, briefly, dumping the prisoners on Trieste, then decided it would be dangerous. The Commonwealth had a manpower shortage. Taking the POWs back to Wolfbane wouldn't have *that* much of an impact, but every little bit helped. "And then set course for home."

"Aye, Captain."

Christopher grinned at the commissioner, enjoying the sour look on the man's face. They'd scored a victory...a tiny victory, true, but still a victory. The Commonwealth's shipping crisis wouldn't be made any better, either, by the loss of three freighters. If nothing else, they'd have to redeploy escort units to the sector, if they wanted to send more freighters along the front lines. There weren't *many* raiding squadrons out there, but the Commonwealth wouldn't *know* that...

He watched the shuttles detaching, heading to the enemy ships. The crews would be treated well, of course. Who knew? They might decide to join the Wolves. There was certainly no need to make their imprisonment unpleasant, was there? The ships themselves were the prizes, along with their cargo…whatever it was. He'd make sure the prisoners were well-treated until after the war.

"Captain, we received a manifest from the first freighter," the communications officer reported. "They're carrying farming supplies: equipment, tools and bioengineered seeds."

"Doubtful," the commissioner said. He sneered at the communication officer's back. "It's a cover for something else."

Christopher was inclined to agree, for once. Farming supplies in the middle of a war? He shrugged, keeping his doubts off his face. They'd find out when the ships were carefully searched, just to be sure. Who knew? Perhaps they *were* farming supplies. If the seeds had been bioengineered specifically for Trieste, which was possible, they'd probably be useless elsewhere. He might have to decide to dump them on the planet or not.

"Tell the infantry to check," he ordered. There was no point in telling the commissioner that he thought the asshole might be right. "We'll find out then."

A victory, he told himself, firmly. They'd destroyed two enemy warships and captured three freighters, all for minimal damage. The repairs wouldn't take *that* long. *A victory we can boast about, no matter how small.*

His smile widened. Admiral Singh *would* be pleased.

CHAPTER TEN

"Hurry," Jasmine urged. "Time is running short."

"Shut up," Meade grunted. She didn't look up from her work. "This is delicate!"

Jasmine watched, feeling a flicker of grudging admiration. As prickly as Meade was - and she *was* prickly - she was a *very* good engineer. Her careful manipulation of her tools was actually *working*. The FTL modulator she'd been given was well beyond *Jasmine's* ability to repair, even though she'd practiced repairing nearly everything in the Marine Corps' inventory. But *Meade* was working calmly, carefully restoring the modulator to working order…

"Done," Meade said. She slipped her tools back into her belt and looked up, challengingly. "What do you think?"

Duncan Patrick, another auxiliary, bent over the table to examine the device. "It'll get a starship back into Phase Space," he said, after a moment. "But it won't last forever."

"Unfortunately not," Meade agreed. "The stress of dropping *out* of phase space probably won't help. I'd be surprised if it lasts for more than one trip."

Jasmine met her eyes. "Why?"

"I had to strip out some of the shielding to do the repairs," Meade said. Her voice was very calm, but Jasmine thought she detected a hint of mockery. "The influx of FTL radiation won't do the modulator any good at all. I'd expect it to decay at a frightening rate."

She cocked her eyebrow. "Are you now confident that I actually *earned* my certificates?"

"Yeah," Jasmine conceded. "You did very well."

"Damn right," Meade said.

Jasmine kept her expression blank with an effort. Meade had come back, as expected, and gone into lockdown without any protest. And then she'd brushed up on everything from shooting to basic engineering, proving - quite thoroughly - that she had *definitely* earned her certifications. Meade didn't have what it took to be a marine, Jasmine suspected, but she *was* a very good engineer. She'd have no trouble proving herself when they finally reached Wolfbane.

"We'll be boarding the freighter at 1400," she said, bluntly. She glanced at Patrick, then at her two fellow marines. "You have two hours to get a last lunch, rewrite your wills and then get some rest. If you have any letters you want to write before we depart, get them done and hand them over to the base's censor."

"Aye, boss," Thomas Stewart said, cheerfully. "Not that I have much to leave behind..."

"I'm sure *someone* will appreciate your wages if you're no longer alive to spend them," Henry Parkinson put in. "I'm leaving mine to the company funds."

Jasmine held up a hand. "Report to the shuttlepad at 1400," she said, before the argument could get any further out of hand. "Dismissed."

She watched them go, resisting the urge to rub her forehead. Stewart and Parkinson, at least, had served with her before. She had faith in them, but Meade and Patrick were unknown factors. In theory, they had all the qualifications and experience they needed; in practice, they'd never been really tested. Or maybe she was just being bitchy. On Avalon, the auxiliaries had garnered quite a bit of experience under fire.

And Meade has been doing better, she thought, as she turned and walked out of the exercise room. *She'll cope fine, I hope.*

The complex was large, but almost completely empty. There were no permanent residents, save for a handful of maintenance staffers who lived on the base and apparently had no lives outside it. Jasmine hoped they were being paid well for their services - a year in lockdown, whatever else happened, would be far from pleasant. And yet, given the complex's vast library and other facilities, perhaps they were far from bored. She certainly *hoped* that was true. Bored marines tended to cause trouble.

She stopped outside an unmarked door and knocked, sharply. There was a long pause, just long enough for her to start to worry, before the door opened, revealing General Mark Haverford. He was trembling like a leaf, sweat clearly visible on his forehead. The treatments he'd been given to change his DNA, just enough to spoof any detectors on Wolfbane, had unfortunate side effects. He was just lucky, Jasmine considered, that he hadn't had a reaction bad enough to confine him to bed. He'd be over it, she'd been told, by the time they reached Calomel.

"I have looked better," he said, as he stepped back to invite her in. "But I suppose I have looked worse too."

Jasmine studied him, thoughtfully. His appearance hadn't been changed *that* much, but the different hair colour and the slight - very slight - changes to his cheeks and eyes would be enough to fool any automated facial recognition program. Anyone who'd known him in the military would *probably* be fooled, as long as Haverford was careful. They'd certainly not connect him, automatically, with their former comrade.

"You look younger," she said, as she closed the door. "Are you ready to depart?"

"I will be, once my legs stop trembling," Haverford said. "Are *you* ready to depart?"

Jasmine nodded, wordlessly. She'd checked and rechecked their supplies, then written her last letters and updated her will. It wasn't as if she was carrying very much with her, in any case. A handful of forged ID chips, some Trade Federation currency, a couple of sidearms that could have been purchased almost anywhere along the Rim…there was nothing about her, save for her body, that screamed *marine*. And no one was going to get a close look at her naked.

Unless they have pickups in our cabins, she reminded herself. Starship crews often quietly monitored their guests, just in case. Hotel staff did the same, although often with more perverted motivations. She was used to having no privacy - Boot Camp had cured her of any physical modesty she'd had - but being spied on when she was undressing could prove disastrous. *We will have to be very careful.*

"I've gone through everything I remember from the last few years," Haverford added, after a moment. "We should be able to make contact, once we reach Wolfbane."

And if we can't, we need to find ways to disrupt their war effort, Jasmine thought. Stewart and herself were the only ones who knew that Colonel Stalker intended to attack Wolfbane itself. Everyone else assumed they were going to undermine Admiral Singh and spark off a revolution. *And who knows what we'll do with you then?*

"Let us hope so," she said. She glanced around the tiny room. "Do you have anything you wish to bring with you?"

"Nothing I haven't already packed," Haverford assured her. "Everything in this room belongs to the base, not to me."

"Good," Jasmine said. She wondered, absently, what would happen to the defector after they completed their mission. Haverford wouldn't have a home anywhere. "Then - perhaps - you would care to join me for lunch?"

Haverford gave her a long look, then nodded. "I'll leave the room unlocked," he said, as he pulled on his jacket. "The cleaning staff can take everything back when we're gone."

Jasmine took one last look around the compartment, then walked with him down to the mess hall. Haverford was clearly in a bad way - he stumbled and fell against her twice, forcing her to hold him upright as they staggered into the giant compartment. It was large enough to feed over five hundred men, but it was completely empty. Jasmine wasn't too surprised. Her team was probably getting a few extra winks of sleep before heading to the shuttlepad.

And we'll have to stay in shape while we're on the freighter, she thought, sourly. *We'll be in transit for a month before we even reach our first waypoint.*

She walked over to the hatch and peered through into the kitchen. A lone staffer was sitting on the counter, reading a datapad. Jasmine cleared her throat, loudly. He jumped, then dropped to the floor and hurried over to the hatch.

"Welcome to *Le Cafe Latrine*," he said. "Would you like something shitty, something foul, or something..."

"Something *edible*," Jasmine said, tartly. Maybe the staff *had* been on lockdown for too long. "Something we can actually eat."

"I'm afraid we don't serve *edible* food," the staffer said. He dropped down and opened up a hatch, producing a pair of sealed meal packets. "I've got steak and chips, hamburger and fries, curry and rice..."

"Steak will be fine, thank you," Jasmine said. She grunted in annoyance. The base was isolated, surrounded by prime hunting territory. There was nothing stopping the base's personnel from going out and bagging a deer or rearing their own chickens. "Just bring it over when you're done."

She sat down, eyeing Haverford thoughtfully. He was still trembling, his hands twitching so badly that she was relieved he didn't have a sidearm. She'd seen a couple of people who'd breathed in too much riot control gas - it did long-term nerve damage, if the victims didn't seek medical attention at once - and they'd looked more in control of themselves. It had to be frustrating, very frustrating, to no longer be in command of one's own body.

"You'll get better," she said, firmly. "It won't last forever."

"I hope not," Haverford said. "You do realise I'm a little old for such treatments?"

"The medics cleared you," Jasmine said. Haverford wasn't a marine, but he wasn't exactly in poor condition either. "And it's better than being caught."

"I suppose," Haverford said. He gave her a sharp look. "Does Singh have any samples of *your* DNA?"

Jasmine made a face. It *was* possible, she had to admit. There were marine records in each sector, records that might not have been destroyed when Governor Brown took control. And Admiral Singh had excellent reason to remember Jasmine personally, after what had happened on Corinthian. The Admiral might even have kept the records from Jasmine's interrogation session under her lair. Jasmine *had* her DNA altered a little, just enough to escape a casual scan, but she knew a deep scan would sound the alert.

They'd know I changed my DNA, she thought, glumly. *And they'd know I had something to hide, even if they didn't know* what.

"I have had my own DNA rewritten, slightly," she said, finally. "None of the others ever had any contact with her."

"Good," Haverford said. "There's no point in taking unnecessary risks."

The food arrived before Jasmine could formulate a response. She removed the tin foil, then stared down at a blackened lump and a mass of soggy chips. It was a law of nature, she reminded herself, that military bases had bad food, even if one was heading off on a suicide mission. She poked the lump carefully - it looked as though the steak had been burned to charcoal - and then tasted it. Surprisingly, it tasted better than it looked.

"As long as we can make contact, the mission should go well," she said, nibbling on a chip thoughtfully. It didn't taste bad, either. "And if we can't…well, we have contingency plans."

She looked up as the door opened, revealing Stewart and Patrick. There was no sign of the other two, something that made her wonder if they were together. She'd thought she'd detected sparks between Meade and Parkinson…and technically, a relationship between them wouldn't be against regulations. But it would be, once they left…maybe she was just being silly. There was no proof they were actually together.

"It tastes better than it looks," she said, as the other two joined them. "Really."

"The bar isn't set very high," Stewart said. He stole one of her chips and nibbled it, grimacing in disgust. "Are they trying to convince us that ration bars are actually worth eating?"

"It's as good an explanation as any," Jasmine said. She had no idea what the food would be like, on the freighter, but it would probably make her yearn for ration bars after a couple of weeks. The freighter would take on as much fresh food as it could, she was sure, yet it wouldn't last. "Or maybe they just don't have a proper chef on the base."

"They should have let us cook," Stewart agreed. He stalked over to the hatch, demanded two more meals, and hurried back to the table. The food arrived two minutes later. "I could do better than this…"

Jasmine shook her head, then finished the steak. "We'll be on the shuttle in half an hour," she said, checking her wristcom. She'd have to replace it with a civilian model before she left the base. "Make sure you're ready to go."

"I've only got four bags of luggage," Patrick said. "Can I book some extra storage space, boss?"

"Hah," Jasmine said. "You only get one bag. You'll have to repack."

"It's that collection of souvenirs," Stewart said. He shot Jasmine a mischievous look. "I told him not to go mad in the shop. He bought mugs and tacky t-shirts and chocolate bars and..."

Jasmine snorted. Marines were usually restricted to one carryall, whatever their rank, but other services weren't always so well organised. She still smiled whenever she recalled the army LT who'd arrived on base with two *giant* bags of luggage and a collection of hunting rifles. The bastard had somehow gotten away with it, too. Of course, he *had* been well-connected and the uprising on Han had started a day or two later...

"You marines," Haverford said. "I don't understand you."

"Of course not," Stewart said. "You're *not* a marine."

"Right now, we're a team," Jasmine said, firmly. She understood Stewart's point - even *agreed* with it - but this wasn't the time. "And I hope *you* only have one bag."

"I do," Stewart said. He finished his meal and pushed the foil aside. "It's a crappy piece of crap from a long-gone spacer's guild, but it'll work."

"So will the papers," Jasmine said. She hoped...they'd been easy to forge, too easy. The Wolves might regard them with a degree of suspicion, even without suspecting that they *had* been forged. It would have been simple enough to get papers from the Trade Federation, but that *would* have attracted the wrong kind of attention. "It'll get us a foot in the door, at least."

"Give them an inch and then a foot," Stewart misquoted. "And then pretty soon you won't have a leg to stand on."

"As long as they don't have a leg to stand on either," Jasmine said. Her wristcom bleeped, once. The shuttle was coming in to land. "Grab your bags, please. It's time."

Meade and Parkinson met them at the shuttlepad, both carrying their bags slung over their shoulders. They looked very *civilian*, Jasmine decided, as she looked them both up and down. It wasn't just their outfits - multicoloured shipsuits, without any starship tags - it was their general attitude. They didn't *quite* slump, but it looked very much as though they *wanted* to.

"Make sure you dump everything that can point to Avalon," Jasmine said. She checked her bag, one final time. Everything she'd packed - from clothes to a handful of cosmetics and tools - could have been found in any spacer's market. "I don't want anything that might lead them straight back here."

"They might be too desperate to care," Meade pointed out. She finished checking her bag and slung it back over her shoulder. "They're already paying well above the odds for trained personnel."

"There's no point in taking chances," Jasmine said. She removed her wristcom, locked it and passed it to the nearest staffer. She'd take the replacement out of her bag once she was on the freighter, then slave it to the freighter's computer network. "We cannot afford to take risks."

"Of course not," Meade agreed.

"We can't," Haverford said, quietly. "The slightest mistake would get us tossed into the fire."

Jasmine nodded in grim agreement. Wolfbane was a police state. She knew, all too well, that police states had their limits, but they'd be passing through too many chokepoints for her to feel entirely comfortable. There *would* be an underground, there *would* be a criminal network they could use to undermine the state, yet it would take time to find it. Until then...

We have to be above suspicion, she told herself, firmly. *They cannot be allowed to take a careful look at us.*

"Get on the shuttle," she ordered. "It's time to go."

She took a last breath of air, peering down towards the fence - and the forest beyond. A faint plume of smoke could be seen, rising up in the distance, but otherwise there were no signs of human life. It was strange to realise that Avalon, for all of its new significance, was still a very underpopulated world. The giant CityBlocks of Earth had each held more people than Avalon...

But the CityBlocks were too big to be comfortable, she thought, grimly. She would never stop giving thanks to God that she hadn't been born on Earth. *And they eventually started to crumble.*

Avalon wouldn't go like that, she thought. Earth had been the centre of a very centralised Empire, ruled by people who had alternatively coddled and repressed their population. Very - very - few people on Earth had dreamed of something better…and those who had dared to dream had often been exiled or killed. Avalon was different, populated by men and women who had fought for their independence and would fight again - if necessary - to keep it. She couldn't imagine it becoming a clone of Earth.

And yet, things can go wrong, she thought. She'd never studied history formally, but she had picked up enough to know that very few people *learned* from history. *We might repeat all the mistakes of the past.*

Stewart cleared his throat. "Jasmine?"

Jasmine sighed and stepped through the hatch. "Let's go," she said. "The sooner we're on our way, the better."

CHAPTER ELEVEN

"The troops are boarding now," General Mathis said. "I've distributed the marines over the troopships."

Ed nodded as he peered down towards the spaceport. Lines of uniformed men - a handful looking the worse for wear after their last night on the town - were walking forward, boarding shuttles with the calm precision of men who'd done it a hundred times before. Sergeants and military policemen strode from line to line, trying to keep everything carefully organised in hopes of avoiding confusion. Ed knew there *would* be confusion - he'd handled enough deployments to know that *something* would go wrong - but his subordinates had the authority to fix problems without screaming to their superiors. Hopefully, everything would be solved without him having to get involved.

He turned to face his subordinate. General Mathis looked surprisingly old, compared to some of the other officers on Avalon, but there was no doubting his competence. He'd commanded a regiment during the Battle of Camelot, then served as Ed's second on Corinthian. Maybe he wasn't the most imaginative officer - the Civil Guard hadn't encouraged its personnel to think for themselves - but he was solid. He *needed* to be solid.

"Our equipment has been loaded?"

"Yes, sir," Mathis said. "I installed everything on *Chesty Puller.* Taking it all the way to…to our destination may be a waste."

"But we'd regret not having it if we needed it," Ed pointed out. He'd been on enough campaigns where the beancounters had refused to allow the troops all kinds of supplies, pointing out that the plans didn't *call* for them. Inevitably, they'd missed the supplies when they actually *needed* them. "I assume the equipment all checked out?"

"Mostly, sir," Mathis said. "A handful of combat suits were deemed non-functional. The engineers believe they can be repaired during the voyage."

"Let us hope so," Ed said. He'd conserved as much of his original stockpile of equipment as possible, knowing that some marine kit would be very hard to replace, but they needed it now. "We're definitely going to have to start building it for ourselves."

"If we have time, sir," Mathis said. "And if we can afford to spare the resources."

Ed nodded, irked. The Empire, for all of its flaws, had had a massive industrial base. The industrial nodes on the Slaughterhouse alone had been sufficient to supply the Marine Corps with everything it needed, from simple bullets and rifles to armoured combat suits and heavy plasma cannons. There had been a time when they'd been *drowning* in supplies, despite the best efforts of the beancounters. But now…

We have to compromise, he thought, sourly. There were too many demands and too few resources, even now. *The industrial nodes that could turn out armoured battlesuits are needed elsewhere.*

He turned back to peer down at the spaceport. A line of armoured vehicles was being driven into the giant shuttles, their drivers waving and cheering as they vanished into the darkened interior. They'd be unloaded again once they reached orbit, the AFVs moved into the vehicle bays and locked down for the voyage. He smiled humourlessly, remembering weeks and months spent breaking down similar vehicles and then putting them back together, learning how they worked on a very basic level. The marines had always been good at repairing their gear on the fly, even during wartime. Their counterparts in the army had never been permitted to learn how to repair their vehicles.

Although they did learn quickly how to bolt additional armour onto their vehicles on Han, he recalled. *They had no choice.*

"The loading should be finished in two days," Mathis said. "Unless something goes wrong…"

"The schedule will slip," Ed said, flatly. He'd known senior officers who'd exploded with rage when they'd discovered that loading wouldn't be completed on schedule after all. They hadn't had any real experience of military affairs. *Ed* had been careful to add some slippage to *his* schedule. "But we should be able to depart as planned."

"Yes, sir," Mathis said.

Ed nodded, sucking in his breath as he saw a group of men cantering towards a shuttle. They looked young, painfully young…he knew, just by looking at them, that they had *never* seen the elephant. They'd probably just been entering their teens when Stalker's Stalkers had arrived on Avalon, too young to fight for either side. Some of them still didn't look old enough to shave. And yet, they'd volunteered for the CEF instead of joining the militia…

Some of them will not come home, Ed thought, grimly. He felt a pang of guilt, mingled with the grim awareness that he couldn't allow himself any sentimentality. *I might have to send some of them to their deaths to save the others.*

He couldn't help feeling a stab of bitter envy. Avalon had been a primitive world, once upon a time. A stage-one colony, barely capable of feeding itself…and yet, it had given its population a lifestyle beyond the wildest dreams of most of Earth's population. Being independent, being responsible…it had been fantastic, even though he knew that it came with its own price. There were no government agencies on Avalon helping people cope with their lives…

But those agencies didn't really help on Earth, he reminded himself. *And Avalon is all the better for their absence.*

He saw two young men laughing and felt another flicker of morbid envy. There was something open and honest about them, something that would never have been possible on Earth. They didn't have to keep their feelings hidden, they didn't have to fear attack at all times, they didn't have to make the choice between being victim and victimiser…they were healthy, truly healthy, on a level few could match. And yet, they probably considered their farms to be boring prisons, they probably feared spending the rest of their lives watching the back end of a mule…they didn't know how lucky they were.

The grass is always greener on the other side of the hill, he reminded himself, dryly. *And you've been at war for too long.*

Mathis cleared his throat. "Sir?"

Ed scowled, silently glad that Mathis couldn't see his face. "I'm sorry, I was miles away," he said. Light-years would be more accurate. "What was that?"

"General Grosskopf is on his way up," Mathis said. "I think he wants a word with you."

"Understood," Ed said. A pair of shuttles were taking off, their pilots flying in perfect formation. He made a mental note to remind the air traffic controllers that the pilots shouldn't be showing off, even if they *had* flown through rather more unfriendly skies. Ed was no stranger to danger, but there was nothing to be gained by running unnecessary risks. "Let him in when he arrives."

The door opened, two minutes later. "Ed."

"George," Ed said, turning to face the older man. "I trust you're ready to take command?"

"Not much left to do here," Grosskopf said. It wouldn't be the first time he'd assumed command on Avalon while Ed and his men headed off to fight elsewhere. "But yes, I'm ready."

"And in a good position to give any attackers a hard time," Ed pointed out. "I think you're in command of the toughest fortress in known space."

He smiled, rather coldly. Once, command of the high orbitals was enough to convince a planet to surrender. Anyone foolish enough to *refuse* to surrender could be hammered from orbit until they gave up or were overthrown by their own people. A planet lacking orbital defences was as helpless as a naked virgin in the Undercity. It simply couldn't put up an effective resistance against a determined enemy.

But now, with force shields and ground-based plasma cannons, the face of war had changed again. Anyone who wanted to take Avalon would have to land troops and defeat the defenders on the ground, unless they wanted to render the planet completely lifeless. And even *that* would be difficult, now. Corinthian had had *one* city covered by *one* force shield and the would-be attackers had lost thousands of soldiers in an ultimately futile attempt to take the city. He dreaded to think just how many people would be killed if the Wolves attempted to take Avalon.

But then, they'd also devastate the planet, he thought. *It will be years before Corinthian recovers from the war.*

"I will certainly make anyone pay for daring to set foot on our soil," Grosskopf said. Like Ed, he was an exile. But he'd come to see Avalon as home. "And we'll be proceeding with training and suchlike, too."

"And preparing the New Slaughterhouse," Ed said. They'd have to come up with a better name, once the training ground was ready. There would never be anything quite like the *original* Slaughterhouse. "I hope it will live up to the old."

"It will be as good as possible," Grosskopf said. "But you won't have complete control, sir."

Ed nodded. He'd considered trying to claim the unsettled continent for the marines, but the council would probably have vetoed the idea. Hell, the Marine Corps probably wouldn't have been able to claim the Slaughterhouse if the planet's terraforming hadn't failed so spectacularly. There *were* a couple of worlds along the Rim that were barely rated habitable - their populations had actually begged to be evacuated, when the Commonwealth had made contact with them - and they *could* be converted into a new training centre, but it would cost far too much. The Commonwealth couldn't afford it.

Not yet, he told himself. *And what we have is more than enough.*

"I look forward to seeing it," he said. It wasn't entirely true. Deciding to build a new Slaughterhouse - or whatever they decided to call it - felt like giving up. The Empire he'd served for all of his adult life was gone. "And I'm sure the new recruits will live up to the old."

"They'll be better," Grosskopf assured him. "They'll learn from the past."

Ed shrugged. The Marine Corps had evolved with the times, yet the *essence* of the corps hadn't changed. The timeless truths of military life - of a tough, professional force that punched well above its weight - hadn't changed since Alexander the Great had built an empire that had vanished in less than a generation. Evil had to be fought, enemies had to be cowed, bullies had to be given bloody noses...those who wanted peace had to prepare for war. If the Empire had remembered that, he considered, it might never have fallen.

"We shall see," he said.

It was an intimidating thought. The Slaughterhouse had been thousands of years old. Its staff had been heir to a tradition that stretched back even longer. But the *new* Slaughterhouse would be *new*. He didn't even know if he had enough marines to keep the ethos of the corps intact when the new recruits arrived. It wasn't going to be easy.

He pushed the thought aside. "You'll take command from this evening," he said. It would have been awkward, on Earth, but the Avalon Knights had discarded a great deal of pointless formality. "I'll be here until the fleet leaves, allowing us to smooth out any problems."

"Yes, sir," Grosskopf said.

Ed nodded. He doubted there would be any real problems. Grosskopf had been in command while Ed had been on Corinthian and, while Ed had been formally in command of the system as soon as he returned, Grosskopf had carried on with his duties. It was well to be careful, to make sure that nothing went wrong, but he didn't anticipate trouble.

And this would have been impossible on Earth, he thought. Grosskopf had a point. They *had* learned from the past. *Here, we know better.*

"Good," he said. He took one last look out of the window, then smiled. "And now, let us turn our attention to other matters."

Mandy had never imagined, not when she'd been a teenager on Earth, that she would ever wind up in command of a starship. She'd certainly never aspired to the military life...hell, she hadn't really had any aspirations at all. She hadn't given any thought to her future until her father had managed to get himself into trouble and by then it had been far too late to separate herself from her parents. She'd only started to take control of her life after she'd arrived on Avalon.

It still terrified her, as she looked around her bridge, that *she* was one of the most experienced naval officers in the Commonwealth. She'd only been a spacer for six years, a mere drop in the bucket compared to some of the Empire's naval heroes. But then, the Commonwealth had practically had to build a navy from scratch. She'd joined almost as soon as she'd escaped from the pirates, then climbed rapidly up the ranks. And yet, she still felt as though she was faking it…sometimes. It was hard, too hard, to convince herself that she actually deserved it.

"Captain," Midshipwoman Tracy Lloyd said. "I have the latest update from the logistics officers."

Mandy took the datapad and scanned the report, trying to conceal her annoyance. The logistics officers weren't quite as bad as the bean-counters on Earth - if the old sweats were telling the truth - but they were still asking irritating questions. The missile loads she'd requested for the coming engagement, it seemed, were just a *little* bit too large for immediate approval. She ground her teeth, reminded herself that the logistics officers didn't know where the squadron was actually going, and tapped out a short note, telling them to check with Colonel Stalker. He'd approve everything she'd requested without a second thought.

Because the colonel actually knows what he's doing, she thought, coldly.

"Make sure they deal with it promptly," she ordered, returning the datapad. "And don't hesitate to use my name if they try to procrastinate any longer."

Tracy saluted, then hurried off. Mandy watched her go, feeling curiously discomforted. Tracy was sixteen, too young to be given any real responsibility on Earth. Mandy hadn't been taken seriously when *she* was that age, although she did have to admit that she'd been a little brat at the time. No one on Earth would have put Tracy to work, not in anything *legal*. Children - and teenagers - weren't expected to earn money. But here…

She was probably working from the day she was old enough to walk, Mandy thought, unsure if she should envy or pity the younger girl. *And she never had to worry about her safety.*

Mandy shook her head. Tracy would have learned how to handle responsibility from a very young age…hell, the girl *was* strikingly responsible. She'd even admitted that she wanted to be the youngest naval captain in history and she might just make it, if she didn't screw up too badly. The Commonwealth Navy was still expanding rapidly. New ships were coming out of the shipyards at an ever-increasing rate.

Her XO cleared his throat. "*Determined* has reported that she's fixed the problem with her drive modulator," Commander Darren Cobb said. "She's ready to depart with the rest of the squadron."

"Once we have the troopships loaded," Mandy said. She glanced at the display, watching the constant flow of shuttles running between the surface and the nine immense troopships. The Commonwealth might have had to improvise its troopships, she knew from grim experience, but the engineers had done a very good job. "How is *that* going?"

"There's been a slight delay, but the loadmaster believes that loading will be complete within the next twenty-four hours," the XO reported. "There'll be a handful of senior officers who have to board after that, of course."

"Of course," Mandy agreed. They were still on schedule, at least. The squadron should be able to set off as planned. "And our crews?"

"Reasonably happy," the XO said. His face twisted into a grim smile. "The thought of going back to Thule pleases them."

Mandy nodded shortly, keeping her face expressionless. The crew believed the deception, then. That was good, she knew, yet it didn't sit well with her. She'd never liked or trusted people who lied to her, even if it *was* in a good cause. She couldn't help wondering just what the long-term consequences of the lie would be. If her crews stopped trusting her, would they be so quick to obey orders? Or would they understand why she and the others in-the-know had lied to them?

But we can't let Admiral Singh get a hint of where we're actually going, she thought. *The bitch cannot be allowed a chance to reinforce her defences before we arrive.*

"We owe Admiral Singh a damn good ass-kicking," she said, pushing her doubts aside. She still had nightmares about having to withdraw from Thule, leaving Jasmine and the remains of the CEF to surrender. Jasmine didn't blame her - Jasmine had issued the orders - but Mandy blamed herself. She should have been able to find a way to win a victory against overwhelming force. "I'm sure she'll enjoy it as much as we enjoyed the one she gave us."

"Yes, Captain," Cobb agreed. He looked at the display. "The fleet should be ready to depart as planned."

Unless something goes wrong, Mandy thought. She'd run a dozen private simulations, altering the parameters at will. Some of them had been less encouraging than others. *It still could.*

She pushed that aside, too. "Then I'll be in my office," she said. She had paperwork to do, lots of paperwork. Bureaucracy grew, it seemed. It was like weeds, growing back no matter how thoroughly the gardener weeded the garden. Given time, it would entangle the Commonwealth Navy and cripple it. "Inform me if there are any changes."

"Aye, Captain," Cobb said.

CHAPTER TWELVE

"Heaven," Ed said.

Gaby laughed. "Parenthood does change you, doesn't it?"

Ed nodded in rueful agreement. Douglas was in his crib, sleeping soundly. That wouldn't last, of course, but he'd take what he could get. The baby would awaken soon enough, demanding food and attention. Douglas was tiny, his head smaller than Ed's hand, yet he ruled the apartment with a rod of iron. His parents - and their maid - had to scramble to take care of him.

But we're not handing him over to a government-run crèche, he thought, coldly. *Or feeding him bottled shit from an overpaid corporation.*

"It does," he conceded. He seemed to have lost the ability to sleep through anything that wasn't directly threatening. Perhaps infant cries had some sort of penetrative capability his mind just couldn't screen out. "You will be fine with him, won't you?"

Gaby elbowed him. "I'll have some help," she said, nodding towards the door. She looked downcast, just for a second. "It won't make me look good, but I'll get by until the end of my term."

"I know," Ed said.

He sighed, wishing - again - that he could stay with her. On Avalon, having a nursemaid was considered a sign of shame. He didn't pretend to understand why. A mother might want to raise her baby personally, to breastfeed the child and put him to bed, but there was nothing wrong with asking for help when she needed it. Gaby would probably be called a bad mother if the population at large realised she'd hired a nursemaid. But what choice did she have?

"*Men*," Gaby said. She rolled her eyes in exasperation. "I won't be the *first* new mother to remain behind while my partner and the father of my child goes to war."

"Yeah," Ed said.

He turned to look down at the sleeping child. The thought of leaving Gaby and Douglas for a few months was horrific. He didn't *want* to go. Douglas was *his* child. On Earth, the father was often a question mark; on Avalon, the father was intimately involved with raising his children from birth to adulthood. Ed had no idea if he'd fathered any children on Earth - his adventures and misadventures with girls had never lasted very long - but there was no doubt about Douglas's parentage. He didn't want to leave Gaby alone with the baby. He wanted to wrap her in cotton wool…

…And she'd go ballistic if I tried, he thought, wryly. *She'd hate it.*

"I will be fine," Gaby said. Ed turned to look at her. "And if you get back in time, you can even help me move to the farm."

"Of course," Ed said.

He leaned forward and kissed her. "I wish…"

Gaby gave him a sharp look. "You're not allowed to indulge in wishful thinking," she said, dryly. "Leave that to the opposition politicians."

Ed nodded, swinging his legs over the side of the bed and standing. He wanted to make love to her, to say goodbye in a manner that would leave them both with a nice warm glow, but he knew that was impossible. Gaby's doctor had warned her to avoid intercourse for a few weeks, just to give her body time to heal from giving birth. Ed thought the doctor was exaggerating - the birth had apparently been trouble-free - but he wasn't about to put her life at risk just to satisfy himself.

Douglas twitched, then started to cry. Ed hesitated, waiting to see if the baby would go back to sleep, then sighed and reached into the crib. Douglas looked up at him, his dark blue eyes trusting, as Ed picked him up and cradled him against his chest. The baby was so tiny, yet perfect. It was still impossible to believe that Douglas would grow into a toddler, a boy, a teenager, a man…

"You're good with children," Gaby said. She gave him a tired smile as she opened her blouse, revealing her breast. "And Douglas likes you."

"I'm his father," Ed said. It wouldn't have meant *much*, on Earth. His stepfathers - not that they'd ever been married to his mother - had largely ignored him. He supposed he should be grateful. He'd heard more than enough horror stories about abusive parents and stepparents as he'd grown older. "But right now, he doesn't know me from Adam."

"He'll know you when he's nine months old," Gaby said. She took Douglas and pressed him to her breast. "My cousin's little boy loved everyone until he was seven months old or thereabouts. All of a sudden, he wouldn't trust anyone apart from his parents…it lasted for about six months until he got over it."

Ed frowned. "What happened?"

"It's normal," Gaby said. "Babies suddenly realise that the world is divided into their parents and everyone else. And then they cling to their parents until they grow more comfortable with other people."

"Oh," Ed said.

He sat down next to her, feeling torn. He didn't have to go, did he? Mathis could command the troops; Joe Buckley could command the marines. He could stay behind, with his partner and his child, while his men went off to fight and die. But he couldn't do that, not without hating himself for the rest of his life. He couldn't ask them to go into danger while he stayed safe at home.

"I have to go," he said, quietly.

He took a breath. "When I get back," he said, "we'll move out to the farm."

Gaby nodded. "I'll see you soon," she promised. "And good luck."

Ed reached out and kissed her, wishing he could do more. Gaby kissed him back, then looked down at the child. *Their* child. Ed promised himself, silently, that he'd ask her to marry him when he returned home. Marriage wasn't something he'd ever considered on Earth - getting a marriage licence alone was a nightmare - but here…it was a sign of commitment, a sign that two people were serious.

We had a child, he thought, as he walked backwards. *We cannot be any more serious.*

He took one last look at her and his son, then turned and walked out of the door. The building felt cold and empty, even though he knew it was an illusion. The lower floors were crammed with offices, occupied by the men and women who made the government work. And yet...it was all he could do to keep going. He didn't want to go, he didn't want to leave, he didn't want to be away for months...

It was never so hard to leave before, he thought. *Was it?*

He shook his head as he reached the private stairwell and headed up. He'd had nothing left on Earth, nothing keeping him tied to his home. And then he'd been a marine, moving with other marines...he'd never felt as though he was leaving someone behind, when they'd moved from world to world. He'd never really been tied down for more than a few months at most, even on Han. The handful of lovers he'd taken had never been more than brief flings...

But now...now, he felt as though he was abandoning Gaby.

An aircar was waiting on the roof, its door already open. Ed climbed inside, closing the door behind him. The automated system bleeped, displaying a flight plan, but Ed deactivated it and took the controls for himself. Earth's automated ATC system had caused more than its fair share of crashes - some deliberately orchestrated to get rid of people the government found inconvenient - and he didn't really trust the system. The WebHeads might *claim* the system was secure, but Ed wasn't so sure. Anything could be hacked, given enough time.

He forced himself to relax as he took the aircar into the air and headed north, making sure to key his ID into the IFF system. Being shot down by the automated defences protecting Castle Rock would be annoying, to say the least. Camelot seemed to have grown even *larger* since he'd landed his shuttle after returning from Corinthian, a new set of prefabricated housing apartments clearly visible near the water. He peered down, noticing the hundreds of families that had come to the beach...that, too, was something that would never have happened on Earth. Anyone foolish enough to swim in Earth's poisoned seas would deserve everything they got.

The radio buzzed as he crossed the ocean, heading directly for Castle Rock. He identified himself, knowing it wouldn't be enough for the duty officers. Sure enough, a pair of nasty-looking helicopters - their weapons clearly visible under stubby wings - materialised to escort him to the nearest landing pad. The security officers were very apologetic, after they confirmed his identity, but Ed didn't mind. He'd have been more upset if they allowed an unchecked aircar far too close to Castle Rock.

Emmanuel Alves met him at the shuttle, looking tired. Ed wondered, as he nodded tightly to the reporter, just what he'd been doing in lockdown. Marines were fairly used to staying in their barracks - and lockdown wasn't too different - but Alves had probably hated every moment of it. Just being allowed to walk to the shuttlepad would have seemed heavenly, Ed thought. Alves didn't know how lucky he was.

"Colonel," Alves said. "Shall we go?"

Ed nodded. "Yes," he said. He took one last look at Castle Rock, then boarded the shuttlecraft. "Let's go."

The Imperial Navy had laid on a big song and dance, Mandy had been told, whenever a superior officer graced a starship with his presence. She'd actually flipped through some of the protocol books, back when she'd been bored; she'd been astonished by how much effort starship crews were expected to put into greeting officers, even ones who were only visiting for a short while. Thankfully, the Commonwealth Navy hadn't bothered to develop such formalities for itself. All Colonel Stalker had to do, when Mandy met him and his companions at the airlock, was salute the flag, then her.

"Colonel," she said, once the reporter was dispatched to his quarters. "Welcome onboard."

"Thank you," Colonel Stalker said. "I trust that all is in readiness?"

Mandy nodded. Colonel Stalker wasn't as intimidating as some of the younger marines she'd met, but there was something about him that made her want to avoid *disappointing* him. He was…she wasn't sure how to put it into words. He was so confident, so sure of himself, that he had no *need* to boss or bully to get his way. His smile had been nice, when they'd first met, yet there had been a hard edge behind it that told her not to mess with him. Now…he looked harder, as if the stresses of the war were slowly getting to him.

I'm not the only one who was pushed upwards at breakneck speed, she reminded herself, grimly. *Colonel Stalker went from being in command of an understrength company of marines to commander-in-chief of an entire military machine.*

"Loading is complete, both troops and supplies," she said, as she led him to the bridge. "We can depart at any time."

Colonel Stalker's expression, if anything, grew grimmer. "And the first waypoint?"

"We'll be there in five days," Mandy said. "The others should meet us there."

She groaned, inwardly. The other squadrons had been given sealed orders, instructing them to head to the first waypoint, but she was grimly aware that too much could go wrong. She couldn't help thinking that they were trying to be too clever, despite the risks. Admiral Singh finding out where they were going would be bad, but losing a squadron because it didn't make the RV point in time would be worse.

And we don't even know what we're facing at Titlark, she reminded herself. *We might still be outgunned.*

She stepped onto the bridge. The crew glanced at her, then stared at Colonel Stalker. Mandy shook her head in droll amusement, then motioned for the colonel to take one of the spare seats. She took her own seat a moment later, silently noting the crewmen who didn't hurry back to their duties. Colonel Stalker's presence had been unexpected, at least to her crew, but they *were* on the bridge. The next time they were distracted, it might prove fatal.

"Communications, alert the squadron," she ordered. "We will depart in five minutes."

"Aye, Captain," the communications officer said.

Mandy leaned back in her chair, forcing herself to relax. Nothing would go wrong. They'd leave the system, following a least-time course to Thule; they'd alter course once they were on their way, secure in the knowledge they couldn't be tracked through Phase Space. And then they'd link up with the rest of the fleet and head directly to their *true* target. Admiral Singh wouldn't know what had hit her.

"The squadron is ready," the communications officer reported. "All ships - warships and troopships - are standing by."

"Take us out," Mandy ordered.

She watched the display as *Defiant* slowly moved out of orbit. Local space was crowded, hundreds of starships, industrial nodes and habitats orbiting Avalon or floating around the primary star…it was hard to believe, even now, that it was the same system she'd entered, seven years ago. Then, the system had been practically empty; now, it hummed with life, with everything necessary to make sure that Avalon and the Commonwealth survived and prospered. And *she* had played a role in making it happen…

"We'll cross the Phase Limit in nineteen hours," the helmsman said. "The freighters are slowing us down."

"It can't be helped," Mandy said. The warships could go faster - her cruisers were the fastest things in known space - but the troopships needed to be protected. "We'll get there soon enough."

She glanced at Colonel Stalker. He was looking at the display, an odd look on his face. It took her a moment to realise that he was feeling wistful. She wondered, absently, just what he'd left behind on Avalon. And then she remembered that he'd had a baby…

Poor man, she thought. *Her* father had stayed with her mother. It had never seemed unusual until she'd realised that the upper middle classes were very much the exception on Earth. No doubt Colonel Stalker wanted to stay with his son. *We'll be back soon.*

But she knew, all too well, that that wasn't true.

The intercom bleeped. Gaby stabbed it with a finger. "Yes?"

"Madam President," the dispatcher said. "*Defiant* and her squadron have left orbit. You wanted to be informed."

"Thank you," Gaby said, shortly. She had given that order, hadn't she? Tiredness was affecting her ability to function, more than she cared to admit. God knew she'd had her fair share of sleepless nights during the war - she'd been woken and warned to flee more than once - but Douglas was wearing down her resistance. "Inform me when they cross the limit and vanish."

She closed the connection without waiting for a response, then looked down at her child. Her heart swelled with love, with an affection that seemed to transcend the love she felt for her partner or her planet. And yet, she knew Douglas had been an accident. Getting pregnant outside of wedlock, when she couldn't care for the child as much as a mother should, risked her reputation. Getting pregnant and then not getting married…

I don't regret it, she thought. She liked to think that it had been that night they'd shared in the mountain hut, although the timing suggested that Douglas had been conceived in Camelot. Her birth control implant had run out ahead of time. *I don't regret it, but I will have to deal with it.*

She shifted the baby as gently as she could, then reached for her datapad. Her staff were handling routine matters - she'd trained them well - but she couldn't remain detached from her office indefinitely. What could she do then? Resign from politics, at least as long as it took for Douglas to go to school? Or try to balance her work with her life, governing the planet and raising a child? She wasn't sure she could do both. If she'd had a longer term ahead of her, she might just have resigned.

If I don't get forced out of office, she reminded herself. She'd checked the statistics. She wasn't the only woman who'd had a surprise pregnancy. But she was the only one, as far as anyone knew, in a government post. *They'll say I'm a bad example.*

She rubbed her head in annoyance. She'd had to cut her hair short and her scalp itched. It didn't make her feel any better. She'd wanted children, but she'd wanted to plan them ahead of time. Perhaps Ed had been right, when she'd told him that she was expecting. Perhaps the Old Council, damn them, had wanted a population boom. It was the sort of thing they would have done.

Douglas shifted against her, then started to cry. She hastily pushed him against her breast, relaxing when she felt him starting to suck milk. She didn't know how she was going to split her time, not when there were too many demands from both sides. And yet, she couldn't resign either. It would weaken the Commonwealth if its Head of State left before the end of her term.

And we have too few precedents to draw on, she thought, tiredly. She couldn't help a yawn as Douglas slipped back into sleep. *I can't let myself be forced from office for this.*

She picked up the datapad again, cursing under her breath. There was no help for it. She'd have to depend on the nursemaid and hope, desperately, that she could weather the political storm. Perhaps she could get some sympathy votes…

Sure, her own thoughts mocked her. *And perhaps pigs will fly.*

CHAPTER THIRTEEN

"We cannot go on like this," Daniel said.

Nadia nodded in agreement. She'd applied to enter one of the technical colleges as soon as Governor Brown had opened them, thinking that it would open the doorways to a good job and a chance to rise high in the corporate world. But three years of intensive study - and coping with instructors who snapped and snarled at anyone who didn't come up with the right answers - had worn her down. Nothing she'd done on Wolfbane had prepared her for the college, not really. The students had been utterly unprepared to take on the challenge.

She took a sip of her beer as she looked around the room: seventeen students sitting on the wooden floor, nine boys and eight girls...the foundations of a protest movement. Or so she'd been promised, when she'd been invited. She'd heard that other protest movements had come to sticky ends - the protesters had been quietly rounded up and exiled to stage-one colony worlds - but this one was different. They'd spent far too long in the technical college, hadn't they? The government couldn't exile them without shooting itself in the foot.

"And so we have to go on strike," Daniel added. "We have to show them that we're serious."

Nadia felt the shock running around the room. Going on strike was taboo on Wolfbane, unsurprisingly. A world ruled by corporations wouldn't want its workers to strike for better conditions, would it? But *students* going on strike wouldn't present an immediate threat, would it? The corporations might try to negotiate rather than merely crush the strikers with overwhelming force, once word got out. They certainly wouldn't want to discourage students from attending technical colleges.

"They'll know we're serious," Susan said. She'd dyed her hair white, the week after she'd entered the college. The instructors had suspended her until she'd reluctantly agreed to allow her hair to go back to its usual mousey brown. It had been a harsh lesson for everyone. The colleges didn't allow their students to step out of line. "But they might expel us."

"They can't expel *all* of us," Daniel pointed out. "There are over five *thousand* students in our campus alone."

Nadia sucked in her breath. Daniel was right, yet...not *all* of the students would agree to strike. The older students, the ones who'd been screwed by the system, were even more determined to gain qualifications than any of the younger ones. But even if *half* of the students went on strike, the campus would have a serious problem. They might just agree to concede a few demands rather than risk the strike getting out of control.

"We will be peaceful, but firm," Daniel said. He looked around the room. "If each of you speaks to a single friend, and brings him along to the next meeting, we can expand slowly until we have enough people to spark off a strike. Make sure you pick someone you trust..."

"I'm not sure I trust anyone that much," Nadia said.

"You came here," Daniel pointed out.

Nadia shrugged. She knew she was on the verge of failing and being kicked out, no matter how hard she worked. She had never realised just how much she'd never been taught - just how much the former government had wanted to keep from her - until it was too late. Her aptitude tests insisted she would make a good WebHead, but she just couldn't grasp the underlying technical concepts. She'd be lucky to get a job fixing personal computers, not writing programming for military or corporate datacores.

She chewed on a strand of blonde hair, wishing she had the money or connections to just walk out. A life on the government teat sounded very good right now, even though Admiral Singh had been cutting back on social benefits with savage intensity. The former government had made solemn promises, promises that Governor Brown and Admiral

Singh had chosen to ignore. She didn't know what would happen if she left the college, particularly if she didn't have any real qualifications. Some Job Assignment Board asshole would probably decide her willowy body and silky blonde hair qualified her to be an exotic dancer… and it was a short step from there to whore. She *needed* some proper qualifications…

…But she didn't know if she was going to get them. She worked and worked, but she felt as though she was getting nowhere. Coming here, coming to a room Daniel had hired for the evening, was her first step outside the campus and her dorms for *months*. She hadn't even been able to go home for a night, just to check on her family. God alone knew what had happened to her parents and siblings.

She dragged her attention back to Nancy as the older girl spoke with quiet intensity. "We have to make a stand now, while we still can," she said. "Otherwise…that will be the end."

Nadia snorted. She wanted a week or two of sleep. Anything else would be a bonus…

There was a sharp knock on the door, an authoritative *rap-rap-rap* that made them all freeze in horror. Only the police made such sounds, entering houses and apartments at night just to make sure that everyone knew they *could*…Nadia glanced around, frantically, as Daniel tapped his lips, sharply. She barely heard him mutter instructions to play dumb as panic yammered at the back of her mind. They'd been caught…

The door exploded inwards as soon as Daniel undid the bolt. A line of black-clad policemen streamed into the room, two of them shoving Daniel to the floor while the remainder surged towards the others, barking orders. Nadia tried to rise, but it was far too late. Strong arms grabbed her, pushed her down and wrenched her hands behind her back. She screamed in pain, but the policeman ignored her. His knee held her down as he wrapped a plastic tie around her wrists, pulling it tight enough to cut off her circulation. And then she was yanked up and thrust against the wall.

"Keep still," her captor growled.

Nadia froze. Hamish was bleeding…it looked as though his jaw was broken. Beside him, Nancy and Seven were looking stunned, their eyes vacant as though they'd checked out of reality altogether. They were both from higher social classes than herself, Nadia recalled, as her captor frisked her thoroughly. They'd both enjoyed a certain immunity from police raids until they'd joined Daniel's protest movement…

This isn't fair, she thought, as her captor's hand lingered on her bum. She wanted to scream, but she knew no one would come to help. *We didn't even get started.*

She felt tears pouring down her cheeks as the policemen smashed their way through the room, tearing open cupboards and ripping up floorboards with an intensity Nadia could only admire. A small collection of papers were waved in front of her face - some forbidden literature and political pamphlets, something that would get them in real trouble - and then dumped on the floor. She kept glancing over her shoulder, half-hoping that someone - anyone - would come to their rescue. Perhaps the instructors would appear and call the policemen off, now their students had learned their lesson.

Daniel gasped in pain. A policeman walked over to where he was lying and casually kicked him in the head. Nadia stared, unable to look away…had she just seen Daniel *die?* Her mind couldn't quite comprehend it. She'd seen violence, she'd seen people get mistreated, but she'd never seen someone killed like *that*. He…

"Get your eyes to the wall," a policeman barked.

Nadia obeyed, hearing him moving up behind her. A moment later, she felt his hands slipping into her trousers, pushing them and her panties down to her knees. She closed her eyes as he pushed up against her, his penis rubbing against her bare skin, trying to pretend that it wasn't happening…

It didn't work.

Captain Joshua Forster lit a cigarette and waited outside the meeting hall as the prisoners were half-marched, half-carried down to the penal van. The boys looked shell-shocked, those who were in any state to notice what was going on; the girls were weeping, wailing and whining, their trousers at half-mast as they were shoved into the door. He sneered at one blonde girl, who was frantically telling herself that it wasn't real, that nothing was happening, then nodded to his subordinates. The doors were slammed shut, cutting the prisoners off from the outside world.

He turned to look at Sergeant Fanucchi, who looked pleased. The ugly little man had had a string of complaints against his name, mainly for sexually assaulting female prisoners, but none of them had ever come to anything. Fanucchi had a real nose for sniffing out trouble, even where it was least expected. The students who'd been plotting against the state didn't know how lucky they were, how lucky they'd *been*. *They* hadn't had to fight their way up from the gutter in a world that only cared about results.

"Subversive literature, sir," Fanucchi said, holding out a set of papers. "They concealed it under the floorboards."

"Very good," Joshua said. He took the papers and skimmed them, quickly. They were nothing more than extracts from a set of banned books, save for one which claimed to be a true history of the war. He felt dirty just for looking at them. *Some* people really *didn't* know which side their bread was buttered on. "Did they have anything useful to say?"

Fanucchi smirked. "They asked us to do it again and again," he said. "I promised we'd see them again in the cells."

"I'm sure you will, if you slip the prison staff the right bribe," Joshua said. He'd had HQ run a check on the prisoners, while his men had their fun. Not that it mattered *that* much, not now they'd been caught in the act. Their families would disown their bastards for fear of being tarred with the treasonous brush. "Just make sure you do it before they get shipped off to some shithole on the other side of the galaxy."

He smiled as he walked into the meeting hall and peered into the devastated room. The entire complex would have to be searched, of course, but they'd already caught the ringleaders. He didn't know why the students had decided to betray the state, or why they thought they could get away with it…all that mattered was that they'd been arrested, that they were on their way to the nearest penal world. It was a shame, almost. Some of those girls had been quite pretty, the type of girls who had been utterly untouchable when he'd been a teenager.

And if they'd kept their heads down, he thought, *they would have been giving me orders soon enough.*

"Ah…Captain," a voice said. "About the reward…?"

Joshua turned. The hall supervisor was standing there, looking as if he wanted to be somewhere - anywhere - else. Joshua couldn't help a flicker of disgust at the overweight man, mingled with grim amusement. The bastard had taken money from the students, then betrayed them to the police. But then, reporting subversion was everyone's job. A man who could be proved - who was even accused - of knowing about subversion and doing nothing might join the subversives in jail.

And he won't survive a penal world, Joshua thought, as he met the man's eyes. *He'll be cooked and eaten by the others within a day.*

"The reward," Joshua repeated. "You think you deserve a reward?"

He leaned forward, then smirked. "You'll get your reward by the end of the day," he said, nastily. "Suitably taxed, of course."

The supervisor nodded, clearly too terrified to speak. His immense belly was shaking like jelly. Joshua dismissed him with a wave, knowing the man wouldn't dare to complain. Garnishing the reward money was a long-standing police privilege, one of the few privileges of an underpaid and underappreciated job. And *he* - not his men - would get a segment of the money. *They'd* just have to content themselves by having fun with the prisoners.

He turned and strode out of the door. A handful of students were watching from a distance, ready to duck into the alleyway if the policemen came after them. Joshua shrugged, unconcerned. Let them see, if they wished, that a subversive cell had been broken, that the boys had been beaten into submission and the girls raped. They'd take note and think twice before joining the subversives themselves.

"Get us back to the station," he ordered, as he climbed into the front seat. He could hear a faint whimpering coming from the rear of the van, but he ignored it. The subversives had to learn, sooner rather than later, that their lives were no longer their own. "We have work to do."

"Yes, sir," the driver said.

Joshua smiled as the engine roared into life. They had orders from higher up the food chain - right from the very top, he'd been told - to crack down hard on subversives. Everyone *knew* the subversives were working their way into the state, preparing to bring everything the government had built crashing down in ruins. The cell he'd cracked, the cell he'd arrested… he'd be promoted for uncovering its existence. And then…

He smirked. There would always be subversives. And they would always be rooted out.

"Police uncovered another cell of subversives, Admiral," Paula Bartholomew said. She held out a datapad. "A cluster of technical college students, between nineteen and twenty-two years of age. The police currently have them in detention."

Rani gritted her teeth. There had been too many challenges to her authority over the last two months, too many subversive cells popping up and asking questions…every time she smashed one, another rose to replace it. And the hell of it was that the *really* dangerous ones couldn't be stopped so easily. The subversives themselves weren't a problem; the directors, the big corporations, *were* a problem.

"That makes thirty-seven cells uncovered within the last week," Paula added. "We still don't have a handle on how subversive papers are being distributed…"

"Through the datanet, one would assume," Rani said. Wolfbane's datanet was a mess. It was more organised than Earth's datanet, she had to admit, but the bar wasn't set very high. A single message couldn't be traced unless the WebHeads got lucky. "Make sure the subversives are interrogated before being put in front of a wall and shot."

Paula hesitated. "Admiral…these are young men and women," she said. "Would it not be better to have them exiled…"

"Have them shot," Rani repeated, coldly. The students had betrayed her. Governor Brown might have started the technical colleges, but *she* had made them work. She'd ensured the students had a good chance at proper jobs, at doing important work for their planet…and *this* was how they rewarded her? "March them out, put them in front of a wall and shoot them."

"Yes, Admiral," Paula said.

Rani scowled as she turned to peer out the window. The city seemed quiet, but she knew it seethed with resentment and hatred. She knew she wasn't popular…it seemed she wasn't feared either. *That* would have to change. And yet, she knew that fear alone wasn't enough to make people work for her. She needed to apply the carrot as well as the stick.

She shook her head, tiredly. She'd wanted to be powerful. And yes, she *was* powerful. But she was now riding a tiger. If she tried to stop the beast, it would devour her; if she tried to jump off, she might be injured and devoured…she was stuck, held in place by the power she'd gathered. Governor Brown had been able to convince people - corporate directors in particular - to work with him. *She* had no such talents.

"Give me the report," she ordered, without looking back.

Paula passed her the datapad. Rani took the device and read the report, quickly. Normally, something so small would have been handled by one of her subordinates, but she needed to stay abreast of progress. She wasn't sure she trusted anyone else to handle the search for subversion anyway. And if it meant delaying matters while it was brought to her attention…

She scowled as she finished reading the report. It was blunt, almost brutally honest. There were none of the euphuisms and half-truths she'd grown used to from the Imperial Navy. And yet…she shuddered at her own lack of concern. Hadn't there been a time when she would have vetoed mindless brutality? When she would have insisted that prisoners, even subversives, be treated well? When she would have executed a rapist instead of putting him to work?

Her wristcom bleeped. "Admiral, *Powerhouse* and her squadron have just returned home," Colonel Higgs said. Rani frowned. Higgs wouldn't have told her that, now, unless there was bad news on the way. "Captain Christopher Brookes is gloating over his success."

Rani felt her blood run cold. "What *kind* of success?"

"He attacked an enemy convoy and destroyed it," Higgs said. His voice, as always, was calm and composed. She welcomed it, even as she feared what he would say next. "It was apparently a great victory."

"I see," Rani said. Cold ice was rapidly replaced by rage - and fear. If word was already spreading…she couldn't allow that, could she? "Have him arrested at once."

Paula started. "Admiral?"

"See to it," Rani ordered sharply, ignoring her aide. Paula was a civilian at heart. She wouldn't understand, couldn't understand, just how dangerous matters had become. "I want him off his bridge as soon as possible."

"Aye, Admiral," Higgs said. "I'll see to it personally."

CHAPTER FOURTEEN

Captain Christopher Brookes ignored the commissioner's silent fury as *Powerhouse* and her consorts glided towards the docking station. The man had been a grumbling presence ever since *Powerhouse* had set course for home, muttering under his breath about imprudence and treacherous commanding officers every time he laid eyes on his charge. Christopher had ignored him, refusing to rise to the bait. He'd destroyed two enemy warships and captured three freighters - which could be pressed into service - for minimal cost. His crew was already looking forward to going on leave and gloating about their one-sided victory.

"They're ordering us to dock on the lower pylon," the communications officer said. "There's an officer boarding to inspect the ship."

Christopher allowed himself a tight smile. An officer…Admiral Singh herself? He'd seen her once, but he'd never spoken to her privately. The chance to put his case for promotion directly to the highest authority on Wolfbane was not to be missed. No doubt the commissioner would whisper poison in her ear, but Admiral Singh was an experienced naval officer. She'd understand the significance of what he'd done, even if the groundpounder didn't. Admiral Singh wouldn't listen to a groundpounder over a starship captain.

"Very good," he said. "Helm, take us into dock."

He glanced at the XO. "Assume command," he added. "I'll be at the main airlock."

"Aye, Captain," the XO said.

Christopher glanced at the commissioner, who glowered back at him. The man didn't seem to know if he wanted to go to the airlock to greet the newcomer or stay on the bridge, as he was technically supposed to do. Regulations weren't clear on what procedure was to be followed, not when the commissioner was supposed to do both. But then, the commissioners were a relatively new innovation. No doubt matters would sort themselves out in time.

Powerhouse felt different as he made his way through the hatch and down to the main airlock. The entire ship seemed to be holding its breath in anticipation. Christopher couldn't help smiling at the thought. The crew knew they'd have a few days of leave in the orbital fleshpots, even if they decided not to go down to the planet itself. They'd be off on leave as soon as the new crew took over, drinking in the bars and telling lies about smashing a hundred enemy ships without taking a single loss. No one would believe them, but no one would care.

A dull thump echoed through the ship as she docked, followed by a series of shudders as the airlocks matched and mated. Christopher reached the airlock, hastily straightening his uniform. There hadn't been time to don his dress uniform, unfortunately, but Admiral Singh would understand. Formal ceremonies were normally announced at least a week in advance so the crews had a chance to wash the decks, clean their uniforms and do everything else necessary to ensure they presented a good impression. He'd known senior officers who'd downgraded the entire ship because they'd spotted a speck of microscopic dust.

The airlocks hissed open, slowly. Christopher took a deep breath, breathing in the air from the station. It tasted faintly of oil, but it was different. *Powerhouse* had good air filtering systems - she wasn't a stinking pirate ship - yet her atmosphere had been starting to feel a little stale. No doubt the filters would have to be swapped out - again - after the crew returned from leave. There were too many shortages of things the bean-counters deemed unessential.

Which goes to prove they know nothing, he thought, crossly. He was in a good mood, damn it. He wasn't going to allow the thought of beancounters to spoil his day. And yet, it was hard to escape the thought. *If the filters start to fail, the air will turn poisonous very quickly.*

He straightened as four men strode into the ship, then frowned. They were shore patrolmen in red uniforms, led by a Provost Marshal. Their hands rested on the pistols in their unbuttoned holsters, ready to draw them at a moment's notice. For a moment, his eyes refused to believe what he was seeing. Could they be securing the ship before Admiral Singh arrived? Or…?

The Provost Marshal stopped in front of him. "Captain Christopher Brookes?"

He spoke with the air of a man who already knew the answer. Christopher felt his blood run cold. He was in trouble, somehow. The commissioner had sent a message ahead of him…somehow. No doubt he'd bullied a communications officer into sending a message as soon as *Powerhouse* returned to realspace, then wiping it from the datacore. Christopher promised himself revenge, as soon as possible. He'd explain himself to Admiral Singh. Once she understood what he'd done, everything would be fine.

"Yes," he said, finally.

"You are under arrest," the Provost Marshal stated. "You will be taken from this place and held until a court martial board can be organised. Any attempt to escape my custody will be held against you…"

Christopher barely heard the Provost Marshal as he finished the rest of the speech, then snapped on the handcuffs. His head was spinning helplessly. How could things have gone so sour, so quickly? Admiral Singh didn't know what her commissioners had done, he told himself firmly. He'd have a chance to appeal to her personally, afterwards. The Provost Marshal pushed him through the airlock, ensuring he didn't have a chance to speak to any of his crew. A small army of military policemen waited on the far side, ready to assume control of *Powerhouse.* Christopher felt his heart sink. Whatever had happened - whatever was going on - someone had definitely put the boot in. He might never have a chance to contact *anyone.*

"Remain here," the Provost Marshal said, shoving him into a tiny cell. "You will be contacted."

Christopher spun around as the hatch slammed closed. "What about the cuffs?"

There was no answer. Christopher tested the cuffs, flexing his muscles against the metal. It didn't give, of course. They didn't have to be made from hullmetal to be effectively unbreakable, at least to an unaugmented human. He'd heard rumours about enhanced superhumans who could snap steel bars as though they were made of paper, but he'd never actually seen one outside a poorly-written flick or two. They were probably just rumours.

Christopher glanced around the cell, composing himself with an effort. He was innocent. He'd done his duty and nothing more. He wasn't going to surrender to fear, not when he had *nothing* to fear. He sat down on the bunk. They wouldn't leave him in the cell for long, he was sure. They'd have to remove the cuffs, if nothing else. And then he'd have a chance to explain himself. He was going to be fine…

…But the cell was barren, save for a bunk and a chamberpot, and the four walls were closing in.

"*Powerhouse* has been secured, Admiral," Paula reported. "Her crew have been transferred to secure holding facilities until their ultimate fate can be determined, save for their commissioner. He was happy to produce a report condemning Captain Brookes for multiple offences against good order…"

Rani nodded, stiffly. She'd thought she was beyond guilt. She'd done what she needed to do to survive, right from the start. And yet… Christopher Brookes had done a good job, whatever else could be said about him. Destroying two tiny warships wouldn't materially affect the balance of power, but it *was* a victory. His only crime was being *too* good at self-promotion for her comfort.

And that is all that matters, she told herself. *I don't need a new threat.*

She looked up at Paula. "And the popular reaction?"

"Muted," Paula said. "So far, no one outside a small group knows that Captain Brookes has been arrested. We will make sure that doesn't get out."

"Of course," Rani said. Captain Brookes was *very* good at self-promotion. His crowing had spread across the system before her PR staff had been able to put a lid on it. No doubt there would be trouble if the general public realised that their new hero had been arrested. She'd have to make very sure that *that* never got out. "Do you have media strategies in place?"

"Yes, Admiral," Paula said. "Captain Brookes will be - officially - promoted and reassigned to a heavy cruiser. That ship will later be reported lost to enemy fire."

And Brookes will become a martyr, Rani thought. *A person we can use to encourage the war effort.*

"Very good," she said.

She could stop it, she knew. A word from her would be enough to stop the court martial in its tracks. Christopher Brookes could be rewarded for his deeds instead of being punished for daring to *win*. She could cover everything up, give him a bigger ship…shoot the snotty commissioner instead or reassign him to somewhere cold and desolate. It didn't have to go so badly wrong…

But she knew she had no choice.

"Have him convicted, then shot," she ordered. Brookes was too dangerous to be allowed to live. Besides, his death would serve her well. "Keep me informed."

"Yes, Admiral," Paula said.

Christopher had always had a good sense of time. It was nearly an hour, by his reckoning, before the hatch was slammed open and two military policemen appeared. They caught his arms, dragged him to his feet and bundled him through the hatch, marching him down the empty corridor and into a large meeting room. He felt his heart sink as he saw the three officers waiting for him, sitting behind a table and wearing their dress uniforms. The lack of greeting, even of acknowledgement, proved he was in trouble.

The guards shoved him into a chair, cuffed his hands to an iron ring and then stood behind him. He could hear their breathing, just loud enough to be disconcerting. A subtle way of reminding him that they were there, he wondered, or were they just being rude? It was hard to think clearly with that noise in the background. Perhaps they wanted him off balance.

A fourth officer emerged from a side room and took up a position at one end of the table. Christopher felt his heart sink still further as he took in the man's appearance, noting the neatly-trimmed beard, clean uniform and perfect bearing. A REMF, then. A man who had never seen the elephant, who had made a career of serving his superior officers…the nasty part of Christopher's mind wondered if the man kissed their asses or if he went further. It wouldn't be the first time someone had traded sexual favours for advancement. Admiral Singh had cracked down on it, when she'd taken command, but she hadn't managed to eradicate it either.

"Captain Christopher Brookes," the fourth officer said. Christopher looked at him. His nametag read MCINNERNY. "You are charged with wilful defiance of orders, reckless endangerment and conduct unbecoming to an officer and a gentleman. How do you plead?"

Christopher felt his mouth drop open. It was several minutes before he was able to muster a response.

"If this is a formal court martial," he said finally, "I should have a representative and a notification of the charges…"

"You have just been informed of the charges," McInnerny said. "This court martial has been summoned in accordance with the Military Jurisdiction Act. You must enter a plea."

Christopher forced himself to think. The Military Jurisdiction Act was so long and complicated that practically anything could be justified, if one used a little imagination. It had actually been superseded by later legislation, if he recalled correctly…coming to think of it, as a holdover from the Empire, it could probably be put aside completely. But somehow he doubted the court would accept that reasoning.

Shit, he thought, numbly.

McInnerny leaned forward. "You must enter a plea."

Christopher ground his teeth. McInnerny had a voice that grated on the soul.

"I plead Not Guilty," he said. He lifted his head, meeting McInnerny's eyes. "And I will defend myself on all of these charges."

McInnerny turned to face the other officers, the judges. "Captain Brookes was ordered to raid the Trieste System," he said. "He had strict orders to avoid contact with enemy forces that posed a genuine threat to his command. Upon discovering such forces, Captain Brookes saw fit to ignore his orders and recklessly plunge his command into an engagement they could easily have lost..."

"But we didn't lose," Christopher said. He tried to keep the sneer from his voice, but he suspected it was a lost cause. "We won."

"You had orders to avoid engagements with significant enemy forces," McInnerny snapped, harshly. "Why did you choose to engage the enemy?"

Christopher felt his temper start to fray. "A person with *genuine* experience," he said, "would realise that the two enemy ships posed only a minor threat to my command. I had a crushing advantage. Indeed, I not only obliterated two enemy ships...I captured three freighters as well."

McInnerny reddened. Christopher's barb had struck its target.

"You also expended a significant number of missiles," he pointed out. "Your ships were not in a good position to defend themselves as they withdrew from the system."

Christopher spoke directly to the judges, ignoring McInnerny. "If I had chosen to avoid engagement on those grounds," he said, "what would I be expected to do when *this* system comes under attack? There was no reason to believe that there were any significant enemy forces at Trieste - we certainly weren't attacked as we left the system. These charges are bullshit."

The lead judge scowled. "You will comport yourself in a manner befitting your rank," he said, sternly. "This is a court of law."

Christopher felt cold as McInnerny bombarded him with question after question, steadily painting every one of his decisions in the worst possible light. This was *no* court of law. It wasn't even a proper court martial. It was a kangaroo court, one that denied due process in favour of laying the groundwork for a guilty verdict. If Admiral Singh knew what was being done in her name…his blood turned to ice as he realised, dully, that she *must* know. She'd even signed off on it. He was being thrown to the dogs and he didn't even know *why*.

"This court finds you guilty on all charges," the lead judge said, finally. McInnerny smirked, a smirk that made Christopher want to hit him. Again. "You will be taken from this place, allowed to write one final letter and then executed without further delay."

"I appeal," Christopher said. He knew it was futile - there was no appeal - but he had to try. "I did my duty and…"

The judge raised his voice. "Remove the prisoner!"

Christopher braced himself, planning to lash out the moment they released him from the chair. But the guards knew that trick. They shackled him first, ensuring that he could barely walk without falling over. McInnerny and the judges watched as he was half-dragged out of the courtroom and back to his cell. He thought he heard a faint snigger as the door closed.

He sagged, forcing them to carry him. He'd expected to be rewarded, not…not put in front of a kangaroo court and executed. He'd done his duty…he'd thought he was doing the right thing. He'd thought…

"I don't understand," he said. "What did I do wrong?"

The guards didn't bother to answer.

"It is done," Paula said. "Captain Brookes is dead. The cover stories are firmly in place."

Rani rubbed her forehead, tiredly. She'd gone back to her suite, hoping to catch a few hours of sleep before the next crisis. She should have known better. There was always something for her to handle, something that only *she* could approve…she wished she could trust her subordinates with more authority, but she knew she couldn't. Now, more than ever, she had to keep her grip on power.

"Very good," she said. She cut off Paula's next words with a glower. "Go."

She watched Paula flee, feeling bitter guilt gnawing at her soul. Christopher Brookes hadn't done anything wrong, not really. He'd shown bravery and determination, he'd scored a tiny victory that would boost morale…but he'd also proved himself to be very good at blowing his own trumpet. She couldn't risk having a rival, not now. Too many people were plotting against her for *that*. Brookes might not have *planned* to replace her, but she knew that others might have seen him as a potential figurehead. She'd had to kill him before it was too late.

He didn't deserve to die, she thought. Was she any better than Admiral Bainbridge? He'd tried to destroy *Rani's* career just because she'd turned down his advances. *But I had to kill him.*

Rani sighed. No one knew better than *she* just how easy it was to mount a coup, particularly when the target was too stupid to realise the possibility. And *she* didn't have any real legitimacy, neither on Corinthian nor Wolfbane. Her rule was upheld by military force. Very few people gave a damn about her personally. Why should they? She hadn't been their ruler long enough for simple inertia to give her a certain legitimacy. And the corporations were already trying to limit her power.

She undressed, slowly. She'd thought herself one of the good guys, once upon a time. She'd wanted power - true - but she'd also wanted to use it for more than her own glory. She could have built a paradise, if she hadn't needed to fight to defend her position. And, somewhere along the way, she'd stopped caring about anything else. Christopher Brookes was just another sacrifice to her power, another person removed and executed because he could pose a threat. She couldn't trust anyone.

Sighing, she climbed into bed.

Alone.

CHAPTER FIFTEEN

"This planet stinks," Meade commented.

"It's better than breathing in the stench of dead bodies," Jasmine pointed out, as they stepped out of the shuttle. The heat struck her like a physical blow. "Or having to empty a septic tank in the middle of a firefight."

Meade shot her a sharp look. "Has anyone actually had to *do* that?"

"Probably," Jasmine said.

She glanced around, taking a long breath. Meade was right. The atmosphere *did* smell foul: burning hydrocarbons, toasted rubber, the scent of too many humans in too close proximity...and something else, something *alien*. Calomel was only marginally habitable - really, it should have been classed as uninhabitable and terraformed. The atmosphere was breathable, thankfully, but the planet's biochemistry was strikingly hostile to humanity. Growing crops on Calomel was almost impossible.

And eating anything you find is a good way to put yourself in hospital, if you're lucky, she reminded herself. The guidebooks had been very clear. *Nothing* was edible, even after repeated boiling. Eating one of the nicer-looking fruits would result in nerve damage at the very least. *No wonder no one was interested in actually settling the world.*

She glanced at the rest of the team, then led the way towards the settlement. Hundreds of shuttles roared overhead, reminding her that Calomel was a nexus for legal and semi-legal trade. Anything could be found on Calomel, apparently. She was surprised the Wolves hadn't tried to shut it down, although the briefing papers had made it clear that Calomel was useful to them as well as their enemies. No doubt the planet's rulers, whoever they were, hoped the war would go on forever. Whoever won might take advantage of the peace to settle accounts with Calomel.

The settlement itself looked like a mess, a hundred prefabricated buildings mingled with the remains of freighter crates and military tents. Dozens of people milled around, mostly older men or women. Jasmine rather suspected that the women were actually younger than they looked, but life on Calomel had worn them down. They'd probably been kicked out of the brothels, she decided. The pimps might consider them largely worthless now they'd lost their looks. She ground her teeth, knowing it was yet another injustice she couldn't tackle.

We'll come back here, one day, she promised herself. *And we can try to make things better.*

She knew, all too well, that it was a promise she wouldn't be able to keep. She'd seen too many injustices during her career, from child brides to young boys turned into eunuchs, to believe they could *all* be handled. The Commonwealth had written laws that cracked down on the nastiest injustices, but she suspected that some of them had merely been driven underground. People on the margins of interstellar society didn't care for its niceties. The women who'd been sold into prostitution might have been sold by their families, their parents believing that sacrificing one child would be enough to save the rest.

A man stepped out in front of them. "New in town?"

"Yes," Jasmine said. She tried to keep her voice level, but it was hard. "Can you point us to the nearest recruitment office?"

The man gave her a long look. "Spacers?"

"From *Porcupine*," Jasmine said. "We're looking for new berths."

"Two rows down," the man said. "Good luck."

He sounded as if he didn't quite believe her. Jasmine wasn't too surprised. Partnerships weren't *that* uncommon in place, but six people travelling together was a *little* odd. She'd done her best to cover for it - their paperwork made it clear that *Porcupine's* captain hadn't been able to pay them all - yet she knew it was a potential flaw in their cover story.

Jasmine nodded her thanks, then led the way down the street. It grew hotter as the sun rose in the sky, baking the dusty street and blanching everything in view. There was something oddly *faded* about the recruitment officers, even the Trade Federation's verified shipping agent. She couldn't help thinking that *anyone* who stayed on Calomel for long would eventually be worn down by the heat and poisonous vegetation. Even fresh water was a pain in the ass.

They probably don't eat anything more than ration bars, she thought. *And whoever controls the food supply has this planet in a vice.*

"That's the Wolfbane office," Haverford said, quietly. He pointed to a small wooden building. A wolf banner flew over it, hanging limply from a flag post. "They'll probably arrange shipping, if we manage to convince them to take us as a group."

Jasmine nodded. They'd already agreed to go in as a group. A normal starship would probably balk at hiring all *six* of them, but the Wolves wouldn't care. She read the sign outside, promising good rates for trained and experienced crewmen, then opened the door and walked inside. It was mercifully cool. A tired-looking man sat at the desk, playing with his datapad. He looked up at them, his eyes widening with surprise. Jasmine guessed he didn't have many visitors.

"We're off *Porcupine*," she announced, holding out her datachip. "We hear you're looking for trained crewmen."

The man took the chip and plugged it into his datapad. She couldn't help thinking that he looked as faded as the rest of the settlement, as if he'd been on Calomel too long. He'd probably pissed someone off, she decided. There was nothing on Calomel that might make his exile bearable, not down on the surface. She'd been surprised to discover that the Wolves hadn't opened an office in orbit.

More expensive, she thought, dryly. *Buying a couple of compartments on a makeshift station probably costs more than they want to spend.*

"Uh...welcome," the man stammered. He sounded as though he hadn't used his voice in a very long time. "You have...you have certifications in starship maintenance and basic engineering?"

"I do indeed," Jasmine said. "I took the first set of exams on Rockhole and the second on Quanta."

The man raised his eyebrows. "And you are together? All six of you?"

"We're a group marriage," Jasmine lied, smoothly. It wasn't *that* uncommon in the Trade Federation. Group marriages ensured that children always had someone to look after them, even if their biological parents died. "We don't want to be split up."

"Which you would have to be, if you wanted to go to a normal freighter," the man said. He wasn't entirely ignorant, then. "If you sign up with us, you'll be shipped back to Wolfbane and assigned to posts there. I don't *think* you'll be split up, but there would be no promises."

Jasmine made a show of silently consulting the others, then turned back to him. "That would be fine," she said. "What jobs and benefits can we expect?"

The man launched into a long and tedious speech about everything they could expect, ranging from ample health benefits to citizenship… if they wanted it. Jasmine doubted he had many takers, no matter how good it sounded. Spacers rarely wanted to work on a planet, not when they were used to the freedom of deep space. Anyone who went to Wolfbane might wind up trapped, if they weren't careful. It was hellishly easy to get into debt.

And please don't throw me in the briar patch, she thought, wryly.

"An apartment will be assigned to you for the first six months," the man concluded. "You'll then be able to take out a loan for a more upscale apartment."

"That sounds good," Jasmine said. It *did* sound good, if one didn't care about returning to space. She'd thought she'd heard all of the tricks to trap unwary spacers, but the Wolves had clearly invented a few new ones. "When do we leave?"

The man worked his datapad for a long moment. "The *Lagos* is leaving for Wolfbane in two days," he said. "I'll arrange for you to have passage, all of you. That should give me time to check your references and certifications."

"Of course," Jasmine said. She paused. "We will need an advance."

She smiled, inwardly, at the greedy look on the man's face. Of *course* they'd need a cash advance. They wouldn't be signing up with the Wolves if they weren't terminally short of cash. Being kicked off their ship, even through no fault of their own, meant they were obviously penniless. And being penniless on a world like Calomel meant certain death, unless they found jobs very quickly.

"I can offer you five hundred credits now," the man said. He reached into his drawer and produced a handful of cash-chips. "Consider them a signing bonus."

He collected their datachips, then smiled. "I'll put your details on the datanet," he said, dryly. "Report back here in two days for pickup."

Jasmine nodded, curtly. The man wasn't really taking a risk. They'd agreed to go to Wolfbane. If they refused to go, or tried to sign up with someone else, they'd be blacklisted forever. The interstellar traders might dislike planetary governments, but they disliked cheats and claim-jumpers even more. Not, of course, that she had any intention of cheating the Wolves. She *wanted* to go to Wolfbane.

"We'll see you in two days," she said.

"Take rooms at the Ganymede," the man advised. He picked up a piece of paper and sketched out a set of directions. "Tell the innkeeper I sent you. He won't overcharge you."

Much, Jasmine thought. There would be a kickback, of course. *But at least he'll know where to find us.*

She nodded goodbye, then led the way back out of the building. The air was even hotter, somehow. She looked around, but the streets were largely deserted. The only people in sight were hidden under giant hats. Shaking her head, she took a look at the map and led the way down the street. The Ganymede was just on the next block. She wasn't surprised, somehow, when she saw the prostitutes waiting just outside the inn.

"I hear music," Stewart muttered. "*Bad* music."

Jasmine shrugged as she opened the door. The music was louder now, blaring out a drumbeat that obscured most of the lyrics. She rolled her eyes - she'd never been a music fan - and looked around, her eyes instantly adapting to the gloom. A handful of men sat at tables or perched against the bar, drinking steadily; a couple of women moved from table to table, looking worn down by experience. A gust of cooler air washed across her face, making her look up. The ceiling was covered in fans. She could hear them rattling alarmingly as they tried to banish the heat.

A waitress looked up, saw them and hurried over. She would have been pretty, Jasmine thought, if she hadn't slathered so much makeup on her pale face. Her shirt was open, revealing a pair of breasts; her skirt was so short that she could barely move without revealing her buttocks. She was young, but looked and moved like an older woman.

"Welcome," she said. "What can I get you?"

"Rooms for six," Jasmine said. She held up the cash-chips. "And dinner, afterwards."

The waitress nodded. "If you'll follow me…"

Jasmine glanced around as the waitress led them to a stairwell, half-hidden behind a giant statue of…*something*. The stairs were wooden; they creaked alarmingly as the waitress walked upstairs, shivering under her tread. Jasmine told herself that it was perfectly safe, even though she knew it probably wasn't. The innkeeper had clearly skimped on safety when he'd built his inn.

"We only have two large rooms," the waitress said. "Do you mind sharing?"

"We can go three to a room," Jasmine said. "It will be sufficient."

The waitress nodded and opened the first door. Jasmine peered inside, resisting the urge to make sarcastic remarks. Two beds, neither one particularly big; a bathroom smelling of something foul, a window frame that looked so weak that one good tug would pull it out…she'd slept in worse places, but most of them had been in war zones. They'd need more blankets, she told herself. But the bedding didn't seem to be clean either.

"It will do," she said, dropping her carryall on the bed. Beggars couldn't be choosers. "We'll be down for dinner soon."

"Just order at the bar," the waitress said, after showing them the second room. She collected the tip Jasmine offered her with practiced ease. Hopefully, she'd make it vanish before her superior demanded a cut. "Good luck."

Jasmine snorted as the waitress headed back down the stairs. "Thomas, you stay with Meade and I," she said, crisply. "The rest of you can have the other room."

"Understood," Stewart said. He looked around. "Not the safest of places, is it?"

Jasmine was inclined to agree. There was a lock on the door, but she was fairly sure she could pick it with her eyes closed. Not that the door itself was much tougher. The designer had used balsa wood. One good kick would be more than enough to smash a hole in the wood. She rather suspected the innkeeper would probably try to search their possessions when they were out, no matter what he said. He would be paid double if he found something incriminating before they boarded the freighter and headed to Wolfbane.

"Looks that way," she agreed, dryly.

She searched the room carefully, looking for bugs or other hidden surprises. There were no technological surveillance devices, as far as she could tell, but there *was* a knothole in the wooden wall that could be used to spy on them. If someone crawled along a hidden passageway and peered through the chink in the wall…

"Make sure you don't do anything you shouldn't," she said, after blocking the knothole. She was damned if she was *letting* them spy on her. "We'll have someone in here at all times."

"Of course," Stewart agreed. "Is there actually anything to *do* here?"

"Repairs," Meade said. She jabbed a finger at the rattling fan. "I'd bet good money there's shit here that needs repaired."

Jasmine was inclined to agree. "If you can find a few side jobs, do them," she said. It would keep Meade occupied for a day or so. There was nothing *else* to do on Calomel. "Until then…dinner time."

"Good idea," Stewart agreed. "I'm hungry."

"You're always hungry," Parkinson teased. "I'll stay here, with the luggage."

Jasmine nodded. She didn't *think* the innkeeper would actually *steal* from them - on a rough world, it would be asking for rough justice - but it was well to be sure. Their toolkits alone would be worth their weight in gold to the right person. She took one final look around the room, then led the way downstairs. The bar seemed to have grown louder, somehow, even though the number of people hadn't changed. She shook her head and sat down, beckoning the waitress.

"We only have reprocessed meat," the waitress said, holding out a faded menu. It was covered in pictures of food, but Jasmine would have been astonished if any of them were actually available. They looked too good. "Our water is clean; our beer is homemade…"

"Five beers, then," Jasmine said. She wasn't sure she trusted the local water, no matter what the innkeeper and his staff claimed. Marines did have all kinds of enhancements to make it harder to poison them, but there was no point in taking chances. "And I'd like a burger, please."

The waitress took their orders and scurried off. Jasmine sat back and waited, allowing her eyes to wander around the bar. There was a nasty vibe to the air, although not one suggesting the prospect of imminent violence. The patrons were too ground down to do more than drink and mutter… she wondered, absently, what most of them *did*. They had to do *something*, didn't they? Calomel was hardly the kind of world to give charity.

"The fan keeps rattling," Meade said, rising. "I'll go fix it."

She rose, striding over to the ancient device - it looked so old that Jasmine could readily believe it predated the Empire - and pulling a sonic manipulator from her belt. Jasmine watched, her eyes narrowing as she saw a man rising from his chair and heading over to Meade. His eyes were fixed on her rear as she bent over the fan, carefully dismantling the protective net. A moment later, he grabbed her ass…

…And she spun around, punching him in the face.

Jasmine tensed, half-expecting the rest of the bar to leap to the man's defence. It wouldn't be the first time someone had done just that, either because they didn't understand what was actually going on or because they just wanted a fight. But…instead…the patrons didn't show any reaction at all. They weren't angry or gloating or…they just didn't care. Life had worn them down too badly to care.

The waitress reappeared, carrying a tray of food. Jasmine saw her smile, just for a second, as she saw the groaning man. Clearly, he'd been making a nuisance of himself for weeks, perhaps months. No one really gave a damn, not really. She wished she was surprised. The settlement was a black hole, sucking in anyone who dared to stay too long. She was silently relieved that *she* wouldn't be staying.

"Here's your food," the waitress said. "Tuck in."

Jasmine took a bite. Her burger tasted like cardboard. The catsup and mustard tasted worse.

"It could be worse," Meade said. "We could be eating Civil Guard rations."

"Probably," Haverford said. "Or we could be eating prison food."

Jasmine scowled and took another bite. It wouldn't kill her. That was all that mattered, she told herself firmly. And besides, she *had* eaten worse.

And we'll be starting the most dangerous part of the mission in two days, she reminded herself. *Food won't be a concern then.*

CHAPTER SIXTEEN

"Colonel Elbridge has definite ties to Mouganthu," Lieutenant Jammu Foxglove reported, carefully. She was Emma Foxglove's sister, the only reason Rani had seen fit to promote her into her personal counterintelligence unit. "He was followed to Mouganthu Tower, where he spent two hours doing…doing *something*."

Rani gritted her teeth. Colonel Elbridge wasn't *important*, not in and of himself, but his ties to Mouganthu made him dangerous. And she couldn't even remove him without risking a major confrontation. Mouganthu had every right to patronise officers, to assist them in developing their careers…Governor Brown, damn him, had set precedents Rani had to follow.

"Keep an eye on him," she growled. Perhaps they could arrange an accident. "Let me know if he does anything outside the scope of his duties."

She glared down at the picture on the datapad. Colonel Elbridge was handsome enough, in a bland kind of way; his record was good, but not good enough to suggest an exceptional officer. Hell, he *was* the kind of person who'd sell his soul to a corporation in exchange for promotion. Normally, she wouldn't even have blamed him for trying…although she wouldn't have felt inclined to tolerate it. But now, she *had* to tolerate it.

He was careless, she thought. *And what does* that *mean?*

Colonel Elbridge had been *very* careless. Going straight to Mouganthu Tower had been more than enough to draw her attention, which meant… what? Colonel Elbridge wasn't stupid, was he? *Mouganthu* certainly wasn't stupid. They had to know that their meeting would alert her, which meant...were they trying to decoy her? Colonel Elbridge might be intended to draw her attention *away* from more competent threats. She might waste time and energy obsessing over him while the *real* threat moved into position.

Or they might want me to judge him as worthless, she thought, sourly. Paranoia was a survival skill, but...it was a pain, sometimes. *Which way do they want me to look?*

"Admiral, we could promote him up and send him to a worthless military base," Jammu offered. "That would neutralise the threat."

"Perhaps," Rani said. She'd have to give it some thought. Colonel Elbridge *might* not realise that his promotion was no reward at all, but his backers would certainly smell a rat. "For the moment, keep an eye on him."

She looked at Paula. "Do you have the latest set of reports from the security forces?"

"Four more cells of subversives, uncovered in the city," Paula said. "They've all been cleaned out, as far as we can tell."

"That's what they said last time," Rani said. She'd lost track of the number of men and women she'd sent to the firing squad or exiled to stage-one colony worlds. "And yet new cells spring up everywhere."

"Yes, Admiral," Paula said. "But we are keeping them down."

Her wristcom bleeped. "Admiral, Lieutenant Foxglove is requesting an immediate interview," she said. "She says there's been a major breakthrough."

Rani looked up, hopefully. "Order her to come in," she said, dismissing Jammu with a glance. "I'll speak to her at once."

Lieutenant Emma Foxglove looked tired, when she entered the office. But there was a faint smile on her face that, for the first time in far too long, made Rani feel a little better. The war wasn't lost, not yet - not at all. Losing at Corinthian had been embarrassing - and there was no easy way to shift the blame onto someone else - but Wolfbane was far from defeated. She was damned if she was just giving up.

"Admiral," Emma said. She held out a datachip. "We just received the latest set of reports from our sources on Avalon. The enemy is attempting to launch an offensive of its own."

Rani leaned forward. "The target?"

"Thule," Emma said. "All our sources agree on it."

"I see," Rani said. She tapped her console, bringing up the starchart. Thousands of tactical icons were scattered around, each one representing a starship or a battle squadron. Wolfbane itself was surrounded by hundreds of icon, blurring together into a featureless mass. "And what do they say?"

"The enemy intends to recover Thule," Emma said. "Their fleet may already be on their way."

Rani stroked her chin. Thule…it didn't seem likely, somehow. The Commonwealth *had* been beaten at Thule, true, but…somehow, she doubted they were driven by a desire for bloody revenge. Thule was no longer particularly important, not after a full-scale war and the destruction of most of its infrastructure. She'd withdrawn half of the forces assigned to Thule for the ill-fated drive on Corinthian.

Losing Thule would be annoying, she thought. The enemy was practically guaranteed a victory, unless she acted quickly. Their propaganda would turn it into a major victory, given the chance. *But it would hardly be decisive.*

"We should react," Paula said. "If we could get reinforcements there in time…"

"It would be useless," Rani said. Thule was worthless now. "There's no point in throwing good money after bad."

She leaned forward, thinking hard. The enemy *had* scored a major victory. There was no point in trying to hide from *that*. And they planned to capitalise on it by liberating a useless world? She didn't *think* so. Given time, she'd rebalance her forces and resume the offensive…they knew it as well as she did. No, they'd need something a little more decisive if they hoped to win the war.

They're not afraid to gamble, she thought. *And Thule is a pretty safe bet.*

"They're not going to Thule," she said, softly. "That's a decoy."

Emma frowned. "Admiral, our sources all agree…"

"Our sources helped prime us to walk right into a trap," Rani said. She hadn't forgotten just how badly she'd been misled over Corinthian. "Either they lied to us or they were lied to."

She studied the display, shaking her head slowly. "They're not going to Thule."

"We know they were preparing an operation," Emma said. "Admiral, where *are* they going?"

Rani said nothing. Where would *she* go, if she was in their shoes? A direct strike on Avalon - or Wolfbane - would be one hell of a gamble. It might shorten the war. But where else *could* they go?

"Titlark," she said, finally.

Emma coughed. "Titlark?"

"Yes," Rani said.

She pointed to the glowing star - and the blue shipping lines leading to it. "It's our forward base," she said. "We run convoys through the system all the time. We built up one hell of a stockpile of weapons and supplies there. Taking the base out - either capturing or destroying it - would give us a bloody nose."

"Yes, Admiral," Emma agreed.

"We'd have to rebuild our stockpiles, if nothing else," Paula said. "That would set the war back a few months..."

"More like a few years," Rani said. Titlark *was* the most logical target. There were other fleet bases, but none of them so crucial to the war. Even if she regained control of the system in a hurry, she'd still lose the supplies and any convoys unfortunate enough to pass through the region. "We need to reinforce the base..."

She stopped, studying the display. The enemy would have the system under observation, of course. She'd done the same, back before the war had actually started. They'd see the reinforcements and either back off or come up with a better plan. But if they didn't *know* the system had been reinforced...they'd come in, fat and happy. They wouldn't realise they'd been rumbled until it was too late.

"No," she said. "We're going to ambush them."

She closed her eyes for a long moment. She needed a victory, a decisive victory. Smashing the enemy fleet would give her *that*. And it would convince her enemies on Wolfbane to back off, just long enough to let her win the war. The only real danger lay in leaving Wolfbane herself. Did she dare leave the corporations unsupervised?

And if I don't go, she thought, *I might wind up with a second Christopher Brookes.*

She scowled at the thought. The truth - that Brookes had been executed - *had* been buried, but he already had a growing personality cult and fan club. A handsome young war hero…how could he *not* be popular? It was sheer luck that the media had accepted the story about him being promoted without demur. There were limits to how badly she could strong-arm them without the reporters suspecting that something was wrong.

No, that's not the worst that could happen, she told herself. *The worst is that whoever I put in command of the fleet comes back intent on unseating me.*

She felt her scowl deepen as her head started to pound. She wasn't *blind* to the problems caused by the political commissioners, even though she *needed* them. Most of her commanding officers were too busy looking over their shoulders to pose a threat to her - Christopher Brookes had been an exception, damn him. Sending a fleet out supervised by the commissioners *was* asking for trouble. No, she had to take command personally.

"Paula, inform fleet command that I want to detach four battle squadrons and flanking elements for immediate redeployment," she ordered, curtly. Assuming the enemy took a least-time course to Titlark - the only wise assumption - she should get there a day or two before them. "And make sure they're armed with the latest weapons. I want full missile loads and supplies."

"Yes, Admiral," Paula said.

"And order them to conceal as much as possible," Rani added. "I don't want any spies *here* getting a whisper of our true intentions."

"Yes, Admiral," Paula said, again.

Rani took a long breath. "I'll be taking command personally," she added. "You and my inner circle will remain here, supervising matters."

Paula looked pale, but she nodded. There wasn't any choice. She was a bureaucrat, not a fleet commander. And besides, she was strikingly unpopular. She couldn't undermine Rani without risking her own life.

The same could be said for many of her other officers. Their careers - and lives - depended on her.

And if the corporations do decide to get uppity, she thought coldly, *I'll have enough firepower with me to make them regret it.*

She smiled at the thought. Plastering Wolfbane with KEWs would feel good, although she knew it would practically *guarantee* a Commonwealth victory. But a civil war would also guarantee a Commonwealth victory. If the corporations decided to stab her in the back, she resolved, she'd make them pay. It would cost her everything, but she'd make them pay.

"I'll discuss the matter with the directors later today," she said. "Until then..."

She looked at Emma. "I want a full breakdown of conventional enemy forces," she ordered. "Don't assume they're sending a single squadron. Assume the worst - that they're making a serious attempt to take Titlark. And then start making plans to deny the base's facilities to the enemy if we lose the engagement."

"Aye, Admiral," Emma said. "I'll get right on it."

"And have your staff analyse everything we got from our agents," Rani added. "See if there are any oddities about the reports."

If they all say the same thing, her thoughts reminded her, *someone is definitely trying to set us up.*

She smiled, coldly. Rumours had a habit of growing and mutating as they passed from mouth to mouth. The sources might all agree on the same general points, but the details would be different...if everything matched, someone was spreading false rumours and lies deliberately. And that meant they were trying to mislead people...

Paula cleared her throat. "Admiral," she said nervously, "what if you're wrong?"

Rani was in too good a mood to snap at her. "Thule is not a particularly important target," she said. She'd have to make sure the occupation forces CO received secret orders, just in case. "If they really are planning to attack Thule, it will cause us some embarrassment and little else. We'll order the occupation forces to retreat if they see a powerful enemy fleet bearing down on them."

"There will be no time to evacuate the people on the ground," Emma pointed out.

"They can fight to the last," Rani said. She'd pulled the best infantry units out long ago. The ones she'd left behind were untrustworthy. They would probably have defected if the enemy hadn't made it clear that anyone who fell into their hands would be killed and their bodies mutilated. "The starships are more important."

She shrugged, feeling chipper. "I'll depart tomorrow afternoon," she said. "By then, we'll have taken steps to secure our position here."

"Yes, Admiral," Paula said.

Rani raised her voice. "Dismissed."

She leaned back in her chair as her officers retreated, leaving her alone. Perhaps, she considered, she hadn't been entirely honest with herself. She *did* need to be there - she was the only one she could trust to command the fleet - but it was more than that, wasn't it? It was a chance to get out of the fortress and get to grips with the enemy. The prospect of death in battle was less terrifying, somehow, than remaining on Wolfbane, growing more and more isolated every day.

If I win, I'll have a chance to come out ahead, she thought, coolly. She'd be gone for a month, at least. It shouldn't be long enough for her enemies to put together a coup. *And if I lose, it won't matter anymore...will it*?

It was a bitter thought. She'd sacrificed hundreds, perhaps thousands, of lives, just to stay in charge. She didn't know the names or faces of the men and women, the boys and girls, she'd ordered killed. They haunted her dreams, mocking her. Some of them had deserved it, perhaps, but others had been in the wrong place at the wrong time. And some of them - like Christopher Brookes - had expected to be rewarded. They hadn't realised that she couldn't let them live.

And yet, she couldn't stop. She was *still* riding a tiger, she was *still* unable to get off without being killed...she had to go on. Part of her even *hoped* for a clean death, somewhere in the inky darkness of space. It was better than she'd given any of her enemies, really. Her lips twitched at the thought. Death would be the end.

But what do you get, her own thoughts mocked her, *if you stay alive?*

Rani sighed. She had no answer.

Rising, she banished the depression and strode over to the window, peering over the brightly-lit city. She had to win. Whatever happened, she had to win.

And she couldn't allow herself to care, any longer, about *how* she won.

Nadia sat in her cell, her naked body shaking helplessly.

She'd lost all track of time, since she'd been thrust into the tiny room. She had no idea how long she'd been in the cell, how long it had been since she'd been arrested. It felt like months, perhaps years…her life had shrunk, rapidly, to the cell's four walls. The beatings, the rapes…she'd thought, at first, that the policemen were trying to break her, but it had rapidly become clear that they were merely having fun. She didn't know how long she could endure, not really.

But we were just talking, she thought. *We didn't do anything*! *We didn't do anything*!

She looked up, bleakly, as she heard the cell door rattling. The police didn't bother to take any precautions with her - why should they? She'd tried to fight, the first few times, but they'd just beaten her bloody and raped her anyway. She twisted, hoping that if she submitted it wouldn't be so bad. Some of the policemen seemed to like hurting her, but others just wanted to spend themselves. How far had she fallen, she asked herself bitterly, when she was *glad* for a gentle rapist?

Two policemen stepped into the cell. One held a pistol in his hand. "On your feet," he growled. "Now!"

Nadia felt a flicker of hope, mixed with dull horror and resignation. Her life was over. It would be over even if they marched her to the door and kicked her out onto the streets. Her family wouldn't want to take her back, the college certainly wouldn't want to take her back…what could she do? She forced herself to stand, despite her aching body. She'd ache much more if she gave them an excuse for yet another beating.

The policemen eyed her as though she was just a piece of meat. She shuddered, dully, at the coldness in their eyes. She'd known men *looked* at her since she'd matured - and she'd enjoyed and hated it in equal measure - but this was different. To them, she was just an object...not a woman. She wasn't even *human*, as far as they were concerned. She was...

"Turn around," the policeman said. His eyes never left hers. "Kneel."

Nadia did as she was told, struggling not to collapse as she knelt down. They probably wanted to cuff her...or something. She found it hard to care. Her thoughts were fragmented, drowned out by the growing pains in her arms and legs. Nothing was broken, as far as she could tell, but she was *sore*.

"You have been found guilty of subversion," the policeman said. She felt something cold and hard pressed against the back of her neck. A gun, she realised numbly. They hadn't come to cuff her or rape her. They'd come to kill her. "The sentence is death."

It was almost a relief, Nadia thought. She closed her eyes as she felt the trigger slowly being pulled. At least there would be no more pain...

CHAPTER SEVENTEEN

From nearly five light years away, Mandy knew, there was little to separate Titlark from any of the other stars glowing against the inky blackness of interstellar space. The star was just a pinpoint of light…in truth, she wouldn't even have known she was looking at the *right* star if her computers hadn't identified it for her. Her task force could have been thousands of light-years out of place for all she knew.

"All ships have returned to realspace," Commander Darren Cobb reported. They stood on the bridge, looking at the display. "They're signalling for orders."

"Tell them to prepare to move," Mandy ordered. Four weeks in transit had worn down her crews, even though her officers had worked hard to vary their duties. "We'll be sending *Sneaky* into the system shortly."

"Aye, Captain," Cobb said. "Do you still mean to accompany her?"

Mandy nodded. Captain Karin Hughes wouldn't be too pleased to have her superior officer on her bridge - Mandy wouldn't have been pleased, if the roles had been reversed - but she'd do as she was told. Mandy wouldn't be an awkward guest either, she promised herself. She wouldn't allow any confusion over who was in command. Besides, the Commonwealth Navy would back Captain Hughes if push came to shove.

"I'll be back before you know it," she said. "And if I don't come back, Colonel Stalker and Commodore Mountbatten can decide what to do next."

"You'll be back soon enough, I am sure," Cobb said. He grinned. "Do you want the corridors swept or the bulkheads repainted while you're gone?"

Mandy smiled. "Give the crew a few hours to relax," she said. This far from Titlark, there was almost no chance of being detected, let alone ambushed. The Wolves would have to get impossibly lucky to discover the task force, let alone organise an attack before she took her ships to Titlark. It was the sort of thing that only happened in bad flicks. "And make sure the tactical staff run the final set of simulations."

She glanced at the timer, feeling cold. It was impossible to be *sure*, of course, but the Wolves *should* have picked up the rumours about Thule by now. Assuming the timing worked out, they *should* have dispatched reinforcements to the system - and Titlark, their closest major fleet base, was the only place they could have been dispatched *from*. But she knew, all too well, that interstellar warfare rarely rewarded anyone for trying to be clever. It was quite possible that the Wolves had never picked up on the deception, let alone decided to act on it.

Or they might have decided that it was too late to reinforce Thule, she thought, grimly. *Or that the planet isn't worth holding.*

She shrugged, dismissing the thought. There was no point in brooding over the possibilities, not when there was too much work to do. She had five battle squadrons and their flankers under her command, enough firepower to blast her way through Titlark's defences and capture the planet. And, if she *did* run into something she couldn't handle, she should be able to alter course and break contact before it was too late. She wouldn't allow herself to be trapped.

Space combat can be intensely frustrating when the two sides are well-matched, she thought, ruefully. The pirates had always made a point of not picking on someone bigger than them, but the Commonwealth didn't have that option. *And if we are beaten off, we may not be able to continue the offensive.*

She glanced at Cobb. "Make sure that all of our maintenance schedules are up-to-date, then load missile racks," she ordered. "We'll move as soon as I return."

"Aye, Captain," Cobb said. "We'll be ready."

Mandy nodded, although the tension refused to fade. She *always* felt nervous before a battle, always felt as though something was going to go wrong. Perhaps it was just another legacy from her time on the pirate ship, where failure had been harshly punished…the Commonwealth Navy, at least, didn't shoot officers for failure. But *someone* would have to be the scapegoat if the operation went badly wrong. Mandy wasn't blind to just how much political capital had been spent on the operation, quite apart from the material aspects. A complete failure could bring down the government.

"Inform Colonel Stalker that I will be departing within the hour," Mandy said. "And ask if he wishes to accompany me."

She leaned forward, studying the live feed from the other ships. She felt almost as though she was deserting her command, even though she knew she wasn't. Cobb could handle the bridge. He was practically a commanding officer in his own right. She'd have just long enough to make sure there weren't any fleet issues that required her attention before departing. The other commanding officers could probably deal with most issues on their own, but she wanted to be sure. They didn't have time for a major dispute on the brink of a full-scale engagement.

And I really should move to the CIC, she thought, numbly.

It wasn't something she wanted to do. She didn't *want* to give up command of a starship, even though she was balancing those duties with fleet command. And yet, as the fleets grew larger and the stakes rose higher, she knew she couldn't continue to balance the duties indefinitely. She'd either have to surrender command or accept a demotion.

We do have more commanding officers now, she told herself. The training programs were nowhere near as comprehensive as the Imperial Navy's academy - the old sweats insisted that this was a good thing - but they *were* churning out new officers and crewmen. Hell, she'd worked hard to make sure that crewmen could rise to the ranks, if they wished to become mustangs. *I don't have to hold two hats.*

She shook her head. She'd have to make her decision soon, after the battle. And then…

"Colonel Stalker has declined your offer," Cobb reported. "He's wished you luck."

Mandy nodded. "You have the bridge," she said. "I'll see you when I get back."

It was easy, Ed had discovered long ago, to get bored in transit. Troopships - even the giant MEUs the Marine Corps had once deployed - weren't really designed to keep the troops entertained, not when every last square inch was either accommodation or storage. He'd made sure to keep the troops busy, running through combat drills or brushing up on background knowledge, but he knew it hadn't been enough. The handful of fights - and offenders who'd received NJP instead of being dragged in front of their ultimate CO - bore mute testament to that.

He sat in the observation blister, staring out at the stars. Jasmine and her team *should* be on their way to Wolfbane by now, assuming that they'd managed to get passage on a freighter from Calomel. He was sure she'd succeeded, but…he had no way to know if she actually *had* succeeded. There was no way to know if she was on her way or if she was stuck on Calomel…or if she'd been discovered in transit and killed. He wanted an update, but he knew he wouldn't get one. Jasmine was on her own.

Not quite on her own, he reminded herself. *She does have five others with her.*

He snorted as he scanned the unblinking stars. He'd always hated micromanagers. He'd always hated their demands for constant updates and their hectoring and their conviction that they knew better than the man on the ground, but now…now he thought he understood them a little better. It wasn't easy to send someone countless light years away, then sit back and wait for an update. Jasmine was completely isolated, completely cut off from him…she was outside his control. He trusted her - certainly more than any of the micromanagers had ever trusted *him* - but he still wanted to know what was going on.

There are too many moving parts in this plan, he thought, sourly. They'd simplified the original concept as much as possible, but he was glumly aware that too much could still go wrong. *She might never make it to Wolfbane.*

He shook his head, firmly. They'd gone through a multitude of contingency plans. Jasmine would hijack a freighter, if necessary, if there was no other way to leave Calomel. And then she'd head straight back to the

Commonwealth to report failure. It wouldn't sit well with her - it wouldn't sit well with *any* of them - but at least they'd know. They could start coming up with a new plan…

And even that will take time, he thought. *It might be months before we knew the full story - and by then, the enemy might have mounted a counter-attack of their own.*

He leaned forward, pressing his face against the transparent material. The remainder of the squadron was out there somewhere, but the starships were invisible against the darkness. It was easy to believe that *Defiant* was alone, that he was standing in the only safe place for hundreds of light years…he sighed, remembering one of the more tedious lectures he'd endured at OCS. Humanity simply couldn't comprehend the distances between star systems, the lecturer had insisted. Modern technology had only made it worse.

Ed nodded, slowly. Alexander the Great had built an empire, but it had barely been half the size - and far less developed - than the Roman Empire. And the Roman Empire had been tiny compared to the British Empire. And the British Empire would have vanished without trace when compared to the first interstellar empires. And yet…those empire-builders, he thought, would have understood the problem he faced. They'd often had to wait weeks or months for answers to their questions…

He scowled. Two people on Earth - or Avalon - could hold a real-time conversation easily, thanks to the wonders of technology. But as the gulf between them grew wider - if one person was standing on Earth and the other on Mars - it took longer and longer to send a message and wait for a reply. The Grand Senate had needed over a year to send a message to Avalon and receive a reply. They hadn't been able to micromanage and they'd hated it.

Which didn't stop them from trying, he thought, ruefully. He'd known commanding officers who'd glanced at the messages, then done whatever they thought best anyway. The really good ones had been able to conceal their defiance long enough to actually win the war…although it had never lasted. There had always been *someone* willing to betray them for money or rank. *They ruined the Empire because they refused to let the man on the spot make his decisions.*

It was more than that, he knew. The Grand Senate had been so used to instant communications - on Earth - that they'd never really comprehended the gulf between the stars. They should have done, he thought, but...most of them had never left the Sol System, never even ventured as far as the moon. They'd never quite grasped the immensity of interplanetary space, let alone interstellar...they hadn't realised just how badly they were hampering themselves.

That won't happen to us, he promised himself. *We'll learn from the past.*

He smiled. What had Professor Leo Caesius said?

"Those who do not learn from the past are condemned to repeat it," he'd said. "Those who *do* learn from the past are condemned to watch helplessly as *others* repeat it."

But we're not helpless, Ed thought. He'd worked hard to make sure that Avalon and the Commonwealth understood the mistakes of the past. *We can ensure that the same mistakes are not repeated.*

And come up with new ones instead, his thoughts mocked him. *Who knows what will change as technology advances again?*

His wristcom bleeped. "Colonel," Gwendolyn Patterson said. "We completed the preliminary set of combat tests. We're a little rusty."

Ed nodded, curtly. His company - or what was left of it - hadn't fought as a unit for nearly five years. He'd deployed platoons to reinforce the Knights or fight behind enemy lines, but nothing more complex. Marines were good, the best of the best, but even *they* got rusty when they didn't have a chance to exercise. Stalker's Stalkers would be in trouble if the Corps Inspector ever paid them a visit.

If the Corps Inspectorate still exists, Ed thought. The Slaughterhouse was gone...he had no idea what had happened to Major General Jeremy Damiani and the remainder of the Terran Marine Corps. He didn't want to consider the likelihood that *he* might be the senior surviving marine in the entire galaxy, but he had to admit it *was* possible. *We might be the only combat unit left intact.*

He told himself, firmly, that it was unlikely. But the thought kept gnawing at his mind.

"I'm on my way," he said. *He* was a little rusty too, if he was forced to be honest. He'd spent too much time behind a desk and too little on the field. He was still fit, still healthy, but he'd started to slip. "We'll run through the basic set of exercises again."

"Aye, Colonel," Gwen said. "Your suit is waiting for you."

Ed nodded. He *needed* to exercise. And besides, it would keep him from brooding.

And if the company needs to be deployed, he thought, *they'd better be ready for it.*

———

"I used to think that I'd never have a real career," Midshipwoman Simone Perkins said. She struck a dramatic pose as she perched on her bed, fluffing her short blonde hair with one hand. "And now…look at me."

Emmanuel Alves smiled as he filmed her. Interviewing junior officers and crew wasn't the easiest job in the world - some of them were suspicious of the media while others were too trusting - but it was better than sitting in his cabin doing nothing. Besides, there was a reasonable chance that some of his interviews would become background material or even documentaries. The Commonwealth Navy didn't have a recruitment problem - now - but that might change.

"You seem a little young to be an officer," he said. "How old were you when you joined the navy?"

"Sixteen, officially," Simone said. She shrugged. "To be honest, I was one of the unregistered. I think I'm eighteen now, but…"

"Your birth was never registered," Emmanuel said. It wasn't exactly uncommon. The Old Council had recorded births to make sure they knew who was meant to be paying off their family's debts. Several thousand children had been kept off the rolls until after the war. "Do you like the navy?"

"It's…different," Simone admitted. She waved a hand at the bulkhead. "Sharing bunkspace with a dozen others isn't easy, not after growing up in the countryside. But there is a comradeship that you don't get anywhere else."

Emmanuel looked around. He'd thought his cabin was small, but the middy bunkspace was *tiny*. The bunk beds looked as though they were intended for children, not grown adults. He had the feeling he couldn't have slept in one without being very uncomfortable. His legs were just too long. Simone was a *little* shorter, but not by much.

"I'm glad to hear it," he said. "What do you *do* every day?"

"We have a basic schedule," Simone informed him. She shot him a flirtatious look. "What do *you* do every day?"

"Write stories and reports that hardly anyone will ever read," Emmanuel said. It wasn't entirely untruthful. He had a good reputation, as far as his readers were concerned, but there was just so *much* news flooding the datanet that nearly everyone got flooded out. "And waiting for the exclusive that will define my career."

"Sounds boring," Simone said. She grinned. "But I've been told to enjoy boredom."

Emmanuel nodded in agreement. Boredom was bad, but being shot at was worse. Jasmine had told him that the military life was divided between boredom and danger…the two never really met. Simone was right. Whatever broke the boredom would be far worse. *Defiant* was going to war. There would be casualties, ships would be lost…one of them might be *Defiant*.

Simone glanced at her wristcom. "I'm on duty in an hour," she said. She winked. "Fancy a quickie?"

Emmanuel stared at her. He'd never been propositioned before, not like that. He honestly wasn't sure if she was serious or not. Hell, *she* might not be sure if she was serious or not. It might be a joke, a trick played on a reporter…or it might be real. And yet…

He shook his head. "I'm in a relationship at the moment," he said. He wasn't even sure what the rules *were*, when it came to sex on ships. There was no way he was in her chain of command, but he could influence her career. "Thank you for the offer, but…"

Simone shrugged. "You're welcome," she said. She didn't *sound* hurt. "You do know you could be dead in the next couple of days?"

"I know," Emmanuel said. "But if I don't die in the next couple of days, I'll have to live with what I'd done."

"A common problem," Simone said. She winked, again. He had the very definite feeling that she wasn't serious. "I'll just go hit up one of the soldiers."

She paused. "Don't put *that* on the interview," she added. "It'll look bad."

"I suppose it will," Emmanuel said. Simone's bunkmates might find it amusing, but her commanding officer would probably take a different view. "Don't worry. I'll keep it to myself."

"Thank you," Simone said. "But you can run the rest of the interview."

"Oh good," Emmanuel said. "I'd hate to think you lured me here under false pretences."

CHAPTER EIGHTEEN

"Local space is clear, Admiral."

Rani nodded as she sat in the CIC, watching the display. She knew she should rest, she knew she should be in her cabin, but she found it hard to sleep. Titlark was in an excellent position, at least for mounting offences into enemy territory, yet the oddities in the system meant that attackers could actually get quite close to the base without being detected. Indeed, if there was a major downside to the system, it was that the enemy ships might be able to withdraw if they saw the ambush before it was too late.

"Keep us under cloak," she ordered. The enemy couldn't be allowed to know that she was waiting for them. If, of course, she was right and the enemy *was* heading for Titlark. She'd had plenty of time to second-guess herself during the voyage from Wolfbane. "Do we have any updates from the sensor network?"

"None," Commander Julia Robinson reported. "There are no hints that the system is under observation."

And that proves nothing, Rani thought. *A careful spy could remain undetected indefinitely.*

She leaned back in her chair, enjoying the sensation of being on a starship. There were no corporate whiners or ungrateful little brats on the battleship, just trained and experienced crewmen who understood the realities of interstellar warfare. She didn't have to worry about knives in the dark, about assassins coming to put an end to her life…she could relax and enjoy herself while waiting for the enemy. It almost made her regret that she'd taken control of Wolfbane, after Governor Brown's death. She'd had no choice - she would have been killed if she hadn't made a bid for the brass ring - but she still mourned what could have been.

"I assume there's been no update from Admiral Howarth," she said. "Or have I missed something?"

"No, Admiral," Julia said. "He hasn't sent any update."

Rani nodded. Admiral Howarth was the only person on Titlark Base who knew that her battle squadrons were lurking within the system. Telling him was a risk - there was no way to know if one of his staffers was a spy - yet she'd had no choice. He'd actually argued quite strenuously to be allowed to bring his defences to full alert, but Rani had vetoed it. She didn't want to discourage the enemy from attacking, after all.

Unless they bring their entire fleet, she thought. *That might make things difficult.*

She scowled at the thought. She'd stuffed her ships with the new weapons, but she knew - all too well - that technological concepts didn't always work out in real life. The Commonwealth might have already devised countermeasures, even if they didn't know how far her own researchers had progressed. They could hardly be blind to the implications of their own technology. Rani felt cold ice curling through her veins as she contemplated the problem. The Commonwealth was likely to have a major advantage for the foreseeable future, one that couldn't be offset easily. And if they came up with a silver bullet...

All the more reason to end the war as quickly as possible, she mused. *And that means destroying their fleet.*

She rose. "Keep the fleet cycling through the training exercises," she ordered. "I'll be in my office."

"Aye, Admiral," Julia said.

Rani smiled as she stepped through the hatch and into the compartment. It was smaller than the office she'd taken from Governor Brown, but it felt...safer. She sat down at the desk as the hatch hissed closed behind her, keying her terminal to bring up the latest set of reports from the courier boats. This close to the front, she could actually make decisions that might have a genuine impact on the war. The enemy had a raiding force operating in a nearby system and Admiral Howarth wanted to detach a battle squadron to deal with it. Rani considered the concept for a moment, then shook her head. It would have to wait until after the battle.

She forced herself to relax as she read the latest updates from Wolfbane, even though she knew they were three weeks out of date. Nothing had happened, yet…more accurately, nothing had happened three weeks ago. The uncertainty was enough to drive her mad, she knew. She needed to be in too many places at once, if she wanted to stay in power indefinitely. Or she needed a partner who could actually command respect. But she didn't know who she could use who wouldn't try to unseat her…

Or mess up the balance of power, she thought. She'd underestimated just how carefully Governor Brown had built his government. By positioning himself as the mediator, he'd secured his own position. *She* didn't have that option, not any longer. And allying herself closely with one of the corporations would merely unite the others against her. *They won't allow one of their competitors to build up an unchallengeable power base.*

A new update blinked up on the display. A scan-sat, positioned along the edge of the fluctuating phase limit, had reported a brief flicker of energy that might - might - indicate the presence of a cloaked ship. Rani felt a flicker of excitement, mingled with the grim awareness that it might just be a random background fluctuation. Deploying the scan-sat network had been a costly gamble, even though it might have paid off. There was no way they could cover the entire star system.

And the message itself is already an hour out of date, Rani reminded herself. *The enemy ship could be anywhere.*

She keyed her console. "Assume it's a real ship," she ordered. "Run a set of passive tracking exercises - passive only. Don't let them know we spotted them."

"Aye, Admiral," Julia said.

"And then deploy a set of additional sensor platforms," Rani added. "I want to see the enemy as soon as possible."

She closed the connection, then forced herself to think. Her instincts told her that the sensor flicker was real, even though she knew she couldn't prove it. And that meant the enemy task force had to be near. There was no point in bringing the fleet to battle stations, not yet, but she could make some preparations. The enemy wouldn't have risked detection - even though the odds were vastly against being detected - unless they were ready to move.

And then there will be no more sneaking around, she thought, as she brought up the in-system display. *Just a clean honest battle against an open foe.*

She smiled. She knew the risks, she knew she might not survive the day, but still...

...She was quite looking forward to it.

It had been nearly two years since Mandy had last entered the Titlark System, shortly before the Wolves had attacked Thule and started the war. She'd only probed the system because she'd had a hunch the enemy might find a use for it. According to the somewhat outdated files from the Imperial Navy, Titlark had been visited once, briefly surveyed and then simply abandoned. There was nothing there, apart from a handful of asteroids and a couple of comets the red star had captured thousands of years ago. It might attract pirates or survivalists, but not the Imperial Navy. But, if one ignored the absence of anything usable, it was within a handful of light years of Thule.

And she'd been right, she recalled.

Titlark was odd, by any reasonable standard. A dark system circling a dull red star...it should have been predictable. It shouldn't have had any surprises. And yet, the phase limit fluctuated, seemingly at random. The Commonwealth Navy hadn't had the time to carry out a full survey, let alone invite researchers to try to puzzle out the mystery...as far as she knew, the Wolves hadn't bothered to do any research either. She tossed the problem over and over in her head for a long moment, then dismiss it. The mystery could wait until after the war.

She sat on the bridge, watching as Captain Karin Hughes issued a quiet stream of orders to her crew. *Sneaky* was tiny, barely larger than a corvette. And yet, she was almost completely undetectable even without the cloak. The Commonwealth Navy had designed her for sneaking into enemy-held star systems, reasoning that long-range active and passive sensors were likely to keep improving. Mandy couldn't help feeling that the designers had been quite right. Titlark didn't seem to be on alert, but…

Three battle squadrons and flankers, she thought. The enemy ships showed up clearly on the display. They weren't even trying to hide. *They're clearly doing some reconsolidation.*

She sucked in her breath as she studied the two enemy battleships. The Imperial Navy had designed them to be indestructible, lining their hulls with heavy armour and cramming hundreds of missile tubes into their bulk, although she knew from experience that they could be beaten. Admiral Singh had probably made sure they were refitted with the latest sensors, too. The Imperial Navy had skimped on refitting its ships, but *they* hadn't had to fight a major war. Mandy knew from bitter experience that *not* refitting ships when there *was* a war on was asking for trouble.

Beyond them, there were a handful of new-build heavy cruisers and battlecruisers. Mandy studied them with interest, wondering just what Wolfbane's designers had invented. The Commonwealth Navy had come up with all sorts of ideas, although they hadn't had the time or resources to turn them all into reality. She couldn't help thinking that the heavy cruisers looked larger than they should be, while the battlecruisers were smaller. Perhaps it was a good sign.

"The base itself has expanded," the sensor officer said.

Mandy nodded in grim agreement. The original settlements had been nothing more than asteroids, inhabited by cultists. They'd probably been unceremoniously evicted by the Wolves when they arrived. Now, the asteroids had been turned into space docks and storage depots - there were even a pair of shipyard slips, probably intended to allow repair crews to work on damaged starships. She made a mental note to mark them out for special attention, if they had to fall back and abandon the system. The repair crews were worth their weight in whatever precious metal one cared to name.

She shuddered. How far had they fallen, she asked herself, when she was calmly contemplating the slaughter of defenceless men? She'd had to do bad things - evil things, perhaps - when she'd been a pirate slave, but now…now she shouldn't have to make those decisions. And yet, cold logic told her that slaughtering the repair crews would only help the Commonwealth. It was her duty.

It was her duty...and she hated the very idea of it.

"Captain, I'm picking up a flight of shuttles heading to the nearest comet," the sensor officer added. "They'll pass along our flight path in twenty minutes."

"Give them a wide berth," Captain Hughes ordered. "And prepare to cut power and go doggo."

"Aye, Captain."

Mandy tensed. The shuttles weren't going to be *that* close to them, but their presence *was* alarming. Had they been detected? Were the enemy trying to get a lock on them? Or was it just a coincidence? *Sneaky* was *very* sneaky. The enemy would have to get incredibly lucky to detect her, as long as the crew were careful.

They could have another cloaked ship shadowing us, she thought. *Sneaky* hadn't detected anything following her, but that meant nothing. *We can't use our active sensors without being detected.*

She braced herself as the shuttles flew closer.... and then flashed onwards, heading directly to the comet. A coincidence then...she hoped. The comet did contain a lot of raw materials, materials the Wolves would need if they wanted to keep the system running. Mining it *did* make sense. And yet...

"Take us towards the base," Captain Hughes ordered.

Mandy glanced at her. Captain Hughes seemed unflappable. Mandy was impressed, even though she *knew* the odds of being detected were very low. The bridge crew spoke in whispers, the slightest sound made everyone jump...as if the noise could somehow echo across the vacuum and alert the enemy. And yet, Captain Hughes remained calm. She didn't look as though anything worried her.

She turned her attention back to the display as Titlark Base grew closer. It was surrounded by a network of defensive stations and automated weapons platforms, although nowhere near as many as she'd expected. But then, Titlark wasn't a planet. Mandy rather suspected that the Wolves had seen it as nothing more than a temporary base, never intending to turn it into a permanent headquarters. It had grown as the war stalled, more and more ships being funnelled through the base instead of making their way directly to more habitable star systems. She had no doubt that the Wolves found that irritating…

"Commodore," Captain Hughes said, quietly. "We probably can't go any closer."

"Very good," Mandy said. She had to remind herself not to whisper. The enemy couldn't hear them. "We have enough data, I think."

Captain Hughes showed no reaction. "Then we can alter course and sneak out of the system," she said. "I dare say we'll be back with the fleet in three hours."

Mandy nodded. "See to it," she ordered. She picked up her datapad. "I'll start reviewing the data now."

She forced herself to relax as Captain Hughes started issuing orders to her crew. They'd sneaked into the system and collected the data they needed…she could relax, now. The data in front of her was everything she needed to plan an offensive, trapping the enemy ships against the base. They'd have to decide between fighting - and being smashed - or retreating, leaving her to ravage the base at leisure. She hoped the enemy commander would have the sense to surrender, when he saw her fleet bearing down on him.

I don't want to kill thousands of men because they can't be allowed to live, she thought, grimly. *Or because their commander is too foolish to surrender.*

She sighed. It wouldn't be long now.

"Only three battle squadrons," Ed mused, as he studied the report. "They're badly outgunned."

"Yes, sir," Mandy said. She looked tired. Ed hoped she'd managed to catch a nap on *Sneaky* as she inched her way out of the system. "We should have a two-to-one advantage in both numbers and firepower. More, perhaps, if they don't have any new weapons."

Ed nodded. Titlark wasn't a shipyard or a major industrial node, but taking the base out would hurt the Wolves. At the very least, they'd have to slow their planned counteroffensive while they struggled to compensate for its loss. The ships were more important - they'd be hard to replace within the year - but he doubted the enemy commander would stick around for the fight. Unless he thought Admiral Singh would shoot him for cowardice in the face of the enemy…

"We'll leave the troopships here," Mandy added. "I'll take the battle squadrons into the system and engage the enemy. If we're lucky, we can sneak up to their defences while cloaked and open fire from point-blank range."

"Do your best," Ed said. Ninety-seven starships, even cloaked, would generate a lot of turbulence. The odds were against escaping detection indefinitely, particularly as they got close to the base. "And watch for unpleasant surprises."

"We will," Mandy assured him. She rubbed her forehead. "They're clearly not expecting an attack."

Ed shrugged. No military force could remain on alert forever, no matter what politicians thought, but Admiral Singh would have trained her people to react to sudden attacks. He'd had the same training drummed into his head at Boot Camp. They'd know what to do…he hoped Mandy could trap the enemy ships, but he knew better than to count on it. War was a democracy, after all. The enemy got a vote.

"Don't take it for granted," he warned. "They'll have contingency plans."

Mandy glanced at her wristcom. "We'll bring the fleet to full alert now, then move out in thirty minutes," she said. Her fingers tapped a command into the wristcom. A moment later, sirens began howling. "Will that be suitable?"

"It will do," Ed said. He met her eyes for a long moment. "I'll watch from the CIC."

"Yes, sir," Mandy said. She showed a flicker of amusement. "I hope you enjoy the show."

She saluted, then turned and left the room. Ed shook his head, wonderingly. She was so bloody *young*. Or at least she *looked* young. Mandy was twenty-five, if he recalled correctly, but she was grappling with responsibilities that would normally go to someone a decade or two older than her. And yet…he sighed, knowing there was no choice. Avalon hadn't started with a vast array of experienced personnel. Even now, the Commonwealth was desperately short of trained officers. It would take years to build up a suitable reserve.

And you were seventeen when you went to Boot Camp, he reminded himself. He could have gone at sixteen, if his mother had signed the right papers. *And you were leading men in combat when you were twenty.*

Sure, his own thoughts answered. *And you - and she - had to grow up fast.*

He reached out and keyed the display, focusing on the base. Titlark had to be taken out, if the war was to be won. Even if the rest of the operation failed, taking out Titlark would slow the enemy counteroffensive… he scowled, remembering how the justifications had been hashed out time and time again. They knew it had to be done…

It will be done, he told himself. *And then we can proceed to the real target.*

CHAPTER NINETEEN

Admiral Gordon Howarth knew, without false modesty, that he wasn't a particularly good commanding officer. He'd been a desk jockey for nearly a decade before Governor Brown had taken control of Wolfbane, then found himself promoted up the chain to Admiral when he'd been assigned to Titlark. He hadn't expected the assignment to last very long, either, but the war hadn't gone *precisely* as planned. Titlark had wound up becoming more than a simple jump-off point for the invasion.

He sat in the CIC of *Lutheran* and eyed the display, unable to admit to the fear gnawing at his heart. Admiral Singh was out there somewhere, waiting for an attack that might never come…that *would* come, Gordon feared. Three battle squadrons were a formidable force, he was sure, but the enemy would know what they were facing. Indeed, if the vague sensor reports actually *were* cloaked ships prowling the system, the enemy would know *precisely* what they were facing. And they'd bring along more than enough firepower to compensate…

We should be making preparations to abandon the base, he thought, grimly. *It wouldn't be* that *hard to move all the essential people out of the system.*

Admiral Singh had flatly vetoed the idea, forbidding Gordon to discuss either her presence or the impending attack with any of his officers. She was concerned about security, apparently; she'd made it clear that she expected the secret to *remain* secret. *Gordon* was concerned about the lives of his crew, about the men and women who would be captured or killed if Titlark fell…Admiral Singh had refused to listen to him. There was nothing he could do, but obey orders and hope for the best.

He resisted the urge to pace as he waited, knowing he didn't dare go to his office or sleeping quarters. Admiral Singh would not be amused if the base went to alert because he wasn't in place to stop it. And yet, he knew that waiting for something to happen was wearing him down. A handful of orders, a few warnings…he could have alerted his crews without alerting any spies in the system. But the Admiral had been very clear. *No one* was to know until it was far too late.

Wonderful, he thought. He'd argued as much as he dared, even though he knew that Admiral Singh had a lethal temper. *We could win the battle and yet a single missile, striking the right place, could ensure we'd lose the war.*

The display beeped. He sat upright, sharply.

"Report," he snapped.

"Admiral, long-range sensors are detecting flickers of turbulence," Commander Rupert said, slowly. His face paled as he turned to face his commander. "Computer analysis suggests it's a cloaked fleet."

"Show me," Gordon ordered.

Rupert worked his console. A red haze appeared on the display, heading directly towards the base. Gordon felt sweat prickling down his back as he silently calculated the vectors. It was impossible to be sure - they didn't have a solid lock on anything - but it looked as though the unknown ships would be entering the outer edge of detection range in thirty minutes. He rather suspected that the enemy would assume they'd be detected at that point, no matter what they did.

"They're sneaking up on us," he said, slowly. "Can you get an accurate ship count?"

"No, sir," Rupert said. "I'd say they have somewhere between seventy and a hundred and fifty ships, but that's just an estimate."

Gordon nodded. He might not be an expert, but he *did* have a fairly complete military education. That much turbulence could mean a large fleet of small ships or a relatively small number of capital ships. Admiral Singh's intelligence staff hadn't been able to suggest just how *many* ships would be coming at them, but Gordon *was* fairly sure they wouldn't send a single squadron to face his three. They'd want at least five battle squadrons to give them a reasonable shot at victory.

"Pass the word quietly - and I mean *quietly* - to the rest of the ships," Gordon ordered. The Admiral wouldn't be pleased, but he couldn't leave his fleet commanders *completely* in the dark. If nothing else, their sensor crews would pick up the enemy soon enough. "I want them ready to go to battle stations at a moment's notice."

"Aye, sir," Rupert said.

Gordon smiled, then keyed his console, sending a private message to Admiral Singh. He didn't know where she was - not precisely - but he knew where she would be when the shit hit the fan. If she managed to get behind the enemy ships, they'd be trapped between two fires, forced to decide between trying to take out the base or trying to flee. Gordon rather hoped they'd choose the latter. Quite apart from maximising the odds of his personal survival, it would also limit the damage the enemy could do as they retreated.

"The squadrons have responded, sir," Rupert said. "They're standing by."

"Then set quiet alert throughout the ships," Gordon said. His squadrons weren't concentrated as much as he would have liked, but the ships *were* close enough to cover each other if the enemy had a secret weapon. "And prepare to go to full alert on my command."

"Aye, sir."

"The enemy ships are continuing their course towards the base," Julia reported. "There's no sign that they know they've been detected."

Rani nodded, feeling an odd thrill of excitement. She'd gambled…and she'd won. She'd been right! She'd deduced *precisely* where the enemy would attack. Whatever the outcome, whoever won the coming engagement, she'd been right. The corporate beancounters and their naval lackeys could suck on it, as far as she was concerned. She hadn't lost her strategic acumen after all. None of those stuffed shirts could have done what *she'd* done!

She forced her glee down, reminding herself that she could celebrate *after* the battle. The Commonwealth ships were heading straight for the base, under cloak. It wasn't a bad move - there was little point in dancing around when both sides knew the only possible target - but it was careless. They hadn't even launched drones to cover their flanks.

That will change, the moment they drop their cloaks, she reminded herself. *And if we're too close, they'll move to evade us.*

She sucked in her breath as the three sets of vectors converged, mentally fighting and refighting the engagement. The timing had to be precise for maximum effect. If she caught the enemy at the right moment, she could be reasonably sure of shooting their ships to pieces before they could either escape or obliterate the base. And yet, even if they didn't cooperate long enough to let her get the perfect shot…

"Contact the fleet," she ordered. "The battle squadrons are to move out as planned."

"Aye, Admiral," Julie said.

Rani nodded. Her ships were cloaked, the enemy ships were cloaked… but, unlike her, they didn't have access to a network of sensor platforms. There was a very good chance that their tactical computers would ignore any turbulence they happened to detect, particularly when it was right behind them. Rani's starships would be masked by the enemy's own sensor turbulence.

And even if they do notice us, she thought, *it's already too late to escape an engagement.*

She silently updated the projections as the three fleets began to converge. Admiral Howarth was in place, fat and happy…a target the enemy could not resist. Rani *knew* it was a trap and even *she* had problems telling herself that she shouldn't try to engage. Three battle squadrons were a tempting target, particularly when the crews might well be a little rusty. The opportunity to smash them could not be missed.

"We will be at Point Hammer in twenty minutes," Julia reported.

"Very good," Rani said. She smiled, coldly. "Warn the fleet. We will open fire early if we believe we've been detected."

"Aye, Admiral," Julia said.

"There's no sign the enemy ships have detected us," the sensor officer reported. "They're just sitting there, waiting to be thrashed."

Mandy shot a reproving look at the back of his neck. The enemy might not have detected them - yet - but they hadn't dispersed their squadrons. *That*, at least, wasn't a surprise. Not splitting up the squadrons had been standard procedure for the last thousand years, if not longer. And Titlark *was* on the front lines. The enemy might not know that an attack was underway, but they'd be foolish not to prepare for the possibility.

"Keep a sharp eye on them," she ordered. "They'll see us before we can get into point-blank range."

She forced herself to think as the range steadily narrowed. What would *she* do, if she detected an enemy fleet heading towards her? It would depend on the size of the fleet, something the enemy couldn't know until she dropped the cloak. A smart commanding officer would bring his ships to alert, then wait to see what he was facing. But a paranoid officer might just try to open the range a little, maybe even abandon the base. It would get him in trouble, she suspected, if his superiors took a dim view of it, but it would give him a number of additional options.

They'll see us when we cross the outer edge of their defences, she thought. *We can't avoid detection once we reach there, if we do manage to reach it without setting off any alarms.*

"We will drop the cloak and engage at Point Alpha," she said. It was one of a number of possible options, but it gave her the greatest flexibility. It would also give the enemy a chance to escape, which would force them to decide between landing a few blows on her ships or running. Hopefully, they'd hesitate long enough for her to land a few blows of her own. "Their battleships and heavy cruisers are priority targets."

"Aye, Captain."

"Admiral," Captain Winslow said. "I respectfully request that we bring the ships to battle stations now."

"Denied," Gordon snarled. He understood Winslow's concern - he even shared it - but orders were orders. The enemy *had* to be allowed to slip in closer to the base, limiting their chances of escape. "You are not to bring your ships to battle stations."

Winslow eyed him with utter contempt. It was the sort of expression, Gordon noted, that would probably have had other commanding officers relieving Winslow of command and tossing him through the nearest airlock. As it was...Gordon didn't really blame Winslow for being concerned. The closer the enemy ships came, the greater the chance that they'd give his ships a mauling they couldn't escape.

"Admiral," Winslow said. His tone was flatly insubordinate. "I..."

"Shut up," Gordon said, sharply. He felt, just for a second, as though someone else was speaking through him. "You have your orders, Captain. Carry them out or I'll find someone else who will."

He closed the connection, wondering just what Winslow would do. The man wasn't an idiot - he knew that mutiny would lead to his certain death, particularly when there *was* a plan. But he also knew that his ship and crew were facing an incredibly powerful enemy force. He had to wonder if Gordon was too scared to run, too scared to admit that he was outgunned...

...And that Gordon's fear might get them all killed.

Not that he would be too far wrong, Gordon thought. His lips twitched, as though it was actually funny. *Would it be better to die at enemy hands or be hung for deserting my post?*

He shook his head, looking at the display. The enemy would cross the outer edge of his sensor network in five minutes. At that point, they'd smell a rat if they weren't detected, if his fleet didn't go to battle stations. At that point, they'd get themselves ready for a last stand and hope - desperately - that Admiral Singh would come to their rescue.

"Captain," the sensor officer said. "We'll be detected in two minutes."

Mandy nodded. Despite herself, she was surprised they hadn't been detected earlier. She was honestly wondering if the enemy had abandoned

Titlark - perhaps under the impression that *Thule* was going to be attacked - and left a handful of sensor drones in place of the relocated warships. *They* wouldn't go to alert - they couldn't.

And if they are decoys, she asked herself, *where are the real ships?*

"Stand by to engage," she ordered. She'd find out soon, whatever happened. "Drop the cloak in two minutes."

"Aye, Captain," the tactical officer said.

Mandy glanced at the status display, quietly assessing their chances. Her combined squadrons mounted more than enough missiles on their external racks to give the enemy a very bad day, even though the enemy point defence was probably very good. God knew the Commonwealth had given them lots of practice. Their heavy ships would be damaged, if not destroyed, by her first salvo. And if they *did* somehow manage to evade her shots, the remainder of her missiles would slam into the base.

"Prepare to transmit the surrender demand," she ordered the communications officer. The enemy would probably render their base and warships useless before surrendering, if they chose to give up without firing a shot, but at least she wouldn't have to kill thousands of people. "Transmit it as soon as we decloak."

"Aye, Captain."

Mandy silently counted down the last few seconds. The enemy should have noticed them by now, surely. She had six battle squadrons, nearly a hundred ships. None of the heavy vessels were *really* designed to be stealthy. It didn't quite make sense, unless she was flying into a trap. Or if the enemy ships were actually decoys…

"Decloaking…now," the tactical officer said.

"Deploy drones," Mandy ordered, curtly. "Prepare to engage!"

"Signal sent," the communications officer said.

Mandy nodded. On the display, the enemy ships were slowly coming to life. She felt a flicker of relief, mingled with concern. Something wasn't quite right. The Wolves weren't *quite* as advanced as the Commonwealth, but they were very far from stupid. They should have seen her ships before they dropped their cloaks.

"No response," the communications officer reported. "I'm not picking up any chatter at all."

"Idiots," Cobb muttered.

It didn't make Mandy feel any better. The enemy knew - now - that they were badly outnumbered. They should be trying to retreat. Instead, they were just floating in space...she would have been *convinced* they were drones if the ships weren't coming to life in front of her. She was tempted to back off, or to ask Colonel Stalker for advice, but she knew she couldn't do either. The buck stopped with her.

"Tactical," she said. "Are our missiles locked on target?"

"Yes, Captain," the tactical officer said. "We are ready to engage on your command."

"Fire," Mandy ordered.

At least Winslow isn't screaming any longer, Gordon thought, as his ships ramped up their drives and weapons. The enemy were close, but not close enough to do real damage *whatever* he did. *We have other things to worry about.*

"Admiral," Rupert said. He sounded alarmed. "The enemy is locking weapons on us."

"Stand by point defence," Gordon ordered. Admiral Singh *could* have let him drill the point defence officers, couldn't she? Thankfully, most of his commanding officers had held regular drills anyway. There was a war on, after all. "Prepare to engage."

He sucked in his breath as the enemy opened fire. The display seemed to fuzz for a long moment as the tactical computers struggled to determine just how many missiles had been fired at them, then assign targets to the point defence network. It was an impressive salvo, easily ten times larger than anything he'd seen before the start of the war. But then, the Empire had never needed to do more than send a battleship to overawe any space-based opposition. Resistance in space had been minimal since the Unification Wars.

Everything has changed, he thought. *And nothing will ever be the same.*

"Enemy missiles will enter point defence range in two minutes," Rupert warned.

"Return fire," Gordon said.

"Aye, Admiral," Rupert said.

"And order the base crews to evacuate," Gordon added. The missiles would go on to blow the base to atoms, if he wasn't mistaken. Now, at least, he could try to save his crews. "And to set the self-destruct charges, just in case."

"The enemy ships are returning fire," the tactical officer said.

"Activate force shields, stand by point defence," Mandy ordered. The enemy's missiles looked pitiful, somehow. Three battle squadrons couldn't match the sheer volume of missiles she'd fired at them. They hadn't even had time to load their external racks! And yet, she had the nagging feeling she'd missed something. "And…"

"Captain," the sensor officer said. "I'm picking up a sensor distortion! Behind us!"

Mandy felt her blood run cold. "Evasive action," she snapped. They'd been suckered, lured into a trap. *She'd* been tricked. She'd seen what she wanted to see. "Stand by to alter course!"

And then the first enemy ships started to appear on the display.

"Drop the cloak," Rani ordered. "Drop the cloak and prepare to engage."

She took a moment, just a moment, to savour the sheer delight of luring the enemy into a deadly trap. They saw her now, too late. She'd expected - feared - that they would see her when they had a chance to evade, but now… they couldn't escape without running the gauntlet. They might get a few ships out of the trap - the timing hadn't been entirely perfect - yet their confidence would never recover. She'd already scored one victory…

…And now it was time to score another.

"Fire," she ordered.

CHAPTER TWENTY

"Incoming missiles," the tactical officer reported. "I'm…I'm picking up over a *thousand* missiles."

Mandy nodded. She wanted to panic - she could hear panic yammering at the back of her mind - but there was no time. She took the panic and locked it out of her mind, then studied the display. Her ships were trapped between two enemy forces, unable to escape without engaging at least one of them…

And then the other one takes us up the ass, she thought, grimly. *We're in trouble.*

"Force One is launching a second salvo," the tactical officer warned. "Force Two is preparing to follow suit."

Mandy nodded. There would be time to contemplate the disaster later. Right now, she needed to concentrate on survival - and escape.

"Swing ships," she ordered. Taking the system was no longer possible, not without taking heavy - and potentially catastrophic - damage. The missiles she'd launched would inflict enough damage to force the enemy to rebuild, in any case. "Put the force fields between us and Force Two."

"Aye, Captain."

"Alter course," Mandy added, keying her console. Her starships were moving at incomprehensible speeds, but everything was still happening so slowly. "Put us on a least-time course to the phase limit."

"Aye, Captain."

Force One and Force Two will have a chance to join hands, she thought, as her ships slowly began to alter course. *But that might just buy us some time to escape.*

Admiral Singh will know that, her own thoughts answered. *She won't let us off the hook so easily.*

"Deploy combat ECM drones," she added. She'd hoped to keep them in reserve - the sooner the Wolves saw them, the sooner they'd come up with countermeasures - but her fleet was now fighting for its life. "Order the point defence to engage as soon as the enemy missiles enter weapons range."

"Aye, Captain."

"And prepare to return fire, targeted on Force Two," Mandy added. "I want to cripple as many ships as possible."

They don't have force shields, she reminded herself. She knew the Wolves would duplicate them - eventually - but they didn't have them *now*. The Commonwealth still had a formidable edge. Her ships might have been trapped - they *had* been trapped - but she'd give the enemy a mauling they'd never forget. This time, the enemy couldn't back off unless they wanted her to escape. *And that's the last thing they want.*

"Missiles ready, Captain," the tactical officer said.

"Fire," Mandy ordered.

"The enemy ships have returned fire," Julia reported.

"As expected," Rani said. The Commonwealth ships had been surprised - they wouldn't have flushed their external racks so quickly if they'd known she was there - but they were recovering rapidly. Their answering fire looked paltry compared to her huge barrage, yet she knew not to underestimate it. The Commonwealth's missile warheads were dangerously advanced. "Order the point defence crews to stand by."

She leaned forward, watching avidly as her missiles flashed towards their targets. The Commonwealth ships were altering course slowly - as she'd predicted - but they couldn't get out of range before it was too late.

Their ships were already starting to blur into a haze as their ECM came online - they'd improved that *again*, she noted - yet it wouldn't be enough to save them from a beating. Even swinging their force shields around wouldn't help.

We should be glad they haven't figured out how to encase an entire ship in a bubble, she told herself, dryly. *That would make the entire battle unwinnable.*

Julia coughed. "Admiral Howarth's force has taken a hammering, Admiral," she reported, nervously. "The enemy missiles have also done immense damage to the base."

"As expected," Rani said. She'd hoped to preserve the base, but all of her simulations had suggested that the enemy would have an opportunity to wipe the facilities out before they were destroyed. "Order his remaining ships to continue to push the enemy away from the base."

And if they soak up fire, she thought coldly, *so much the better.*

"Our missiles are entering engagement range," Julia said. "The enemy point defence is engaging now."

Rani nodded. The enemy thought they only had to cope with *two* problems, *two* waves of missiles coming from two different directions. They hadn't seen her first surprise yet...

She smiled, coldly. The Commonwealth Navy was about to get a very bloody nose.

Midshipwoman Maggie Dawson cursed the day she'd volunteered for 'special duty' as her pinnace raced towards the enemy fleet. She'd never felt g-forces in space, never felt as if the acceleration was squashing her back into her chair, until she'd boarded the pinnace for the first time. The tiny craft was little more than engines and targeting computers, with a crew compartment thrown in as an afterthought. She hated to think what the g-forces might be doing to her body, let alone the possibility of suddenly becoming irradiated if the drive field went out of tune. There were *reasons* most starships couldn't pull such speeds. The prospect of a catastrophic drive or compensator failure was terrifyingly high.

You volunteered for this duty, she reminded herself, sharply. The pressure on her chest seemed to be increasing, although she wasn't sure if she was imagining it or not. There was no such thing as a *partial* failure where compensators were concerned. A failed compensator meant instant death. *And the reward will be worth it...*

"I have enhanced targeting locks," Midshipman Timothy Peaks said. "The enemy ships are in my sights."

"Then update the missiles," Maggie snapped at him. The pinnace didn't *look* like an incoming missile. She'd been assured that the enemy point defence wouldn't target them automatically, although she wasn't sure if she believed it. The enemy would *certainly* target them once they realised what the pinnace actually *did*. "Hurry!"

"Missile locks updated," Peaks assured her. "You want to go for dinner tonight?"

Maggie bit off a harsh response as she felt the pinnace shiver underneath her. She had no idea if Peaks was serious or if he was just trying to defuse the tension, but she really didn't care. The pinnace crews were bound by the same rules on fraternisation as everyone else in the navy, even though there was a good chance none of them would survive long enough to claim their promised rewards. Being jumped up a grade or two had sounded like a good idea at the time...

She gritted her teeth, watching the display update. The tiny electronic brains that told the missiles where to go simply weren't very smart. No one wasted advanced sensors and targeting systems on missiles that would obliterate themselves along with their targets, something that made the missiles depressingly easy to fool. *Starships* carried much more powerful targeting systems, but they had to operate at a distance from the enemy fleet or risk being wiped out. They just couldn't control their missiles from a distance.

But we can tell the missiles where to go, she thought. The idea had seemed a better one *before* she'd actually seen the pinnace. Theory told her it should work; experience told her that there were probably bugs in the system that would need to be ironed out. *And we can see through much of the chaff.*

"I'm preparing to alter course," she said. Flying the pinnace through the outer edge of the enemy's point defence zone was probably safe enough - the enemy had other problems - but there was no point in taking chances. The enemy *would* target the pinnace as soon as they realised what it was doing. "Brace yourself."

"Braced," Peaks said.

Maggie turned the pinnace, feeling the g-forces tugging at her again. The engineers assured her that they were harmless - just a little bleed-over from the enhanced drives - but she had her doubts. Bleed-over was rare, very rare. It was almost always a warning sign that the compensators were about to fail. She had the nasty feeling she was going to look like she'd lost a fight when she got back to the mothership and tore off her pressure suit. She'd been black and blue after some of the training exercises.

"Missiles heading to their targets," Peaks said. "The enemy decoys aren't working."

"Very good," Maggie said. "Watch for any last minute surprises."

"Of course," Peaks said. "I'm already trying to steer them around the force shields."

"Captain," the tactical officer said. "The enemy missiles are behaving oddly."

Mandy blinked. The enemy had messed up the timing, just a little. Force One - now a twisted mess of its former self - had expended most of its missiles on her decoys, rather than hitting her ships. It was something, at least. She'd managed to get the point defence realigned before Force Two's missiles roared into their engagement envelope, as well as getting the force shields in place. Combined with the decoys, it should give her a reasonable chance of getting most of her ships out of the trap before it was too late.

"Explain," she ordered.

"They're not going for the decoys," the tactical officer said. "They're heading straight for the ships."

"That's impossible," Cobb said. "*Some* of them should be going for the decoys."

Mandy shrugged, forcing herself to remain calm. There were very definite advantages to *not* having been an Imperial Navy officer before the collapse, even if it did come with disadvantages. For one thing, she didn't believe that weapons and defensive technology had reached a point where it could no longer be improved. Or, for that matter, that her technology would always be superior.

"Adjust the point defence and force shields to compensate," she ordered. "Take out as many of the missiles as you can."

Her eyes narrowed as she studied the display. The missiles were showing curiously *intelligent* behaviour, rather than the normal rush to slam themselves into their targets as quickly as possible. They were ignoring the drones, evading the point defence...even trying to avoid expending themselves uselessly against the force shields. It was almost as though a live human or an advanced tactical computer was directing their flight.

They're too far from the warships to be steered remotely, she thought. The speed of light delay would be enough to render orders hopelessly out of date by the time they reached their destination. *Unless they've somehow managed to improve their communicators...*

She forced herself to think, watching the missiles roaring towards her ships. There was no way the enemy could steer the missiles from their warships, yet...yet they were doing it, somehow. Impossible? Or was it a trick of some kind? Surely, if the enemy had made a breakthrough, they would have used it as soon as possible. Improved missile guidance systems might not seem as sexy as advanced weapons and force shields, but they might prove as decisive as logistics.

"Impact in twenty seconds," Cobb warned. "Some of the missiles are burning out."

"Thank God for small favours," Mandy said. The enemy hadn't managed to improve missile drive technology, if nothing else. Dozens of missiles were losing power, either going ballistic as the drive systems failed or being ripped apart by their own engines. They just weren't designed to endure such stress. "Keep an eye on the ballistic missiles, just in case."

A new icon popped up in her display. "Captain, this is Armstrong in Tactical," a voice said, grimly. "We have a theory."

Mandy made a face. In hindsight, she should have commanded the battle from the CIC. She couldn't be *both* captain and commodore. "Go ahead."

"The enemy deployed a small craft with their missile swarm, perhaps more than one," Armstrong informed her. Mandy glanced at her display as Armstrong sent an update, pointing to a tiny craft skimming around her point defence engagement range. "It's tiny, but big enough to carry targeting computers and missile uplinks..."

"...Shit," Mandy thought. The concept had been discussed, if she recalled correctly, but it had come to nothing. Everyone had agreed that it was effectively suicide. The tiny craft's drives would be under immense stress. The slightest mistake would result in utter disaster and the death of the crew. "They made it work?"

"Yes, Captain," Armstrong said. "We think they brute-forced their way through the problems."

"Devious bastards," Mandy said. The enemy ships had already launched a second barrage of missiles. "Pass the data to the targeting sensors. Those craft are to be marked priority targets."

"Aye, Captain," Armstrong said. He paused. "They're out of energy weapons range..."

And they're unlikely to be foolhardy enough to fly into it, Mandy thought. The tiny craft - she felt a flicker of admiration for the pilots - didn't need to go much closer to her ships to do their job. They were already close enough to see through her ECM and keep the missiles updated. *We have to take them out.*

"Tactical, lock shipkillers on them," she ordered. "Take them out."

"Aye, Captain."

"Incoming missiles," Cobb said.

"All hands, brace for impact," Mandy snapped.

She gritted her teeth as the enemy missiles entered terminal attack mode and lunged forward, burning out their drives as they threw themselves on her ships. Laser heads exploded, sending beams of ravening force into her starships; contact nukes slammed against her hulls, damaging her armour and shaking her ships. She shook her head, feeling - again - a flicker of the old terror. On the ground, nuclear warheads were devastating; in space, they were barely noticeable. It didn't look as though the enemy had made any significant improvement to their warheads, thankfully…

"*Onslaught* and *Patton* have taken heavy damage," Cobb reported. "*Brilliant Light* and *Dawn of Empire* have both been destroyed, along with seven flankers…"

Mandy gritted her teeth. *Brilliant Light* and *Dawn of Empire* had been battleships, two of the five captured from Admiral Singh. She wasn't surprised they'd soaked up fire, even though they weren't the deadliest warships in her fleet. Admiral Singh and her peers probably still considered them the queens of the spaceways. And yet, naval combat had moved on. Losing the crew was going to hurt the Commonwealth Navy a great deal worse than losing the ships.

She forced herself to watch, coldly, as the damage mounted up. Warships could take one hell of a pounding - she knew from bitter experience - but the Wolves had inflicted a great deal of damage. Her point defence had been weakened, perhaps fatally. The next barrage would inflict more damage, the third would inflict more still. And while she'd hurt the enemy, it might not be enough to save her ships…

"Continue on our current course," she ordered. The enemy had taken a pounding too. It wasn't enough to stop them, but it might just give her a chance to escape. "And continue firing."

"Aye, Captain."

"Two battleships have been destroyed, Admiral," Julia reported.

"Good," Rani said. Technology was advancing, but battleships were still formidable - and intimidating - weapons of war. The Commonwealth Navy hadn't even *started* building battleships for itself, as far as she could tell. She could see their logic - quantity had a quality all of its own - but she could also see their weaknesses. Their ships couldn't soak up as much damage as hers. "And the second wave of missiles?"

"Inbound," Julia assured her. "The special warheads are in the lead."

Rani leaned forward. If the scientists were correct…

The enemy has already taken a bloody nose, she told herself, firmly. *And now we're going to crack their skulls.*

"Captain," the tactical officer said. "I'm picking up some odd reports from the point defence computers."

Mandy glanced at him. "Odd reports?"

"Yes, Captain," the tactical officer said. He sounded perplexed - and worried. "Some of the missiles appear to be brushing off direct hits."

"*What*?"

"They *are* being hit," the tactical officer assured her. "They're just not being taken out."

Mandy forced herself to think. Decoys? She'd never heard of an ECM decoy so small it could be mounted on a missile, although the Wolves *had* proven themselves to be dangerously inventive. Those missile-guiding craft might have tipped the balance of power in their favour. If they'd managed to con her point defences into wasting time firing on decoys instead of real missiles…

"Pass the data to Armstrong," she ordered. It didn't make sense. If the Wolves really *had* come up with something new, they'd *surely* have found a better use for it. The prospect of a piece of technology being captured and reverse-engineered was not to be dismissed. Admiral Singh or whoever she'd put in command of the engagement *had* to be *very* confident of actually *winning*. "And…"

She braced herself as the missiles closed in. The decoys were doing a damn good job, she had to admit…yet, there was something odd about the readings. Something that didn't quite make sense. Sometimes, the missiles vanished; sometimes, they just seemed to shrug off the blows and keep going. What were they *doing*? Something was nagging at the back of her mind, something she'd seen…

"*Invincible* is under heavy attack," the tactical officer warned. On the display, dozens of missiles were angling towards their target. "She's altering course to evade enemy fire."

"Move *Formidable* and *Defender* up to support her," Mandy ordered. The battlecruiser needed support. She didn't dare risk having her modern ships disabled. They'd have to be abandoned and destroyed before the enemy could capture them. "And then consolidate our formation as Force One falls behind."

"Aye, Captain."

Mandy nodded. The enemy had wised up, perhaps. Targeting her heavy cruisers and battlecruisers would cause more harm in the long run. But only five missiles looked likely to make it through *Invincible's* defences and slam home. They'd do harm, she knew, but not enough to matter. The missiles struck their target...

...And *Invincible* vanished from the display.

CHAPTER TWENTY-ONE

For a moment, Mandy flatly refused to believe her eyes.

Invincible was - had been - a modern battlecruiser. Her hull was composed of the latest alloy of hullmetal, a material that could shrug off a nuclear explosion; her point defence and damage control systems second to none. She and her sisters were the most advanced starships in known space. And yet, she'd been blown into an expanding cloud of debris and plasma by a single hit. It was impossible…

It happened, she told herself, sharply. *Deal with it*!

She found her voice. "What happened?"

"The missile exploded *inside* the ship," the tactical officer managed. He sounded as shocked as she felt. "It punched through the hull and exploded inside the ship."

Mandy stared at him. Hullmetal was the single strongest material known to exist. It had been *designed* to take a pounding. Even a laser warhead had problems cutting through solid hullmetal. And yet, *Invincible* had been casually blown to dust. None of the crew had survived. They hadn't had anything like enough warning to take to the boats.

Her console bleeped. "Captain," Armstrong said. "We have a theory."

"Hit me," Mandy said.

"They've devised their own force shields," Armstrong said. "They mounted them on their missiles."

"That would be incredibly costly," Cobb objected.

"No, sir," Armstrong said. "The effect wouldn't last for long, but they *could* use it to protect a missile *and* create a…a force shield that acted like a monofilament blade. They cut through the hullmetal and put a warhead *inside* the ship."

Mandy nodded. It made sense, for the moment. Maybe they'd discover Armstrong was wrong - later - but right now it was the best idea they'd had. And it explained why the missiles had been so resilient. They'd been shooting at force shields instead of decoys. No *wonder* the missiles had survived.

"Adjust our point defence patterns to compensate," she ordered, grimly. It wasn't going to be easy. Hitting a shielded missile meant firing from a different angle...she'd have to open her formation, which would make her flankers easy targets. "Helm, concentrate on building up speed."

"Aye, Captain," the helmsman said.

Mandy sat back as the enemy unleashed another wave of missiles. Now they knew what to look for, the sensors could pick out missiles that carried their own force shields...primitive, compared to the ones that protected Mandy's ships, but dangerous. She silently complimented Admiral Singh or whoever had come up with the warheads, even though they were devastating her ships. The Commonwealth Navy hadn't even *thought* of using force shields to punch through hullmetal.

That will change, she thought. *But right now we have to fight without it.*

"We'll be across the phase limit in one hour," the helmsman said.

Mandy nodded. "Pass the word," she said. "Any starships that cannot keep up with the fleet are to be abandoned, then destroyed."

Cobb's eyes went wide. "Captain...?"

"There's no choice," Mandy said. She didn't want to leave anyone behind, but she couldn't think of an alternative. The Wolves were relatively civilised, at least. Mandy's people would go into POW camps, rather than being raped and murdered. "And that includes *this* ship, Commander."

She sat back, watching as the enemy missiles started to close in. There was no point in lying, least of all to herself. The battle was lost. All she could do was extract as many units as possible before the end came. And if that meant sacrificing herself, she'd do it...

And the colonel will have to move to another ship, she thought, grimly. *I can't let him fall into enemy hands.*

"Target their small craft," she ordered, shortly. "See if that gives us some more options."

"Aye, Captain."

Rani felt a hot flash of exultation as she saw the enemy battlecruiser die. One hit…one hit had been enough to blow the enemy ship to atoms! Part of her mourned the end of everything she'd learned in the Imperial Navy; the rest of her cheered, knowing it meant that she'd won the battle. The corporate dictators could count their money and play their political games, if they liked. She'd just won the most significant naval engagement of the last fifty years.

"Continue firing," she ordered. She didn't have *that* many special warheads left, but the enemy didn't know that. Besides, she had enough to do more damage before the remaining enemy ships managed to escape. "Aim to cripple the enemy ships."

"Aye, Admiral," Julia said.

A dull shiver ran through the battleship as a missile slammed against her armour. Rani tensed, then relaxed. For now, she had a decisive advantage. It wouldn't last - she briefly considered taking her fleet directly to Avalon, before the Commonwealth learned what had happened at Titlark - but it would be enough. The Commonwealth didn't have missiles that could vaporise an entire battlecruiser with a single shot.

She forced herself to relax as the enemy ships started to run. They *were* picking up speed at an alarming rate, but they couldn't outrun her. Unless, of course, the newer ships abandoned the older ships…Rani wondered, absently, if her opponent had the nerve to do just that. It would be a costly decision, but it would preserve most of her modern firepower.

"*Thunder* took four hits in quick succession," Julia warned. "She's falling out of formation."

"Leave her," Rani ordered. The cripple was of no concern. Either she survived the battle - in which case she'd be repaired afterwards - or she died, soaking up an enemy missile that might do real damage if it struck a different ship. "Order her crew to do whatever repairs they can."

"Aye, Admiral."

Rani nodded, watching the display like a hawk. The enemy ships were concentrating their defences, trying to swat down her missiles as they roared towards their targets. It wasn't a bad tactic - the Commonwealth's point defence systems were irritatingly good - but it wasn't enough to stop the *special* missiles. She was more concerned about the way they were angling their force shields. Her missiles would have to get ahead of them, somehow, if they wanted to strike their targets.

And the command and control craft worked like a dream, she thought, wryly. *The enemy took a beating they weren't expecting.*

She allowed her smile to widen. She'd won. Whatever happened, she'd won. No one could take that from her…

…And, when she got home, she could settle accounts with her enemies.

"The next wave of missiles is entering control range," Peaks reported.

Maggie nodded as she swung the pinnace back towards the enemy ships. Red lights kept flickering up in front of her eyes, only to vanish before she could come to grips with them. It was obvious that the drive units were under considerable pressure, but thankfully - so far - they appeared to be coping. The enemy ships were in a much worse state. As she watched, a destroyer fell out of formation and exploded into a ball of flame.

"Take control," she ordered, pushing the craft forward. She felt, just for a second, as through someone had punched her in the belly. She was *definitely* going to be black and blue afterwards. "Get them to their targets."

"There's a solid wall of force shields blocking them," Peaks said. Maggie could hear the frustration in his voice as he grappled with the control systems. "They're blocking a straight-line flight path."

"Surprise, surprise," Maggie said. "You'll just have to be a little twisty to get them in."

Peaks muttered something unpleasant, just loud enough for her to hear, as he struggled with his console. A wave of…*something*…passed through the ship, making them both yelp in pain. Maggie clenched her teeth against the sensation, trying to remain focused on flying the pinnace. They were already alarmingly close to the enemy's point defence engagement range.

And they might manage to pick us off with a lucky shot, Maggie thought. The pinnace was tougher than the average missile, but flimsy compared to a destroyer, let alone a full-sized battleship. A single hit would probably be enough to disable the craft, if they were lucky...she knew, all too well, that their chances of survival were minimal. *We're definitely too close to them.*

"Got the missiles roaring forward, then dropping back," Peaks reported. "It's not perfect, but..."

"No," Maggie agreed. The force shields weren't *bubbles*. The enemy would have a fair shot at the unshielded parts of the missile as they flew past, then reversed course. "I..."

She cursed as her threat receiver lit up, screaming the alert. Two missiles - full-sized shipkillers - were heading directly for the pinnace. She stared in disbelief, then hastily altered course as the missiles closed in. Using shipkillers against her pinnace was massive overkill, but it was the only realistic tactic...she reminded herself, again, that the Commonwealth was revoltingly ingenious.

"They really don't like us," Peaks observed. Maggie felt her head start to spin. She hadn't felt so bad since she'd flown in an aircraft during basic training. The pilot had been a madman and the craft itself probably predated the Empire. "I...fuck it..."

Maggie heard him vomiting behind her. She clenched her mouth shut, resisting the urge to throw up herself. The entire craft was spinning...yet her sensors insisted they *weren't* spinning. She held on to the control stick, trying to keep her distance from the missiles. If they detonated too close to her, she would be in real trouble...

The missiles exploded. Maggie flew straight for as long as she dared, bracing herself even though she knew it was silly. They'd been *just* far enough from the blast to survive. She allowed herself a sigh of relief, turning the craft slowly in space. Her head was still spinning...she felt a stab of pain that seemed to knife right through her.

"Fuck," Peaks said. He coughed, helplessly. "Can we go home now?"

Maggie tried to ignore the stench drifting through the air. "I don't know," she said, as she checked the display. They'd flown some distance away from the battle during their desperate flight from the missiles. "I..."

She pushed the stick forward. An instant later, alarms started to sound. The drive field was twisting out of shape, lashing against the hull itself. Radiation alarms were going off...she felt her skin start to crawl, even though she *knew* that losing drive containment would have killed them both instantly. And yet...she stared in disbelief, then grabbed for the ejection lever as the hull started to crack and shatter under the impact. But it was too late...

"They've taken out the pinnaces," Julia reported. "Our missiles are reverting to their normal attack patterns."

"Understood," Rani said. She'd hoped to keep the secret a little longer, but the enemy weren't *stupid*. She had known they'd figure out what was happening and take countermeasures. It was unfortunate that it had happened so quickly, but it couldn't be helped. "Continue firing."

She smiled, coldly, as the enemy fleet continued its retreat. A number of ships *would* make it over the phase limit and escape - she rather suspected that couldn't be helped, unless the enemy decided to reverse course and go down fighting - but they would have taken one hell of a beating. Hell, they *had* taken one hell of a beating. She'd been hammered too, but she had far more ships to deploy against them. Given a couple of months - first to stamp her dominance on Wolfbane and then to gather the rest of her fleet - she could strike directly at Avalon. It would be risky, but the risk had already been minimised.

And after Avalon falls, the rest of the Commonwealth will wither and die, she told herself.

"They're redeploying drones," Julia warned. "We cannot isolate them from the enemy starships at this range."

"And we don't have any more pinnaces," Rani sighed. It *was* unfortunate, but it couldn't be helped. She made a mental note to ensure that the pinnace crews were remembered with honour. They'd helped her win the battle and the war. "Deploy additional drones and sensor platforms of our own."

"Aye, Admiral."

Rani leaned back in her chair. It was a stern chase now - and a stern chase was always a *long* chase - but the enemy were definitely in retreat. And they couldn't outrun her without abandoning their slower comrades. A handful of cripples had already been abandoned, lagging behind the main enemy fleet. Maybe they'd surrender or maybe they'd just try to strike a final blow before they were blown away…it didn't matter. Either way, she'd already won.

"Launch SAR shuttles to pick up the enemy crews," Rani ordered. Having prisoners to parade back home would go down well. Perhaps she could march them down the street, showing the population that the enemy were not *gods*. Technologically advanced or not, they could be beaten. "And inform the infantry that the prisoners are to be treated well, as long as they behave."

"Aye, Admiral," Julia said.

"They're continuing to fire," the tactical officer reported. "But our drones are proving far more effective now."

"Good," Mandy said. She hoped the drones would even the odds a little. She'd already lost too many ships. Two battleships, three battlecruisers, five heavy cruisers, nineteen flankers…she'd lost more tonnage, in a single engagement, than the entire navy had lost in eighteen months of war. "Keep angling them to soak up enemy fire."

She forced herself to remain calm. The enemy had scored a victory, but she would get most of her ships out of the trap. And yet, the damage was continuing to mount up. Her crews would need weeks, if not months, to restore her ships to their former condition. The original plan - to head directly to Wolfbane - would have to be scrapped. She wasn't sure if they shouldn't just reverse course and retreat to Avalon as soon as they crossed the phase limit.

"*Magnificent* just lost two drive nodes," Cobb said, quietly. "She's at risk of losing a third."

"Order her to hold position as long as possible." Mandy ordered. "And if she does lose a third drive node..."

She winced, inwardly. Captain Patel had been one of her friends, back when she'd been living with the RockRats. Like her, he'd been promoted rapidly as the Commonwealth Navy struggled to build up its manpower base. And yet...she didn't want to abandon him, but she knew she might have no choice. She couldn't sacrifice the entire fleet for one man.

"If she falls out of formation," she ordered, "she is to be abandoned and scuttled."

"Aye, Captain," Cobb said.

Mandy hated herself at that moment, hated the person she'd become. She couldn't think of her friends as numbers, she couldn't sacrifice them for the greater good...and yet, she had no choice. She had no choice...she told herself, again and again, that she had no choice. But she didn't want to believe it. She felt as though she was betraying the young man she'd met and befriended, years ago. He'd been fun...

And now he might die, she thought. *And there's nothing I can do about it.*

On the display, the enemy fleet belched yet another volley of missiles.

"Admiral," Julia said. "We're starting to run out of missiles."

Rani turned to glower at her. "Are you sure?"

She shook her head in irritation before Julia could try to think of an answer. Of *course* Julia was sure. Missile loads were automatically tracked and monitored by the fleet's datanet. If the fleet was running out of missiles...

"Order the fleet to continue firing," she ordered.

She brought up the data on her console and studied it, grimly. Her ships had expended ninety percent of their missiles during the engagement. Imperial Navy tactical doctrine called for keeping at least five percent as a reserve at all times, just in case the fleet ran into something it couldn't handle. And yet, if she gave the order to end the engagement…

"We could try to reload," Julia suggested. "The base's missile stockpiles are largely intact."

"Not during an engagement," Rani said.

Her lips quirked in bitter amusement. She'd been a very junior officer when Admiral Ying had tried to do just that during an exercise, showing off his crew's skills. The resulting explosion had severely damaged a battleship and destroyed a replenishment ship. Ying had been put in front of a court martial and cashiered. He would have been shot if he hadn't been *very* well connected. It said something about just how *badly* he'd screwed up that his connections hadn't been enough to save him from a dishonourable discharge.

"Keep firing until we reach five percent, then hold fire," she ordered, curtly. The enemy might guess the problem, but she doubted they'd be keen to reverse course and continue the engagement. They'd be running short too. "And alert the fleet train. We'll need to reload our magazines as quickly as possible."

"Aye, Admiral," Julia said.

Rani watched, feeling oddly numb, as the missile fire slacked, then wilted altogether. The enemy ships kept moving, not even slowing long enough to try to determine if they were being tricked. As soon as they crossed the phase limit, they vanished…she knew she could continue to chase the enemy ships, but the odds of *catching* them were very low.

I won, she thought, as the last enemy ship flickered into phase space. *I won…*

"Signal all ships," she ordered. "Stand down from battlestations, then start repairs."

"Aye, Admiral," Julia said.

"And send a further signal," Rani added. She smiled, coldly. "Today, we met the enemy…and kicked his ass."

It was not, she admitted, the most *dignified* of statements. But she felt it fitted.

And besides, after the victory, no one would dare to suggest otherwise.

CHAPTER TWENTY-TWO

"Nineteen ships destroyed, nine more damaged so badly that they'll have to be sent home," Mandy said, quietly. "The remainder took varying levels of damage too."

Ed nodded. He could hear the bitter self-reproach in her words, mingled with the grim awareness that some armchair admiral back home was likely to blame her for the entire catastrophe. She was probably right, he thought. There had never been any shortage of people willing to question the military's decisions from hundreds of light-years away, even though they rarely had any real military experience. Even Avalon had a handful of armchair admirals on staff.

He shook his head, slowly, as he studied the display. He'd seen devastation before, far too many times. He'd seen cities blighted by war, he'd seen towns and villages levelled for being in the wrong place at the wrong time...he'd watched, helplessly, as countless bodies were lowered into mass graves and buried, their names and faces left unrecorded. And yet, looking at the damaged starships, he couldn't help feeling a shiver running down his spine. The Empire had lost battles, but it had never lost the war; the Commonwealth, smaller and poorer, might just *have* lost the war.

"It wasn't your fault," he said, quietly.

"I was in command," Mandy said. "It *was* my fault."

Ed gave her a reassuring look, although he knew it wouldn't be enough. No one had seen the trap until the jaws had begun to swing shut. Mandy had walked right into it, true, but so had everyone else. How had

Admiral Singh even known to *set* the trap? Only a handful of people had known that Titlark was the target, none of whom would have talked. And yet, Admiral Singh - Ed was mortally sure Admiral Singh had been in command - had definitely set a trap. She wouldn't have bothered to cloak her ships if she hadn't been expecting to be attacked.

Either something leaked, somehow, or she didn't fall for the deception, he thought, pushing the matter aside. It would require careful consideration, later. *Right now, we have more important concerns.*

He looked at Mandy. "How badly did we hurt them?"

"We wiped out two of Force One's battle squadrons," Mandy said, reciting from figures that were burned into her mind. Ed knew that sensation all too well. "The third took a beating - I suspect it'll be disbanded altogether. We also took out seven or eight ships from Force Two and damaged a number of others, although it's harder to be sure. And we devastated the base."

Ed saw a flicker of horror cross her face and nodded in understanding. Killing enemy combatants had never been a problem - and he had no trouble whatsoever with killing terrorists - but slaughtering non-combatants had always hurt. Cold logic told him that the base and its personnel needed to be removed - not *killed, removed* - yet his heart told him that slaughtering them would be wrong. They were marines, not monsters. And Mandy didn't have anything *like* his experience...

"Titlark won't be supporting the war effort for a while," Ed said, coolly. That was *something*, at least. Not enough to make up for the disaster - and it *had* been a disaster - but perhaps it could be spun as a victory. "How long until the fleet is ready to move?"

Mandy gave him a sharp look. "Apart from the ships that need to be sent home, we can repair most of the damage within the next ten days," she said. "But sir...is there any point in launching a second attack?"

"Not on Titlark," Ed agreed. They'd been rumbled. He didn't know how, but it had happened. Admiral Singh would have ordered convoys to avoid the planet, whatever the outcome of the engagement. Going back and smashing what was left of the base would be highly satisfying, but militarily useless. "We may have to go elsewhere."

Mandy looked tired. "There are no other reasonable targets for dozens of light-years," she said. Her eyes flickered around the CIC. "Where do you want to go?"

"We'll discuss that later," Ed said. "For now, get the repair crews to work and then get some sleep."

"I can't sleep," Mandy protested. She yawned, despite herself. "Colonel, I have to be awake and..."

She yawned, again. Ed hid his grim amusement with an effort. Mandy had been awake for nearly thirty-six hours, perhaps longer. She'd have drunk enough coffee - perhaps even taken a stimulant - to be seeing things by now. He'd done it himself, back when he'd been a young officer. It had never been a pleasant experience.

"Go to your cabin and sleep," Ed said. "That's an order."

Mandy *could* have argued that *she* was the captain, that *no one* could give her orders on her ship. Instead, she turned and shuffled off. Ed watched her go, feeling a flicker of grim concern. Mandy had made at least one mistake, even though it was probably not the one she was blaming herself for. Trying to command both the ship and the fleet at the same time had been a mistake. And it was one she should have corrected long ago.

You felt the same way too, he reminded himself. It was a bitter thought, but one he had to accept. *You wanted to be commander of the company, even as you were commander of an entire military.*

He sighed as he checked the datapad. The list of missing, dead and wounded was growing longer as bodies were recovered or confirmed missing. Over two thousand officers and crew had already been reported dead and the list was *still* growing. It wasn't the end of the world, he knew, but it felt that way. The Commonwealth Navy had had its collective butt soundly kicked.

And that leaves us with the very real possibility of losing the war, Ed thought. There was no escaping it. *And that means we have to gamble - again.*

"The base is beyond repair," Julia said. She sounded tired, but happy. Rani didn't really blame her. "The engineers think we'll need to dismantle the remaining structures and rebuild them from scratch."

"Or shut down the base for good," Rani said. Titlark *was* in a good position for launching offensive operations into the Commonwealth, but the war would soon be over. "We can move operations to Thule or Gethsemane if necessary."

"Yes, Admiral," Julia said.

Rani shrugged. "And the fleet?"

"Twenty-one ships are significantly damaged," Julia reported. "The remainder are reloading their magazines now. I believe that the latest estimate stated that the majority of the damage will be repaired in less than five days…less, perhaps, if we carry out the repairs while underway."

"We do need to take word home," Rani said. She could have dispatched a courier boat, but she would have preferred to be present - with her fleet - when the news reached Wolfbane. It might keep someone from doing something stupid. "Order the engineers to put a repair schedule together, then start work. I want to be heading home in two days."

"Yes, Admiral," Julia said. "And the base?"

Rani hesitated. "Have the remaining crew transferred to the fleet train," she ordered. "We'll abandon the base, for the moment. Make sure there are enough decoys scattered around to keep them from noticing any difference."

She glanced at the starchart. She'd sent messages to the nearest star systems, ordering them not to send anything through Titlark. It was still *possible* that anyone who took the system would be in a position to intercept a freighter convoy, if someone hadn't got the word on time, but unlikely. Abandoning Titlark wouldn't be *that* much of a sacrifice. The base was largely destroyed, after all.

And we'll be heading straight into enemy space once my position is secure, she thought, wryly. *We won't need Titlark any longer*.

"Strip the remaining facilities of anything we need," she added, quietly. "We don't want to *waste* anything."

Julia yawned and tried to hide it. "Yes, Admiral…sorry, Admiral."

"It's quite all right," Rani said. *She'd* been an ops officer, once upon a time. "Just one more task and then you can go catch up on your sleep."

She smiled at Julia's hopeful expression. Julia really was *too* young to hide her eagerness.

"Alter the records so that Captain Christopher Brookes died in combat here," Rani ordered, shortly. "Make it clear that it was a *heroic* death. He was a brave man who gave his life for the cause, etc, etc. His body did not survive, of course."

"Of course," Julia agreed.

Rani dismissed her with a nod. Captain Christopher Brookes would have a *great* afterlife, she told herself. It was the very least she could do. He *had* been a brave man, after all; a skilled starship commander who should have gone far...who *would* have gone far, if he'd been a little more understanding of the political realities. Rani had had no choice, but to kill him...

And I won, she told herself. *I won the battle.*

She sighed as she rose and headed for her suite. Perhaps she should have waited. Perhaps she should have merely confined Christopher Brookes to his quarters for a few months, just to see what happened. But she knew that wouldn't solve anything, not in the long run. If she'd freed him, he would have emerged an embittered man. And her career was proof of just what a single embittered officer could do.

I'm still riding the tiger, she thought, bitterly.

The new weapons had performed as well as she'd expected - in some cases, *better* than she'd expected. There would be time, during the voyage home, to sit down with her analysts and work out just what had and what hadn't worked, then devise new tactics and countermeasures for when the enemy deployed such weapons themselves. And yet, she knew there was still a very good chance of losing the arms race. If she failed to win the war in the next six months, she might lose instead. The Commonwealth's industrial base was smaller than hers, even after her shipyards had been damaged, but their researchers had proven revoltingly ingenious.

Colonel Jason Higgs met her outside her quarters. Rani nodded to him, then opened the hatch. She trusted him as far as she trusted anyone - he'd been with her since Corinthian - but she knew better than to trust anyone completely. *Everyone* had their breaking point, everyone had their price…and everyone had their ambitions. Colonel Higgs might want something, one day, that she wouldn't be able to give him. Perhaps he, too, would want to rule an empire.

She scowled inwardly, keeping her expression blank. Dictatorship was *hard*. She needed to keep everything balanced, everything supporting her primacy…Governor Brown had made it work, when he'd taken over. *Rani* was all too aware that she might easily lose control at any moment, no matter how carefully she covered herself.

"Jason," she said, sitting down on the sofa. "We won."

Higgs cracked a slight smile. "We did," he agreed. "There was no pro-enemy movement, as far as I could tell."

Rani nodded, studying him thoughtfully. Higgs appeared to be in his late thirties, although a combination of rejuvenation treatments and cosmetic surgery made it impossible for anyone to guess his real age. The hints of maturity on his face suggested he was older. *She* knew he was in his early fifties. And yet, there was something about him that made it hard - if not impossible - to remember his face. There were so many classified sections of his file that she'd had second thoughts before taking him on.

But he has had ample opportunity to kill me, Rani thought. Oddly, the realisation made her feel better. *And I am still alive.*

"Sit down," she said, nodding to a chair. "How's morale?"

"Soaring," Higgs informed her. "We won, did we not? The crew *knows* we won, too. My…agents…haven't reported any dissatisfaction, not even the usual grumbling. That will change, of course."

"Of course," Rani agreed. Spacers grumbled about everything, from the food to duty rosters and emergency crew reshufflings on short notice. She would have been more concerned if they *hadn't* grumbled. "You don't think there's any cause for concern?"

"Not on the ships," Higgs said. "*Off* the ships…"

"I know," Rani said. "They don't like me."

"No," Higgs agreed. "They don't."

Rani smiled as they fell into a contemplative silence. She knew she wasn't *liked*, but now…who cared? The corporations would have to act in unison to bring her down and *that* wasn't going to happen. They'd be too scared of accidentally triggering a full-scale civil war in the midst of an *interstellar* one. And now she'd won a victory, they'd be concerned about throwing away the advantage she'd gained them.

"We will be able to move more firmly against…dissenters when we return home," she said, finally. "And then we will be in control."

Higgs tilted his head. "It would be better to allow them the illusion of power," he said, calmly. "They can do significant damage in the long run."

"Perhaps," Rani said. She didn't *want* to allow her enemies *any* illusions. People who held illusions tended to do stupid things because they believed the illusions were *real*. "We shall see."

She leaned back against the sofa, feeling tired. And yet, she didn't *want* to sleep. She was too keyed up to sleep.

"We have to work with them," Higgs pointed out. "There is no way they can be easily replaced."

"Perhaps," Rani said. She met his eyes. "Are you going back on duty?"

Higgs blinked at the sudden shift in tone. "I'm always on duty," he said, seriously. It was true enough. "But I was planning to catch some rest later."

Rani rose. "I'm going to bed," she said. "If you want, if you like, join me."

She strode towards the hatch, not looking back. It had been too long since she'd let herself relax, so long since she'd had a lover…or even a casual partner for a one-night stand. On Trafalgar, she hadn't dared; on Corinthian, she'd had too many other problems. Now…

The hatch hissed open. After a moment, she heard him rise and follow her.

"Well," Simone Perkins said. "Not such a pretty face any longer, am I?"

Emmanuel hesitated, unsure what to say. Simone was lying on a bed, surgical packs taped to her arms and upper body. Her face was badly scarred, so badly that it was a minor miracle that she'd survived long enough for her shipmates to put her in a stasis tube. It would be weeks, perhaps months, before she was fit to return to duty, let alone have the surgery that would restore her face.

"I saw myself," Simone said. Her voice sounded old. "You don't have to lie."

"I wasn't going to lie," Emmanuel said. In truth, he wasn't sure if *that* was a lie. He wasn't sure what he should tell her, if anything. "You will get better, won't you?"

Simone lifted a hand to her face. Emmanuel couldn't help noticing that it was badly scarred too. He wasn't even sure what had happened. *Defiant* had been hit several times during the battle - thankfully, with conventional weapons - and she'd been on duty...perhaps she'd just been too close to one of the hits. But surely that would have killed her outright...

"The doc says I'll be fine, once my skin regenerates," Simone said. "But it will take time, apparently. I may be going home."

Emmanuel winced. He'd known that war had a cost. He'd learnt that the hard way, on a dozen worlds. And yet, looking at Simone, he learned it once again. The brilliant young girl he'd met had been replaced by a bitter woman, a stranger who just didn't care. She would get better, physically. He'd seen people with worse injuries who'd made a full recovery. But would she recover mentally?

"They're moving some of the wounded over to the transports," he said. One of the modified colonist-carriers was nothing, but stasis pods. The wounded would be suspended in time until they could be treated properly. It wasn't an ideal solution, but at least the wounded wouldn't feel time passing. "You might be going with them."

"I want to leave and I don't want to leave," Simone said. Her voice was bitter. She moved her head, very gingerly. "I don't want to feel as though I'm running out on everyone."

"You're injured," Emmanuel pointed out. Her face twisted. It was hard to be sure, but he thought she'd given him a nasty look. "No one will blame you for leaving."

"I'll blame myself," Simone said. Her face twisted, again. "I was the fool who got hurt and..."

"...Needs to sleep," a voice finished. "I'll give you a sedative."

Emmanuel looked up. A doctor had materialised behind them. He looked tired, as tired as Emmanuel felt. Emmanuel rose - there was no point in trying to argue - and slipped away from the bed. Simone would recover, he was sure. But she'd never be the same again.

"Five more confirmed dead," a voice said, as he passed an office. "Two more transferred to the stasis cells."

Emmanuel shuddered. He'd expected to record a victory. Instead, he was counting the cost of a defeat. There was no point in trying to hide from the truth. The Commonwealth Navy had taken one hell of a beating. How many men and women had died in the brief, but disastrous battle? How many more would never be the same again?

He shuddered, again. He'd spent his whole life in pursuit of the truth. But right now, he didn't think he wanted to know.

CHAPTER TWENTY-THREE

"We kept the system under observation," Mandy said, quietly. She sat in the conference room, studying the report from *Sneaky*. "The majority of the enemy fleet pulled out thirty-six hours ago."

"Unless it slipped back into cloak," Commodore Van Houlton said. His hologram seemed doubtful. He'd never really liked her and she knew it. "They might be waiting to ambush us again."

Mandy kept her face carefully expressionless. Colonel Stalker had supported her, but it was clear that not all of her subordinates thought she'd done a good job. And she knew they were right. She'd lost engagements before, but never so badly. Morale was in the pits and it wasn't likely to get any better in a hurry.

"They've left decoys behind," Commodore Henderson countered. "They probably took their fleet elsewhere."

"Perhaps," Mandy said. She cleared her throat. "Colonel?"

Colonel Stalker leaned forward. "There is nothing to be gained - now - by returning to Titlark and trashing the place," he said. "We *did* succeed in crippling or destroying most of the facilities. Given how we were ambushed" - his face darkened, for a second - "we must assume that they've already rerouted their convoys around Titlark. The system is now effectively worthless."

"Unless we get lucky," Henderson commented. "There's always *someone* who doesn't get the word."

"It would be too much to hope for," Colonel Stalker said. His eyes swept the compartment, moving from face to face. "We would tie up the remainder of our strength for far too long."

Mandy nodded in grim agreement. Admiral Singh had - somehow - known they were coming. She'd had ample opportunity to make sure her people knew to avoid Titlark in future, at least until they knew the battle's outcome. And now the base was crippled, there was little point in reclaiming the system. Titlark's importance had been an accident of interstellar geography. That importance was now gone.

"We still have a formidable force," Henderson said. "And they won't catch us the same way twice."

"Unless they have some even *newer* weapons," Van Houlton muttered. "We *invented* the damned force shields, sir. And yet we never considered using them to punch through armour."

"We can duplicate their missiles fairly quickly," Mandy pointed out. "My tactical analysts think we can even improve on their design a little."

"Not quickly enough to help us," Van Houlton snapped. He looked directly at Colonel Stalker. "Colonel, we must withdraw and regroup."

Mandy felt a hot flash of anger. Colonel Stalker was - technically - the senior officer, but *she* was in command of the squadron. Van Houlton was appealing over her head, to someone who wasn't a naval officer and never would be. And yet…Colonel Stalker had far more military experience than all three of the other officers put together. She might have to defer to his judgement.

No wonder the Imperial Navy spent so long sorting out questions of precedence and command, she thought, dryly. *They had problems like this all the time.*

"No," Colonel Stalker said. His voice was very calm. Only someone who knew him well would have caught the edge in it. "That's precisely the *last* thing we should do."

He tapped his terminal, displaying a starchart. "Right now, Admiral Singh thinks she's won. She caught us by surprise and gave us a bloody nose. And yes, there's no point in trying to hide from that truth. But that doesn't mean we're beaten. We have to take the offensive again, now."

Van Houlton looked perplexed. "Colonel," he said slowly, "we took a beating."

"We can repair most of the ships," Colonel Stalker countered. "By the time we reach Wolfbane, Commodore, our ships will be in fighting trim again."

Mandy concealed her amusement as Van Houlton started to splutter. "Wolfbane?"

"Yes, Commodore," Colonel Stalker said. "It is the sole remaining target."

"It would be risky," Henderson said. "They might have deployed their new weapons to cover their homeworld. And even without them, Wolfbane is heavily defended."

"Exactly," Colonel Stalker said. "The last thing they'll expect is to be attacked."

"With good reason," Van Houlton said. "Colonel, pressing an offensive against Wolfbane is *suicide*!"

Colonel Stalker cocked his head. "It will be risky," he said, nodding to Henderson. "But we *cannot* afford to give them time to recover. Admiral Singh will have all the time in the world to rearm her forces, then take the offensive. And when she does, she will do it with a considerable advantage. Tearing the guts out of Wolfbane may be the only thing capable of keeping her from tearing the guts out of *us*."

Mandy nodded, slowly. Colonel Stalker was right. Wolfbane *still* had a considerable advantage, despite the damage Jasmine had done to their shipyards nine months ago. Giving Admiral Singh a chance to consolidate her victory would mean certain defeat. And yet, Van Houlton also had a point. They would be risking her entire fleet on a headlong charge into the enemy's defences.

"First, we will have a chance to cripple both their mobile forces and their industrial base," Colonel Stalker said. "Second, we will…encourage dissatisfied members of her regime to overthrow her. The prospect of watching their planet being overrun may push them into joining the winning side."

"Assuming we are the winning side," Van Houlton muttered.

Colonel Stalker ignored him. "And third, we will knock enemy morale back down," he concluded. "We *cannot* let them regain their balance and retake the offensive."

Van Houlton cleared his throat. "Colonel, I understand the logic," he said. "But we will be taking an immense risk."

"As you have said," Colonel Stalker said.

"But perhaps not enough," Van Houlton insisted. "Colonel, we would be operating on a logistics shoestring, nearly a month from the closest fleet base and two months from Avalon itself. We would certainly be out of touch with home for quite some time. Admiral Singh might have launched her own offensive towards Avalon..."

His voice trailed off. "I understand your concerns," Colonel Stalker said. "I believe, however, that we have no choice."

He paused. His voice hardened. "This isn't a council of war," he added, coolly. Mandy felt a shiver running down her spine. It was easy to forget, at times, that Colonel Stalker's affable nature hid a very dangerous man. "The decision is mine, mine alone. And I have decided that we will throw the dice one final time."

Mandy swallowed, hard. She took a moment to compose herself before speaking.

"I believe we can depart within the day, sir," she said. "We'd just need to update the repair schedule and transfer spare parts and crews."

"See to it," Colonel Stalker said. "We'll drop out of phase space at some point close to Wolfbane, just long enough to catch up on repairs."

Van Houlton looked pale, but determined. "Colonel...are you going to send word back to Avalon?"

"We are already dispatching a handful of ships back home," Colonel Stalker said. "One of them will take a message to the council."

"Yes, sir," Van Houlton said. He paused. "Shouldn't we also be trying to determine how Admiral Singh knew we were coming?"

"That's a problem for another time," Colonel Stalker said. "For the moment" - he nodded to Mandy - "we have a departure to plan."

Mandy nodded back. "Yes, sir."

Ed had never *liked* the idea of inactivity, even as a young man. He'd always craved something to do, something to keep himself occupied. Boot Camp had built on that, if only because there was always something to do on base or out in the field. The thought of taking the offensive felt good, although he knew the risks. If anything, Commodore Van Houlton had understated them. Ed wasn't gambling with a platoon or even the entire company. He was gambling with the entire Commonwealth.

But there's no choice, he reminded himself, again. He'd talked it through with Gwendolyn, making sure his own need to do something wasn't driving his thoughts. *We have to retake the initiative somehow.*

He listened, politely, as Mandy outlined the repair schedule for the remaining naval squadrons. She'd done a good job of reorganising the ships, then pushing the tactical staff to come up with countermeasures for the enemy's new weapons. It was almost a shame that he had to read her the riot act…he knew, deep inside, that he should have done it earlier. But he'd chosen to stay his hand. It had been a mistake.

"We'll depart in seven hours," Mandy finished. "Dismissed."

She leaned back in her chair, looking tired. Ed studied her, noting the signs of physical and mental tiredness. He didn't blame her, not really. Mandy hadn't really started to grow up until she'd been exiled to Avalon. It was odd to realise that their birthplaces hadn't been *that* far apart. But Mandy had been one of the lucky ones. She'd been born in what might as well be a very different world.

"You did well," he said, softly. "Not everyone copes so well with defeat."

Mandy didn't look at him. "You've never been defeated in your life."

"I had my ass kicked more times than I care to think about at Boot Camp," Ed said. It was true. The Drill Instructors had worked hard to make sure the recruits made mistakes and learned from them. "Things go wrong, regularly. It's how you cope with them that matters."

"Yes, sir," Mandy said.

Ed cleared his throat. "You'll be handing command of *Defiant* to Commander Cobb," he said, flatly. "And commanding the fleet from the CIC."

Mandy turned her head to look at him. Her voice was flat, as if she was too tired to feel anything. "*Defiant* is my ship, sir."

"You cannot command a starship *and* the entire fleet," Ed said. "It worked - barely - for squadron command. It cannot work for a larger fleet."

He sighed, inwardly. Avalon's manpower shortage was a serious problem. Mandy, who'd grown up in a decidedly non-military family, was *still* one of the most experienced naval officers at his disposal. They were rushing people up the ranks, forcing them to hold down two or more jobs... it was a policy, he knew, that would eventually lead to disaster. Perhaps it *had* led to disaster. Mandy had been torn between two competing sets of responsibilities.

"I understand, sir," Mandy said.

She sounded hurt. Ed wasn't really surprised. Mandy had never gone to the Naval Academy, never worked her way up the ranks. She'd be lucky to be a lieutenant if she'd joined the Imperial Navy and followed a traditional career path. Her youth - and lack of family connections - told against her. Avalon had been the making of her...

But she didn't get some of the training she needed, Ed thought. *She never learnt to respect her own limits.*

He shook his head, mentally. Ideally, Mandy would have been given a year or two of shore leave and therapy after being taken prisoner by pirates. She'd been surprisingly well-treated, but she'd still been a prisoner, still forced to assist the pirates...hell, she might have been shot if she'd been rescued by the Imperial Navy. Instead, he'd had no choice, but to put her back in the navy. He was just too short of experienced officers.

"You will have a chance to take command again afterwards, if you wish," Ed said. "It *will* mean a demotion..."

"I accept," Mandy said. She gave him the ghost of a smile. "I don't care about the demotion."

Ed nodded. A demotion from flag rank would have meant the end of her career, in the Imperial Navy. For Avalon...there was something to be said for putting commodores and admirals back in their command chairs on a regular basis. Why not? It had worked for the Marine Corps. The Corps had worked hard to ensure that its senior officers never lost their touch.

"I'll inform Commander Cobb after we depart," she added. "I hope that's okay."

"It will do," Ed said. Mandy and her XO would have three weeks to get used to the new arrangement. It wasn't going to be easy. Normally, a new commander or flag officer would be assigned to a whole new unit. But that wasn't an option now. "I'll promote him personally, if you like."

Mandy smiled, tiredly. "I'm sure he'll like it."

Ed nodded. "Very good," he said. "Go get some sleep."

"You keep telling me to get some sleep," Mandy said. She rose. "Is that a tradition in the Marine Corps?"

"Yep," Ed said. He smirked. "Sleep, sleep and sleep again, for tomorrow you might be in the middle of a forty-eight hour firefight."

Mandy giggled. "Eat, drink and be merry, for tomorrow we may catch some disgusting skin disease?"

Ed snorted. "Eat, drink and be merry, for tomorrow the sergeants will smell alcohol on your breath and shout extra loud just to ram the point home."

He sighed. Joker had said that, hadn't he? He wondered, not for the first time, what had happened to his old friend. Joker had transferred to a different company after OCS and headed off to bang heads together on a planet with an unpronounceable name. And then he'd vanished when Avalon had lost touch with the Empire. God alone knew what had happened to him.

Mandy saluted and left the compartment. Ed watched her go, remembering the teenage brat he'd met on Earth. Mandy had been pretty enough, he recalled, pretty enough to attract attention from some of the younger marines...but he doubted she'd ever had an original thought in her head. She'd been spoilt rotten by her mother, utterly unprepared for her family's sudden change in fortune. Ed had doubted Mandy would survive on Avalon. He'd rarely been so glad to be wrong. The teenage brat had grown into a fine young woman.

Who's on the edge, just like the rest of us, he thought.

He looked back at the starchart, silently contemplating the problem. Admiral Singh could *not* be allowed to retake the offensive. And *that* meant knocking her off-balance, as hard as possible. Devastating Wolfbane was the key to winning the war, either by crippling her ability to rebuild her forces or convincing her former partners to take her out and sue for peace. But it wasn't going to be easy.

The responsibility is mine, he told himself. *And we have to move fast.*

He sighed. The Commonwealth was starting to crack under the strains of war. It had never really been *designed* for war, certainly not a long conflict. Gaby had warned him that there *was* a peace party, one composed of men and women who believed the Commonwealth needed to sue for peace before it cracked asunder. Once she left office - or earlier, if Douglas demanded her attention - there would be an election. God alone knew who would win.

It was ironic, he admitted, in the privacy of his own mind. He'd learned to despise politicians during his career, but the politicians on Avalon were actually *respectable.* They weren't *professional* politicians. They'd fought in wars, helped to rebuild their planets…they knew the hard truths that the Grand Senate had forgotten long ago. And yet, they also knew that the war was slowly tearing the Commonwealth apart. They sought peace because it was better than war.

Peace is not freedom, he reminded himself. *And they know it too.*

He tapped the console, deactivating the starchart. They would roll the dice one final time before the end. And if they were lucky…

And if we're not lucky, he thought, *at least we'll make sure they know they've been in a fight.*

"We have entered phase space, Captain," the helmsman said. "We're on our way."

"Very good," Mandy said. She looked around the bridge, silently memorising every detail. It wouldn't be *hers*, the next time she set foot on it. "Commander Cobb. Please will you join me in my office?"

She glanced at the tactical officer. "Mr. Graves, you have the bridge."

Her office wouldn't be *hers* any more either, she recalled, as she stepped through the hatch and into the small compartment. Thankfully, she'd never bothered to decorate. The photograph of her family on the desk was the only real personal touch. Clearing the room wouldn't take more than a few minutes.

"Commander," she said, sitting down on the chair. Commander Cobb took the sofa. "I…"

Mandy paused, feeling awkward. She honestly wasn't sure how to proceed.

She cleared her throat. "Commander, I…you will assume command of *Defiant* from 2200 tonight," she said. "Colonel Stalker will pin the badge on you. And then…the ship will be yours from that moment on."

"I…thank you," Cobb managed. He sounded as if he was trying, very hard, to hide his delight. Starship command was *everyone's* dream. And yet, he was taking it from her. He had to wonder if Mandy had been *ordered* to surrender command to him. "Captain, I…"

"You're a good man," Mandy said. She forced her voice to stay level. It wasn't his fault. "I am sure you'll make me proud."

"Thank you," Cobb said.

Mandy reached into her pocket and removed a single silver star. "This was taken from *Sword*, after she was disabled," she said. It had belonged to an Imperial Navy officer, once upon a time. She didn't want to think about how the pirates had acquired it. "Colonel Stalker insisted I should keep it."

She held it out to him. "I'd appreciate it if you wore it," she added. "It would mean a great deal to me."

Cobb took it. "It would be my honour."

Mandy nodded. She told herself, firmly, that she had to be happy for him. Cobb deserved a promotion…

And he can concentrate on the ship, she told herself, firmly. *That's all that matters right now.*

CHAPTER TWENTY-FOUR

"You might be working out here," Captain Cleveland said. "What do you think?"

Jasmine shrugged as she studied the display. Captain Cleveland had been flirting with her during the voyage, testing her patience more than she cared to admit. His collection of chat-up lines were so bad that she was honestly surprised someone hadn't sewn his mouth together long ago. He was hardly the first freighter captain she'd met who'd had an inflated view of himself, but he was in a class of his own.

And to think the six of us are supposed to be married, she thought. *Aren't freighter captains meant to honour marital vows?*

"It's a very active system," she said, dryly. "I'm sure the six of us will find jobs here."

She kept her real concern to herself as *Lagos* made its stately way towards Wolfbane. The last time she'd visited the system, she'd destroyed an entire shipyard…but, if anything, the level of interplanetary operations seemed to have doubled. The sensors on the freighter were hardly mil-grade, yet they were still good enough to pick out hundreds of mining camps scattered across the system. Wolfbane itself was ringed by dozens of industrial nodes, all humming away placidly. She doubted it was as *efficient* as Avalon - large corporations were rarely interested in finding newer and better ways to do things - but it was still alarming.

And there are fewer warships in orbit than I expected, she thought. *That might not be a good sign.*

Captain Cleveland cleared his throat. "You're *sure* you don't want to stay with me?"

Jasmine shook her head, hiding her amusement. Captain Cleveland thought he was doing her a favour - and, if she'd been a *genuine* engineer looking for work, he would have been. Sure, she *was* supposed to be married, but there were ways to cope with that. Poly-marriages rose and fell all the time as newcomers entered and older folks left. But it didn't matter. Getting down to the surface was more important than anything else.

"Very well," Captain Cleveland said. He sighed, dramatically. "Grab your bags, then assemble at the primary airlock in thirty minutes. We won't be docking for long."

"Understood," Jasmine said.

She walked through the hatch and down to the cabins. They'd been given the best quarters on the ship, which wasn't saying much. The cabins were tiny, barely large enough to hold a couple of bunk beds apiece. Jasmine found it hard to care. The floor was clean, the bedding was fresh and the toilet didn't smell. She'd slept in worse places.

"Get packing," she called, as she passed Stewart's room. "We're being kicked off in thirty minutes."

She stepped into her cabin. Meade was sitting on her bed, reading her datapad. Her carryall was positioned next to her, looking suspiciously clean. Jasmine hoped that wouldn't attract too much attention from the security officers, when they passed through the checkpoint. It was uncommon for spacers to lug new bags around for long. They *always* got dirty.

"I've had a job offer," Meade said. She grinned. "The engineer wanted me to stay."

"I'm sure he wanted more than just your skills," Jasmine said, dryly. They had to be careful what they said on the freighter. She'd checked the compartment for bugs, of course, but she was all too aware that they might have missed something. "What did you say?"

"I could hardly desert my family," Meade said, in mock offence. "And they can't take us *all* on."

Jasmine nodded as she picked up her carryall. She'd been careful not to carry anything that might arouse suspicions, but she checked it again just to be sure. The Wolves had already had an infiltrator make his way to the surface and assassinate Governor Brown. They'd be very careful not to let that happen again.

And they're going to be out of luck, she thought. A dull rattle ran through the ship as it powered into orbit. *They won't see us at all.*

She licked her lips. In theory, passing through security shouldn't be a problem; in practice, she was painfully aware of just how much could go wrong. And while they weren't entirely unarmed, she knew their chances of fighting their way out were precisely zero. Security checkpoints were bottlenecks, places *designed* to keep even the most heavily-armed intruders trapped until they could be captured or killed. Even *marines* wouldn't be able to escape.

Unless they really screw up, she thought. *And that's not likely to happen.*

She glanced at Meade. She'd undone the upper buttons of her shirt, exposing the tops of her breasts. Jasmine had to admit that it would probably divert attention from anything she happened to be carrying. Security goons were rarely very well trained. They'd prefer to spend their time ogling attractive guests instead of doing their job. For once, Jasmine thought, she wouldn't complain about it.

"Let's go," she said. "Time is not on our side."

"It never is," Meade agreed.

General Mark Haverford shivered as he walked through the airlock. It was cold, cold enough to make him wish he'd worn his jacket. The spacer's garb he'd been given just wasn't warm enough. He kept his face impassive as they hurried through a second set of airlocks. The air didn't get any warmer when they reached the checkpoint. A handful of guards were already there, waiting for them. Their expressions were far from welcoming.

"Welcome to Wolfbane," the leader said. He wore a uniform that made him look like a naval admiral. Mark silently wondered which corporation had been given the contract for planetary security and why. "Wait here. When I give the order, walk through the gates and into the security compound. Follow all orders until you reach the far end. Any misbehaviour will result in arrest and possible detention."

Mark smiled, inwardly. *Welcome home…*

He waited until his name - his false name - was called, then walked through the door. A pair of guards greeted him, then took his ID card and tested it against their files. Mark tensed, despite himself. They shouldn't be able to detect a forged ID, he was sure, but if he was wrong…

"You're an engineer," one of the guards said. He was a surprisingly fat man. There was no nametag on his uniform, so Mark mentally dubbed him Fatty. "You have some very good qualifications."

"Thank you," Mark said. He was grimly aware of the other guard running scanners over his body, then opening the carryall and scanning his possessions. "We're looking for a job here."

Fatty winked. "What's it like, being in bed with five others?"

Mark felt himself flush. "It doesn't work like that," he said. "We don't all share the same bed."

"I wish I could do that with my wife," Fatty said. He laughed. "Stupid bitch thinks I hog all the blankets."

"We swap partners," Mark told him. "We're a family, you see."

"I don't," Fatty said. "How do you cope when two of you want to fuck the same girl?"

"We manage it," Mark said. Jasmine had made him read up on polymarriages. He silently blessed her foresight. He'd never imagined being asked so many odd questions. "But the girls can choose for themselves, too."

"Just like my wife," Fatty said. He brayed with laughter. "She's been choosing not to have sex with me for the past year!"

"I don't blame her," his companion said. He held up a device from Mark's toolkit. "What is this?"

"It's a sonic screwdriver," Mark explained. There was a story behind the name, but he didn't know it. "I use it for undoing screws and removing components."

"Very interesting," Fatty said. His tone suggested it was nothing of the sort. "Put your hand on this panel, please."

Mark braced himself as he touched the panel. If something had gone wrong, if the DNA resequencing hadn't worked, he was trapped. Fatty would call for reinforcements, then arrest the whole lot of them. His DNA was on file. Admiral Singh would have made sure of it, if she knew he'd defected. He rather assumed she'd suspect the worst…

The device pinged. "No record of you," Fatty grunted. Mark did his best not to sag in unspoken relief. "Very good, my man."

He jabbed a finger at the door. "The girl outside will give you some paperwork," he said, as the door hissed open. "Make sure you fill it out, then wait. Your partners will be along soon."

Mark nodded and hurried through the door, trying to conceal his relief. A young woman in a black uniform passed him a set of papers and a pen, then pointed him to a desk. Jasmine was already sitting down, writing carefully. Mark sat next to her and started to work his way through the paperwork. Wolfbane, it seemed, wanted to know their entire cover story, from start to finish. Mark couldn't help wondering if they were just trying to trip unwary visitors up.

"We met on Crisco," Jasmine muttered. "And married there."

"Ouch," Mark muttered. He groaned, inwardly, as he filled out his form. The slightest discrepancy would attract attention. Thankfully, Jasmine had forced him to memorise their cover story in great detail. "And got kicked off our ship on Calomel."

The others joined them, looking displeased. Mark didn't blame them. He had no doubt that Fatty had questioned them too. Meade, in particular, looked like an angry cat. Mark shot her a reassuring look, then returned to his paperwork. It took nearly an hour to finish writing and then check it against the other forms. By the time they were finished, he had remembered why he'd come to loathe paperwork.

He half-expected another set of questions, but instead they were merely led through a second set of security gates, where they met a young woman in a green uniform who introduced herself as a guide. Mark studied her with interest, noting the way she held herself. She was just a little *too* neat to be a guide. He silently made a bet with himself that the young lady actually worked for the security forces.

"Welcome to Wolfbane," the young woman said. She actually managed to make it sound convincing. "I'm Talia. My job is to get you settled in, then start you off on a round of interviews. Ideally, you'll all have jobs by the end of the week."

"You move fast," Jasmine commented. Her tone was so neutral that Mark couldn't tell if it was a genuine compliment or not. "Do you already have an apartment lined up for us?"

"We have several," Talia said. She turned and walked towards the nearest door. "You can pick and choose, if you like."

"Nothing is too good for an engineer," Meade said.

Talia nodded. "You're important people," she said. "We do want to welcome you properly."

Mark followed her down the corridor and into the elevator. Unusually, Wolfbane's orbital tower had its elevators in the centre of the structure, rather than running down the outer edge so the passengers could watch the view. The elevator car itself was barren, save for a set of chairs and a large drinks machine positioned in one corner. Save for the six of them and Talia, it was deserted. Mark couldn't help wondering if they'd been separated from other travellers or if there were truly so few people visiting Wolfbane these days. The new security requirements probably put casual visitors off.

The elevator lurched, then started to fall. "We'll be down in thirty minutes," Talia said. "I'll take you to the car once we arrive."

Meade sat down, crossing her arms under her breasts. "We're going down fast," she said, dryly. Stewart hurried over to the drinks machine and started to order something. "How do you balance the g-forces?"

"I think it has something to do with compensator fields," Talia said. She looked oddly embarrassed. "I don't know the details. I'm not an engineer."

And that, Mark thought silently, *explains precisely why the Empire fell.*

Jasmine was silently relieved as the elevator car finally reached the surface. It was oddly crude, compared to the orbital tower elevators she'd seen on Earth; she'd heard creaking noises, accompanied by slight shifts in the compensator field. There was no way to know for sure, but she'd bet good money that whoever was in charge of the orbital tower was skipping basic maintenance. The war effort had probably dragged all the *good* techs into space.

Which is why they were so glad to get us, she thought. Going through security had been unpleasant, but she'd honestly expected worse. Security goons were notorious for abusing their power, particularly over young and vulnerable female tourists. *They have a very real shortage of experienced technicians.*

She followed Talia out of the door and into a small office. A set of ID cards were already on the table, waiting for them. Talia picked them up and passed them around. Jasmine sighed as she saw her photograph, rolling her eyes in annoyance. She looked criminally insane, if not dead. The police would probably take one look at the ID card and arrest her on suspicion.

"Keep these with you at all times," Talia said. "They're your key to everything - your bank accounts, for example, are accessed with the card. Pop them into a standard reader for a full description of what you can do with them. Failure to produce them on demand will result in arrest and possible detention. Losing one will result in a very hefty fine."

And they're probably tracking us too, Jasmine thought. It wouldn't be *hard* to install a tracking chip in the ID card. Earth had experimented with a similar scheme, once upon a time. Wolfbane certainly had the tech base to make it happen. *We'll have to take one of the cards apart to see how it works.*

"We've given each of you a basic expense account, with a small balance," Talia continued. "You'll be required to repay anything you spend if you don't get a job in the next couple of weeks. Should you require a more complex account or a bank loan, discuss it with your employers first. They may be willing to help smooth the way."

Jasmine nodded, listening as Talia outlined more and more rules and regulations. Wolfbane was starting to sound like a somewhat less populated version of Earth. It was a relief, almost, when Talia led them outside and helped them into a large aircar. Jasmine took a seat by the window and watched, grimly, as the aircar rose into the air. Wolfbane *did* look an awful lot like Earth. It was certainly as heavily regulated as Earth.

"Your first apartment is in the Henna Skyscraper," Talia said, as the aircar flew over the city. "If you don't like it, we'll move to a couple of others…"

"I'm sure it will be fine," Jasmine said.

She studied the city carefully, trying to get a feel for its mood. It didn't look good, she thought. There were too many armed guards on the streets, watching for trouble. The civilians themselves looked listless, moving from place to place with a drab slowness that sent chills down her spine. There were few women on the streets, she noted. *That* was always a bad sign.

The aircar landed on the skyscraper and they walked down to the apartment. It was large, larger than Jasmine had expected. There was a kitchen - instead of the standard food processor - a bath and six large bedrooms, each one with a double bed. Someone was *definitely* trying to welcome them. She rather suspected that a group of *real* engineers would be either flattered or intimidated by the apartment. They'd be expected to work hard in return.

"It will do," Jasmine said. Once Talia had gone, they'd have to search the apartment for bugs. She had no doubt the building was infested. Foreigners would be closely watched at all times. "We'll be very happy here."

Talia beamed. "I'm sure of it," she said. "Your resumes have already been forwarded to recruitment offices. You'll be hearing from them by the end of the day."

Jasmine made a show of looking at her wristcom. "We'll get some rest," she said. "And then see what we find to eat."

"Very good," Talia said. "There's a set of restaurants on the lower levels and some more outside, if you wish to explore."

She bowed, politely. "Call me if you have any questions. I'm available every hour of every day."

Which probably means you have an office somewhere within this building, Jasmine thought, wryly. It was another complication, but she couldn't say she hadn't prepared for it. The *real* problem would be avoiding getting hired. *That* might be a major headache. *They will expect us to start work as quickly as possible.*

"Unpack, if you like," she said, cheerfully. They'd know she *really* meant they were to hunt for bugs. "And then we'll get something to eat."

She walked into her bedroom, dumped the carryall on the bed and started to unpack, taking the opportunity to look for bugs. There didn't seem to have been *any* attempt to hide them, she discovered. Three bugs were close to her bed - she wondered what the security officers expected to hear - and two more were positioned by the door. She made a mental note to keep looking - she might have been *meant* to find the obvious bugs - and then hurried back out. Meade and Stewart were exploring the kitchen together, poking through the stasis fridge.

"I fancy a cup of coffee," Stewart said. He moved his hands in a motion Jasmine recognised, indicating that there were at least five bugs in the kitchen. "How about you, Jazz?"

"Coffee would be great, thanks," Jasmine said. "Make sure you get a shower before we go out."

"Of course," Stewart said. He made another signal. *Bugs in the bathroom.* "I can't *wait* to explore."

Jasmine groaned, inwardly. Bugs in the bathroom...optical pick-ups, she suspected. They'd be harder to deal with than audio bugs. The bastards who'd hidden them probably wanted a show.

She pushed the thought aside. "Neither can I."

CHAPTER TWENTY-FIVE

Jasmine had once heard a particularly unpleasant world described as a prison camp above ground and a mass grave below. She had no idea if Governor Brown or Admiral Singh had bothered to slaughter their enemies in vast numbers, but she couldn't help comparing Wolfbane to a giant prison camp. A day of covert observation and datanet probing was enough to confirm that the planetary population was under very close surveillance indeed.

But watching everyone all the time is beyond the security forces, she thought, as she walked down the darkening streets. The sun was setting, plunging the city into night. Haverford followed her, trying to look inconspicuous. *There's just too many people to watch.*

She smiled, thinly. It hadn't taken *long* for Meade and Patrick to figure out how the ID cards worked, then spoof them. As Jasmine had expected, they *did* broadcast a regular 'I am here' signal to the planetary security network, allowing guests to be tracked without making it particularly obvious. But it had rapidly become clear that half the population didn't carry ID cards on a regular basis, making it harder for the security forces to keep track of them. Once they'd ditched the cards, moving around without being followed was easy.

As long as we don't attract attention, she reminded herself. There seemed to be armed guards on every intersection, marching up and down and glowering at anyone who looked too closely at them. Jasmine wasn't too impressed. It was a show of strength - but that was *all* it was. *The guards are scattered across the city.*

Tryon City was on edge, she thought. The guards couldn't stop people from talking, whispering in hushed voices. Jasmine had heard countless rumours, ranging from massive defeats in interstellar space to hundreds of people who'd simply vanished. Everywhere they went, viewscreens blared exhortations to hard work and dedication, reminding the general population that the war was in their lands. Jasmine rather hoped that was true, if only because the Wolves were bound to lose. The listless civilians, drinking when they weren't working, didn't seem particularly inspired. She had a feeling that some of them - perhaps most of them - had given up.

Most of them don't have the skills to be useful, she thought. *And getting the training they need isn't going to be easy.*

She stopped, allowing Haverford the chance to catch up with her. "Are you sure about your friend?"

"He's still alive and in place," Haverford said. He sounded confident, but Jasmine could tell he was faking it. Haverford had deserted nearly five *months* ago. A lot could change since then. "And he owes me."

Jasmine sighed. She would have been happier vanishing into the underground - it wouldn't be hard - and trying to build up a revolutionary army from scratch, but she knew that wasn't an option. She'd learned enough in a day to know that Admiral Singh's forces would squash any unconnected rebel force like bugs. Admiral Singh might be away - Jasmine hadn't been able to determine *where* she'd gone or when she'd return - but her lackeys would happily do the dirty work for her. Reading between the lines, it was clear that Admiral Singh's bully boys had already started to exceed their orders.

"I hope you're right," she said, as they reached a small bar. A grim-faced bouncer stood outside, his arms bulging with implanted enhancements. "Do you have the passcodes?"

Haverford nodded. Jasmine braced herself, one hand touching her wristcom, as they walked up to the bouncer. If they were caught, she'd send an emergency signal first...the others would know she'd been caught and clear out before it was too late. After that...well, they had their orders. They'd just have to proceed without her.

We need more time, she thought. Haverford spoke quickly to the bouncer, exchanging passcodes. *But we don't have time.*

She groaned, inwardly. They'd already started to receive job offers. Most of them looked reasonably good - *would* have been good, if they'd been *real* techs. Wolfbane was so desperate for engineers that the corporations were happy to agree not to break up the poly-marriage. Jasmine suspected that the pressure to take a job, any job, would start to grow stronger within the next few days. By then, they needed to make contact with potential allies and either join them or slip underground.

The bouncer opened the door. Haverford led her into a small room, dominated by privacy cubicles. Jasmine reminded herself, carefully, not to trust them completely. The planetary security services probably knew about the bar, even though they hadn't seen fit to shut it down. They might well have settled for quietly monitoring the establishment instead, watching to see who made use of it. She'd just have to hope they hadn't attracted too much attention.

It was easier last time, she thought. *But then, we were sneaking down from orbit instead of registering at the gates.*

A thin man - apparently in his early forties - was sitting at the bar, nursing a mug of beer. He looked up at Haverford, then nodded curtly and motioned to the stairs. Haverford nodded back and followed him up the stairs, Jasmine bringing up the rear. Her ears started to hurt as she passed through a privacy field, one designed to disrupt audio bugs. It should work, she thought, unless the bugs were hidden within the counter-surveillance devices themselves. It was a very old trick.

"General," the man said. His voice was warm, but very composed. "Welcome home."

"Thank you," Haverford said. He glanced at Jasmine. "This is Barker, an old friend."

Jasmine gave them both a sharp look, then started to check the room. There didn't seem to be any bugs, as far as she could tell, but that meant nothing. She didn't have enough equipment to be entirely sure they were unobserved. And who knew who Barker was *really* working for? He might be one of Admiral Singh's spies.

I guess we'll know if we get arrested tonight, she thought, sourly. She sat down next to Haverford, facing Barker. His face was too perfect to be natural, while his clothes were probably expensive. *And even if we don't get arrested, it means nothing.*

"General," Barker said. "Aren't you going to introduce me to your friend?"

Haverford glanced at Jasmine. "This is Jazz," he said. "She's a friend."

Barker nodded. "I heard you were killed on Corinthian," he said, bluntly. "And yet here you are, alive."

"Reports of my death were nothing more than lies," Haverford said. Jasmine snorted. He leaned forward. "What *were* you told about me?"

"That you'd been killed heroically leading a charge," Barker said. "There was a funeral and everything."

"Admiral Singh is a liar," Haverford said. "But then, I guess you already knew that."

Barker studied him for a long moment. "I wouldn't say *that* too loudly," he said. "Even here…"

Jasmine met his eyes. "What *is* this place?"

"A place for secret deals and chitchat," Barker said. "Totally secure, of course. The officer in charge of the district is on the take. Nothing gets reported out of here unless the owner gives the word."

And I can believe as much or as little of that as I like, Jasmine thought. Corruption was epidemic in police states - people didn't rise to power in police states without a certain degree of self-interest - but she couldn't take it for granted. *This isn't a simple dinner between two crime lords.*

Barker looked back at her, evenly. "And who are you?"

"A friend," Jasmine said.

Haverford cleared his throat. "Do you still have that *in* with Director Mouganthu?"

"Yeah," Barker said, slowly. "I was saving it for a rainy day."

"We need an introduction," Haverford said. "A way of meeting him, perhaps, without being observed."

Barker's eyebrows crawled upwards. "I would have thought your name alone would be enough to get you a meeting."

"But not enough to be sure," Haverford said. "Can you arrange us a meeting?"

"It might be doable," Barker said, after a long moment. "But it wouldn't be easy."

"We can pay," Haverford said.

"I have no doubt of it," Barker said. His eyes rested on Jasmine for a long moment. She had no doubt that he knew that she was a soldier, even if he didn't know she was a marine. And *that* would be enough to tell him where she was from. "I'm sure Mouganthu will pay too."

He leaned forward. "I'll have to make some calls," he added. "Is there anything else you want?"

"Perhaps later," Haverford said. "And you only get paid afterwards."

Barker eyed him, sourly. "People should be more generous these days," he said. "How much are you offering?"

"Ten thousand Trade Federation credits," Haverford said. "But only afterwards."

"Twenty thousand," Barker said. They haggled backwards and forwards for several minutes before settling on thirteen thousand. "I need to make a couple of calls. Give me a moment."

He rose and hurried off. Jasmine watched him open the door and vanish, feeling a cold shiver running down her spine. Barker was clearly smart, smarter than he let on. He'd seen a man return from the dead, a man his government had *told* him was dead…and he knew, probably, that Jasmine had come from the Commonwealth. Admiral Singh would reward him beyond the dreams of avarice if he betrayed them…

She glanced at Haverford. He didn't seem concerned. Jasmine hoped he was right not to worry. Being dependent on a single man - someone she didn't know and didn't trust - didn't sit well with her. She didn't dare let herself be captured, not again. If Admiral Singh knew who she was, she would be assured of a very long and painful death.

Barker returned, looking surprisingly composed. "I called in a dozen favours," he said. "I'm to take you directly to Mouganthu Tower. Give me a moment to arrange an aircar."

Jasmine's eyes narrowed as Barker walked back out of the room. "What does he *do*?"

"He's a fixer," Haverford said. "He...organises meetings and contracts, all strictly on the down low. The type of man who can find a way to cut through a pile of red tape and get you whatever you want, for a price..."

"Of course," Jasmine said, slowly. She knew the type. "And he can get us an interview with Mouganthu? Immediately?"

"He has a good reputation," Haverford said. "Mouganthu probably thinks we're looking to make a commercial deal with him."

Barker opened the door. "Come on downstairs," he said. "The aircar is waiting."

Jasmine followed him, feeling tense. The passageway seemed to be closing in on her. It was a relief when they reached the bottom of the stairs. An aircar was sitting there, its console blinking with lights. She moved to take the controls, then stopped herself. Wolfbane - and all other heavily-populated planets - didn't allow aircar owners to fly their own craft. The ATC system would handle the flying.

She leaned back and forced herself to relax as the aircar rose into the air, listening as Haverford and Barker talked in quiet voices. They'd been friendly, she realised; friendly enough to tease each other gently. She wondered just how they'd become friends in the first place, then decided it didn't matter. She had quite a few friends - and a lover - who weren't marines.

Tryon City was ablaze with lights, from towering skyscrapers and corporate towers to the brooding shape of the fortress. The building had surprised her, when she'd first seen it. There was no way Admiral Singh or Governor Brown had known about giant force shields, not when they'd started work on the giant fortress. But she had to admit it made a certain kind of sense. The fortress was in the middle of a city. Anything powerful enough to vaporise it would kill hundreds of thousands of innocents too.

As long as one's enemies are squeamish, she thought coldly, *the fortress has a perfect defence.*

She felt a flicker of dark hatred as she peered towards the fortress. Admiral Singh had had an impressive record, once. Now she was a monster, as monstrous as the pirates or the terrorists she'd faced on a dozen worlds. It was clear, all too clear, that she'd turned Wolfbane into a police state, all the while using the planet's population as her human shields. Admiral Singh had to go. There was no way around it.

But getting into the fortress won't be easy, she told herself. *And the Admiral hasn't even returned to the planet.*

"That's Mouganthu Tower," Barker said, curtly. The aircar altered course, avoiding the massive fortress. Jasmine could practically *feel* anti-aircraft missiles tracking their every move, just *waiting* for them to do something stupid. Flying over the fortress would be the last mistake they ever made. "We'll be landing at the priority pad."

"Very good," Jasmine said.

Mouganthu Tower slowly came into view as her eyes adapted to the blazing lights. It was immense, easily one of the largest buildings within view...although tiny, compared to one of Earth's CityBlocks. She could easily imagine thousands of people living and working within the corporate microstate, isolated from the rest of the planet...it was Earth in miniature, once again.

And it wouldn't be a very comfortable environment for anyone who refused to toe the party line, she thought. *The entire tower is a corporate fiefdom.*

Jasmine sucked in her breath as she peered down. It was hard to be sure - her eyes weren't adapting well - but the tower seemed to be rising out of utter darkness. She could only make out a handful of lights. There would be slums down there, she was sure; places for the poor, hiding in the shadow of their betters. Wolfbane might have adapted better than most to the post-Empire universe, but there were still poor and helpless people on the surface. They didn't have a hope of finding jobs, let alone a better place to live or a chance for a brighter future.

She glanced at Haverford, noting his grim expression. He was good at hiding his feelings, but she could tell he was concerned. Making contact like this was always a risk. Mouganthu had an excellent motive to turn against Admiral Singh - they'd discussed it often enough, during the planning stages - yet Mouganthu himself might not agree with them. If they were wrong, they'd be trapped...

The aircar touched down. She gritted her teeth as a set of corporate guardsmen appeared from the shelter, weapons in hand. Barker opened the hatch and stepped out, keeping his hands visible at all times. The guards scanned him, patted him down and then motioned for Haverford and Jasmine to follow him out of the aircar. Their pat-down was professional, Jasmine noted. She couldn't help feeling that that was a good sign.

"Leave your weapons here," the guard ordered. He held out a secure box. "You can recover them when you return."

Jasmine hesitated - she'd rarely been unarmed since she'd reached adulthood - but she couldn't blame the guards for insisting. Haverford had already removed his pistol and dropped it in the box. Sighing, Jasmine followed suit. The guards checked the weapons, then motioned to the door. Barker led the way, confidently. He'd been here before.

The guards kept a wary eye on them as they made their way down the corridor and into a giant arboretum, crammed with trees. Jasmine looked back at them, thoughtfully. They were *very* professional; their eyes watching for threats, their hands hovering near their belts, ready to draw their shockrods or pistols. She didn't *think* they were ex-military, but they'd definitely had some training.

And they're presumably paid by the corporation, she thought. She'd encountered corporate security officers before, but they'd always been a very mixed bag. Some had fought well, some had folded when the going got tough, some had been little more than hired thugs. *Their loyalties lie with their paychecks.*

She blinked in surprise as she heard water trickling down from high overhead and splashing into a pool, crammed with golden fish. A small bridge crossed a tiny stream, leading into another copse of trees. The guards stopped, but motioned for the three of them to cross the bridge and enter the grove. Jasmine frowned, then stared as the trees parted, revealing a wooden desk. The arboretum wasn't outside the office, the arboretum *was* the office. She couldn't help feeling impressed as she took in the design. The desk looked as though it was growing out of the ground.

"Director Mouganthu," Barker said. His voice was very respectful. "Please allow me to introduce General Haverford, who was reported dead, and Jazz."

Mouganthu rose, slowly. He appeared to be about fifty years old, his brown hair slowly shading to grey. His face looked sagged, as if he couldn't be bothered either taking proper care of himself or getting cosmetic surgery. And yet, he held himself with a dignity that screamed *Old Money*. He was, as far as Wolfbane was concerned. Mouganthu Industries had been one of the original founding corporations, five hundred years ago. Jasmine's own family could count their history back a thousand years, but they'd never been so rich or well-connected. Mouganthu was a man who was used to power and wealth.

And Governor Brown was able to work him into a balanced system, Jasmine thought. She wished, suddenly, that she'd had a chance to meet him. *He must have been a very capable man.*

"General Haverford," Mouganthu said. His voice was cultured. He sounded almost as though he'd just stepped off a shuttle from Earth. "I attended your funeral."

He looked at Jasmine. "And you are?"

Jasmine took a step forward. It was time to gamble.

"I'm from the Commonwealth," she said. "And I come with a proposition."

CHAPTER TWENTY-SIX

If he was forced to be honest - which he was, in the privacy of his own head - Director Herman Mouganthu would have freely admitted that he didn't *like* Admiral Singh. Her burning ambitions had been easy to see, even when she'd been kowtowing to Governor Brown. Herman admired the sheer nerve she'd shown in taking control, after Governor Brown's unfortunate demise, but at the same time it worried him. Admiral Singh simply didn't know where to stop. Ambitious people rarely did.

It worried him, more than he cared to admit to anyone outside his tight-knit circle of corporate friends and allies. Ambition was not always a good thing. Someone might rise high and determine to rise still further, threatening the power structure the corporations had built. An ambitious man, all too aware that the decks were stacked against him, *might* become a useful asset - or a dangerous enemy. Herman had squashed any number of ambitious men in the past, knowing they represented a threat. He had very few qualms about squashing Admiral Singh too.

But it might be difficult, he thought, wryly. *She has a powerful force to protect her.*

He kept his face expressionless as he contemplated his visitors. Barker was a man who had carved out a niche for himself, a man who was content to allow himself to be used as long as he benefited from it. General Haverford - a man who'd been reported dead - had been loyal to Governor Brown, something that spoke in his favour. And the newcomer...she claimed to be from the Commonwealth. Haverford's presence suggested she was telling the truth.

The newcomer seemed inclined to wait for him to break the silence. She looked patient, as calm and composed as if she were waiting on a parade ground. There was none of the supplication he was used to seeing, none of the half-concealed desperation from men - or women - who needed his help. Indeed, she didn't even seem *aware* of her own femininity - or how it could be used to win his favour. She was either incredibly confident in herself, like one of the female directors who didn't *depend* on him, or she'd had some very good combat training. Herman was no expert - he had people for that - but he'd bet a sizable fortune that she was a soldier.

"You say you have a proposition for me," he said, studying the woman. She looked back at him evenly, something he found impressive. Very few women - or men - could meet his gaze. They were all too aware of how much power he possessed. "What do you have to offer?"

"An end to the war," the woman said. Her ID card said her name was Jasmine. Herman assumed it was a false name. "And one that leaves Wolfbane's social structure largely intact."

"I see," Herman said. She wasn't lying, he thought, but she wasn't being very forthcoming, either. He was fairly sure she wasn't a trained negotiator, let alone a diplomat. That made her an odd choice for diplomacy, unless something else was going on. The records his security staff had pulled from the orbital tower made it clear that Jasmine wasn't alone. "An interesting offer, to say the least."

He leaned forward, curious to see her reaction. But she showed no sign of concern.

"I'm a busy man," he said. His looming bulk normally intimidated people. He was torn between amusement and disappointment. "Shall we, as you say, cut to the chase? What are you offering?"

"The war ends," Jasmine said. "Wolfbane either joins the Commonwealth or remains outside it, but with full trading and emigration rights. The remainder of your…*empire*…gets the same offer."

"And Admiral Singh gets the chop, I assume," Herman said. "Or should we just send her into exile?"

"We want her removed from power," Jasmine said. "Anything beyond that is up to you."

"We *did* win an empire," Herman pointed out. "Why should we not *keep* it?"

Jasmine looked back at him, evenly. "And is it worth the cost?"

Touché, Herman thought.

He allowed a flicker of his annoyance to show. Governor Brown had convinced the corporations that a period of expansion and consolidation would put Wolfbane on a secure footing. But most of the worlds they'd invaded and occupied were liabilities, either bitterly resentful of losing their newly-won independence or simply lacking anything worth the effort of taking. Too many worlds required assistance to survive in the post-Empire universe, assistance that was a drain on Wolfbane's coffers. And the handful of worlds that *weren't* useless caused their own problems.

They want to be treated as equals, he thought, sourly. *And that threatens the balance of power.*

"Perhaps not," he conceded. "But tell me...how do we know you won't seek revenge for the war at some later date?"

"On one hand, we would let bygones be bygones," Jasmine said. "Governor Brown is already dead. Admiral Singh would be...removed. Beyond that...we wouldn't seek anything more than the evacuation of the occupied worlds and a handful of navigational treaties. There would be little to be gained by resuming the war at some later date."

She tilted her head, slightly. "And besides...what happens if Admiral Singh *wins* the war?"

Herman kept his face impassive, even though he knew it was a solid hit. The war had been a mistake, right from the start. He should never have agreed to support it. Defeat would mean the end of the world, as far as the corporations were concerned, but victory wouldn't be much better. Admiral Singh - or her successors - would have enough power and prestige to bring the corporations to heel. He had no doubt she'd do it, too. She couldn't stand the thought of anyone having enough power to weaken her, perhaps even to bring her down.

And yet, an armistice had problems too. The Commonwealth had advanced, leaving Wolfbane struggling to catch up. How long would it be before the Commonwealth came up with something completely new, something that shattered the balance of power? And how long would it be before Wolfbane became a backwater, as free movement took experienced and ambitious men and women away from their homeworld? The conscripted workers would want to go home, of course. Others, others who saw no reasonable way to build a career or a business of their own, would follow. Wolfbane would have to change if it wanted to attract and keep talent…

We could forbid people from leaving, he thought. *But that would cause problems too.*

He scowled. Emigration had served as an escape valve, once upon a time. There had always been a minority who hadn't been content to stay in their place, a minority who'd needed to be…*encouraged*…to leave. He hadn't begrudged them the cost of a starship ticket, either. It was far cheaper than putting down a riot - or an uprising. But now, the escape valve was closed and the pressure was starting to build. His security staff were reporting that more and more underground groups were springing into existence, despite the best efforts of the police.

"Very well," he said. "But tell me…why should we negotiate now?"

Jasmine's face didn't change. "Right now, you're in a position to bargain," she said. "You're strong enough to convince even our hard-liners that peace is better than war. That might change."

"It might," Herman agreed.

He leaned back, thinking hard. Admiral Singh had taken command of the fleet and left, going…somewhere. If she lost the battle, she might lose enough ships to ensure that the war was lost with them. There would be little room to bargain if the Commonwealth Navy attacked Wolfbane, either occupying the system or ravaging it from end to end. Losing the industrial nodes and cloudscoops would be enough to bring the entire planet to a screeching halt. Wolfbane would starve, even if the war ended immediately. There weren't *that* many algae farms on the planet. He doubted his subordinates would remain loyal if their families were starving.

"It might not change," he said, after a moment.

"Wars are fluid things," Jasmine said. She sounded as though she was speaking from experience. "They go backwards and forwards until one side gains a decisive advantage, then they end. Either the Commonwealth wins, in which case you'll no longer have any bargaining chips, or Admiral Singh wins, in which case you'll have to get used to having her boot on your neck for all eternity."

"She won't hesitate to crush you, when she thinks she can do it," Haverford put in. "You're the sole remaining threat to her power."

Herman conceded the point with a nod. Governor Brown had played the game. He'd understood that the corporations would nominate and patronise military officers, ensuring that no corporation - or governor - could gain a decisive military advantage. Admiral Singh had been far less tolerant, far less inclined to accept officers with divided loyalties. She'd purge as many of the corporate-backed officers as she could, if she ever had the chance. And she had thousands of loyalists of her own.

A civil war would be disastrous, he thought. *And yet, if we failed to remove her from power in a single stroke, we would have a civil war.*

He doubted he had enough officers under his control to carry out a coup. Admiral Singh had been careful, very careful. He only had one agent within the fortress, someone who wasn't in a position to stick a knife in Admiral Singh's back. If everything went as well as could be expected, he *might* manage to secure control of a handful of orbital fortresses...

...And then get his fortresses blown away by the navy.

"I will have to discuss it with others," he said, slowly. The corporations would have to move as a body. That wasn't going to be easy. Tallyman and Hernandez would probably cooperate, but Admiral Singh had been working hard to court both Straphang and Wu...both of whom had suffered badly during the recession. And the other six corporations had their own problems. "I can't do it alone."

Barker looked surprised, although he tried to hide it. Haverford seemed oddly amused. He'd know there were limits to corporate power, even though they were often hard to see. Hell, he'd *been* a client officer. Governor Brown had promoted him personally. And Jasmine showed no visible reaction. Herman wondered, absently, just what her story actually *was.* It was bound to be interesting.

"Time is not on your side," Jasmine warned. "If you could take over before Admiral Singh returned..."

Herman shook his head. His tactical staff had discussed all the options. Admiral Singh *had* to be killed - or at least trapped - or she'd have too many options for retaking the offensive and regaining control. He had no doubt she'd call down KEW strikes on the corporate towers if she felt she had no choice, despite the certainty of massive civilian casualties. Admiral Singh's security forces had demonstrated a frightening lack of concern for civilian lives over the past few months. Why would their ultimate superior feel any differently?

"She has to be trapped," Herman said. He had no idea *what* Admiral Singh would do, if she found Wolfbane closed to her, but he doubted it would be pleasant. "And everything would need to be planned carefully."

"That would run the risk of her catching on," Haverford warned.

"We know," Herman said, dryly. Admiral Singh had been trying to place agents within his tower for months. He hoped his security forces had managed to keep them all out, but he knew there was no way to be *sure*. A single agent in the wrong place would blow the entire secret wide open. Admiral Singh would certainly try to strike first if she believed she was under threat. "We will just have to live with it."

He met Jasmine's eyes. "Are you empowered to negotiate with us?"

"Within limits," Jasmine said. There was absolute assurance in her voice. "If you want something outside those limits, you'll have to wait for someone with more authority to arrive."

Herman nodded. That was fairly common - or it had been, before the Empire had collapsed into rubble. The negotiator would have considerable latitude, with orders to get the best deal he could…within the preset limits. And his signature would be considered legally binding, once the deal had been made. But anything outside the limits would need to be sent home for confirmation.

And that would take at least a couple of months, he thought.

"I'll discuss the matter with my fellows," he said. He'd have to hold a dinner party and invite everyone. Normally, it wouldn't be a problem; now, it might be seen as a sign of impending trouble. There was no way Admiral Singh's goons could miss all twelve corporate directors meeting in a single place. Thankfully, they'd probably be reluctant to take action while she was absent. "I trust you'll be attending?"

"I'll be happy to make my pitch to the group," Jasmine said. "But security is important."

Herman nodded. "You won't be introduced to anyone, apart from the directors," he said. He shot Barker a sidelong look. "Barker will ensure that you are fully briefed."

"It would be my pleasure," Barker said.

As long as you are paid, Herman finished, silently.

"You and your...*friends*...will be offered jobs within the tower," Herman added. "That will give you sufficient excuse to remain here."

And under my control, he thought.

Jasmine's eyes flickered, then narrowed. Herman wondered if she was *surprised* he knew she wasn't alone. It hadn't been *hard* to match her ID card to one issued to a group of newcomers, then to track their activity. They'd been given a number of very good job offers, but - so far - none of them had actually accepted. It was more revealing, perhaps, than she realised.

"Two of us will work here," Jasmine said. "The others will go... elsewhere."

Herman kept his face expressionless. He didn't *like* the thought of Commonwealth agents operating outside his control. He was unfortunately aware that their interests didn't match his. And yet, he couldn't stop them. Indeed, in some ways, it would be *better* if they didn't all work at his tower. The security forces would ask fewer questions if the agents were caught.

"Very well," he said. He tapped his console, ordering his secretary to make the arrangements. There were so many departments in the tower that no one would realise - at least for a while - that Jasmine and Haverford weren't doing any actual *work*. "Is there anything else I can offer you?"

"We may require money and ID cards," Jasmine said. She looked oddly annoyed, just for a second. She was clearly not someone who liked asking for charity. "We'll ask for anything else we need."

Or make contact with forgers, Herman guessed. There was a thriving black market trade in forged IDs, as well as everything else. His security staff kept an eye on that too. *And you'll probably try to make contact with other underground groups too.*

"Very good," he said, instead. "I'll arrange for a dinner party, probably in two days. By then, you should have received our job offer - just accept it. I'll see to it that you get invited up here when you arrive."

"Of course," Jasmine said.

"My staff will ensure that you are returned home," Herman added. It wouldn't be hard to put together a cover story. Jasmine and her friends were already being headhunted. "And I'll see you later."

Jasmine nodded. Herman couldn't help a flicker of genuine interest. She spoke to him as an equal. Very few people spoke to him on even terms.

"We'll be in touch," she said. "And thank you."

Herman watched them go, feeling cold. They'd *talked* about removing Admiral Singh, they'd planned a possible coup…but this was different. Admiral Singh would call them traitors, if she ever found out. She'd be right, too. Herman knew that not everyone on the Board of Directors would go along with him, if *they* found out too. He'd committed himself to jumping on a tiger and riding it to an unknown destination.

It would be easy, he knew, to alert the security forces. Jasmine and her comrades could be arrested or killed before they had a chance to burrow out of sight. Hell, he could just…*accidentally*…blow their aircar out of the sky. He'd never have to admit what he'd done…

But he knew, too, that this was their only chance. The war had to be stopped before it was too late. Victory or defeat, nothing would ever be the same again.

He tapped a switch, bringing up a holographic image of his great-great-grandfather. Hank Mouganthu had been a hard-boiled son of a bitch, according to his biographer. Herman had been astonished to discover that the first volume had been written when the old bastard had still been alive. Hank Mouganthu had even written the foreword, gleefully admitting that he'd worked his way to the top through ruthlessness, determination and a handful of knives planted in backs. Herman knew that Hank Mouganthu would never have tolerated Admiral Singh, not for a moment.

Unless he thought she could be seduced, he thought, wryly. Hank Mouganthu's womanising had been extraordinary. *But he would have seen her as a danger.*

He sighed. He'd sat on the fence long enough - they'd *all* sat on the fence too long. He knew, now, that the war could be ended on decent terms. And that was all that mattered.

And if this be treason, he thought wryly, *let us make the most of it.*

CHAPTER TWENTY-SEVEN

"I feel ridiculous," Jasmine muttered.

"You look exotic, My Lady," the maid said. "I'm sure you'll be the belle of the ball."

Jasmine gave her a nasty look, then peered at the hologram. The changing room didn't have anything as simple as *mirrors*, it seemed. Instead, hidden cameras watched her from all angles and projected a hologram she could manipulate at will. She could turn it around and inspect her back, if she wanted, just to make sure that everything was perfect. It made her feel ridiculous.

She sighed, inwardly. The blue dress was surprisingly demure - it flowed down from her neckline to her knees - but it was tight enough to make her feel self-conscious. Her olive skin, dark eyes and muscular arms *might* have given her an exotic air…she shook her head, hoping that her comrades never saw the images. It was hard to imagine anyone looking *less* like a marine.

There are Pathfinders who are supposed to blend in with the natives, she reminded herself, as the maid escorted her out of the chamber. *They manage it, somehow.*

She heard the party before she saw it, the sound of piano music drifting down the corridor and inviting her onwards. Hundreds of men in black suits drifted around the ballroom or leaned against the walls and chatted, accompanied by hundreds of women in gorgeous costumes. The men had it easy, she noted, as she descended the stairs into the ballroom. They all wore the same suits, although she couldn't help noticing that some of them were of a finer cut than others. The women wore different dresses, each one seemingly unique. She hadn't seen so much bare flesh on display in her entire life.

The music grew louder, inviting couples onto the dance floor. She accepted the offer of a dance from a handsome young man, allowing him to lead her through the steps of a very simple dance as she surveyed the room, silently matching names to faces. Most of the guests were minor industrialists, but a handful were important officials who had proven amiable to bribery. She did her best to listen to the chatter as the dance came to an end, then politely declined the offer of a second dance. The young man shrugged and hurried off.

She *was* attracting attention, she noted, as she made her way through the room. Eyes turned to follow her, some more knowingly than others. She had the uncomfortable feeling they *knew* she was faking, even if they didn't know *what* she was faking. She just didn't have the skill to blend in with the rich men and women, let alone pretend to be one of them. The dress she wore - the dress she'd been loaned - probably cost more than her entire salary. She doubted that anyone in the room really understood the cost of war…

Or what life is like, for those on the streets, she thought. *They're isolated from the real world.*

"The Admiral has offered us a set of contracts," a dark man was boasting. "Someone is going to have to rebuild those shipyards - why not us?"

"Someone will also have to refurbish them," his partner pointed out. "You can't do that without help."

A hand touched her arm. Jasmine frowned.

"Begging your pardon, My Lady," a waitress said. "Your presence is requested in the Green Room."

"Of course," Jasmine said. It was a relief. "Please, show me the way."

The Green Room, it seemed, was blue. *Everything* was blue, from the walls to the chairs and tables. Jasmine wondered, as she stepped inside, just who'd named it and why. Mouganthu himself sat at the table, flanked by two men she recognised from Haverford's detailed briefings. Director Louis Tallyman and Director Manual Hernandez, two men equal in power and wealth to Mouganthu. They looked very different - Tallyman was thin as a rake, while Hernandez was unbelievably fat - but their expressions were identical. She reminded herself, sharply, that she had to take them seriously. They hadn't been *guaranteed* their posts when they'd been born.

"Jasmine," Mouganthu said. His eyes focused on her face. "Please, be seated. My…friends…have some questions."

"Of course," Jasmine said. She sat, carefully focusing her mind. There were twelve major corporations in all. Winning over three of the directors - and convincing the others to stay on the sidelines - would be a major victory. "How may I be of service?"

"You can start by explaining what guarantees you propose to offer us," Tallyman said. "If, of course, the war comes to an end."

Jasmine smiled, then repeated the same speech she'd made to Mouganthu. The corporations would have their world and their society, if they wanted to keep it; they'd have access to the Commonwealth's growing markets and free trade zones. She suspected they'd have trouble competing in the long run - unless they made a number of changes, which would be just as troublesome - but they'd have a better chance of prosperity. Admiral Singh would certainly not allow them so much latitude. Jasmine dreaded to think what would happen if Admiral Singh tried to crack down on the corporations.

"A pretty speech," Tallyman said, when she'd finished. "And how do we know you'd keep your word?"

"We *are* your competition," Hernandez agreed.

"You would still have enough firepower to make restarting the war - or even locking you out of our markets - a dangerous gamble," Jasmine pointed out. "And even if we tried, we *couldn't* lock you out of our markets."

Assuming you have something we want to buy, she added, silently. *Adapting to new technology may be impossible for you.*

She leaned forward. "Right now, the situation is unstable," she warned. "If we crush your navy and occupy your system, we will not be so inclined to make you a good offer. On the other hand, if Admiral Singh wins the war, she's not going to be inclined to leave you in power either. You're a permanent threat to her position."

"All the more so because the bitch has nothing behind her, but naked force," Hernandez growled.

Jasmine nodded.

"You are asking us to take one hell of a gamble," Tallyman mused. "If we lose...we lose everything."

And that wouldn't be too bad, for the Commonwealth, Jasmine thought. *A civil war that saps your strength would be delightful.*

She kept her face expressionless. "You are already on course to lose everything," she said, bluntly. "There is no *victory* for you. You can accept a truce that allows you to keep *something* or try to deal with whichever side wins the war."

"Admiral Singh can be manipulated," Tallyman said.

"Not for long," Hernandez countered. "She won't hesitate to strike at us if she thinks she can get away with it."

"And she might, if she wins the war," Mouganthu said. "She'll have no trouble finding others to run our corporations."

"That'll degrade them," Tallyman insisted.

"We'll be dead," Hernandez said. "I don't think it will matter."

He shrugged. "All she has to do is start breaking up the corporations," he added. "It won't be long before there'll be no one left who can generate the power to challenge her."

"Perhaps," Tallyman said. He sneered at Jasmine. "It seems to me that we are being asked to commit suicide on your behalf."

"You have the choice between doing something now or being at the mercy of the victor," Jasmine countered. Tallyman *had* a valid point, she conceded. A failed coup would bring on a civil war at the worst possible time. "Doing nothing is *also* suicide."

"True," Hernandez agreed. "But what happens if all hell breaks loose?"

"It will break loose, sooner or later, whatever happens," Mouganthu said. "The security forces are provoking *real* trouble..."

"Which can be crushed," Tallyman snapped.

"But that will cost us," Mouganthu said.

He took a breath. "Let us be brutally honest," he said. "The war was a mistake. We have secured almost none of our gains *and* we have suffered a major defeat. Governor Brown is dead and his successor has none of his restraint - or understanding. Removing Admiral Singh and taking control of Wolfbane may the only chance we have to preserve *some* of our possessions."

"You believe we should do this," Tallyman said. It wasn't a question. "Do you think the risks can be handled?"

"There are always risks," Mouganthu said. "But yes, they can be handled."

"I hope you're right," Tallyman said. "I will need to consider it. Carefully."

He rose. "As do I," Hernandez said. He lumbered to his feet. "I'll be in touch."

Jasmine watched them go, feeling cold. If either of them wanted to betray her - and she knew it was one possible solution to their problems - it would be almost pathetically easy. A quick message to the security forces and all hell would break loose. Jasmine had formulated *some* escape and evasion plans over the last two days, but she knew they were far from perfect. And she didn't dare let herself be captured…

"I didn't expect an immediate commitment," Mouganthu said. "They'll need time to think."

Jasmine raised her eyebrows. "As do you?"

"Yes," Mouganthu said. "I cannot move alone."

"A lone man can assassinate a leader," Jasmine said. "But he cannot hope to manage what follows."

She sighed, inwardly. Carl Watson *had* assassinated Governor Brown. There was no doubt of that. She'd been there when the operation was planned. But Admiral Singh had managed to take control of Wolfbane in the aftermath, rather than civil war or a corporate-dominated government. Their next attempt had to be better planned.

"True," Mouganthu said. He looked up. "The next set of guests will be arriving in a minute."

Jasmine had never liked diplomats. In her experience, diplomats had a habit of surrendering hard-won military victories in exchange for worthless pieces of paper. And yet, as she chatted to dozens of corporate managers and their representatives, she found herself feeling a curious flicker of respect for the diplomats. Saying the same thing over and over again, often using the same words, was tedious beyond belief; shooting down the same objections, time and time again, was frustrating as hell. And yet, she had to carry on.

And so few of them are prepared to commit themselves, she thought, darkly. She knew why - she understood their position - but it was frustrating as hell. *They'd prefer to sit on the fence than do something bold.*

"I have to speak to a couple of people in private," Mouganthu said, after a particularly annoying pair of managers. "You can wait here."

Jasmine sighed, inwardly. Her head was starting to thump. Perhaps she'd discovered a new form of torture, particularly for young recruits who wanted to be *doing* something all the time. She wondered, idly, if she could convince her Drill Instructors to use diplomatic talks as a replacement for push-ups. But then, diplomatic talks probably wouldn't help to build muscles…

They'd help build endurance, she thought. *And that would be useful too.*

She shook her head. It *was* a silly thought.

Haverford entered, looking grim. Jasmine scowled at him. Technically, he'd had an invite to the party as well, but there was too great a chance of someone recognising him. Or so he'd claimed…Jasmine rather suspected he'd done it to get *out* of the party.

"They're not committing themselves," she said.

"I'd be more concerned if they were," Haverford said. He sat down and poured himself a glass of water. "They'll want to try to build an alliance before agreeing to anything."

Jasmine made a face. "And if they agree to betray us instead?"

"We'll cross that bridge when we come to it," Haverford said. He shrugged. "Right now, they won't *want* to betray us. They'll see the value of having underground links to the Commonwealth."

"I hope you're right," Jasmine said.

She rubbed her eyes. She'd spoken to over fifty people, fifty people who now knew there was a plot afoot. Mouganthu might believe they were all trustworthy - and Haverford backed him - but she wasn't so sure. The larger the group, the greater the chance that someone wouldn't see eye-to-eye with everyone else. And if that person reported to Admiral Singh, they were in deep trouble. Admiral Singh wasn't the sort of person to let grass grow under her feet. She'd strike first, as hard as she could.

"We will see," Haverford said. He grinned. "Do you want to dance?"

"We'd better wait for him," Jasmine said. "Do you know who he's meeting?"

Haverford shook his head. "Too many movers and shakers here," he said. "It could be anyone."

I don't get paid enough for this, Laura Blackstone thought sourly, as she made her way through the ballroom. *There isn't enough money on the entire planet to pay for this.*

She gritted her teeth and kept moving. Wearing a skirt so short that the slightest breeze would be all too revealing was bad enough, but the constant gropes and lewd invitations were worse. Her right breast was aching after one young man who'd had too much to drink had pinched it hard while his companions had laughed and cheered him on. She'd known better than to object, too. No one was invited to a party in Mouganthu Tower without being - at least - minor corporate royalty. She'd be on the streets in a heartbeat if anyone complained she hadn't showed a willingness to do whatever she was told. Thankfully, she'd been too busy serving drinks to be lured into one of the side rooms. She knew that some of the other maids weren't so lucky.

Perhaps I should just report him to my other superiors, she thought. *Or even forge a report.*

She knew she didn't dare do anything of the sort - Planetary Security would be less than amused with a false report - but the thought still made her smile. She'd been in the job for five months and the only thing that kept her going was the grim certainty that, sooner or later, she'd see something that could be reported to her bosses. The corporate world was *crammed* with backstabbers and traitors, men and women who would betray the entire planet if they somehow came out ahead. She might never be able to watch - let alone admit her involvement - when they were executed, but at least she'd *know*.

A hand slipped under her skirt and squeezed, hard. Laura plastered a smile on her face, not daring to look at her assailant. Dumping her tray of drinks on his head would be satisfying, but it would get her sacked too. Instead, she took a step forward, watching the older men and women as they flowed in and out of the ballroom. Her trained eye spotted a number of patterns that worried her. The movers and shakers were talking, privately. And *that* meant they were nervous.

She glanced towards a fat oaf who was laughing, braying like a drunken bull. His companion - a young woman from serious money - looked awkward, torn between embarrassment and horror. Laura would have felt sorry for her, if she hadn't known the poor girl had options. But… her companion wasn't even *trying* to hide his nature. None of his fellows tried to keep things private for long. She could have made a mint on the stock market, just from what she'd overhead, if she'd had the cash to start.

And the really big movers and shakers are all having private meetings, she thought, silently making a mental list. She *knew* it was something, even if she didn't know *what. And each of the meetings is being held separately.*

She composed her report to her superiors as she carried her empty tray back to the table. She didn't know what it meant, but *they'd* know. She'd love to be there when the stormtroopers raided the tower, arresting the corporate pigs and tossing them out of the windows. They were monsters, plain and simple; monsters who deserved to suffer for their crimes. She would enjoy watching them fall.

And if they get shot instead, she thought, *it will be almost as good.*

She sighed, inwardly, as she heard a crash. A half-drunk man had stumbled into a waitress, knocking her tray of drinks to the floor. Laura hurried over to help, cursing the man under her breath. Instead of helping - or fucking off - he was screaming at the girl, berating her for not keeping her balance. The fact he'd crashed into her didn't seem to have penetrated his mind. Laura eyed him as she arrived, fixing his face in her mind. Her superiors probably wouldn't notice - or care - if she named him as one of the co-conspirators.

And he'll be hung, she told herself. She picked up the pieces of glass carefully, cursing the corporations under her breath. They didn't *have* to make their glasses out of *glass. They could have used transparent aluminium instead.*

She finished scooping up the glass and hurried to the nearest door, nearly bumping into a tall woman in a blue dress. Laura's eyes widened as she caught a glimpse of her, unable to avoid noticing the exotic features. A relative, she assumed, or perhaps someone from one of the occupied worlds. She curtseyed hastily, then hurried onwards. The dress the stranger wore was definitely too costly to belong to a courtesan, yet she didn't hold herself like corporate royalty. Perhaps she was a bodyguard. She was certainly far too muscular for anyone's tastes. Laura pushed the thought aside. She doubted the newcomer was important.

Only a few hours left, she told herself. The party was due to end at one o'clock, but she knew it would probably last longer. She was going to be shattered in the morning. *And then I can make my report.*

CHAPTER TWENTY-EIGHT

"The Admiral left me in charge," Paula Bartholomew said. "You can make your report to me."

"An interesting twist on the orders she left *me*," Lieutenant Emma Foxglove sneered. "I was under the distinct impression that the council was meant to *share* authority."

Paula winced. She was ruefully aware that Admiral Singh *didn't* trust her completely - and really, why *should* she? Paula had betrayed both her former boss *and* the Commonwealth Navy. Admiral Singh might make use of her - Paula had nowhere else to go - but she wouldn't *trust* her. There was no way she'd leave Paula with supreme power when she had to leave.

"Yes, we are," she conceded. She'd never liked Emma and she had a feeling that Emma felt the same way about her. "And we are also meant to share intelligence."

"That would leave me with *less* intelligence," Emma jibed. She grinned at Paula's angry expression, then sobered. "I've had four intelligence agents reporting secret meetings between seven of the twelve corporate directors."

Paula's eyes narrowed. A single corporate director enjoyed wealth and power on a staggering scale. *Seven* of them were enough to challenge Admiral Singh herself, if they worked in unison. She knew from experience that it wouldn't be easy for *anyone* to get them to work together, but someone was clearly trying. And that meant...what?

Admiral Singh isn't here, she thought. In theory, she had authority over the remaining starships and the orbital defences. In practice...she wasn't sure she wanted to test her authority that far. *They might be plotting to move against her.*

She met Emma's eyes. "Do you know what they were saying?"

"No," Emma said. For once, she sounded completely serious. "I wasn't able to get an agent into any of their meeting rooms. They're locked down as tight as a princess's bedroom."

"Thank you for that image," Paula muttered. She cleared her throat. "The Admiral isn't here - and they're meeting. That *can't* be a coincidence."

"No," Emma agreed. "But we can't deal with them, either."

Paula nodded, grimly. Admiral Singh would have to authorise any move against the corporate directors. They were too important for *Paula* to challenge openly. She knew better than to try. Admiral Singh would happily throw her to the dogs if it was the only way to save her power base. It was what Paula would have done, if their positions were reversed. All she could do was wait and see what happened.

"Get more agents into their towers," she ordered. "And see if you can intercept their communications."

"Not going to happen," Emma said. "They've started a total hiring freeze. No one has been hired in the last week, not for the towers themselves. No catering staff, no waitresses, no whores...no one. I haven't been able to get anyone else through the defences."

Paula gave her a sharp look. "What about suborning someone who's already inside?"

"Not particularly easy," Emma admitted. "Corporate Security keeps a fairly solid lock on them at all times."

"Fuck," Paula said, quietly.

She looked down at her hands. She'd seen enough political, bureaucratic and corporate intrigue to be fairly sure they were only seeing the tip of the iceberg. The corporations had been improving their counter-surveillance techniques long before Governor Brown had taken control of Wolfbane and turned it into an empire. There was no way Emma could *guarantee* getting someone through the endless vetting and background checks, although that wouldn't stop Paula using it against Emma at some later date. She *had* to stay in Admiral Singh's good books.

"We do have a rough idea of who's involved," Emma offered. "At least, we know who went where and when."

Paula shook her head. It wouldn't be enough. It wouldn't be anything *like* enough to justify a crackdown, not against seven corporate directors. Even *trying* - without some very strong evidence - would probably spark off a civil war. Admiral Singh might come home to find that the entire system had turned into a battleground.

We could try to grab someone and make him talk, she thought. *But even that wouldn't be enough to head off a civil war.*

She looked up. "Perhaps we're approaching this from the wrong angle," she said. She was so desperate for ideas that she'd lower her defences and share her thoughts with her hated rival. "What if we start transferring military officers around at random?"

Emma looked doubtful. "It *would* break up any cells they'd happened to form," she said, slowly. "But it would also play merry hell with military efficiency. Admiral Singh would not be pleased."

"She wouldn't be pleased if we lost Wolfbane, either," Paula snapped. "What happens if they gain control of the high orbitals?"

"Then we're fucked," Emma said, practically. She shrugged. "Of course, they might hesitate to blow up the fortress from orbit. Their towers would be taken down too."

"Unless they evacuated them," Paula countered. "The towers aren't *necessary*, are they?"

"No," Emma said.

Paula rose and walked to the window. The sun was rising slowly, mocking her. She hadn't slept for nearly thirty hours. "Is there *anything* we can do?"

"We can tighten security," Emma said. "Put more guards on the streets, double or triple the patrols running through the sensitive zones..."

"That's not enough," Paula objected. "There *has* to be something more we can do."

She looked at the corporate towers, glinting under the rising sun. A small army of infantry would be enough to seal the towers off, then storm them. The corporate royalty wasn't really *necessary,* was it? She could have authority passed down to their juniors, to men and women who'd been held down by those with better breeding and family ties. She'd been one of them, once upon a time. They'd be forever grateful if they were given a chance to rise to the very highest levels.

But it would spark off a civil war, she thought, darkly. *And who knows who would come out on top*?

Her expression darkened as she peered at the streets. There were guardsmen clearly visible, marching up and down the road to remind the civilians that any unauthorised meetings would be brutally crushed. But who knew which guards were truly loyal to Admiral Singh? Far too many of them had ties to the corporations. There was no way to tell who was loyal and who would turn on her when his masters gave the orders.

"Tighten security," she ordered. "Get some additional security units onto each of the orbital fortresses, too. If they try to take over, they can be stopped."

"One hopes so," Emma agreed.

Paula scowled. Emma Foxglove had been with Admiral Singh since Corinthian. She had no ties to Wolfbane, nothing to interfere with her loyalties to her mistress. And yet, *could* she be trusted? Paula didn't know. Emma might just have ambitions of her own. Coming to think of it, Emma might easily think that *Paula* had ambitions too. And she'd be right.

"She'll be back soon," she said. They'd survived four weeks without Admiral Singh. So far, there hadn't been any open defiance. But that might be about to change. "And when she arrives, she can decide what to do next."

Assuming she wins, she thought. Judging by the suddenly sour look on Emma's face, she probably had the same thought. *Defeat might mean the end of everything.*

"Good," Emma said. "She can make the final call."

Jasmine hadn't been particularly surprised to discover that Wolfbane had *very* strict gun-control laws. Governments that suspected their populations might want to overthrow them were careful to make sure that weapons were kept out of civilian hands. She *also* hadn't been surprised to discover that there were hundreds of thousands of unlicensed weapons in the criminal underworld. The only people who ever really paid attention to gun-control laws were the type of people the government didn't need to worry about.

She studied the masked students as she talked them through using assault rifles. They were keen, but they knew nothing about using guns - or other weapons, for that matter. They'd learnt how to hide themselves a long time before she'd arrived - she gave them credit for that - but they were terrifyingly ignorant in plenty of other ways. They just didn't have the kind of experience she'd taken for granted.

But they didn't have good teachers, either, she thought. Her mask itched. She resisted the urge to remove it. *They had to catch up in a hurry.*

"Make sure you keep the safety on at all times, except when you're ready to fire," she ordered. The abandoned warehouse had been converted into a makeshift firing range, but she was grimly aware that *someone* would probably hear the gunshots. "Remember the three rules at all times."

She watched them work the unloaded guns for a long moment and sighed inwardly. They just didn't have time for anything more than a quick and dirty tutorial. The students would probably be swatted aside, if they went up against trained and experienced troops. Cold logic told her that it was necessary, but sentiment told her it was a waste. The young men and women in front of her had never had a real chance at life.

"Very good," she said. It was a lie. Her firearms instructor would have broken down crying if he'd seen some of her students, if he hadn't picked them up and physically removed them from his classroom. "Your cell leaders will be issued with ammunition. Make sure you keep it under very close guard."

She smiled as she led the way to the next set of tables. "You'll notice that almost everything here can be obtained easily," she said. She'd purchased it herself, just to be sure. In theory, everything was tightly rationed; in practice, the system was easy to beat. "You won't have any difficulty obtaining it for yourselves."

"That's cleaner," a student objected. "What's the point of it?"

"Simple," Jasmine said. "You turn it into explosive."

She talked them through the entire procedure, then distributed pages printed from *The Alchemist's Cookbook*. She'd been amused to discover copies of the text - banned almost everywhere - floating around the planetary datanet, as if the hacker community had amused itself by distributing them at random. The students would be arrested and jailed for life - or exiled - if they were caught with the text, but under the circumstances it didn't matter. Their captors would have some problems deciding just *what* charge to put on the official record.

"Be very careful when you do this," she said, after demonstrating several other possible techniques. Some of the students had practical experience in chemistry labs - or kitchens - but others were effectively virgins. "If something goes wrong, the results will be lethal."

The students nodded in unison. Jasmine wished, just for a moment, that she could see their faces. But she knew it wasn't possible. The student leadership had reinvented the cell structure, doing their level best to ensure that *no one* - not even themselves - knew *everyone* who was involved. Jasmine knew that *her* students would teach others...she just hoped they were careful. Turning household cleaner and bleach into explosive - and using it to power an IED - was extremely dangerous.

And some of the students will be extremely dangerous too, she thought. She'd heard stories about advisory teams who'd taught the locals how to fight, only to discover that the locals weren't inclined to be puppets. *The ones who survive their mistakes will learn from the experience.*

She scratched her itchy face as she finished the lecture. "Any questions?"

A young man stuck up his hand. "Is there anything we can do about riot gas?"

"It depends," Jasmine said. "A wet mask - even a cloth over your face - and goggles *might* provide some protection, if you're lucky. If the police start deploying gas that is absorbed into your skin, you're fucked unless you have protective gear."

"I thought there were drugs that helped with that," the student said.

"I don't know if you could get the *specific* drug you'd need," Jasmine said. "There are some standardised counter-gas injections, but they're not always effective. The policemen will have the specific counter-injection before they march out."

She sighed. "Next?"

A young woman coughed. "I saw a movie where a girl my size knocked out a man *his* size," she said, jabbing a pale finger at a male student who was large enough to pass for an artilleryman. "How did she do it?"

"She had the scriptwriter on her side," Jasmine said, wryly. The students chuckled. It was hard to be sure, but the girl looked a little put out. "I'm serious - someone scripted that fight in great detail."

The girl's masked face leaned forward. "What do you mean?"

Jasmine silently damned scriptwriters and flick producers under her breath. "As a general rule, very few people understand *real* violence," she said. "The first blow is often the last, if delivered with enough force. Even when it isn't, the force might be enough to disorient you and ensure that the *second* blow is the last. And the average woman is generally weaker than the average man. In the real world, without rules or a friendly scriptwriter, he'll kick her ass soundly. It's as simple as that."

She took a breath. "It takes years of training for someone my size to fight effectively," she added. "I was taught to fight dirty, to go for the balls or the throat or anywhere that might increase the power of my blows. And I tell you that, if I had to fight a man with the same training, he'd beat me like a drum.

"If you have a chance to run, take it. If you have to fight, go for the balls or somewhere vulnerable and *don't* hold back. Take him down. Once you start fighting, you have to finish it or be finished."

The young woman didn't look convinced, judging by her stance. Jasmine knew she probably *wouldn't* be convinced until she encountered real violence for herself. She'd probably go into the fight, certain she could win…

"It's time to go," Jasmine said. "Pass on what I taught you - and be careful."

She turned on her heel and hurried out of the warehouse, scooping up her bag as she passed through the door and into the alleyway. Stewart was waiting for her, as agreed; she dumped the mask into the bag, then pulled her overalls off to reveal an engineering uniform. It had been hot, wearing two layers, but necessary. She smoothed down her hair, closed the bag and followed him onto the street. There was nothing left behind to connect her with the student rebels.

"No enemy movements," Stewart muttered. "We seem to have gotten lucky."

Jasmine shrugged. Three weeks on Wolfbane, three weeks spent training the locals and negotiating with corporate directors…it made her want something to happen. The longer they remained on the planet, the greater the chance of being detected. Even now, with Mouganthu helping to cover for them, the odds of being detected were still growing higher and higher. The enemy had clearly taken steps of their own to watch for trouble.

But they haven't stumbled across us yet, she thought. *And it won't be long before the Colonel arrives.*

She kept her concerns to herself as they walked past a giant marble statue of the Childe Roland. Jasmine had never met the young Emperor - she had no idea what had happened to him, either - but she doubted the sixteen-year-old had been anything like as mature as his statue suggested. He looked more like a dignified thirty-year-old man than a teenager.

"We'll be going back to the tower tonight," she said. It was mid-afternoon by her watch, although it felt later. "Perhaps he'll have gotten further."

"Perhaps," Stewart said. "Or perhaps he's setting us up."

They walked into the skyscraper and climbed the stairs, level by level. Jasmine was glad of the exercise, even though it was alarmingly clear that hardly anyone *else* bothered to use the stairs. The steps were covered in dust. She led the way through the door as they reached their level, then pressed her ID card against the scanner. The door clicked open, inviting them inside.

"Honey, we're home," Stewart called.

Meade was sitting on the sofa in her underwear, a computer balanced on her lap. Jasmine opened her mouth, then closed it again. There was no point in telling Meade off, not when she'd been digging into the enemy computer network. She'd already isolated the apartment from the local surveillance network, although Jasmine knew better than to take that for granted. The enemy might easily have set up another network without linking it to the datanet.

They'd still have too much data to sort through in a hurry, she told herself. *As long as we are careful, we should be fine.*

"I got a link into the communications grid," Meade said. She looked up, her eyes alight with mischief. "We can get a message out, if there's anyone there to hear it."

"Good," Jasmine said. They'd have to signal the Colonel, once he arrived. "Can they talk back to us?"

"Probably," Meade said. She *sounded* confident. "We'd just have to tell them where to send the message. I've got a tap into a pre-established data address, but I don't know how secure it is."

Her computer bleeped. "Hang on."

Jasmine frowned. Meade sounded…worried.

"What?"

"One of my flags just sounded the alert," Meade said. She bent her head over the console, fingers flying over the keyboard. "I think…"

She broke off. Jasmine reached for her pistol. If they were about to be attacked, she needed to be ready to fight. "*What*?"

Meade looked up. "Admiral Singh has returned," she said. Her face was very pale. "I'm…I'm afraid it's bad news."

CHAPTER TWENTY-NINE

"We're picking up a standard welcoming message," Julia reported. "They're welcoming you home."

Rani relaxed, slightly, as the verification codes popped up in front of her. Leaving Wolfbane had been a calculated risk. There had always been the possibility that her enemies would take control of the planet in her absence or that one of her trusted subordinates - insofar as she *had* trusted subordinates - would take advantage of the opportunity to mount a coup. But it looked as though no one had tried anything stupid while she was gone. She couldn't help feeling relieved.

"Inform them of our victory," she ordered. She'd had plenty of time to prepare a bulletin that hit the right notes. The Commonwealth Navy had been routed after a long battle. A number of heroic officers - including Captain Brookes - had been killed, but the enemy had been defeated. And Rani was the sole architect of the victory. "Transmit the signal over the entire system."

"Aye, Admiral," Julia said.

"And then inform the fortress that I will be landing as soon as possible," Rani added. "I'll be meeting with my officers to discuss future offensives into enemy space."

She leaned back in her chair, allowing herself a moment of wry satisfaction. There was no longer any need to be diplomatic. Victory had vindicated her, vindicated her control over Wolfbane and its growing empire. The Commonwealth had taken a beating. It would take time for the enemy to recover and by then her forces would be attacking Avalon itself. She'd win the war...

...And then she'd have all the time she needed to stamp her will on Wolfbane itself.

"It doesn't look good, Jazz," Meade said.

Jasmine paced the apartment. "What do you have?"

"The Wolves intercepted our forces as they attacked Titlark," Meade said. She looked up, cocking one eyebrow. "Our forces were attacking Titlark?"

"Need-to-know," Jasmine said. She and the other marines were the only ones who knew that *Thule* had been a decoy. "What happened?"

"They kicked our ass," Meade said. "Admiral Singh's after-action report makes it clear that they booted us back out of the system, in pieces. We lost the battle."

Jasmine sucked in her breath. Mandy - and Colonel Stalker - had been on those ships. Were they dead? Or were they recuperating, trying to decide what to do next? Jasmine had no doubt that Colonel Stalker would want to resume the offensive as soon as possible...but could he? The fleet might have been hammered so badly that the survivors *had* to return to the Commonwealth. Admiral Singh had certainly felt secure enough to bring the fleet home.

Although she'd want to gloat over her victory, Jasmine thought. *And make sure her subordinates don't have enough time to start plotting against her.*

She turned to look at Meade. "Are they telling the truth?"

"I'm not sure," Meade said. She paused. "I'm running verification programs against their reports, Jazz, but they've had plenty of time to fake things. We might not be able to pick up a hoax before it's too late."

Jasmine nodded. Admiral Singh had ample incentive to claim she'd won, *whatever* had happened. But Admiral Singh *also* knew that her ships were riddled with spies. A lie - or even a minor exaggeration - would be detected, sooner rather than later. She had a great deal to lose if she chose to lie blatantly, didn't she? The corporate directors would not be impressed.

"The programs haven't picked up any obvious glitches," Meade said. "It still doesn't prove anything, but..."

"I know," Jasmine said. Given time, someone could easily put together a false narrative and promote it to the universe. The Empire's media complex had specialised in turning defeats into victories, just by making sure that no disagreeing viewpoints were ever heard. It would be relatively easy to ensure that nothing got through that called the story into question... but not here. "We have to assume the worst."

She poured herself a cup of coffee as she thought, fast. Admiral Singh had scored a major victory. Indeed, she'd scored a bigger victory than she knew. Jasmine had to assume that the plan to strike at Wolfbane itself had been delayed, perhaps cancelled altogether. And if that were the case, what then? Should they try to sneak off the planet before it was too late or continue with the original plan, minus the attacking fleet?

Too many people know we're here, she thought. She was fairly sure that Mouganthu was the only director who knew their precise location, but she didn't dare count on it. *If they choose to back Admiral Singh instead...*

It would be fairly easy to vanish, she thought. Wolfbane had an extensive criminal underground and an entire population of unregistered people. The six of them could go underground and hide, or try to purchase passage off-world. But that would mean abandoning their corporate allies and all hope of winning the war. Admiral Singh, she was sure, would use the victory as an excuse for a clampdown. Her enemies might not be able to muster the power to stop her before it was too late.

"The verification programs still haven't found any glitches," Meade said. "They're even showing footage from the battle itself."

Jasmine felt her heart sink. Faking *that* was risky. There was always someone ready to point out the smallest glitch, the smallest flaw in the footage that would allow them to unravel the narrative and brand it a fake. That they hadn't...Admiral Singh had either won a great victory or she was very confident in her fake. Somehow, Jasmine doubted it was the latter.

The door opened. Stewart entered the apartment.

"It's on all the news channels," he said. Jasmine didn't have to ask *what* was on all the channels. "Apparently, there's going to be a street party."

"Lots of parties," Meade agreed. "Invitations are flying around like flies on shit."

Jasmine rubbed her eyes as she sipped her coffee. There was no point in trying to deny the truth any longer. The original plan had failed spectacularly. Titlark might be devastated - the reports hadn't said anything about what had happened to the base, which made her suspect Mandy had landed a number of devastating blows - but the Commonwealth Navy had been defeated. And *that* meant that they were on their own.

"Contact Mouganthu," she said. "Tell him we need to meet."

"He might not want to meet with us," Stewart warned.

"It's possible," Jasmine agreed.

She put her cup down on the sideboard, gently. Mouganthu hadn't known about the planned attack on Wolfbane. Jasmine had been careful not to even *hint* at the possibility. Logically, nothing had changed… apart from Admiral Singh scoring a decisive victory. Perhaps Mouganthu would prefer to pull in his horns and wait to see what happened before recommitting himself. And if that happened…

We might need to nudge him along, she thought. *That* would be dangerous. Mouganthu was no fool, whatever else he was. *And if we can't do that, we might have to vanish completely.*

"Thomas, get ready to vacate the apartment," she said. Thankfully, they'd had enough time to set up a couple of safe houses that weren't - as far as she knew - on anyone's list. "If we have to go underground, we'll go underground."

She looked at Meade. "See what else you can draw out of the datanet," she added. "And look for any flaws in their story."

"Teach your mother to suck eggs," Meade said rudely. "I know what I'm doing."

"Glad to hear it," Jasmine said. "And make sure you're ready to leave at a moment's notice too."

"Welcome home, Admiral," Paula said. "And congratulations."

Rani nodded. Paula had arranged a big reception for her, including a welcoming committee and a planned dinner for the movers and shakers. Rani had enjoyed the welcome more than she'd expected, although she wasn't looking forward to the dinner. Gloating over her victory was fun - she hadn't had an unambiguous victory for a long time - but she needed to move to capitalise on her victory before it was too late. Her enemies wouldn't stay quiet for long.

"Thank you," she said. "How are the people taking it?"

"There are spontaneous victory parties and parades all over the planet," Emma Foxglove told her. "All genuine, of course."

"Of course," Rani echoed. She strode to the window and peered out. Throngs of people were dancing in the streets below. "And the bad news?"

Paula hesitated. "There's...*something* going on, Admiral," she warned. "It may be troublesome."

Rani was almost relieved. Silence did not, in her experience, mean safety. It generally meant that someone was plotting something, someone who hadn't been noticed by her security forces. Indeed, given just how many plots her security forces had broken up - and how many subversives had been arrested - she feared that the survivors had learnt how to keep themselves unnoticed. It was their only hope of remaining hidden long enough to strike.

"I see," she said. "Details?"

She listened, coldly, as Paula stumbled through an explanation. Meetings between corporate directors, all held under tight security. Rumours of subversives being trained in military tactics and armed... armed by whom? The arrest of a handful of ex-students who'd confessed to downloading terrorism and insurgency manuals and trying to learn from them...even a handful of policemen being arrested and executed for selling weapons and protective gear to subversives. It all added up to a deadly plot.

And client officers having more and more meetings with their handlers, she thought, coldly. *They're plotting something.*

"I had extra troops sent to the orbital fortresses," Paula finished. "But our attempts to raise new units have been hampered. We don't know who we can trust."

"That has always been true," Rani said. She lifted her eyes, picking out the corporate towers against the skyline. "They're plotting *something*."

She cursed the corporations under her breath, savagely. Didn't they realise she'd just won a great victory? The way to Avalon lay open, if she had time to muster her forces and take advantage of it. She couldn't stop *now*. And yet, the corporations feared her. They'd be concerned about just *how* she'd use her victory. Given time, they'd find a way to strike at her from a distance…

I can't afford to give them time, she thought. *I have a window of opportunity and I intend to use it.*

"That is my read on the situation," Emma agreed. "I do have a number of potential suspects on the list. We could take them out now and delay their plans…"

Rani shook her head. "There's no point in going after the weeds," she said. "We have to deal with the main threat."

Paula started. "Admiral, I have to warn you…"

"…That it will cause economic trouble?" Rani finished. "Yes, it will. But we have to cut the head off the snake."

She closed her eyes for a long moment, recalling the reports she'd read during the slow approach to Wolfbane. The industrial nodes had stockpiled thousands of missiles, ranging from conventional warheads to hundreds of the newer designs. Rani knew from bitter experience that consumption was *always* greater than predicted - her squadrons had practically shot themselves dry during the Battle of Titlark - but there should be enough weapons on hand to allow her to hammer the Commonwealth Navy a second time. She could tolerate a short period of economic disruption.

"Emma, put together an operation," Rani ordered. "There are two targets - the corporate towers and the industrial nodes. I want them both secured, with their inhabitants held prisoner. Those who are willing to work for us will be rewarded, those who are not will be…*discarded*."

"Mouganthu has announced a party for tomorrow evening," Emma said. "I believe that most of the corporate directors will be there. If we strike there first, before anywhere else, we'd have them all in the bag. We'd certainly block any attempt to strike at us or launch a counter-offensive."

"Particularly as they're the conspirators," Paula added. "The remaining five directors appear to be sitting on the fence."

Rani had her doubts. Mouganthu and his ilk had *never* liked her. Even Wu and Straphang would replace her in a heartbeat, if they thought they could get away with it. But picking a fight with all twelve directors at once was asking for trouble. If the five fence-sitters *stayed* on the fence, she'd leave them alone for the moment. They could be rounded up and their corporations broken later.

And once the corporations are broken up, they won't be able to challenge me any longer, she thought. *And they may even start innovating again.*

"Put the operation together," she ordered. "Mouganthu Tower is to be targeted first, followed by the remaining towers. Make sure that all communications are jammed."

She paused, contemplatively. "And warn the troops to *try* to take prisoners," she added. "I want the directors and their families alive."

"Of course," Emma said. "It's astonishing how cooperative people become when you hold their families prisoner."

Rani nodded, feeling…odd. When had *she* resorted to hostage-taking? Holding partners and children hostage had always seemed wrong. But now…she sighed, inwardly. She did what she needed to do to make sure she didn't lose power and die. And if that meant taking hostages and being ready to kill them…

I do what I have to do, she thought. *And that's all there is to it.*

"Admiral Howarth will remain in command of the fleet," she added. She was tempted to move operations back to her battleship, but she knew that would be an admission of weakness. Besides, the fortress was still secure. "The crew is having some well-deserved leave."

Emma looked concerned. "Admiral, is it *wise* to have the crew on leave?"

"*Some* of the crew on leave," Rani corrected. She shrugged. Emma had a point, but *Rani* needed to consider the morale issue. Her crewmen had won a great victory. Surely they deserved to join the street parties, too. "Wise or not, we have no choice."

She turned away from the window. "We have an opportunity to strike now," she said. "I do not intend to waste it."

"Aye, Admiral," Emma said.

Rani nodded. Emma would do as she was told. She'd never liked the corporate directors, let alone their habit of conducting business under tight security. Paula didn't seem so enthused, but Rani knew she understood. Besides, the corporations were her enemies. She simply wasn't liked or trusted outside Rani's inner circle.

And afterwards, she can help break up the corporations into more manageable entities, she thought. *It will give her a chance to broaden her mind.*

It was astonishing, Jasmine noted as she made her way down the street, just how infectious a party could become. Street vendors were giving away alcohol and snacks, music was blaring from overhead speakers...even the policemen were joining in the dancing. Spacers were swaggering down the streets, girls on their arms...she could see happy couples in the alleyways, too excited or too drunk to care that they were in public. Older men and women were shaking their heads in amusement, while children ran freely through the crowds, chased by their parents.

She listened carefully as the spacers bragged to everyone within hearing range. The stories were all wildly exaggerated - spacers were the same everywhere - but there was an unmistakable ring of truth in their words. Admiral Singh could *not* have convinced so many men to lie, let alone kept them reciting the same story. No, there *had* been a battle and the Wolves had won. There was a honest jubilation in their storytelling that erased her last remaining doubts. The Wolves had won a major battle.

A hand grabbed her arm. "Hey," a half-drunk spacer said. His breath smelt of cheap rotgut and lighter fluid. She couldn't help thinking of some of the improvised explosives she'd been teaching the students to make. "You want to come celebrate?"

He tugged her towards the alley. Jasmine considered allowing him to pull her into the darkness, then snapping his neck and vanishing before anyone realised he was dead. It would be easy, yet it would also be far too revealing. The policemen might turn a blind eye to pickpockets and sneak thieves working the crowd - Wolfbane's police forces were far more concerned with political subversion - but she doubted they'd ignore a murder. And if she left any clues behind, they'd track her down easily.

She yanked her hand free, then darted into a mass of dancers before the drunkard realised that she'd gone. He'd have no trouble finding *someone* willing, she thought, as she slipped through the crowd and out onto the pavement. The local women seemed to be out in force, giving themselves to the victors. Jasmine snorted as she passed a hot-dog stand - the stench of half-cooked meat assaulted her nostrils - and hurried down the street. A handful of students could be seen in the distance, handing out subversive pamphlets. Jasmine hoped they had the sense to vanish when the policemen came after them.

Back to the apartment, she told herself, firmly. She didn't think there was anything to be gained by working the crowd any further. The enemy victory had been confirmed. *And then start planning.*

She glanced up as another flight of shuttles roared overhead. Admiral Singh appeared to be giving *all* of her crews shore leave. Jasmine wished she'd known in advance, if only because there might have been a way to take advantage of it. Undermanned ships might be easy targets. But she hadn't…

We've had a setback, she conceded, privately. There was no point in trying to hide from the truth. *But it isn't going to stop us.*

CHAPTER THIRTY

"No," Herman Mouganthu said. "This is *not* good news."

"She won a *real* victory," Tallyman agreed. "She's now in a very strong position."

Herman nodded, curtly. He'd thought that outright - unambiguous - military victories were a thing of the past. The Commonwealth-Wolfbane War had certainly had its fair share of *ambiguous* victories, where one side captured a star system but the other side managed to retreat with most of its mobile firepower. It was just too hard, he'd been told, to force the enemy to fight unless one attacked a target the enemy *had* to defend. The enemy had too many options to evade an unpromising engagement.

But Admiral Singh *had* won an unambiguous victory. His tactical analysts all agreed that she'd given the Commonwealth a *very* bloody nose. The Commonwealth Navy would need time to replenish its losses and revise its tactics, particularly in the face of newer weapons and defensive systems. Hell, the analysts had made it clear that enemy morale was likely to suffer too. They'd always enjoyed a major tech advantage, even when they hadn't had the numbers. That advantage was now gone.

"She might win the war," Hernandez agreed. "And then...where will *we* be?"

"In deep shit," Herman said. An Admiral Singh who was constrained by necessity was one thing - she *needed* the corporations, no matter how much she loathed them - but one who had a free hand was quite another. "I don't believe that anything has really changed."

"Except she's won a major engagement," Tallyman pointed out. "She now has the prestige to wage war on us."

"Suicide," Hernandez grumbled. "She'd have to be mad."

"She cannot be blind to our efforts," Herman countered. His staff had done everything they could to conceal his preparations, but he had no doubt that far too much had leaked. Admiral Singh knew they were planning something, even if she didn't know what. "We cannot afford to delay."

"She's on the ground," Hernandez said. "We can get to her."

"If we can take the fortress," Tallyman objected. "If she remains in power, she can call down doom on us."

"Then we need to prepare to move now," Herman said. He glanced at his watch. "We'll speak to the others as the evening wears on."

"Of course," Hernandez agreed. "And then…when do we move?"

"As soon as we can," Herman said. It would be a gamble. He'd hoped for longer before the balloon went up. "And once we start, we can't stop."

Hernandez snorted. "We've already compromised ourselves, in her eyes," he said. "I doubt she would care if we stopped now."

"No," Tallyman agreed. "We're committed."

Jasmine kept her expression blank as she wandered through the ballroom, sipping her wine and speaking briefly to a handful of guests. The food was expensive, the wine was literally irreplaceable now that Earth had been scorched clean of life…and yet, it felt like she was attending a funeral rather than a party. There was none of the sheer *zest* she'd seen on the streets, none of the willingness to throw off dignity and party, not even the leering looks that trailed after every half-way attractive woman…the movers and shakers of Wolfbane didn't seem to take *any* delight in their leader's victory. Jasmine couldn't help thinking that it probably wouldn't please Admiral Singh at all.

But then, Admiral Singh's victory weakens their position, she thought. *They know it too.*

She allowed her eyes to roam the ballroom, silently gauging opinion. The older men and women were talking together in hushed voices, allowing the youngsters to dominate the dance floor. But even the young men looked crushed by events, moving around on the floor as if they were automatons or zombies. The young women looked like flowers, yet their faces were pale and wan. Their expensive dresses were wasted. The only people who looked to be enjoying themselves were the children, too young to understand what was really going on…and yet, even *they* were quiet. They could pick up on the sombre mood even if they didn't know *precisely* what was going on.

Poor kids, she thought. Their parents had spoilt them rotten. *They don't have a hope.*

She shook her head as a trio of young boys - they couldn't be older than seven - ran past her, leaving a set of tired-looking nannies in their wake. Jasmine turned away and walked over to the giant window, peering over the city. Hundreds of shuttles and aircars were flying around, their lights clearly visible as they rose and fell. Admiral Singh was bringing down nearly two-thirds of her crew to join the parties, she'd heard. Oddly, that made Jasmine think better of her enemy. A *real* sadist would deny her crew shore leave, even after their great victory.

But it works in her favour, she reminded herself. *Everyone knows the victory is real, now.*

A maid touched her arm. "My Lady," she said. "Your presence is requested."

Jasmine nodded, curtly. She'd been expecting the summons all evening. Mouganthu and his allies - and cronies - had been meeting for hours, no doubt trying to decide what they should do in response to Admiral Singh's victory. They were committed, Jasmine had argued, but she wasn't sure she'd convinced everyone. Too many of the corporate directors and their allies were used to living in a universe that sheltered them from the consequences of their own mistakes. Governor Brown might have smiled and said 'boys will be boys.' Admiral Singh was unlikely to be so forgiving.

She turned and headed towards the door, silently glad she'd thought to wear something a little more practical. The skin-tight suit showed off her curves to an extraordinary degree, but at least it covered her. And she'd been able to stick a small pistol in her handbag. It made her feel better, even though she was sure that she wouldn't be able to escape alive if

Mouganthu decided to turn on them. But at least she could make him pay for his treachery.

"Hey," a child shouted. "Look!"

Jasmine turned as she reached the door. A shuttle was hovering beside the tower, far too *close* to the tower. She tensed, one hand digging into her handbag, as a wave of force slammed into the windows and blew them inwards. Screams echoed through the ballroom as pieces of flying debris found targets, followed by crashing sounds as black-clad men plunged through the window and landed on the floor.

An amplified voice boomed through the air. "GET DOWN ON THE GROUND! HANDS BEHIND YOUR HEADS!"

Jasmine turned and ran down the corridor as she heard the sound of more windows shattering, followed by stunners being fired. Someone had probably offered resistance…or maybe the policemen had just decided to stun the aristocrats anyway. She'd seen policemen on corrupt worlds come to resent their masters, eventually turning on them or merely looking the other way when the lynch mobs arrived. Not that it mattered, she told herself. The police wouldn't have raided Mouganthu Tower without Admiral Singh's permission.

The building shook as she reached the door. Alarms were going off now, sounding oddly muted. Someone had clearly hacked the tower's defences - or worse. The automated air defence systems would have shot down the police shuttles, if they hadn't been taken offline or sabotaged. Mouganthu had rats in his tower…she shook her head in annoyance. There would be time to think about that later.

She threw the door open. Mouganthu was standing, staring around wildly; there was no sign of anyone else, not even his secretaries or aides. She hoped the other corporate directors had had a chance to escape before the police had launched their raid…by now, they'd be installing a ring of steel around the tower, just to make sure that no one could get out without being captured. And then they'd search the tower from top to bottom. She had to get out before the ring of steel was firmly in place.

"This way," she snapped. She keyed her wristcom, sending Stewart and Haverford instructions to run. Mouganthu *had* to be kept alive. His survival was now her priority. "Come on!"

"There's an emergency shaft to the bottom," Mouganthu said. He started towards a painting that covered half the wall. "This way..."

"They'll be watching it," Jasmine snapped. She'd seen enough of the local police forces to know they were thugs, but reasonably well-trained thugs. Cutting off the obvious line of retreat would be second nature to them. "This way!"

Her wristcom bleeped. Stewart and Haverford were making their way out of the building - she hoped, grimly, that they'd have the sense to go to ground afterwards. God alone knew where *else* was being targeted. Admiral Singh was almost certainly going after *all* the corporate directors...in hindsight, Jasmine wondered if the shuttles had brought down troops instead of spacers going on leave.

It doesn't matter now, she told herself, firmly. *Later.*

She grabbed Mouganthu's hand. He was trembling like a leaf. Jasmine wasn't surprised. He might be a corporate shark, but he'd never seen real combat. He'd never faced death or killed a man...he'd never even issued *orders* to kill a man. She yanked him forward, heading for the servants entrance. Hopefully, the hidden passageways wouldn't be closed so quickly...

And if they are, she thought as she drew her pistol, *I can't let them take either of us alive.*

Captain Joshua Forster shook his head in disbelief as he strode down the ramp, through the shattered window and into the ballroom. This...*this*... was how the corporate directors and their cronies lived? Everything, absolutely everything, smacked of unimaginable wealth and power. The food on the table, the dresses worn by the women, the scantily-clad waitresses and maids...the wisps of silk one young woman wore had probably cost more than his entire salary. And yet...

A young man stared at him, staggering to his feet. "Do you know who I am? You can't treat us like this..."

Joshua shoved his shockrod into the young man's chest and triggered it. The young man doubled over, screaming in pain. Joshua smirked as his victim crashed to the floor, his entire body twitching helplessly. A kick in the groin would probably have been kinder. He briefly considered stunning the asshole, but decided that would be *too* kind. He'd seen too many women trashed by aristocratic scum like this shithead to feel any mercy.

His gaze swept the room, alighting on a handful of women. Their dresses were in tatters, falling off…it was a shame, almost, that his superiors had made it clear that none of the aristocrats were to be harmed more than strictly necessary. Shocking a loudmouthed fool was one thing, molesting a woman was quite another. He shrugged as he looked away, hunting for a particular person. Whoever captured Herman Mouganthu would be promoted on the spot. But there was no sign of him.

"Cuff them," he ordered. He doubted his men had anything to fear from the aristos - they were too stunned to offer any real resistance - but it would make their new position clear to them. They were prisoners now, not the lords and masters of all they surveyed. "And find Mouganthu!"

He peered at the faces, silently matching them to the files. There would be someone who knew everyone, someone who could be…*convinced*…to talk…ah.

A dark-skinned man stared at him as Joshua stomped over, trying to look defiant. The act would have been convincing, if his hands hadn't been shaking so badly. Joshua lifted his shockrod, then pointed it at the woman lying next to the man. His wife? His daughter? His partner or lover or whore? It didn't matter. The man's flinch was enough to tell him that he cared for the bitch.

"I want Mouganthu," he said, sharply. He pushed as much naked menace into his tone as he could. "Where *is* he?"

"I don't know," the man said. His eyes were flickering between Joshua and the woman. "I don't know."

He was lying. It wasn't very convincing. Joshua had met hundreds of far better liars.

"I don't believe you," he said. He placed the shockrod against the woman's right breast, twisting it into her clothing until her bare skin was revealed. "Where is he?"

The man folded. "He was in his office," he said. "But I don't know where he is now."

"Very good," Joshua said. He smiled, nastily. "I thank you."

He triggered the shockrod. The woman started to scream.

Joshua laughed.

Jasmine could hear shooting as she dragged Mouganthu down the corridor. The skyscraper played merry hell with her sense of direction, making it impossible for her to tell who was doing the shooting or where they were. Mouganthu's security forces were probably responding to the emergency, but how? She had no doubt they were constrained by a reluctance to harm the guests in the crossfire...

Unless the police are simply shooting the guests on the spot, she thought. She didn't think it was likely, but Admiral Singh had surprised her before. *They might have orders to execute everyone.*

She let go of him long enough to key her wristcom, but there was no response. The tower's internal communications network was down. Worse, there was enough jamming in the air to keep her from contacting anyone *outside* the tower. She tapped a command into the device, hoping to ping Stewart or Haverford, but there was no response. She hoped, grimly, that that meant they were already out of the tower.

"She's mad," Mouganthu whispered. "She'll start a civil war!"

"Worry about it later," Jasmine agreed. She'd memorised the building diagrams. If she was right, they were close to a maintenance blister. She would have preferred to find a landing pad, preferably one with an aircar, but the police would have secured them as soon as they arrived. Besides, an aircar could be forced down easily. "Stay with me."

She opened a hatch and stepped out into the corridor. The sound of shooting - and people screaming - seemed to grow louder, but there was no one in sight. She listened carefully, then crept down the corridor to the maintenance blister. The police probably wouldn't think of it as a possible means of escape. But if they were lucky...

The door was locked. She cursed, then pressed Mouganthu's wrist-com against the electronic lock. It clicked open, revealing a tiny chamber on the edge of the tower. It was open to the elements…she shivered as the wind blew through the entrance, chilling her to the bone. She pulled Mouganthu inside, then closed the hatch. It was unlikely anyone would check the blister until it was too late, but it was well to be careful.

"There should be a safety pack here," she said. Building regulations demanded it - and Mouganthu, she knew, was a stickler. She dug out the heavy antigrav chute, checked the telltales and strapped it on. There was only one, but it should be enough. She strapped the control to her wrist, then tugged him forward. "Don't let go of me."

Mouganthu quivered. "I…"

"Don't let go," Jasmine said. She hoped he'd listen. Normally, there would be straps and webbing, but both of them were lacking. "Close your eyes, if you think it will help."

She wrapped one arm around him and jumped from the tower. Mouganthu screamed as they plummeted down, the air tearing at their clothes. Jasmine worked the control, hoping she hadn't found a new - or old - way to commit suicide. The chute hummed, slowing their fall; a second later, a gust of wind struck them, blowing them away from the tower. Jasmine gritted her teeth as they started to spin, trying very hard not to let go. HALO jumps were a great deal easier when her partner knew what he was doing.

He's probably never jumped out of a building in his life, she thought, as she guided the chute down towards the darkened city. The streets were still thronged with party-goers. She searched for a landing site, hoping to find somewhere deserted. *How many civilians go parachuting for fun*?

The wind pushed and pulled at them as they fell into a side-street and landed neatly on the ground. Jasmine felt Mouganthu shivering against her, his leg stained…she did her best to ignore it, knowing he'd be embarrassed when he recovered enough to realise he'd wet himself. It wasn't an uncommon reaction. She'd been told that two-thirds of the recruits in Boot Camp wet their pants during their first parachute jump.

"We made it," she said, turning to peer up at the tower. The wind had carried them further away than she'd realised. It was a good thing, she told herself. The police wouldn't have a good idea where they'd landed, even if they'd seen the jump. "But we have to move."

Mouganthu looked stunned. Jasmine glanced at him, then returned her gaze to the tower. A whole fleet of shuttles were buzzing around like angry bees, ferrying policemen and probably removing prisoners. Admiral Singh was going to be frustrated, Jasmine was sure. She'd taken one hell of a gamble, but she'd missed the real prize. Mouganthu had escaped…

"Come on," she said. The cold air was starting to bite, but she'd been in worse places. "We have to hurry."

"That…that was…unpleasant," Mouganthu managed. His entire body was shaking helplessly. "Will we have to do that again?"

"I hope not," Jasmine said, lightly. She'd grown to like parachute jumping, but only as a solo sport. "But if we don't get out of here now, all this will be for nothing."

CHAPTER THIRTY-ONE

"We searched the entire building, sir," Lieutenant Glomma reported. "There's no sign of Mouganthu."

Joshua blanched. The tower was immense, but his men were experts in searching large buildings. They'd already located and opened the panic rooms, forcing the inhabitants to come out on their knees. The lower levels had been sealed within minutes, the men moving forward as soon as the shuttles had begun their assault. Mouganthu could not have escaped the building. But it looked as though he had.

There must be a secret compartment somewhere, he thought. *Somewhere so carefully hidden that even we couldn't find it.*

He gritted his teeth as he stared at the prisoners, lying on the floor with their hands bound behind their backs. A rich haul indeed…but the true prize was missing. Mouganthu *had* to be found, the sooner the better. He glared at a young girl in a bright yellow dress - she had to be rich or she wouldn't have risked looking so silly - and then back at the lieutenant. Hopefully, the younger man was smart enough to know the danger.

"Get the rest of the prisoners out of the building and run them through the scanners," he ordered, shortly. "Make sure you check their ID before shoving them into the vans."

He scowled at the male prisoners, none of whom could meet his gaze. Mouganthu *might* have already been captured and simply gone unnoticed, although it was unlikely. He'd tortured enough prisoners to make sure the rest knew that complete submission was their only hope of survival.

He would have enjoyed it, if the taste of failure wasn't at the back of his mouth. The Admiral was not going to be pleased.

"And then get the men to do a floor-by-floor search," he added. "Check for any hidden passageways below the tower too."

"There aren't any on the building plans, sir," Glomma said.

Joshua snorted. "A man as rich as the asshole we're hunting can easily arrange for something to be kept off the plans, Lieutenant," he said. "There could be a tunnel leading down to the sewers too."

His lips twitched. Perhaps that *was* the answer. Mouganthu might have constructed a secret panic room - a lair - and concealed it within a supposedly solid wall. The skyscraper *was* overdesigned for its size, he'd been told. There could be an entire network of rooms and passageways completely disconnected from the remainder of the building. Or maybe Mouganthu had just managed to jump into an aircar and flee before the police raid really got going. His security staff were good, better than Joshua had expected. Caught by surprise, half their weapons still locked in the armoury, they'd still killed a number of policemen before they'd been wiped out. Joshua would have been impressed if he hadn't had to write a final report on each of the dead men personally.

"Yes, sir," Glomma said.

He saluted, then hurried off. Joshua glared after him, knowing that *Glomma* wouldn't have to pay the price for their failure. He should have known better, when the commissioner had offered him the job. Plenty of experience or not, the task of raiding Mouganthu Tower should have been given to someone higher up the food chain. The bastard had probably decided that anyone higher up wouldn't *want* the job. It was *sensitive*.

A young girl screamed as a policeman hauled her to her feet, taking the opportunity to squeeze her breast. Joshua barked orders at him and the policeman backed off, looking alarmingly like a puppy who'd been kicked despite obeying orders. He'd never been punished before for mixing business and pleasure...but no one gave much of a damn about student bitches and whores. *These* prisoners were important. He made a mental note to impress that on the jailors, too. They couldn't be given the normal welcome meted out to anyone unlucky enough to set foot in Wolfbane's prisons.

Damn it, he thought. The sun was starting to glimmer in the distance. His superiors would be wanting a full report soon. He was surprised they weren't already trying to micromanage him. Perhaps they scented trouble and were trying to keep their distance. It was as good a theory as any other. *What do we do if we can't find him*?

His wristcom buzzed. "Sir, we've searched the lower levels," Glomma said. "They're completely empty. All spaces have been accounted for."

"Then check the upper levels," Joshua snarled. It wouldn't be long before he'd have to explain his failure. "Now!"

He paced into Mouganthu's office, looking around in awe - and envy. The bastard had lived and worked in a forest, a forest within his skyscraper…it just wasn't fair. This was a whole different world, a world where the aristocracy got everything and everyone else had to bow and scrape for the tiniest of favours. There was so much money, just within eyesight, that it would have kept him and his entire family alive for centuries. He couldn't even imagine the sheer *scale* of Mouganthu's fortune. The man had been so wealthy that anyone counting it probably had to resort to imaginary numbers…

His fingers curled around his shockrod. Mouganthu had been born into immense wealth and power. He'd never had to work for it, never had to crawl up the ranks, never had to kiss his superiors while kicking his inferiors…no wonder the world was a mess. No doubt he'd been surrounded by women every hour of every day…or men, if he leant that way. There was never any shortage of women willing to whore themselves for money or power or protection from everyone else. Joshua had learnt that lesson on the streets.

The very rich are just the same as the criminal underclass, he thought, wryly. *They just have more money*.

He glared as his wristcom bleeped, again. "Captain," a female voice said, "this is Tucker. I beg to report that the computer datacores self-destructed…ah, before I arrived."

Joshua ground his teeth. Natalia Tucker was a computer expert. It had been made clear to him that he was to be nice to her at all times, if only because she was irreplaceable. Joshua had his doubts about her qualifications, but it hardly mattered. He knew better than to defy his superiors over something trivial. If she'd fucked up…well, at least it wasn't something that could be blamed on him. No doubt Mouganthu had wanted to make sure that nothing fell into enemy hands.

"Make a full report," he ordered, as he turned and walked back to the shuttles. "I'll see you back at the station."

Which should be just long enough for me to think of something to say myself, he thought. He took one last look at the eerie trees, then left the forest behind. *Something that will hopefully not get me arrested or shot.*

"Mouganthu is gone?"

"Yes, Admiral," Emma said. The intelligence officer sounded nervous. "He was definitely in his tower, but he escaped in the chaos."

Rani's eyes narrowed. Mouganthu was a corporate suit, not a soldier. She didn't *think* he had any combat enhancements, let alone the kind of training he'd need to use them properly. A man like that would be used to hiring others to do the dirty work, not doing it himself. No doubt he spoke of 'taking out' or 'removing' instead of killing. How could he have escaped?

She looked up. "Did one of his guards get him out in the confusion?"

"It's possible," Emma said. "We're currently downloading and studying all the security camera footage from the area, but so far we've come up with nothing."

"I see," Rani said. "And the other directors?"

Emma looked pale. "Both of them left the tower shortly before the raid began," she said. "I…Admiral, by now they will know that *something* happened."

Rani nodded. A *properly* run planet would have a datanet that could be controlled and subverted at will, but Wolfbane's datanet was too chaotic for her intelligence staff to control easily. They'd locked Mouganthu Tower out of the datanet, yet that wouldn't be enough to stop others from spreading the news. Hell, if nothing else, merely jamming every signal within the region would be noticeable.

She ground her teeth in frustration. The raid should have worked. She should have had Mouganthu in her hand, along with hundreds of others. Sure, she had prisoners…but she'd missed the big prize. And that meant…trouble. The other corporate directors would assume the worst, even if they *hadn't* been plotting with Mouganthu. Her shot had misfired and *that* would weaken her…

"Find him," she ordered, curtly. She forced her tired mind to work as she turned to the window. "Put the entire city in stage-one lockdown. Flood the streets with policemen and soldiers. Everyone who doesn't have a valid work permit is to stay off the streets until the lockdown is lifted."

"Yes, Admiral."

"And start swapping officers we *know* to be compromised out of command assignments," Rani added. "We can't risk leaving them alone any longer."

Paula coughed. "Admiral, that *will* alert them," she said. "I…"

Rani turned to face her. "Time is no longer on our side," she said. "We have to move and move now."

She cursed silently, refusing to give vent to her frustration. She'd taken a swing at a lethal enemy…and missed. Now, she had to compensate for her misjudgement before the enemy recovered his balance and swung back at her. Mouganthu had been crippled - losing his tower had to hurt - but he still had contacts, client officers and the other directors. And he had nothing to lose. He *knew* she meant to kill him.

"Get the prisoners into a detention camp," she added. "And see if we can use any of them."

"Aye, Admiral."

The safe house was a tiny apartment, inside a housing block that had been built decades ago and clearly seen better days. Jasmine had checked the area carefully, when she'd first rented the apartment, but she made sure to check again before helping Mouganthu up the stairs and into the apartment. They weren't in the worst part of the city - thankfully - but she had no doubt that the reward on Mouganthu's head, when Admiral Singh got around to offering one, would tempt a saint. A few million credits would be enough to set the betrayer up for life.

She held her pistol in one hand as she opened the door, unsure what to expect. Stewart and Haverford knew where to go, if they'd made it out alive. She didn't want to imagine that they might *not* have made it out alive. Stewart was a trained marine…he'd been in worse situations. But even the greatest marine could be brought down by bad luck or sheer random chance.

Mouganthu was shaking. She half-carried him over to the sofa and plonked him down, then walked to the fridge and opened it. A bottle of cheap wine was already there, waiting. She opened it, poured a generous splash into a glass and carried it back to him. Mouganthu drank it gratefully, then looked down at his trousers. The dark stain was nearly gone.

"More," he stammered. "I…please."

Jasmine poured him another glass, without comment. Mouganthu had been through hell, as far as he was concerned. She couldn't even begin to imagine what it must have been like, growing up in the tower, but having to flee one's childhood home *had* to be traumatic. And jumping from the tower had to have been worse. Mouganthu probably felt as though he'd fallen thousands of miles in a handful of seconds.

It wasn't quite that bad, she thought, dryly. *Maybe a few hundred miles.*

Mouganthu coughed. "Fuck," he said. He looked around. "Where… where *are* we?"

"Safe house," Jasmine said. There was a computer terminal on the desk, waiting. Meade had already set it up for secure communications, as well as a few other things. It was hardly the worst place *she'd* been in, but to him it probably looked like a foretaste of hell. "Are you hungry?"

"Scared," Mouganthu said. His hand was shaking. Jasmine took the glass before he could drop it. "What…what *happened*?"

"Admiral Singh decided to attack," Jasmine said, bluntly. "The tower was raided."

Mouganthu sat up. "She's mad!"

"Probably," Jasmine agreed. Or maybe not. Admiral Singh had come *very* close to taking out Mouganthu as well as his tower. If she'd succeeded, she might have lopped the head off the snake before it was too late. "Do you feel up to doing something about it?"

"...I need a shower," Mouganthu said. He stood on wobbly legs, shivering. "Is there a shower here? And spare clothes"

"Through there," Jasmine said. "You'll find some spare clothes in the bedroom. I think they should fit you."

She caught his arm before he could move. "Do *not* attempt to use any of the wristcoms or terminals without me. They'll explode if you don't put the right code into the system."

Mouganthu nodded and stumbled towards the shower. Jasmine wondered, with a flicker of tired amusement, if he actually *could* work the shower. She'd met a handful of recruits from *very* low-tech societies who had never even *seen* a working shower until they'd arrived at Boot Camp. Mouganthu probably had people to turn the shower on and off for him. But she heard the shower start, a moment later. She just hoped he didn't waste all the hot water.

She sat down and flicked on the terminal, entering her codes when requested. Meade had done a *very* good job. The terminal was linked to the datanet, but apparently untraceable unless the enemy got very lucky. Jasmine keyed out a message to Meade - and the others, who should be in the apartment - and then switched to the news channels. Not entirely to her surprise, there weren't any reports about a raid on Mouganthu Tower. Instead, apparently, there had been a fire. The shuttles had merely removed the tower's inhabitants before they could burn to death.

Nice cover story, she thought, sardonically. It might even be believed. A fire in a skyscraper would be an absolute nightmare. More people would be amused at Mouganthu's fire suppression systems failing than anything else. *It's not as if anyone outside the tower had the full story.*

A message popped up in front of her, from Meade. Jasmine let out a sigh of relief as she realised the others were all right, if scattered. Stewart and Haverford had gone to the other safe house, rather than risk going back to the main apartment. It was a good call on their part, Jasmine noted. The police *might* have tracked them as they left the building.

She heard the shower stop as another message appeared. "What now?"

"Good question," she replied. "We'll have to see how the other directors respond."

Mouganthu stepped back into the room. Jasmine glanced at him, then started to giggle helplessly. Mouganthu looked like he'd dressed poorly, his trousers and shirt a size or two larger than he needed. It was a far cry from the expensively tailored suit he'd worn only a few hours ago. But it was all they had. God knew it would attract less attention here than an expensive suit.

"I need to contact the other directors," Mouganthu said. "Can I do that?"

"Yes," Jasmine said. "Just don't tell them where you are."

"There's definitely no sign of Mouganthu," Glomma said. "Sir, every last square inch of this tower has been searched. We have accounted for every possible hiding place."

And the prisoners have been interrogated, Joshua thought. He'd questioned the maids personally, knowing *they* tended to know more than their masters assumed. But promises, threats and outright torture hadn't produced any actionable intelligence. *The bastard gave us the slip.*

"Damn it," he said. "Put the tower into lockdown, then send the remaining prisoners to the camps."

"Aye, sir," Glomma said.

Joshua ground his teeth. They'd failed...and an immense *mountain* of shit was rolling downhill towards him. His superiors had definitely fucked him. They'd known, damn them, that the raid might misfire. He wondered if he'd be arrested himself, the moment he reached the station. The thought scared him more than he cared to admit. There were quite a few prisoners in the camps who'd *welcome* a chance to settle accounts with him. He'd put them there personally.

He walked towards the police van, wondering if there was a way to escape. There *were* cracks in the system, places a wealthy man could hide...but not indefinitely. He didn't need a charge of desertion as well as everything else. He was already in enough trouble. Who knew? The

Admiral might be pleased, even if everyone else was mad. He'd definitely captured a few of her enemies during the raid.

His wristcom bleeped. "Sir, we received a tip-off," the dispatcher said. "Another student subversive cell, readying for action."

"Really," Joshua said. He stepped into the van. "Do we have an address?"

"Yes, sir," the dispatcher said. "It's on the positioning system."

"We'll take it," Joshua said. "Glomma, take us there."

He sat down, silently checking his weapons. The cell was probably nothing more than another bunch of idiot students, but it didn't matter. He felt like cracking a few skulls. And besides, if they were a little more dangerous than the average subversives, it might just make him look good. Perhaps even good enough to escape punishment for his earlier failure…

And it will stop another bunch of subversives in their tracks, he told himself, as the vehicle roared to life. *Who knows? This might even be the big break we need to crack the entire network.*

His thoughts darkened. *And even if it isn't, they're still subversives. They deserve everything they get.*

CHAPTER THIRTY-TWO

"You're supposed to hit me," Patty said.

Stuart looked doubtful. "I don't *want* to hit you."

Patty rolled her eyes. "We're meant to be learning to *fight*," she reminded him. She'd taken a dozen martial arts classes at university, learning how to defend herself. "Hit me!"

"You're wasting your time," Joe called. He peeked into the training room. The sports complex had been abandoned long ago, then reclaimed by the student resistance. So far, it had gone unnoticed. "Your boyfriend doesn't want to hurt you. I'd have thought you'd be worried if he *did*."

Patty coloured. "I just want to learn how to *fight*," she said. She didn't want to admit just how badly she'd been affected by their tutor's casual dismissal of her skills. Women *could* fight. She'd learned that in class. "And he's not helping."

Joe strode into the room, his smile widening. He was bigger than either of them, a year or two older than Patty. Patty felt a flicker of irritation, mingled with a certain amount of respect. Joe was on the verge of graduating. He had more to lose than most of the student rebels. If the rebels won, that was one thing; if they lost, Joe would be imprisoned, exiled or blacklisted for the rest of his life. He was putting everything at risk to fight.

"Very well," Joe said. He bowed, mockingly. "Fight me. I'll let you have the first swing."

"Joe..." Stuart began.

"It'll be fine," Patty said. Up close, Joe looked even bigger. The casual overalls he'd donned didn't hide his muscles. He'd probably chosen a set a size or two smaller than he needed, just to show off. "Don't do anything stupid now."

"*Stuart* isn't the one doing something stupid," Joe pointed out, dryly. His voice turned mocking. "You *sure* you want to do this?"

Patty drew back her fist and swung. Joe darted backwards, then caught her arm and yanked her forward. Patty toppled, only to be caught by him. Before she could react, before she could do anything, he had an arm wrapped around her neck, threatening to choke her. She stayed very still, feeling her heartbeat starting to pound. His body was pressing against hers, holding her tightly. She'd never been so scared in her life.

"I squeeze, you die," Joe said. "Do you understand me?"

Patty nodded, helplessly. She didn't dare do anything else.

"You telegraphed your swing well before you threw it," Joe lectured. "You then overextended yourself, *then* you allowed me to grab you. If I'd wanted to kill you - or worse - I could have done it by now. Do you understand me?"

Patty groaned. She'd been told she was good. Her *trainers* had told her she was good. But Joe had rendered her helpless effortlessly. She hadn't been fast enough to make up for her weaknesses. He could snap her neck if he wanted and she couldn't stop him…

"That will do," Stuart said. "Let her go."

"Your strongest command is my slightest wish," Joe said. He lowered Patty to the floor, then released her. "*That's* why we need guns."

He smirked as she rubbed her throat. "Aren't you going to *thank* me for the lesson?"

Patty glared at him. Her neck hurt, but otherwise…she was unharmed. Humiliated, but unharmed. And yet…she felt *vulnerable*. She'd taken martial arts, she had badges…had she won *any* of those fights? Or had they been as scripted as a flick show? The mere *thought* of thanking him felt absurd, yet…he'd done as she'd asked. She just hadn't known what she'd really wanted.

"Thank you," she growled.

"Use weapons," Joe said. He walked over to the table and picked up a knife. "Next time, let someone get close and bury this in them."

Patty winced. Stuart helped her to her feet and hugged her, tightly. He didn't look pleased, unsurprisingly. Watching Patty get manhandled had to have been unpleasant, all the more so because it could so easily have been worse. Joe could have bruised her skin, broken bones or even molested her, just to make his point. The feeling of vulnerability only grew worse as she leaned against her boyfriend. Was *this* the true nature of the human race? Was society a mask drawn over a world red in tooth and claw, where might made right and the victor claimed the spoils? Did she need a protector? Could she rely on Stuart to protect her?

Her tutors hadn't told her anything about *this*. But then, they'd rarely talked about society and human nature…her thoughts ran in all directions, mocking her. How long had she been vulnerable? How close had she come to being robbed or raped or murdered each time she walked down the street? How foolish had she been to *believe* she could look after herself?

Joe held out the knife. Patty took it, feeling cold. "You can learn," Joe said. "And the first step in learning is admitting your ignorance."

"Thank you," Patty said. She looked at Joe's hulking muscle and shivered. "How…how did you learn?"

"I was born in Falloch," Joe said. "You learn or you die. My mother never went out without a knife up her sleeve."

Patty's eyes opened wide. Falloch wasn't too far from her own birthplace, but it might as well be on the other side of the planet. The district had been deprived for so long that it was a brutal nightmare, ruled by mobsters and terrorised by gangbangers. And *Joe* had been born there? She eyed him with new respect. Everyone knew that Falloch was a hellish place to grow up. How had Joe managed to escape?

"There's no such thing as a fair fight," Joe said. "I…"

He broke off as a bell rang, several times. "Grab your weapons," he ordered. "I think we're about to be raided."

The building didn't look like much, but then they never did. City Records stated that it had been a sports hall, once upon a time, before the owners had gone bankrupt and abandoned the building to the elements. Police records indicated that a handful of homeless families had tried to use the building as a residence, but they'd been rousted out by Campus Security long ago. The building was still intact, even though a handful of vandals had spray-painted subversive slogans on the walls. As a hiding place for a cell of subversives, it had its limits.

Joshua checked his weapon - again - as the policemen clambered out of the van and hastily surrounded the building. The first report hadn't been particularly detailed, but it *had* implied that there were at least twenty subversives within the building. It was certainly large enough to house many more, given time. Joshua had heard enough rumours about rebel cells training for war to believe that there could easily be a small army inside the building. But they were students, not soldiers or mobsters. They'd fold at the first sight of blood.

"Team One goes in through the front entrance," he ordered. The students probably already knew the police had arrived. It wasn't as though they were trying to remain hidden. "Team Two secures the other entrance."

He smiled as he drew his truncheon. He felt like breaking a few heads - and besides, he needed prisoners. God knew he would be in serious trouble, the moment he returned to the station. The communications channels had been oddly quiet since he'd sent the last report from the tower, *de facto* proof that a massive shitstorm was in the air and heading in his general direction. If he could break a rebel cell - if he could capture someone who could lead the police to the inner circle - the shitstorm might just go away. It wasn't much, he knew all too well, but it was all he had.

The air smelt faintly of blood, sweat and the stench of desperation as the policemen approached the entrance. It looked solid - and locked with a heavy chain and padlock - but his experienced eye had no trouble picking out the telltale signs that someone had jimmied the lock. The students hadn't done a very good job of it, he noted. They'd have done better to remove the padlock entirely and replace it with one of their own. Perhaps he hadn't stumbled across a *real* cell after all.

He forced that thought aside. He *needed* a victory. Whatever the cost...

"Go," he ordered.

The first squad picked up the battering ram, then charged forward.

Patty's hands were trembling as she slotted the ammunition clip into the pistol and stepped forward, taking up a defensive position just past the lobby. Stuart held a rifle with a *little* more assurance - he'd been lucky enough to fire a few rounds for training purposes - but otherwise he looked as nervous as Patty felt. Even Joe looked pale in the half-light as he muttered orders, trying to take control of the situation.

"They're going to come through the main door," he whispered, pulling his mask over his face. His voice sounded funny through the rubber. "Give them hell."

Patty swallowed, hard, as she donned her own mask. Her throat was suddenly dry. She'd heard enough horror stories about what happened to subversives when they were captured to *know* she didn't want to be taken alive. The police did horrible things to their prisoners, she'd been told. If she was lucky, she'd *only* be raped and then exiled. Stuart, Joe and the other men would probably be raped as well, if the rumours were true. She found them easy to believe. The police had never shown the slightest hint of compassion towards anyone, as far as she knew. They were drawn from the very dregs of society.

And there was no hope of escape. Joe had checked. The building was surrounded. There were no tunnels, no tricks that might allow them to escape detection long enough to flee into the university or out onto the streets. They'd been detected, somehow...perhaps they'd been betrayed. She'd been warned - they'd all been warned - to keep the existence and membership of their cell a secret, but *something* had clearly leaked out. Perhaps they'd made a mistake using the sports hall. *Someone* might have noticed that it was being put to use.

She elbowed Stuart. "Don't let them take me alive."

Stuart looked back at her. "I won't."

The main door exploded inwards. Patty flinched as black-clad figures swarmed into the building, the leaders carrying a giant object as they ran forward. Joe barked a command and the students opened fire, a ragged barrage that sent a dozen policemen toppling to the ground, dead. Patty stared at the smoking gun in her hand, wondering just how many of the policemen she'd killed personally. How many times had she pulled the trigger? She wasn't sure. The clip was empty, so she ditched it and slotted in a new one…

"Grenade," someone shouted.

Patty barely had a second to register…*something*…flying into the lobby before it exploded, blasting sheets of gas in all directions. She stumbled backwards, hoping the gas needed to be breathed before it took effect. The masks were supposed to protect their faces, keeping the gas from blinding as well as choking them, but the rest of their clothing wasn't anything like so protective. They'd be dead in seconds if the police had used nerve gas…

She peered into the smog as she moved backwards, searching for targets. The police could be advancing right now and she wouldn't know it, not until they loomed out of the smoke. Joe caught her arm and thrust her back, motioning for her to run. Patty kept her pistol raised as she moved, realising that the smog was getting thicker. They wouldn't be able to see each other soon.

Maybe we can sneak out in the confusion, she thought. *And then make a break for it.*

She shook her head. She knew it wasn't going to happen.

Joshua hit the ground - instinctively - as the bullets started flying, rolling over and trying to draw his pistol even as he hid from the bullets. At least five of his men had already been shot and were down, perhaps more. Their body armour should provide some protection, he thought, but it was impossible to be sure. They might well be dead. His career had probably died with them.

He unhooked a gas grenade from his belt and hurled it into the lobby, then pulled an injector tab from his belt and jabbed it into his neck. The gas would still burn his eyes if he didn't don his mask before he entered the building, but it wouldn't have any other effect once the counteragent took effect. Two of his men threw their own gas grenades into the building, amplifying the effect. Joshua would have felt sorry for the rebels if they didn't deserve to suffer worse. The gas was no fun in the open air, but it would be absolutely lethal in a confined space.

"No prisoners," he growled, as his men regrouped for a second offensive. He read bloody murder on their faces and nodded in agreement. "We crush the bastards."

His superiors would be annoyed if Joshua didn't bring home a few prisoners, but he was past caring. The rebel scum needed to *pay*. Who cared what happened to them? And besides, they were armed. Carrying weapons without a permit was an automatic death sentence. He cocked his pistol, checked his body armour and then gave the order. His men opened fire as they crawled towards the building.

"Get down," Joe snapped.

Patty threw herself to the floor as bullets started to snap through the air, punching holes in the walls and knocking pieces of plaster from the ceiling. The gas was still growing thicker, even though they were crawling away from the lobby as fast as they could. She had no idea if the police were blowing it into the building or if it was just alarmingly persistent, but it hardly mattered. She didn't dare remove her mask.

Something *crashed*, in the distance. She tensed, wondering if the policemen had just knocked a hole in the wall. The sports hall hadn't been particularly well built. Its innards certainly weren't standing up to rifle fire. She lifted her pistol as a dark shape loomed into view, almost pulling the trigger before realising that it was another student. Joe caught his arm and pushed him back, just as two policemen appeared. He shot them both before they could react.

"Get down to the basement," he ordered. Patty could barely hear him over the racket. "Smash the vats and set fire to the chemicals!"

Patty nodded and crawled forward as fast as she dared. The air was definitely growing thicker - thankfully, the policemen probably had the same problem. She cringed as she heard the noise of gunshots growing louder, followed by screams. Someone had been hit...she hoped it was another policeman, but she doubted it. The screams sounded feminine...

She reached the stairwell and hurried down. Joe had turned the basement into a chemical lab, brewing all sorts of formulas. It hadn't struck Patty as particularly safe, but there was no way the university officials would allow them to use a *proper* lab. She hesitated as she reached the first set of vats, then shoved them off the table. They hit the floor and shattered, releasing their contents. Foul-smelling steam started to rise as the different liquids mingled. She had no idea if the mixed contents was poisonous or not, but it hardly mattered. Joe had warned her that it would burn.

And destroy the evidence, she thought, smashing the remainder of the vats. White gas was starting to rise from the floor. *They'll never know what we were doing here.*

A policeman appeared at the top of the stairs, pointing a gun at her. Patty froze, then lifted her own gun. The policeman pulled the trigger...

The entire building shook, so violently that the roof started to cave in. Joshua staggered as he dodged a piece of debris, then bellowed for his men to run as the temperature started to rise sharply. The entire building was on fire. He cursed the subversives savagely as he ran to the nearest exit and burst out into the light. The remainder of his team followed, a couple dragging a prisoner between them. The poor bastard had been so badly beaten that Joshua honestly couldn't tell if he was male or female.

He turned, just in time to see the entire building collapse into flames. They flickered green and purple, suggesting that there were dangerous chemicals within the blaze...he cursed, then ordered his men to pull back completely. God alone knew what would happen next…he cursed, again, as he realised that they were being watched. A handful of students were watching them, *judging* them…

"Five men are dead, seven are wounded," Lieutenant Glomma reported. "Nine more remain unaccounted for."

Somewhere within the fire, Joshua thought. Chemical fires were *nasty*. The gas probably wasn't helping either. His missing men were either dead or wishing they were. By the time the fire brigade arrived they would *definitely* be dead. *Fuck.*

He groaned, inwardly. He was dead. His superiors would kill him when they found out just how badly he'd screwed up. One prisoner - who might not even survive long enough to be interrogated - was not enough to make up for five deaths, perhaps fourteen. He'd be lucky if they just shot him out of hand.

"I'm picking up reports of student disturbances," Lieutenant Glomma added. "Do you want to respond?"

Joshua sighed. In all honestly, he didn't have the slightest idea what to do next.

CHAPTER THIRTY-THREE

"Hey, Meade," Danny Harlem - her supervisor - called. "You got in!"

"Barely," Meade said. She made a show of holding up her ID card. "I had to prove I actually had a job before they let me go - *three* times."

"Ouch," Harlem said. He was only five or so years older than her, but he acted as though he was old enough to be her father. "I'm afraid you're needed in the main computer core today."

Meade nodded. "Just let me take off my coat and I'll head straight down there," she said, reassuringly. "Is Bill on his way?"

"I've heard nothing from him," Harlem said. "You might be on your lonesome down there."

"Good," Meade said.

She shot him a smile, then headed for the cloakroom. Harlem might not understand more than a third of anything his staff said, but he wasn't a *bad* boss. Meade had worked for him for four weeks, give or take a few days, and he'd never been unpleasant, let alone tried to get into her pants. She couldn't help feeling a pang of guilt as she removed her coat and hurried down the stairs. There was no way to avoid the simple fact that she was going to betray him, that her actions might get him in real trouble.... that he might die, because of her.

It has to be done, she told herself, swiping through the security door. *There's no choice.*

In all honesty, she would have loved the job under other circumstances. Tech Solutions had the contract for updating the planetary datanet, a task made harder by corporate resistance and constant hacker attacks. Merely replacing the older datanet nodes and archives was the task of a lifetime, one that would have presented an endless series of challenges. It wasn't quite what she'd intended to do with her life, when she'd gone through Boot Camp and attended the Slaughterhouse, but it would have been satisfying. Instead…

She stepped into the giant room. Hundreds of datacores, each one large enough to pass for a small shuttlecraft, were lined up in rows, lights blinking on control consoles that governed each individual system. Cold air brushed against her skin as she passed under a fan, nodding politely to Yasser as he rose from his desk. He was a nerd, one who became tongue-tied every time he had to speak to her. Meade couldn't help finding it a little sad. Yasser could have found a girlfriend easily if he'd had the courage to approach someone who'd appreciate him - and his job.

"The…ah…the government has us tracking down hacks within the network," Yasser managed. He held out a datapad. "I've been supporting their efforts down here."

Meade nodded and scanned the set of instructions. Whoever had written them hadn't known what they were talking about, unsurprisingly. There were so many different systems connected to the planetary datanet that one size definitely *didn't* fit all. She silently translated the words into more practical instructions, then shrugged. The instructions didn't matter. She had a number of other pieces of work to do.

"I'll be fine," she assured him. "Go get some rest."

She put the datapad down, then checked the live feed from the monitoring systems. Someone had installed a set of monitoring systems, then a set of systems to monitor the monitoring systems…it made her wonder if someone had had to use up the reminder of their budget in a hurry. It had probably never occurred to them to simply hand it out to their staff as a bonus.

Yasser looked nervous. "Should…should I even try to go home?"

"The streets are fairly safe," Meade lied. She had her doubts. She'd picked up plenty of police reports about riots and stabbings before she'd left the apartment. But Yasser would probably be safe. The colder part of her mind pointed out that the mission would only be *helped* if he died. He was a *very* skilled computer and datanet technician. "You should be fine."

"I can stay," Yasser said, nervously. "You might need some help..."

"I'll be fine," Meade assured him. "And you need a nap."

She turned her attention to the display as he hurried out of the room, quietly checking each of the datacores one by one. They didn't have access to the military network, but nearly everything else ran through the company's datacores...sooner or later. No *wonder* the hacker community spent so long trying to disrupt any attempt to rationalise the system. A simple modification could turn into a chokepoint that would strangle their community.

An hour passed slowly as she worked, carefully patching up a couple of the more obvious holes in the network. The hackers were out in force today, using codes they'd obtained - somehow - to crack the outer edge of the firewalls. Someone had probably been sloppy with their passwords again, Meade noted. It was astonishing how many people thought that 'PASSWORD' was a good password. Or the names of their children, something that half an hour of research could dig up. Someone was probably going to be in a great deal of trouble, if they were caught.

And if the police didn't have something else to worry about, she thought, as she opened one of the datacores. *They'll have a lot more to worry about after today.*

She smiled as she put the access panel on the floor, then turned her attention to the datacore's interior. A hundred ROM datachips were plugged into the core, each one providing an aspect of the authorisation procedure. She checked for unexpected surprises - like a new authorisation code for removal - then pulled one of the chips out of place. Nothing happened, so she dropped it in the disposal chute and inserted a chip she'd prepared at home. She tensed, half-expecting alarms, but - again - nothing happened. Her sabotage had gone completely unnoticed.

They'll realise what happened, sooner or later, she thought. *But it'll take them time to find and remove the chip.*

Carefully, she replaced the hatch, wiped her hands clean and hurried back to the desk. She had another three hours before she could slip out for lunch, another three hours before the messages and commands she'd uploaded into the datacore could go active. By then, the worm - and the viruses in its code - would have gone viral, using the datacores to spread itself right across the planet. The messages would go first, followed by the virus. And, if she was very lucky, someone would be careless and the worm would slip into the military network too.

All the security in the world is no help if the personnel using it are incompetent, she thought, remembering how network security had been drilled into her head. There were things you *didn't* hook up to the overall datanet if you valued your life and property. *And by the time they manage to remove the worm, it will be far too late.*

She sat down and checked her watch. Three hours to go. And then she would vanish, leaving Yasser and the others one hell of a mess to clear up. She almost felt sorry for them. No matter how hard they worked, it would take them months to remove the viruses and safeguard the system. Admiral Singh would not be pleased.

And she'll have worse to worry about too, Meade thought. *Serves the bitch right.*

"Got a report of a crowd massing at the Dumpster," Constable Oat said. "Students, mainly."

"Joy," Constable Jon Davis said. He didn't like students - he didn't like anyone, save for his husbands and wives - but they were hardly the worst problem right now. There were riots in Falloch and a couple of other shitty areas, for crying out loud. The students might be breaking the lockdown, but they weren't causing trouble. "Let's go chase them back to bed, shall we?"

He tossed his coffee cup out of the window and started the engine, guiding the police car onto the nearly-deserted streets. Being a policeman had guaranteed him employment for the last ten years - even as the economy took a steep dive and hundreds of thousands of workers found themselves suddenly unemployed. He'd once been proud to be a police officer, but not any longer. Too many of his fellows casually boasted of robbing civilians and raping suspects at the back of police vans.

Two years until retirement, he told himself. He was due a retirement bonus, if the department didn't try to garnish it for their own inscrutable reasons. Perhaps he'd buy a house in the country and invite the rest of his poly-family to stay. *Or maybe we should go off-world.*

He turned on the siren, ignoring Oat's complaints. Yes, the students *would* hear them coming. That was the *point.* The young idiots - he'd never met a youngster who wasn't ignorant of the real world - would have ample opportunity to fade back into the shadows before he had to take official notice of their presence. He dodged a food truck with practiced ease, ignoring the nasty look the driver shot him. Harassing truckers was a good way to end up with a black mark on one's record. Rain or shine, the city had to eat.

"Call it in," he ordered, as he turned the corner. "We'll take care of it and then resume our patrol."

"No response," Oat said.

Jon shrugged. The communications network had been so overloaded, over the past few hours, that it was a minor miracle they'd even heard about the student gathering. Something had definitely happened, although he had no idea what. The handful of messages that had been sent in the clear hadn't been particularly specific, while the news media had been completely off the air. He rather suspected *that* meant that no one could decide what lies they were going to tell the public.

He turned the corner and screeched towards the Dumpster. Despite the name, it was a perfectly decent-looking building, a nightclub where student life met the young working professionals who wanted to capture some of their lost youth. Jon felt his lips twitch in disgust at the thought - there was something creepy about a thirty-year-old worker hitting on a nineteen-year-old student, even if it was technically legal - and told himself, again, that *his* family's children weren't going to university. They could go to a technical college and learn a trade.

The students hadn't dispersed, he realised. There was an entire mob of students, male and female, infesting the street. Half of them wore masks, hiding their features…a number of the others wore scarves that covered their mouths. A chill ran down his spine as he realised the students were angry. Their defiant gazes suggested they were no longer scared.

Shit, he thought.

He keyed the megaphone. "THE CITY IS IN LOCKDOWN," he said. A number of students flinched, but others held their ground. "RETURN TO YOUR HOMES. I REPEAT, RETURN TO YOUR HOMES."

The students glared at him. A moment later, pieces of junk started flying through the air and crashing into the car. The police vehicle was bulletproof, but it wasn't designed to stand up to so many impacts. And yet, Jon wasn't sure what to do. He could trigger the gas nozzles or even the guns, but that would be a slaughter. The gas would make the students panic and run, trampling their former comrades under their feet. He'd seen the aftermath of riots before, even the ones that had ended without the riot squad turning up and opening fire. Hundreds of youngsters might end up dead…

Something crashed into the back of the car. The rear window shattered, the framework twisting out of shape. He turned, just in time to see another car pulling back, blocking their line of retreat. The students howled and ran forward, their faces contorted with hatred and rage. Jon had no time to decide what to do before they were swarming over the vehicle, tearing their way into the car with the bare hands. Oat grabbed his pistol and opened fire, but it was too late. A moment later, Jon felt strong hands yanking him back, dragging him out of the police car. He landed on the ground and stared up. Hate-filled faces glared down at him, their feet raising in unison.

Jon closed his eyes.

Paula hurried into Rani's office, her face pale. Rani *knew* it was bad news.

She scowled. She'd spent the morning fielding angry demands from all eleven of the remaining corporate directors, while doing everything in her power to track down Mouganthu before it was too late. The directors hadn't believed her assurances while Mouganthu had refused to be found. Rani didn't *think* the bastard had managed to escape the city, but she wouldn't have bet against it. *Or* against the asshole hiding out in one of the other towers and spreading lies to his former allies.

Paula came to a halt. "Admiral, we're losing control of the streets," she said. At least she wasn't trying to sugar-coat it. "The police are coming under increasingly heavy attack…there are hundreds of reports. The computer network itself is under attack. Gunfire, stabbings…even improvised bombs! This is a planned uprising!"

"It certainly looks that way," Rani agreed.

She forced herself to bite down on her anger and *think.* So far, the various corporate armies - and their clients in the military - didn't seem to be moving, but that could change at any moment. Her grip on power hung by a thread. The riots on the streets weren't threatening, in and of themselves, but there were other problems. She didn't know how far she could trust the military forces outside the fortress.

And I have to stamp on this as quickly as possible, she thought, grimly. *Or else it will get out of hand.*

"Order the police to clear the streets," she said. The communications problems were bound to make that difficult, but it had to be done. "They are authorised to use maximum force."

"Yes, Admiral," Paula said.

Rani gritted her teeth. The timing was appalling. Two-thirds of her starship crews were on the surface, celebrating their great victory. Getting them out of the city and back into orbit was going to be a nightmare. Hell, given how far their enemy had already gone, she had no doubt they'd start targeting the spacers too. It would be a really simple way to put a crimp in her plans.

"And order the spacers to report to the spaceports at once," she added. Getting them out of the city came first. They could be sorted out later, once they were in orbit. "I want them out of danger."

"Yes, Admiral," Paula said.

Joshua had expected to be arrested, the moment he'd returned to the station to report his failure. If there *was* a silver lining in the endless stream of disastrous reports flowing into the computer network, it was that his failure was far from the only one. Someone had sniped a trio of policemen on Bradshaw Gate, someone else had knifed two spacers before being beaten to death…looting, riots and arson attacks were breaking out everywhere. He had no doubt he'd be punished, eventually, but for the moment his superiors just didn't have time.

"Take your squad to Riverside," Colonel Patterson ordered. "The station there is under siege."

"Yes, sir," Joshua said. He'd been based on Riverside, two years ago. The area had been poor, but relatively honest. He found it hard to imagine that *that* much had changed. "I'll deal with it at once."

He picked up a handful of reinforcements, then ordered his men back on the road, pretending not to hear the grumbling from the rear. His men had been on duty for far too long…had it really only been twelve hours since they'd plunged into Mouganthu Tower? It felt like longer, far longer. They needed rest, just as desperately as he needed redemption. And if that meant working them to the bone, he'd work them to the bone.

The streets were deserted. Even the food trucks were missing, something that worried him more than he cared to admit. The computer network seemed to be having problems, garbling genuine messages and spewing spam every couple of minutes. He couldn't track anything happening outside his field of view as he turned into Riverside. The towering apartment blocks looked as deserted as the streets.

A chill ran down his spine. Riverside had always been full of life. But now…

Trouble, he thought. *Where are they?*

A glass bottle smashed against the window, exploding into fire a second later. For a long moment, Joshua's tired brain refused to grasp what had happened. The rebels had graduated to making and using Molotov Cocktails, filling empty bottles with fuel and lighting the fuse before throwing them at their targets. One of them wouldn't be enough to destroy a police car, but several of them…

He cursed as bullets snapped through the air, followed by more flaming bottles. So far, they were safe, but there was no way they could get out of the vans and deploy before it was too late. And then a car, far too close to the second van, exploded with staggering force. The blast picked up the van and slammed it into the nearest wall. It caught fire a second later and began to burn.

"Pull back," Joshua ordered. Nine men were now dead, nine *more* men. "We'll form a cordon outside Riverside and call for reinforcements."

Lieutenant Glomma glanced at him. "But what about Riverside Station?"

"They'll have to take care of themselves," Joshua snapped. How many men had died under his command in the last twelve hours? He was too tired to count properly. "Right now, we have lost control of the streets!"

CHAPTER THIRTY-FOUR

"Are you sure we're safe here?"

Jasmine shrugged. She was surprised it had taken so long for Mouganthu to ask that question. He'd been working the terminal with surprising skill, sending messages to his allies while she'd been monitoring the live feed from across the city. The safe house *was* in a reasonably safe part of the city, but that could change at any moment. Meade's data packet would see to that.

"Safe enough," she said, dryly. "As long as they don't get a lock on our location, they'll need to be very lucky to catch us."

She glanced at him. "Are you ready to move to the next step?"

"Yes," Mouganthu said. He didn't *sound* confident. "You do realise this could go horrifically wrong?"

"Yeah," Jasmine said. She could hear gunshots in the distance. Admiral Singh had been caught off guard, she suspected, but it wouldn't take her long to recover her balance. The fortress wasn't under threat. "We have to move now or the opportunity will be lost forever."

Mouganthu stabbed at a button. "Done," he said. "The signal is on its way."

Jasmine hoped he was right. Meade's virus *shouldn't* intercept their communications, but Jasmine had been warned - repeatedly - that the virus had been designed to mutate, rewriting its code as it passed from system to system. It was the only way to keep countermeasures from isolating the program, then purging it from the computer network. There was a chance - a better than even chance - that some future version of the virus would prove as dangerous to its senders as its targets.

"Now we wait," she said. "Are the other directors standing by?"

"Most of them," Mouganthu said. "They'll move when we are ready. A handful are still trying to sit on the sidelines."

Jasmine wasn't surprised. "They'll wait till they know who's coming out on top," she commented. It wasn't unusual. "Right now, there's too much chaos for battle lines to take shape."

She sat back, shaking her head. It felt...*wrong* to be controlling - or at least launching - a revolution from a quiet little house. She was used to being on the front lines, stabbing deep into enemy territory and launching attacks on the enemy's rear. Instead, she was pulling strings from a distance, without being entirely sure how many of her orders were being carried out. The torrent of reports streaming through the network ranged from cold descriptions of the crisis to exaggerations that were beyond belief.

Here goes nothing, she thought. *We have to keep the pressure on.*

Lieutenant Steve Coughlin had been a loyal officer in the Wolfbane Planetary Defence Network for over ten years, something that surprised some of his subordinates. He was *only* a lieutenant after a decade in the service, despite a sterling record and a seeming reluctance to join the navy or move to the merchant marine. But then, he *had* been promised - by his real superiors - that he'd be amply rewarded when the time came for him to retire. The influence they'd used to secure him his post was enough to prove they could give him more than enough to make up for the low rank and lower pay.

He glanced around the tiny compartment, feeling nervous. Despite everything - Governor Brown, Admiral Singh - he'd never really expected to receive orders to lead a mutiny against his superior officers. It had been a theoretical possibility, nothing more. But the orders had come in, only twenty minutes ago. He and his allies - and he hadn't even known he *had* allies until they'd made themselves known to him - were to take control of Fortress One as soon as possible, then await further instructions.

"Use the stunners first, if possible," he ordered. He didn't have clearance to enter the armoury - in theory - but one of his few assets was an all-access codekey. "Shoot if there's no other choice."

"Understood," Midshipman Haitian said.

Steve winced. Twenty-two officers and crew, none of whom had *known* about the others until now…it wasn't enough to take the entire fortress. Thankfully, merely controlling the CIC would be enough for the moment. Either their masters took the planet, in which case they could be reinforced at leisure, or they didn't, in which case the mutineers were screwed anyway. It was almost enough to make him want to steal a lifepod and escape. Only the certainty that both desertion and failure would get him and his family killed kept him in his place.

"We move," he ordered. His cabin was close enough to the CIC for them to move rapidly, without sneaking through the entire fortress. "Now."

Red lights pulsed from the bulkheads as they made their way towards the CIC. The giant fortress was in lockdown, all non-essential crewmen confined to their quarters. Steve held his stunner at the ready anyway, primed to shoot anyone who wasn't part of the group. Better someone woke up in an hour with a pounding headache than the alert being sounded too early. The CIC crew could not be allowed to seal the hatches before it was too late or the entire operation would fail spectacularly.

He turned the corner nodded. Two infantrymen stood on guard outside the hatch, both looking bored. They didn't know the alert was anything more than a drill. Steve stunned them both, zapping them repeatedly to make sure they'd go down and stay down, then hurried past them to the hatch. Thankfully, the crew hadn't codelocked it. That would have been an utter disaster.

"Be ready," he muttered. "Stunners only, if possible."

The hatch hissed open. Commander Katy Jones turned, her eyes going wide with surprise as she saw the mutineers. Steve stunned her without pity - she was one of Admiral Singh's cronies - and then ran into the room, stunning everyone within sight. A security officer lunged towards the alarm button, too late. Steve zapped him, then strode over to the command chair. Commander Jones hadn't had time to lock them out of the system before it was too late. He placed his pre-prepared datachip in the reader, then brought up the near-orbit display. Several other fortresses were steadily withdrawing from the combined command network.

"Secure this compartment," he ordered. "Put the rest of the fortress into total lockdown."

"I've got control of the weapons, sir," Midshipman Haitian said. "We're ready to fire."

"Stand ready," Steve warned. The fleet would presumably remain loyal to Admiral Singh and her cronies. It might attempt to attack the planet before it was too late. "Exchange command codes with the other fortresses."

"Fortress Five is locking weapons on us," Midshipman Haitian snapped. "She's attempting to access and subvert our parasite OWPs!"

"Lock them out," Steve ordered. Fortress Five was close enough to cause real damage, if it wanted. It would have been targeted for mutiny too, but something might well have gone wrong. The mutinies had been organised on very short notice. "And prepare to fire."

"I've got a link to Fortress Two and Fortress Six," Midshipwoman Sanyo called. "Sir, I think they're attacking the command network directly! The link keeps failing and then recovering."

"Hold us steady," Steve said. "Can you detect the fleet?"

"No change, as far as I can tell," Sanyo said. "They have to know that *something's* wrong."

"Perhaps," Steve said. "I..."

The display flashed red. "Fortress Five is firing," Midshipman Haitian snapped. "Incoming missiles! I say again, incoming missiles!"

"Return fire," Steve ordered. Something had definitely gone wrong. "The OWPs are to provide covering fire!"

He leaned back in his command chair, watching the new alliances take shape and form. One, Two, Seven and Eight had been taken over, while Five, Nine and Twelve were on Admiral Singh's side. And the others... they didn't seem to know which way to jump. Fortress Three appeared to have gone completely dead. The mutineers must have lost the bid to take over the fortress and crashed all of its systems before they were wiped out. Steve had had contingency plans to do it himself.

"Fortress Five is launching a second barrage," Midshipman Haitian reported. "Our point defence is coming online now."

Steve gritted his teeth. "Engage as soon as possible," he ordered. If the fortress took major damage, the mutineers were going to have real problems maintaining control. On the other hand, if the fortress *did* take major damage, maintaining control would be the least of their problems. "Fire at will."

"The enemy have subverted a number of orbital fortresses," Commodore Bradbury reported, grimly. "They're..."

"I can see that, idiot," Rani snarled. Matters had *definitely* flown right out of control. The planet was on the verge of outright civil war while the orbital defence network was fighting its *own* civil war. "Contact the fleet. Order them to prepare to crush the rebel fortresses!"

"Aye, Admiral," Bradbury said.

Rani studied the display for a long moment. The fortress was fairly secure, for the moment, but if she lost control of the orbital defences the end would be just a matter of time. She was too experienced an officer to believe otherwise. Governor Brown had lavished resources on his fortress, but a handful of KEWs would be enough to reduce it to rubble. The only thing keeping the corporations from doing just that was the proximity of their towers.

And they're probably evacuating their towers already, she thought. She'd banned aircar traffic - the ATC network had crashed, anyway - but the corporate directors were unlikely to care. *And once the towers are empty, they can call down fire from heaven and destroy me.*

She thought, rapidly. Had she lost - again? Should she consider evacuating Wolfbane and fleeing corewards? She *did* have a powerful fleet and advanced technology under her command. It would be one hell of a bargaining chip in the right hands. But there was no guarantee of finding a *third* safe harbour. She'd been incredibly lucky to find Wolfbane after escaping Corinthian.

"Contact the garrisons outside the city," she ordered, finally. "They are to advance and put down the rebels by all means necessary."

Paula looked pale. "Admiral, they may not be loyal," she said. "Their officers..."

Rani met her eyes. "Do you have a better idea?"

"...No," Paula said.

"Then we have no choice," Rani said. "We have to use the weapons we've got and *hope*."

She leaned back, reminding herself - again - that there was no *immediate* threat. If she regained control of the streets, if she brought the fleet into orbit to counter the orbital fortresses, she could secure her position. The towers could be blasted from orbit - they, unlike the fortress, didn't need direct hits to take major damage - and she could crush her enemies like bugs. She had no compunctions about ordering KEW strikes against civilian rebels. She'd teach those traitors *precisely* what happened to anyone who defied her.

"Terrorist attack at the spaceport," Commodore Bradley reported. "They took out a couple of shuttles and their passengers."

Rani gritted her teeth. "Tell the guards to secure the area," she ordered. Trying to get the crews back to the fleet was asking for trouble, now the orbital grid was compromised. The fortresses were shooting at each other, but that wouldn't stop them blasting the shuttles as they tried to fly past. "The spacers can wait in secure accommodation."

"Aye, Admiral," Bradley said.

Captain Ryan Schuler strode into the hastily-established command post, cursing his superiors - both sets of superiors - under his breath. The Wolfbane Militia had been a professional force, once upon a time, but the demand for manpower had forced the militia to take thousands of unqualified recruits and train them in a very short space of time. Half the men under his command were barely qualified to pass the first set of tests, while the other half would probably be poached for off-world duty at any moment. The last thing he'd expected were orders to grab his men, issue ammunition and move the entire company down to the makeshift CP as quickly as possible.

And the second set of orders are even worse, he thought, checking the pistol at his holster. *If they intend to put down the rebels, I have to stop them.*

"Captain," General Francis said, curtly. He was an immensely overweight man, puffing on a cigar. "How *nice* of you to join us."

"Thank you, sir," Ryan said, swallowing his annoyance. He had no idea how General Francis had gotten the post, but the fat bastard was dangerously incompetent. Perhaps *that* was why he'd gotten the post. No one considered him a real threat. "Someone blew up the Stark Bridge. We had to come the long way round."

Francis eyed him, then jabbed a finger at the map. Time *really* must be pressing. The general had printed out a paper map and hung it on the wall himself, rather than passing the duty to his aide. Rumour had it that his current aide was a blonde woman with bigger breasts than brains, although there was no sign of her anywhere in the room. Ryan reminded himself that the blonde might not even exist. Francis was hardly the most popular officer in the militia.

"Tryon is in chaos," Francis said. His finger traced out lines on the map. "At last report, a dozen districts were in rebel hands and several more were in chaos. The police forces are holding a line here" - he pointed to a spot that appeared to be in the middle of the river - "and corporate security forces are holding the towers, but that isn't going to last. Our sources tell us that the rebels are gathering their forces for a final push at the towers before it's too late."

Asshole, Ryan thought. *Too fucking ignorant to even think of a good lie.*

"Our orders are to enter the city, then sweep the rebellious districts clear," Francis added, sternly. "Rear forces will be establishing detention camps - rebels who surrender will be sent there, rebels who insist on fighting will be killed. Once we link up with the police, we will reverse course and sweep the districts again. *Everyone* is to be considered a potential rebel until proven otherwise."

Captain Grossman coughed. "Does that include women and children?"

"Everyone," Francis repeated.

Ryan felt sick. He knew better than to believe that women and children were harmless - and he had no reason to doubt that the region was occupied by rebels - but he had no enthusiasm for a kill-sweep. And that was what Francis wanted. Everyone within the district would be killed unless they surrendered...*everyone*. The prisoners might well wind up wishing that they'd fought to the death instead.

He swallowed. "Sir, with all due respect..."

Francis leered at him. "Don't have the stomach, boy?"

Ryan's temper snapped. "I'm not going to kill thousands of innocents for you!"

"Then place yourself under arrest," Francis snapped. "Your XO can take over the company and..."

Ryan drew his pistol and shot Francis in the head. The general stumbled backwards, then collapsed to the ground. Ryan watched him die...

...And then all hell broke loose.

"Admiral, we have a report from the command post," Paula said. "There... there's been another mutiny. A whole *series* of mutinies."

Rani closed her eyes for a long moment. "What. Happened?"

"The reports contradict one another," Paula said, slowly. Rani opened her eyes and glared at her. "At CP1, General Francis was shot, then several other officers opened fire and now entire units are shooting at each other. At CP2, General Weldon killed both of his commissioners and took his entire division into revolt. At CP3..."

"Enough," Rani said. Her voice was very cold. "I don't need the details. What is the overall situation?"

Paula swallowed. "Two-thirds of the militiamen are heading towards the city to reinforce the rebels," she said. She sounded as though she expected to be beheaded, just for being the bearer of bad news. "And they're going to link up with the corporate security forces."

And then attack the fortress, Rani thought. She was starting to understand why some people shot the messenger. There was no hope of convincing the corporate directors to remain on the fence, not now. They'd have to steer the rebels or be destroyed by them. *That would not be good.*

She studied the display, thinking hard. She'd lost. There was no denying it. The only option left was to abandon the planet and escape, taking the fleet with her. Why not? She'd done it before…

Because there's no certainty of finding a safe place to run, her thoughts reminded her. She'd already been through it. *And the fleet would eventually start to break down.*

She paused. *Or I could attack Avalon. It's the last thing they'd expect.*

"Contact the fleet," she said. "Order them to advance against the orbital fortresses and clear space above the city. Once they are in orbit, they are to prepare to provide fire support against the enemy positions."

And be ready to escape, if necessary, she thought. She would have to send the spacers back to their ships in any case. She'd have no difficulty going with them, along with her command staff. And once she was on the ships, her options would begin to open up. *I can bombard the planet into submission or head straight for Avalon or…*

Red icons flickered into life on the display, far too close to Wolfbane for comfort. Rani stared, unable to believe her eyes. They couldn't be friendly, could they? She hadn't ordered any of her other fleets to return to Wolfbane. And yet, who else could they be?

She found her voice. "What are *those*?"

Commodore Bradbury worked his console, then looked up. "It's the Commonwealth Navy," he said. "They're here!"

CHAPTER THIRTY-FIVE

"Get me a direct link to the ground," Mandy snapped. "And inform the advance team that we're here!"

She forced herself to watch as her fleet raced towards Wolfbane. It had been sheer luck - although she wasn't sure if it had been good or bad luck - that they'd been sneaking into the system when all hell broke loose. Right now, her analysts were trying to make sense of an increasingly complicated multisided conflict and not getting very far. The enemy command network appeared to have splintered into at least *six* competing factions, with sides changing on a moment's notice. There was no way to tell who was friendly and who wasn't.

"The enemy fleet is altering position," Commander Andrew Mayflower said. They'd spent the last three weeks preparing for the final battle, but they hadn't expected such chaos. "They're heading for the planet."

"Then adjust our course to intercept," Mandy ordered. The enemy fleet would almost certainly remain loyal to Admiral Singh. It had to be neutralised. If nothing else, smashing the enemy's mobile units would make it impossible for them to resume the offensive. "And keep trying to get through to the ground."

Her eyes narrowed as the display continued to update. Four orbital fortresses appeared to be friendly, if only because the enemy fleet was heading towards them, but it was impossible to tell *how* friendly they were. Admiral Singh's enemies might not be the Commonwealth's friends. The other fortresses were shooting at their fellows, clearly trying to weaken them before the fleet arrived. Mandy hoped the sides resolved themselves before it was too late. A fortress, even one from the pre-collapse days, was a dangerous opponent. Even with force shields, she didn't want to risk challenging an entire *network* of fortresses unless there was no way to avoid it.

"The enemy fleet is continuing on its current course," Mayflower reported. "They're ignoring us."

"They have to know we're here," Mandy said. "Time to weapons range?"

"Seven minutes," Mayflower said. "Unless they have something *else* up their sleeves."

Mandy gritted her teeth. She'd kept her crews busy during the long flight to Wolfbane, trying to make sure they didn't have time to brood, but it hadn't worked. How could it? Morale had recovered, slowly, as the squadrons were repaired, but everyone *knew* the Commonwealth's tech advantage was no longer guaranteed. Not that it had ever been guaranteed in the first place, the more cynical part of her mind noted. Admiral Singh had had every reason to push technological research and development forward as fast as possible. And now Mandy's crews were expecting to discover *more* enemy superweapons as the war raged on.

"They haven't had time to come up with something new," she said, grimly. "We just need to head the enemy ships off before it's too late."

Impossible, Rani thought. *How the hell did they manage to coordinate such an operation across interstellar distances*?

She didn't *want* to believe what she was seeing. The Commonwealth Navy could *not* be entering *her* system. And yet, there was no way to avoid it. The enemy ships - her analysts had already tagged some of them as having been at the Battle of Titlark - must have followed her all the way to Wolfbane. They *couldn't* have coordinated such an operation. It had to be sheer bad luck.

War in the streets, mutiny in the ranks and now an enemy fleet, she asked herself. *What now?*

She felt sweat trickling down her back as she turned to Bradbury. "Order Admiral Howarth to engage the enemy ships and drive them from the planet," she said. "Fortress One is to be tackled later."

"Aye, Admiral," Bradbury said.

Rani turned back to the display, silently cursing her luck. She was in deep - deep - shit. If she could keep the enemy ships back, she *might* manage to retake control of the high orbitals and clear a path to orbit and escape; if she failed, she would lose. The Commonwealth wouldn't have any hesitation when it came to blasting the fortress from orbit. Taking out the corporate towers would only help the Commonwealth in the long run.

Damn traitors, she thought, coldly. *They've betrayed their own world*.

She forced herself to think. She'd built a reputation on thinking her way out of tight spots - a reputation Admiral Bainbridge had casually destroyed - but she couldn't see many options remaining. Her ships were undermanned - thankfully, they'd reloaded their magazines - and most of the orbital defences had been compromised. She could trump some of the threats facing her, but not all of them in combination. Together, they were lethal.

"And record a message for Detachment Nine," she said. It was a gamble, but she was fast running out of other options. "I have some special orders for them."

"Aye, Admiral."

Rani nodded, her eyes flickering around the compartment. Paula looked pale and worn, Emma was showing no emotion…Bradbury was working his console, looking grim. How long would it be, she wondered, before one of them decided to betray her in exchange for their life and freedom? She had no doubt that the thought had already crossed their minds…

"The enemy fleet is altering course," Mayflower reported. "They're heading towards us and shifting into combat formation."

Mandy nodded. The enemy commander - she doubted Admiral Singh was in direct command - didn't seem to be inclined to be subtle. His ships were heading directly towards hers, aiming for a battering match. He had to be *pissed*, she thought. Normally, a defending fleet would fall back on the planetary defences and combine their firepower, but that wasn't an option now. The Wolves had to remain between the Commonwealth Navy and Wolfbane, yet they couldn't go too close to Wolfbane itself. They'd be stabbed in the back.

"Alert all ships," she ordered. "Prepare to open fire."

She tensed as the range dropped sharply. They'd adapted their point defence systems - and even added modifications to deal with enemy pinnaces - but there was no way to know how well they'd work in the *real* world. Nothing went as planned, no matter how carefully she strove to cover all the bases. She'd just have to hope - and pray - that she'd done *enough* to give her ships a fighting chance. The Wolves hadn't had time to come up with more innovations, had they?

"Enemy ships are opening fire," Mayflower reported.

"Return fire," Mandy ordered, automatically. The range was still closing. "Tactical analysis?"

Mayflower coughed. "They loaded their external racks," he said. "I can't separate the new missiles from the old yet."

Mandy nodded. She'd hoped the Wolves wouldn't have bothered to load their external racks - normally, they weren't loaded unless the CO was expecting a battle - but fate had decided to rule against her. Admiral Singh must have been feeling paranoid. Her ships shivered, a moment later, as they flushed their own external racks. The range was still closing. Her opponent, it seemed, wasn't inclined to reverse course and hold the range open.

Which makes sense, if they think they have a decisive advantage, she thought. *But do they*?

"I've isolated five pinnaces," Mayflower reported. "They're keeping pace with the missiles."

"Target them with shipkillers," Mandy ordered. She felt a flicker of admiration for the enemy pilots. Unless the Wolves had made a *real* breakthrough, which seemed unlikely, their pinnaces had to be pushing their compensators right to the limit. Her analysts agreed that there was a very real chance that their systems would collapse under the strain. "Can you isolate some of the advanced warheads?"

"Not as yet," Mayflower reported. He paused. "The enemy ships are launching their second salvo."

Mandy braced herself as the tidal wave of missiles roared into her point defence envelope and began to vanish. Her point defence systems had been improved, after the last battle, and hundreds of missiles were wiped out of space, but a handful of missiles managed to make it through the network and throw themselves against her ships. Her display began to chart a mounting liturgy of destruction as starships were destroyed or damaged by the enemy missiles. The enemy were firing at her flankers, she noted. Their second salvo seemed to be aimed at her capital ships.

Which is smart, she acknowledged. *They'll put their advanced warheads into their second offensive, once they've reduced our point defence.*

"Picking up a signal from the ground," Lieutenant Robins reported. "ID confirmed, Commodore. It's the advance team!"

"Forward it to Colonel Stalker," Mandy ordered. "And see if you can get an update."

She felt a moment of grim satisfaction as her missiles crashed into the enemy formation. The Wolves *had* improved, she noted, but not enough. Her missiles crippled two battleships and destroyed a third, along with a handful of smaller ships. Leaving the enemy flankers alone had been a calculated risk, but it seemed to have paid off. Smashing the enemy's mobile units would be enough to win the war, even if Mandy and her fleet were wiped out. The Wolves would be unable to resume the offensive before it was too late.

"The enemy pinnaces have been destroyed," Mayflower said. "The enemy missiles are still coming."

"Of course," Mandy said, dryly.

The display updated, again. Mandy winced. The enemy *had* launched their advanced missiles, throwing them right into the teeth of her defences. Taking out so many of her flankers had been a gamble - just like hers - but it had worked out for them. She couldn't take out their missiles until they roared into her formation, by which time it would be too late to keep them from inflicting real damage.

"Move the remaining flankers forward," she ordered, coldly. The flankers would take heavy losses - again - but her capital ships would survive. "And continue to engage the enemy."

She forced herself to watch as the enemy missiles tore into her formation. *Triumphant, Spectre, Magnificent* and *Daredevil* were blown into atoms, while *Cavalcade* and *Braveheart* fell out of formation, streaming plasma and lifepods into space. She hoped the enemy would give her crews time to escape before finishing the job…she cursed, under her breath. The hulks would have to be destroyed before she left the system, if she had to retreat. They couldn't allow the enemy a chance to study the remains.

"*Lamington* reports that she's lost four of her drive nodes," Mayflower said. "Her CO is requesting permission to disengage."

"Order her to hold position as long as possible," Mandy said, curtly. The enemy *couldn't* have an unlimited supply of advanced warheads. She'd have lost her entire fleet at Titlark if they had. "She is to keep firing until she shoots herself dry."

"Aye, Commodore," Mayflower said.

Mandy returned her attention to the display. The enemy formation was wavering, although they were holding together remarkably well. She'd inflicted a great deal of damage, enough to convince a normal enemy that the time had come to retreat. But the Wolves *couldn't* retreat. They were defending their homeworld. Admiral Singh might decide to abandon Wolfbane - it wouldn't be the first world she'd abandoned - but her subordinates might have different ideas…

"We received an update from the ground, Commodore," Robins reported. The display updated. A number of fortresses turned yellow, denoting them as allies. Mandy hoped they weren't fair-weather allies. "The…ah…rebels are holding some of the fortresses, but others are remaining loyal or have gone dark."

Surprise, surprise, Mandy thought. If one side thought it was going to lose - and it had the chance - it would do everything in its power to keep the other from taking control of the orbital defences. *And we don't know how far we can trust the rebels…*

"Keep a wary eye on them," she ordered. There were over a thousand crewmen on each of the giant fortresses. It would be dangerous to assume they were *all* friendly. "We'll keep our distance until we're sure…"

Mayflower cleared his throat. "Commodore, one of the friendly fortresses has just been destroyed," he said. "The others are taking heavy damage."

Mandy nodded. Wolfbane's network of orbital defences and industrial nodes was taking a severe battering. Whatever else happened, the planet would need years to rebuild after the war ended. She wondered, absently, just what the rebels were thinking. Did they believe that getting rid of Admiral Singh was worth the price? Or were they thinking the war had already gone too far?

She shrugged. The civil war had already begun. It was too late to have second thoughts.

"The enemy fleet has taken a pounding," Bradbury reported.

Rani nodded. Under other circumstances, it would have been good news. The new missiles had worked as advertised, as had the tactics for deploying them in open combat. But now...every ship she lost reduced her bargaining power, if she had to open negotiations with...*anyone.* The mounting damage was enough to prove - to her, at least - that Wolfbane had lost the war. She closed her eyes for a long moment, conceding the point. It made her next moves so much easier.

"Order the fleet to pull back," she said. "They are to conserve their missile loads as much as possible."

Her lips quirked with cold amusement. The mutinies and uprisings had been well-planned - and the enemy had had a remarkable stroke of luck - but it wasn't *perfect.* They hadn't come close to threatening the fortress, while the mere presence of so many civilians so close to her headquarters prevented them from simply blasting her from orbit. Her position had been gravely weakened - there was no point in trying to deny it - but she still had some cards to play, assuming her guards remained loyal.

And if they all turn on me, she thought wryly, *I'm screwed anyway*.

"Order the loyalists to hold position or withdraw to more defensible locations," she added, coolly. Any formation lacking human shields was doomed, as soon as the enemy secured the high orbitals. "Units that can make it to the outer defence lines are to do so; other units are to hold in place if possible."

Paula nodded. "Yes, Admiral."

Rani keyed her wristcom. Colonel Higgs was already waiting outside with a squad of loyal guards. He'd secure the room, making sure that her subordinates knew they were with her to the end. Maybe they did have plans to turn on her, maybe they didn't. All that mattered was keeping some bargaining chips long enough to make her escape.

I could always turn pirate, she thought, as the guards filed into the room. *Or blast Avalon before they realise where I've gone.*

"Commodore, the enemy fleet is reversing course and falling back," Mayflower reported, slowly. He sounded as though he didn't believe his own words. "They're dropping mines to cover their retreat."

And making it obvious, Mandy thought. *That* was bad tactics unless they *wanted* to slow her down. They probably did. She'd battered a dozen enemy ships into bleeding hulks and the remainder weren't in much better shape. If nothing else, they needed to buy time to patch up the damage and reload their missile tubes. *We can't give them that time.*

"Deploy countermeasures," she ordered. Too many of her own ships were damaged for her to order a quick advance. "And muster every ship capable of matching their speed."

She scowled as she realised *precisely* what the enemy ships were doing. They were falling back on the planet, angling themselves so they'd be shielded from the mutinous orbital fortresses. If she went after them, she'd be exposing herself to fire from the loyalist fortresses as well as the fleet…if she didn't, she'd be giving them all the time they needed to make repairs. And if she tried to take the high orbitals herself, they'd be in a perfect position to intercept her.

And there'll be weapons on the ground too, she thought. *As long as they remain in enemy hands, taking the high orbitals is going to be dangerous.*

"I've reconfigured the formations," Mayflower said. "A third of our ships are going to have to remain behind."

"Detail them to cover the wounded," Mandy ordered. "The remainder of our ships are to give chase..."

A new alarm sounded. "Commodore," Robins said. "Long-range sensors are picking up a *second* enemy formation, heading straight for the planet!"

Mandy swore. "Time to intercept?"

"Four hours," Robins said. "I...there's four battleships and a number of cruisers!"

They want us to see them, Mandy thought. Admiral Singh had probably been planning to retake the offensive as soon as possible. No *wonder* she'd decided to concentrate her forces. It was common sense. She'd definitely not expected the Commonwealth Navy to attack Wolfbane. *If that fleet is in our rear, we cannot push through against Wolfbane itself.*

"Pass the alert to Colonel Stalker," she said. It felt like a bad joke. She'd crippled the enemy fleet - and rebels had broken Admiral Singh's hold on the planet - but now she would have to retreat, leaving the job undone. Perhaps Colonel Stalker would have an idea. "And order the fleet to hold position."

"Aye, Commodore," Mayflower said.

Four hours, Mandy thought. Wolfbane's industrial nodes had already been damaged, but there were hundreds of other targets within the system. The asteroid bases, the remaining shipyards, the cloudscoops... *We could do a lot of damage in four hours.*

She cursed under her breath. The Commonwealth would still win the war. But now...now the cost was going to be far higher.

And it won't be paid by us, she thought. She could withdraw - she would withdraw, once she had smashed the industrial base. Admiral Singh wouldn't be able to catch *her. The rebels will pay the real price.*

CHAPTER THIRTY-SIX

Jasmine could hear shooting echoing over the city as she led the way out of the safe house and down to the corporate security convoy. Tallyman's men looked professional, she noted as Mouganthu clambered into the AFV, but she had no idea how they would handle a real firefight. They weren't noticeably sloppy, yet there was a rote quality to their movements that suggested they hadn't come under attack when escorting a convoy before.

"We have control over the inner city, all the way up to the inner circle," the driver called back, as the vehicle lurched into motion. The escorts fell into formation around them, their guns swinging from side to side. "Some of the districts have been barricaded, but others are still in chaos."

Jasmine nodded. "And the loyalists?"

"Trapped in the inner circle, for now," the driver said. "Unless they've gone to ground outside it."

Mouganthu snorted. "They can't hide for long, can they?"

"Maybe," Jasmine said.

She shrugged. Securing an entire city was always a nightmare, even with plenty of soldiers and a unified command structure. Tryon had hundreds of different forces, ranging from corporate security and mutinous militia regiments to gangsters, students and home-grown defence forces. Getting them all to cooperate afterwards - or simply disarming them - would not be easy. Rogue enemy forces *could* hide their weapons and go to ground for a while, if they were careful. She doubted they could hide for long, but they might have a chance to do some damage before they were rounded up.

The streets seemed to be quiet, too quiet. Parts looked almost normal, if deserted; other parts were scarred and blackened by war, bodies lying where they'd fallen. She hoped that *someone* was picking up the wounded, but she knew it wasn't likely. The hospitals would be overloaded, if they hadn't already been destroyed. Long-term thinkers would consider them important targets. Securing medical supplies might make the difference between life and death.

"Dear God," Mouganthu breathed. They drove past the burned-out remains of a convoy of vehicles, charred bodies clearly visible inside. "Is this real?"

"Yeah," Jasmine said. "This is war."

She kept one hand on her pistol as they drove onwards, glancing from side to side. The narrowing streets weren't very secure…they were the perfect place for an ambush, if someone considered it worth the risk. An IED in the dustbins, then a brief spray of bullets and an immediate retreat…she'd seen it done, time and time again. No doubt, if someone didn't take control quickly, insurgents would learn how to carry out such attacks. The dumb ones would have been killed in the first round of fighting.

"Taking a detour round the plaza," the driver called. "Someone's turned it into a miniature fortress."

Jasmine sucked in her breath, feeling her heart starting to pound. In her experience, unexpected detours always led to ambushes. The enemy might have done something to make the convoy change course… and course changes, on the surface, were always predicable. But she saw nothing, apart from hundreds of armed guards, as they drove into Tallyman Tower and halted in the garage. A pair of young men were waiting for them.

"Fredrick," Mouganthu said, as he climbed out of the car. "It's good to see you again."

"Sir," Fredrick said. He had an oddly-formal way of talking. His eyes flickered over Jasmine, then returned to Mouganthu. "Father is waiting in the war room."

"Very good," Mouganthu said. "Take us to him at once."

Jasmine followed the three men through a series of secure doors - each one guarded by armed men - and then into a large command and control room. She knew, immediately, that whoever had designed it had never been a soldier. It *looked* good, she could tell, but it wasn't very efficient. She'd have sooner worked in a makeshift command post. But it didn't look as though she had a choice.

"Herman," Tallyman said, rising. His command chair looked like something out of a bad flick. "I'm glad you're safe."

"I was very nearly dead," Mouganthu said. He glanced around the room. "You've done well for yourself..."

Jasmine cleared her throat. "Can I have a SITREP?"

"Of course," Tallyman said. He nodded to the other young man. "Major Adders?"

"The situation is as follows," Adders drawled. "Admiral Singh's loyalists have holed up in the fortress. From this position, they are sniping at any visible targets. Our people have been warned to stay out of sight."

"We've had to clear the upper levels," Fredrick put in. "They've been distressingly good at shooting our staff."

Adders nodded, curtly. "Our own forces have established a ring of steel around the fortress," he continued. "We believe we can keep them from breaking out, either on the ground or in the air. Portable MANPADs have been deployed to cover the airspace directly over the fortress. However, we cannot break in without taking serious losses."

"I see," Jasmine said. She rather suspected the corporate directors were unwilling to risk their forces in an attack on the fortress. "And Admiral Singh?"

"Is in the fortress herself, as far as we can tell," Adders informed her. "So far, she's ignored all our attempts to negotiate."

Mouganthu lifted his eyebrows. "You intend to negotiate?"

"We offered her safe passage to a world of her choosing, if she surrendered without a fuss," Tallyman said. "She didn't bother to send a response."

Jasmine turned her attention to the displays as the two directors argued. They were hard to read - another sign that the designer hadn't really known what he was doing - but the overall situation was clear. The uprising had stalemated. Admiral Singh could not win, yet - as long as she remained alive - she couldn't be defeated. And taking the fortress would be hideously costly.

"Stalemate," she muttered.

"Not quite," Adders said. "She's got a relief fleet inbound. ETA four hours."

Jasmine cursed as he adjusted the display. If the timing worked out, Admiral Singh might just come out on top after all. The Commonwealth Navy couldn't defeat both the loyalists *and* the new fleet. That would allow Admiral Singh a chance to take control of the high orbitals and punish the rebels…

And how many of the directors will try to switch sides if it looks like Admiral Singh will win, she asked herself. *She* was intent on weakening Wolfbane, but the corporate directors would probably have very different ideas. *All of them?*

"Get me a link to the fleet," she said. "I need to talk to Colonel Stalker."

"That's another one dead," the sniper said. "You owe me a bonus."

Captain Joshua Forster snorted, rudely. The sniper wouldn't be able to claim his wages, let alone a bonus. His unit had been torn to ribbons and merged with two more units as the police force struggled to cope with an uprising that far exceeded their worst nightmares. By the time the order had come to retreat to the inner circle and set up defensive lines, his body had been aching so badly that he'd practically fallen asleep on his feet. Now, the stimulants he'd been taking made his entire body jumpy.

"Just try to keep them from watching us," he ordered. "I don't want them getting any closer."

He groaned as he surveyed the makeshift defence line. The fortress was heavily defended - there was a hullmetal wall and strong gates - but the policemen hadn't been allowed inside the walls. Instead, they'd resorted to using their vehicles as barricades and digging trenches in the hard ground. It would have been enough to hold off an unarmed mob - his men had long since lost any reluctance to fire on crowds - but nowhere near enough to stop a determined offensive. He was all too aware that supplies were running low and morale was at rock bottom.

And discipline is in the pits, he thought, grimly. *I can't control my men any longer.*

The sniper fired another shot, then muttered a curse. Joshua guessed he'd missed his target, even though he'd been warned to make every shot count. Ammunition, like everything else, was in short supply. A brief hail of shots spluttered back at them, then faded back into the background noise. He found it hard to care as bullets snapped though the air. Part of him wondered if he would be relieved if a bullet struck him. He'd long-since lost track of just how long he'd been awake.

He glanced towards the far edge of the square, wondering if he could sneak out before someone put a bullet in his back. A number of policemen had already deserted, if rumour was to be believed. They'd taken off their uniforms and blended into the streets, no doubt hoping they could hide from any future reprisals. Maybe they were right. Joshua didn't *think* that anyone knew his face. But if he was wrong…

A low rumble echoed through the air as a pair of AFVs drove around the barricades. The younger policemen raised a quiet cheer when they saw the vehicles, but Joshua wasn't so impressed. He'd seen too many of them struck by rockets or blown up by improvised bombs to take any comfort from their presence. The only good news was that they'd probably attract fire, but not for long. They'd be destroyed soon, once the enemy attacked. God knew just how the rebels had obtained so many weapons - the militia had probably been *composed* of traitors - but it didn't matter. All that mattered is that he was trapped.

Lieutenant Glomma appeared, looking haggard. His uniform was torn in a dozen places, blood staining his blue jacket. He looked a nightmare, just like Joshua himself. In calmer times, they'd be severely punished for allowing their uniforms to get so messy. The thought nearly made Joshua giggle. Under the circumstances, there was no point in caring about the state of their clothes.

"Captain," Lieutenant Glomma said. His voice was unsteady. He'd been up almost as long as Joshua himself. "Commissioner Hendry has put you in command of this sector."

"Joy," Joshua said. He couldn't quite keep back a giggle. He'd been expecting the hammer to fall for hours - his superiors knew he'd fucked up by the numbers - but this...this was a brilliant punishment. They *knew* he didn't have a hope of keeping the sector secure, once the enemy started to push. The rebels would kill Joshua for them. "Is there more good news?"

Lieutenant Glomma shrugged. "There's a handful of rebel bitches in the office," he said, shortly. "Do you want a turn?"

Joshua snickered. "Eat, drink and be merry, for tomorrow we will be castrated, shot and dumped in an unmarked grave?

"Something like that," Lieutenant Glomma said. He sobered. "There's no hope of getting out, is there?"

"Probably not," Joshua said. "If we try to run, our own side will shoot us in the back; if we stay, the rebels will kill us. The only hope is the Admiral pulling a rabbit out of her hat."

And then I'll be executed for failure, he thought. He giggled, helplessly. *Failure is the only option.*

Lieutenant Glomma eyed him, severely. "I think you've had too much stimulant juice, sir."

Joshua nodded. He was wired, practically bouncing off the walls. The hallucinations would start soon, if the medics were to be believed. He needed sleep and a purge, probably not in that order. Or perhaps a complete blood replenishment. He couldn't recall *precisely* what happened to people who overdosed on stimulants, but he didn't think it would be pleasant.

We're not meant to have more than one or two cans in a day, he thought. The medics had made that clear. *How many did I have?*

He racked his brains. He couldn't remember. He wasn't sure he even cared.

"It doesn't matter," he said. He nodded towards the distant buildings. The rebels were massing on the far side, plotting to storm the fortress. They might not get through the walls, but that wouldn't make any difference to the police. They'd be torn to ribbons before the Admiral's loyalists counterattacked. "They're coming for us."

"Yes, sir," Lieutenant Glomma said.

"Tell the lads they can have their fun, if they like," Joshua added. Raping subversive women had been one of the perks of the job, but he had the feeling that the rebels would take a far dimmer view of it. The mutilations they'd inflicted on lone policemen proved it. "It'll be the last time."

"Yes, sir."

Ed had realised, a long time ago, that the universe had a grim sense of humour. He'd seen plenty of operations where random chance had made the difference between success and failure, where luck had overwhelmed careful planning...now, he couldn't help feeling that the universe had gone too far. The battle in orbit had stalemated, but the stalemate wouldn't last. Once the newcomers arrived, the Commonwealth Navy would have to retreat.

And we don't even know those ships are real, he thought. Admiral Singh *might* have gotten lucky or she could be trying to trick them. The timing suggested the latter. *They could be drones.*

He made a face as he ran through the calculations. It might not matter. If the ships were real and the Commonwealth Navy retreated, Admiral Singh would reassert control over Wolfbane and punish the rebels. If the ships *weren't* real, Admiral Singh would still have won time to come up with something else. Ed knew, from bitter experience, that just because *he* couldn't see any other options didn't mean that they didn't exist. If nothing else, Admiral Singh might start thinking about preparing to take the planet with her when she died.

The nasty part of his mind pointed out that Mandy was right. They *could* lay waste to the system's industrial base, then retreat to gather reinforcements. Admiral Singh wouldn't be able to rebuild before it was too late. From a coldly pragmatic point of view, letting her crush the rebels would work in the Commonwealth's favour. And yet...honour demanded that they find a way to help the rebels. Whatever their motives, the rebels had risked everything to help the Commonwealth. They had to be helped in turn.

His terminal bleeped. He touched a switch. Jasmine's face appeared in front of him.

"Colonel," she said. "We seem to have a stalemate."

Ed nodded. "Perhaps," he said. "We have to winkle Admiral Singh out of her lair."

"Yes, sir," Jasmine said. "They're refusing to allow us to bombard the city."

"I expected as much," Ed said. The nasty part of his mind pointed out that the rebels couldn't *stop* him bombarding the city. He told that part of him to shut up. "There's no way they can evacuate in time?"

"The city is in chaos, sir," Jasmine said. "Even getting a few thousand people out before it's too late would be difficult."

Ed frowned as a tactical assessment popped up in front of him. He knew better than to believe it was perfect - something was *always* missing - but there was no way to avoid the simple fact that the situation *was* chaotic. There was no way to evacuate the city in less than a week, assuming the various insurgents chose to cooperate. If they didn't, the task would rapidly become impossible.

"We are pulling people away from the inner circle," Jasmine said. "But right now we can't get them much further away."

"It looks like that," Ed agreed.

He cursed, again. The fortress was tough. His long-range sensors had told him things he didn't want to know about its defences. The locals would bleed themselves white trying to get through the outer edge, while there was no way to *know* what was waiting for them inside. Admiral Singh had created a neat little trap. Starving her out was starting to look like the only realistic option, but the incoming ships had removed *that* as a possibility…

Unless we take the offensive, he thought, coldly. There were sixty marines on his ships, sixty marines and all their equipment. *The rebels would back us up, wouldn't they?*

He couldn't help feeling a thrill, even as he forced himself to think logically. The prospect of donning his armour and jumping into a hot zone was tempting, very tempting. And yet, he knew it would be a risk. He'd been reluctant to spend his marines freely even before they'd been exiled to Avalon, with no hope of replacements in the pipeline. He might well be leading the remainder of his company to the grave.

It has to be done, he thought. They'd stormed a CityBlock on Earth, just before they'd been exiled to Avalon. *And we can do it.*

He took a breath. "The company will be jumping shortly," he said. There wouldn't be much time to plan the operation, but they were used to that. "Coordinate with the locals, see what support they can offer."

Jasmine's eyes went wide. "Yes, sir," she said. "And afterwards, I request permission to join you."

Ed nodded. "I'll be landing supplies soon," he said. The plan was already taking shape in his mind. "Suit up, once the suit is on the ground - tell the other two to join you. Your platoon will be assaulting from the ground."

Jasmine saluted. "Yes, sir," she said. "*Semper Fi*!"

Her face vanished. Ed smiled, then called for his command staff. Three hours to plan and execute a mission…they'd done it before, back when they'd been in the Core Worlds. Now…it wasn't going to be easy. They were operating on a shoestring, without half the supplies or back-up they'd had on Earth. And yet, he was looking forward to it…

And yet, he couldn't help thinking that it was going to be their last hurrah.

CHAPTER THIRTY-SEVEN

"Everything is in place, sir," Command Sergeant Gwendolyn Patterson said. "Platoon One is on the ground. Platoons Two through Five are in the air, ready to move. Platoon Six is in the air, ready to reinforce as necessary."

Ed nodded, feeling the Raptor shifting under his feet as he tested his armour. How long had it *been* since he'd worn the combat suit? Four *years*? Or had it been longer? It had been carefully tailored for him, back on Earth, but now...it didn't *feel* like a second skin any longer. He made a mental note to wear it more often, once he returned to Avalon. He'd fallen out of practice.

"Very good," he said. The fortress was a daunting target, but they'd tackled worse. "Order the advance units to begin the offensive."

"Yes, sir."

Rani paced the command centre, feeling impatient. The enemy hadn't moved, suggesting they hadn't fallen for her bluff...or that they thought they had an obligation to defend the planet. Not that *that* would last, once they confirmed that she *was* bluffing. She'd dispatched courier boats to summon reinforcements, but cold logic told her that the battle would be over before they could arrive.

She glanced at Paula. "Has there been any update?"

"No, Admiral," Paula said. Her eyes flicked to the armed guards, nervously. "Just demands for your surrender."

Rani nodded, not bothering to respond. The demands ranged from gentle suggestions that she should resign to demands for unconditional surrender, but she hadn't bothered to respond to them either. There was no way the corporate directors would allow her to go into exile, even though it *would* end the uprising before it could dissolve into chaos. She'd be lucky if she was *only* shot in the head. The atrocities her forces had committed over the last twenty-four hours would be enough to guarantee her a slow and painful death.

Not that they care about the worst atrocities, she thought. *They're more upset that I raided their tower.*

The console bleeped an alert. "Admiral," Bradbury said. "The enemy has…" - there was a short pause - "the enemy has redirected every aircar in the city into our airspace."

Rani gritted her teeth. The aircars would be unmanned, of course. The rebels had probably captured the ATC system, then subverted it. They wouldn't have any trouble taking remote control of the entire fleet and pointing them at her fortress. She doubted they'd do any damage if they were rammed into the hullmetal, but they might distract her guards or weaken her point defence. It could not be allowed.

"Order the point defence to engage," she said.

"Aye, Admiral."

"The aircars are on their way," Meade's voice said, through the earpiece. "They'll be entering engagement range in one minute."

"Understood," Jasmine said. She crouched behind a makeshift barricade, only a dozen metres from the police line. The remainder of Platoon One was behind her. "Order the gunners to engage the moment the point defence crews reveal their locations."

"Will do," Meade said. "Good luck."

Jasmine glanced up, just in time to see the first aircar screaming overhead. Meade had assured her that there were no passengers - the ATC had locked down every aircar in the city, as soon as the crisis began - but she still felt cold as she watched a bolt of plasma blowing the aircar into flaming debris. Others followed, pieces of debris falling from the skies as they died, one by one. Compared to missiles - or even mortar shells - the aircars were slow and stupid, a problem made worse by flying predicable courses. But they were doing their job.

"I have a lock on their point defence guns," Meade reported. "Firing…now!"

"We move in five," Jasmine told the platoon. Her armour hummed around her, ready to engage. "Be ready."

"Admiral, they're firing shells," Bradbury reported. "They're taking out our point defence clusters!"

Rani swore, realising her mistake. Perhaps she should have simply ignored the aircars. The enemy had probably located *some* of her point defence blisters, but not all of them. Not that it mattered now, did it? The mistake had already been made.

"Switch to countering the incoming fire," she ordered. The enemy targets doubled, then doubled again. Drones projecting false images or… or what? Real threats? "And engage with counterbattery fire!"

"Aye, Admiral."

I still have my fortress, Rani thought. *It isn't over yet.*

Joshua ducked low as another aircar exploded, pieces of debris showering down on the police lines. The skies seemed to be ablaze with fire, hundreds of explosions flashing high over their heads. The noise was deafening. He clutched his rifle, hoping - praying - that none of the debris fell on his head. The battle had barely begun and the police lines were already in tatters.

He saw Lieutenant Glomma running towards him, then fall as *something* fell on him from overhead. Joshua stared, shocked into motionless. The buzzing in his head was growing louder - in truth, he was no longer sure what was real and what wasn't. Perhaps the fireworks overhead weren't real too. The ground shook and shook again, but he had no idea if it was real or something his mind had made up. He took a breath and regretted it instantly as the stench of the dead and dying washed through his nose. His stomach heaved. His legs trembled and he found himself on the ground, with no clear memory of how he'd fallen - or even *if* he'd fallen.

Black figures were running forward. Rebels, they had to be rebels. And yet, they didn't *look* like rebels. Armour meant soldiers, didn't it? Joshua gripped his rifle and tried to rise, praying he was aiming the right end at his target. His head was so confused he wasn't sure if he was coming or going. And then, someone kicked the rifle out of his hand and knocked him back to the ground. He cracked his head against the ground and everything went black…

Jasmine barely noticed the policeman as she led the charge into their lines. The barricades hadn't held up at all, not to the artillery and not to the handful of rockets the corporate security officers had fired from the towers. Dozens of policemen lay everywhere, their broken bodies oddly pathetic on the ground. They'd been lucky, she reflected as she hurried onwards. The rebels had openly talked about torturing the policemen to death.

"The drones are starting their charge now," Meade informed her. She was watching through a hundred stealth drones, which were currently taking up positions over the fortress. "Launch and impact in ten seconds."

"Understood," Jasmine said. A pair of policemen were crouched in a foxhole, firing madly in all directions. She shot them both, grimly aware that their *true* role was to soak up bullets while the *real* defenders got ready to fight to the death. "We're ready…"

She glanced at the entrance. It looked *professional*: a pair of guard-houses, an inspection zone and a whole set of barricades designed to deflect the force of any explosion up into the air. Admiral Singh's designer had lined the whole thing with hullmetal, leaving only a tiny number of murder holes. And yet, it *was* a fixed defence. It had its weaknesses.

"Incoming," Stewart snapped.

Jasmine ducked as the HVM screamed down from high overhead and slammed into the gatehouse. There was a colossal explosion, followed by a thunderous roar. The hullmetal had stood up to the blast, but she'd bet half her salary that the inhabitants were stunned by the impact. A handful of smaller missiles followed, each one targeted on one of the murder holes. Some didn't make it into the guardhouses before detonating, but enough did to wipe out the defenders. Jasmine ran forward as soon as the last missile exploded, clutching a pair of grenades in one hand. If there were any defenders left…

No one fired at her as she ran through the inspection zone, then around the back and into the door. The interior was a blackened ruin, everything save for the hullmetal reduced to charred ash. She felt a flicker of sympathy for the defenders - pinned down, they hadn't stood a chance - and then keyed her mouthpiece. They needed to secure the entrance, then break into the fortress itself before it was too late.

"Gatehouse is secured," she said. The enemy were mounting a counterattack, but it had come too late to do any good. "Send the reinforcements."

"Gotcha," Meade said. "They're on the way."

Jasmine nodded as she took up a defensive position, the rest of the platoon taking up positions behind her. Push back the counterattack, then resume the offensive…it sounded simple, didn't it?

And the second wave is already on the way, she thought. The air was growing thick with smog, but she could hear engines moving through the air. *Admiral Singh will be looking at us while the real threat moves into place.*

"The enemy has captured one of the gatehouses," Colonel Higgs reported. He sounded calm, very calm. Rani appreciated it more than she cared to admit. The others were on the verge of outright panic. "They're moving up reinforcements now."

"Move our own troops to counter them," Rani ordered. Her fortress was still holding out, but she'd lost most of her point defence and counterbattery weapons. Thankfully, the enemy seemed reluctant to continue shelling the installation now their troops were storming the walls. "And ready our shuttles for departure."

"I wouldn't advise that," Colonel Highs said. His voice was *still* calm. "The enemy troops have MANPADs. They've already shot down a number of drones. Launching shuttles would be suicide."

Rani cursed, lightly. She was starting to feel cornered. There had to be a way out, but how?

The display flickered, then updated again. A hundred aircraft - no, a *thousand* - were heading directly towards the fortress. Some of them, perhaps almost *all* of them, had to be false sensor images, but a handful would be real. Which ones? She couldn't tell. Her sensors had been badly damaged by the earlier strikes. She didn't even have enough weapons left to fire at *all* of them.

She glanced at Higgs. "What are they doing?"

"Forcing us to keep revealing our point defence," Higgs said, slowly. He paused, just long enough for Rani to start worrying. "Or they're planning a combat drop..."

He swore. "Move the reserve troops to the upper levels," he snapped. "We're about to have visitors!"

Ed watched through the Raptor's sensors as the assault aircraft roared over Tryon City. It wasn't the first city he'd seen that had been turned into a war zone, but there was something uniquely horrific about the plumes of smoke rising from all over the district. Perhaps it was the brooding presence of twelve giant towers and the fortress itself, wrapped in smoke and spluttering green flashes of plasma fire in all directions. Or perhaps it was the grim knowledge that the smoke hid scenes of horror. The civilians down below had had their lives torn apart, now the war had come home.

And none of them did anything to deserve it, he thought. Wolfbane wasn't a democracy, not in any sense of the word. They didn't even *pretend* to be democratic. *They were never asked if they wanted to start a war.*

"Ten seconds," the jumpmaster said. "Nine…eight…"

The fortress was a brooding mass, a giant obscenity that looked to have come from a bygone era. Ed couldn't help comparing it to a wet-navy battleship, bristling with weapons and mistress of all it surveyed. Governor Brown hadn't *known* about the force shields when he'd started work on his headquarters, but he'd somehow crafted a building that was *ideal* for the new face of war. It was sheer dumb luck that Admiral Singh hadn't managed to design and mass-produce her own planetary force shields before the war had reached Wolfbane. Ed dreaded to think of the cost of trying to fight through an entire modern city. Storming a single CityBlock had been expensive enough.

He gritted his teeth as the harness snapped free, sending him plummeting down towards the squat mass. The rest of the platoons fanned out behind him as the enemy, suddenly aware of the threat, opened fire. Ed watched calmly as the ground rose towards him, knowing that he'd have no hope of survival if the enemy scored a direct hit. The swarm of ECM drones would make it harder for the enemy to pick out the real marines amongst the decoys, but he knew they might get lucky. Or get manual gun crews into place to steer the weapons.

His suit flipped, the antigrav field cancelling his fall a split-second before he slammed into the rooftop. A handful of enemy soldiers were swinging around, raising their weapons: the marines killed them before they could fire a single shot. Ed ducked as a plasma blast tore through the air an inch above his head, then fired a rocket back towards the enemy plasma cannon. It exploded into a ball of white fire, vaporising the crew. They hadn't stood a chance.

"The roof is clear," Gwendolyn reported. "Colonel?"

Call me Captain, Ed thought. *Colonels* did not lead missions. He squashed the thought, hard. There wasn't time.

"Find the hatch," he ordered. The enemy would probably have it code-locked. Given time, his hackers could break the lock, but he doubted they *had* the time. The enemy might even have destroyed the control node, rendering it completely unusable. They'd have to use brute force. "And ready the cracker."

"Yes, sir."

Ed nodded, then checked the network. Two marines had been killed in the drop, but the remainder of all four platoons were on the roof, save for one marine who'd missed the roof and dropped all the way to the ground. Ed hastily ordered him to link up with Platoon One, then contacted the rebel commander. They'd have to send reinforcements of their own, just in case the marines were repulsed.

"We found the hatch," Gwen said, curtly. Her voice sounded as if she'd bitten into something sour. "It's sealed."

"Set the cracker," Ed ordered. He couldn't help feeling a flicker of anticipation. He'd never needed to use a cracker before, not even on Earth. They'd been designed to punch through starship hulls, but he'd never encountered a ship that couldn't be boarded through the standard hatches. "Everyone else, take cover!"

"The colonel is on the roof," Meade's voice said. "They're deploying a cracker."

Jasmine nodded as the last enemy counterattack failed, the enemy troops falling back in disarray. Her reinforcements arrived shortly afterwards, occupying the gatehouse and summoning more men to push against the fortress itself. She checked with her men, then nodded to herself. It was time to retake the offensive.

"We're moving onwards," she said. They didn't dare give the enemy more time to think and plan. "Alert me when they detonate the cracker."

"I'm sure you'll see the flash," Meade said. "Just be careful when you detonate yours."

Jasmine nodded as she led the rush towards the main doors, her reinforcements providing covering fire. The enemy had built *more* murder holes into the fortress itself, but they slammed them closed as the marines approached. Jasmine smirked, despite the situation. It was clear the enemy were reluctant to open the murder holes while the marines were close enough to hurl grenades into the fortress.

"The main doors are sealed," Stewart reported. A string of reports flashed up in Jasmine's HUD. The enemy soldiers had been driven all the way into the fortress. Her reinforcements were fanning out, trying to secure the grounds while the marines worked on finding a way into the building. "Cracker?"

"See if you can beat the colonel," Jasmine said. It wasn't a race, but she wanted bragging rights. "Hurry!"

"Cracker alert," Meade snapped. "Detonation in five…four…three…"

Jasmine's visor darkened automatically as, just for a handful of seconds, the world went a brilliant white. The cracker wasn't *quite* a backpack nuke, but it was certainly powerful enough to pass for one. If it hadn't been designed to funnel the blast into its target, the explosion would have scorched the roof and wiped out the entire platoon. As it was…

"The rooftop has melted," Colonel Stalker said. He sounded pleased. "We're going in…now."

Jasmine nodded. It was time to trigger *their* cracker. "Thomas?"

"We're ready," Stewart said. "Cracker alert…twenty seconds."

Jasmine took cover, rolling over to protect her eyes. Her suit screamed warnings as the cracker detonated…she hoped - prayed - that the rebel troops had followed orders and hit the deck as soon as they heard the alert. Blindness could be cured, given time, but it might be *months* before the victims received any medical treatment. She dreaded to think how many people might have been wounded in the last twenty-four hours. Gritting her teeth, she rolled back over to look at the doorway. It was gone.

She stared, shocked into silence. Hullmetal was the strongest metal known to man, yet it was now a molten mass. The interior looked like a melted honeycomb, everything twisted out of shape. Anyone on the far side hadn't stood a chance. They'd been vaporised before they even knew they were under attack. The remainder of the fortress was still intact, but it had lost its first line of defence. God alone knew how long it would take the defenders to muster yet another counterattack.

"Fuck," Stewart breathed.

Jasmine keyed her mouthpiece. There was no more time to waste. Admiral Singh was somewhere within the fortress, no doubt planning her final roll of the dice. She had to be stopped before it was too late.

"This is Platoon One," she said. "We're going in."

CHAPTER THIRTY-EIGHT

"They burned through the hullmetal," Rani said. "How?"

She stared at the wretched display, unable to believe her eyes. She was an experienced naval officer. She *knew* that hullmetal wasn't *completely* invulnerable. Hell, she knew that not *all* of the hull - or the fortress walls - could be wrapped in hullmetal. And yet, she'd believed the fortress invulnerable. She'd clearly been wrong.

"A baby nuke, perhaps, or a shaped plasma charge," Higgs said. He held his wristcom to his lips and spoke briefly into it, then looked at Rani. "The defenders have been hit hard. I'm rallying a counterattack, but it's only a matter of time."

Rani swallowed, hard. "We need to get out of here."

Higgs nodded. "Yes, Admiral," he said, gravely. "An escape tunnel would be very useful right now."

He keyed a command into the console, then passed Rani a jacket. Rani rose and donned it, thinking hard. Governor Brown, for better or worse, had designed the fortress as a completely self-contained unit. There were no hidden tunnels that could be used to escape, no way out save for the upper doors or the shuttlepad. And the enemy were already swarming through the chinks in the defences. She had no doubt it was only a matter of time before they had the fortress under control.

"The rest of you, stay here," Higgs said. "Surrender when the time comes."

Paula gasped. "Admiral, you can't leave us here," she said. "I..."

Higgs shot her. Paula's body hit the ground with an audible *thud*. Rani stared in shock, trying to comprehend what she'd seen. She'd killed before, but never at close quarters. An icon vanishing from the display didn't have the same impact as a lone person shot right in front of her eyes. Bradbury coughed, then froze as Higgs turned to look at him. The rest of the operators stayed as quiet as mice.

They can surrender, Rani told herself. *Paula was the only one who might be shot on sight.*

"Admiral, come on," Higgs said. "We need to move."

Rani took one last look at the control centre, then followed him out the door. His security squad fell in around them, weapons at the ready. They looked tough, but they weren't wearing combat armour. They'd be at a disadvantage when the shit hit the fan.

And if the enemy controls all the exits, she thought grimly, *we don't have a hope of getting out.*

She drew her pistol from her belt and held it in her hand, one finger toying with the safety. If nothing else, she was damned if she'd allow herself to be taken alive.

"They've got powerful disruptor fields up," Gwen reported, as Ed plunged into the yawning abyss. "The drones can't get very far into the building without losing their control links."

"Get them setting up a relay network," Ed ordered. The fortress was immense, larger than any building on Avalon. Even a handful of microscopic drones might make the difference between success or total failure. "And order Platoon Six to reinforce Platoon One."

He landed on the metal floor and looked around. The cracker had melted its way through several layers, leaving the fortress badly damaged. Governor Brown *hadn't* lined the *interior* of his fortress with hullmetal. There was no sign of any resistance, something that didn't surprise him. Anyone exposed to the heat would have been killed instantly, if not vaporised outright. The scorched walls bore mute witness to the sheer power of the cracker.

They'll be in the lower levels, he thought, as they crashed through a series of rooms. He thought they were offices, but it was hard to be sure. The damage wasn't so bad, the further they moved from the entrance, yet it was still staggering. Everything flammable had burst into flames, blazing brightly as he moved from room to room. His suit kept flashing up alerts, warning him that the air wasn't safe to breathe. *There'll be a panic room at the lower levels.*

"The guards must have pulled back," Gwen said.

"Yeah," Ed agreed. It would be nice to believe that they'd already killed all the guards, but he didn't dare take it for granted. "Find the way down..."

He cursed as red lights flared up in his display. Platoon Three had found the stairwell - and an enemy ambush. He snapped commands, ordering Platoon Two to reinforce, just as Platoon Three started hurling grenades down the stairs. The floor shook under his feet and the shooting stopped abruptly. And then there was another explosion.

"They rigged a plasma cannon to blow," Lieutenant Fellows said. "Waters is down, sir."

"Understood," Ed said. The combat suits were good, but they weren't invulnerable. Waters hadn't stood a chance. He pushed the thought aside, bitterly. There would be time to mourn later. "Keep moving."

"They're trying to slow us down, sir," Gwen said, as they blasted their way through a second ambush. The enemy knew the terrain better than the marines and worked hard to use it against them. "They're not trying to drive us out."

Ed nodded in grim agreement. Admiral Singh knew she was trapped. The only thing she could do was throw her people into the fray and hope for the best. Unless she *did* have an escape tunnel, after all... he cursed under his breath, silently promising himself that it *would* end. Admiral Singh would *not* have a third chance to gain supreme power. He would make sure of it, whatever it took. No shuttle would be allowed to leave the planet without being inspected and cleared for departure.

A sane opponent would be trying to surrender by now, he thought. *But she knows she cannot expect any mercy.*

He sighed, inwardly. There was nothing for it, but to keep going...

...And hope that - this time - the bitch was definitely trapped.

"They're in the upper levels, making their way down," Higgs muttered, as the small formation came to a halt. "I can't track the second group."

Rani nodded, feeling sweat trickling down her back. The fortress was supposed to be soundproofed, but she could hear shooting echoing down the passageways. Her wristcom keep flashing updates, each one warning that the enemy had made further progress into her fortress. She was running out of options...no, she *had* run out of options. Her only hope was to escape.

The lights flickered, then dimmed. Her wristcom bleeped up a final alert. The fortress's command network had failed. Rani ground her teeth, certain that Bradbury or one of the others had deactivated it. The fortress's datanet had been designed to survive much worse than rampaging enemy forces tearing their way through the building. A series of nuclear strikes wouldn't be enough to destroy it. And it was completely isolated from the rest of the planet's datanet.

Higgs caught her arm as his men opened the next set of doors. "We need to hurry," he said, grimly. "If they block us now, we're trapped."

Rani nodded. *And if we do make it out*, her thoughts mocked her, *we would still need to get to a shuttle to escape.*

Jasmine launched two grenades down the corridor, then hurled herself forwards as they detonated together. The blast smashed the enemy position, allowing the marines to take out the remainder of the guards before they recovered. Jasmine glanced in both directions - the enemy appeared to be retreating *further* into the fortress - then plunged onwards. The enemy couldn't be allowed time to set up more barricades.

"They're falling back," Stewart said.

Jasmine's earpiece buzzed. "Jazz, I've got local reinforcements plugging the hole," Meade said. "They're ready to flood the lower floors if necessary."

"It may be necessary," Jasmine said. The fortress was *huge*. All sixty marines were rattling around like peas in a pod. The microscopic recon drones were expanding their coverage, thankfully, but the enemy countermeasures were still effective. They didn't have anything like total saturation. "Can you hack their systems?"

"No," Meade said. "I've got a datalink, but the system is heavily secured. I think they have a rotating code-lock sequence based on random numbers and..."

"Keep working on it," Jasmine said, cutting Meade off. She didn't need a long barrage of technobabble to tell her that they'd have to clear the fortress the old-fashioned way. An enemy sniper appeared at the far end of the corridor. She shot him down without hesitation and hurried over his dead body. "Can you update the plans?"

"Not any further," Meade warned. "The fortress was designed by an idiot."

Some idiots can be very capable, Jasmine thought. The fortress wasn't very organised - or efficient - but she had to concede that the design *had* slowed their plunge into its innards. It didn't look as though the designers had bothered to include stairwells that ran from top to bottom. *And whoever designed it may have meant to do it too.*

Meade coughed. "I've noticed they're sending more troops towards you," she added. "They may be trying to cover for something."

"Like Singh's escape," Jasmine said.

She thought, fast. The gates were sealed, covered by local forces. Admiral Singh would be shot down like a dog if she showed her face there. And there were no tunnels, according to the locals. But Admiral Singh might just be trying to sneak out. How? One of the other exits would be her best bet, perhaps...

Admiral Singh won't be alone, Jasmine thought. She'd done close-protection duty during her stint on Han. *She'll have a team of bodyguards. How would they try to get her out?*

Her mind raced. *Not the rear exit*, she told herself. *That's too obvious. They'd go for one of the side exits. And we've had more attacks coming at us from the east.*

She tongued her mouthpiece. "Colonel, we're moving to cover the east side," she said. The locals didn't have a hope of breaking in, unless they used a cracker of their own. "The target might be going out that way."

"Understood," Colonel Stalker said. "We're moving in on the command centre now. Good luck."

"Now," Ed said.

There was a shattering explosion. The solid metal doors blasted inwards, revealing a giant command and control centre. Ed hurried forward, rifle at the ready. The men and women inside were standing against the far wall, their hands where he could see them. Clearly, they'd decided to surrender as quickly as possible. A dead body - a middle-aged woman - lay on the ground, blood leaking from her forehead. There was no sign of Admiral Singh.

He swept the room, matching names and faces to the files stored in his suit's database. A handful of senior officers, all part of Admiral Singh's inner circle; five younger operators, all clearly terrified. Ed didn't really blame them. The operators had nothing to fear from the marines, as long as they behaved themselves, but they knew what the *locals* would do. Ed had heard more than enough horrific reports to know that handing any prisoners over to the locals would be nothing more than execution by proxy.

"Contact your fleet," he ordered, once the room was secure. "Order it to surrender."

An older man - Commodore Bradbury, according to the files - stared at him wildly. "But..."

"You'll be taken into *our* custody if you behave," Ed told him. Bradbury might be dumped on a penal world - or turned into an indent - but he wouldn't be executed out of hand. "If you don't..."

Bradbury sagged. "Very well," he said. "I'll send the orders."

Ed nodded. "Where is she?"

"She left," a bitter voice said. Ed turned to see a young woman, leaning against the wall. "I...she just *left* us."

"I see," Ed said. "Tell me...are you really surprised?"

There was no answer. He hadn't expected one. Instead, he detailed marines to take the prisoners into custody and secure the enemy computer network. If they were lucky, Admiral Singh was still using it, allowing them to track her down easily. If not...Admiral Singh's fleet and the remaining loyalists were already receiving orders to surrender. She could run, she could hide...but she couldn't regain control of the planet. She'd never be a threat again.

And if she runs straight into local hands, he thought, *she'll be executed on the spot.*

Higgs swore. "Admiral, the main network has been subverted," he said. "I'm crashing it now."

Rani glanced down at her wristcom, then deactivated the device and dropped it on the floor. It was a danger now, even when powered down. The tiny monitoring chip would be more than enough to lead the enemy to her, now they had the computer network under their control. Higgs might not manage to crash the system before they locked him out...

The sound of shooting was growing louder. She gritted her teeth as they hurried on, picking their way through a maze of maintenance corridors. There was no way to know where the enemy were or what they were doing, let alone avoid them. She just hoped there was enough confusion outside for them to slip away into the streets, then make their way directly to the spaceport.

"We'll need to slip into the main corridors here," Higgs said. He stopped outside a solid metal hatch and glanced at his men. "Be ready - anyone not one of us is a potential enemy."

We might be shooting our own people, Rani thought. But it didn't matter. They'd betrayed her. They'd *all* betrayed her. *All that matters is getting out.*

The pistol felt slippery in her hand. But she held it tightly, bracing herself.

"Now," Higgs said. The hatch crashed open. "Move!"

Jasmine heard the sound as she slipped down the corridor towards the exit and forced herself to move faster. The enemy attacks had dropped off completely, suggesting…what? That they were running out of manpower or that they were hoping to make a break for it? The command datanet was down, spelling the end of the fight. Anyone left alive would know that the battle was over. The marines had won.

Not quite, she told herself. *Admiral Singh is still free.*

She rounded the corner and jerked up her weapon. Five men - no, *six* - moving with the easy precision of trained bodyguards, surrounding a tall dark-skinned woman. Jasmine had never laid eyes on Admiral Singh before, but she *knew* the enemy commander as surely as she knew her own name. The surge of sudden hatred she felt was overpowering. She could understand why Admiral Singh would want to seize power for herself, but not unleash a war that had already killed hundreds of thousands of innocent people.

"STOP," she barked. "THROW DOWN YOUR WEAPONS!"

Rani barely had a second to realise that they'd been caught before Higgs shoved her hard, sending her falling to the floor. She crawled forwards as her bodyguards started shooting, a brief splutter of fire that ended with their dead bodies falling around her. Rani glanced back and saw Higgs die, the marines running forward at terrifying speed. She rolled over, lifting her pistol, only to have it knocked out of her hand by an armoured gauntlet. A marine hauled her to her feet, searched her roughly and then wrapped a plastic tie around her hands. Rani kicked out, but it was futile. The armour was too strong.

"Got you," a voice said. "Hold still."

Rani saw the stunner. And then the world went black.

Jasmine looked down at Admiral Singh's limp body and shook her head, torn between relief that it was over and an odd kind of disappointment. The end of the war *was* a good thing, but...part of her knew she'd miss it. She'd been a marine for so long that she couldn't imagine a life outside the military. There would be other challenges, she told herself, firmly. Some of them wouldn't put so many lives at risk, too.

She tongued her mouthpiece. "Colonel, we have Singh," she said. "It's over."

"Very good," Colonel Stalker said. "Hold position. We'll escort you out once we have the entire building under control."

Jasmine nodded. Admiral Singh was *the* prize. Everyone would want her. Mouganthu and the other directors would want to kill her personally, while the Commonwealth would want to put her on trial on Avalon before sending her to her death. Corinthian, too, would have a claim on Admiral Singh's life. Or...Jasmine had the feeling that the diplomats were going to be very busy, sorting out just who had the right to execute the former admiral.

And there'll be a big crowd to witness the execution, she though, remembering the captured bandits on Avalon. They'd been publicly hung, just to make it clear that the rules were different now. The planetary council had been horrified, but the public had loved it. *We should sell tickets.*

She pushed the thought aside as more updates flashed up in her HUD. The fortress's remaining defenders had surrendered, the starships and orbital fortresses were being secured...the war was effectively over. Admiral Singh's reinforcements, in the end, had turned out to be nothing but drones. A trick, one that had backfired spectacularly. The remaining outposts - the fleets and garrisons - would have to be rounded up, but that wouldn't take too long. She just hoped that none of the enemy commanders decided to turn pirate.

"It's over," Stewart said, as Platoon Six appeared. "Now the *real* work begins."

Jasmine nodded, then picked Admiral Singh's limp body off the ground and slung it over her armoured shoulder. "We'll get her to the shuttles," she said. Admiral Singh felt slight, as if she was too small to have caused so much trouble. "And then we can relax."

"For now," Stewart said.

"For now," Jasmine agreed.

CHAPTER THIRTY-NINE

"It's time," Colonel Stalker said.

Rani rose, not bothering to offer any resistance as the marines cuffed her hands and shackled her feet. She'd never had any doubt of her eventual fate, after she'd woken up in a cell. The only real question had been just *who* would have the pleasure of executing her and now, it seemed, the question had been answered. She would die on Wolfbane, like so many others.

She felt numb as she shuffled out of the cell, as if she was past caring about her life. She'd done everything in her power to seize power for herself, only to realise - too late - that she had mounted a tiger. She had never believed she had a choice, not after her former superior had destroyed her career because she wouldn't give in to him. The universe was divided into victims and victimisers and, if she had to choose, she'd be a victimiser. It was unpleasant - she acknowledged as much - but it was safer. The meek and powerless did not inherit the universe.

The trial had been nothing more than a formality. She hadn't been permitted to speak, merely forced to listen to a long list of charges. Some of them had been laughable, but others had been deadly serious. She wouldn't have bothered to mount a defence if they *had* allowed her to speak, even when she'd been accused of rounding up young men and keeping them in a personal harem. There had been no hope of any other outcome, but death. *That* had been clear to her from the start. She was too great a symbol of the former regime to be allowed to live.

And besides, I couldn't have disproved most of the charges, she thought. She'd done terrible things to seize and hold power. *They didn't have to work to find me guilty.*

She glanced at Colonel Stalker, wondering what he was thinking. He'd been a loyal officer too, until he'd been sent into exile. The details were vague, but the broad outline was fairly clear. And Colonel Stalker had formed the Commonwealth...the Empire would consider that treason, if it was still around. She wondered, idly, why Colonel Stalker hadn't declared himself a new emperor instead. Didn't he realise that those who picked up power could *never* put it down?

Her legs weakened, suddenly. A marine put out a hand to help her, but she shrugged him off firmly. They'd injected her with all kinds of truth drugs over the last week, forcing her to divulge everything from her first day in the Imperial Navy to her thinking as the war came to an end. She'd told them everything, of course. The training she'd been given hadn't been enough, in the end, to keep them from worming their way around her conditioning and forcing her to talk. She didn't think she'd kept any secrets from them.

Not that it matters, she thought. *There's no hope of escape.*

She sighed. If she had any loyalists left, they were keeping a very low profile. The police had been slaughtered *en masse*, according to her guards; her senior officers had been taken into custody, while their juniors had pledged loyalty to the new regime. She wondered, absently, what had happened to Bradbury and Emma Foxglove. No doubt they'd find room for their talents in the new universe, if they hadn't already been executed. Emma had done enough to make her execution certain...

If they knew what she did, Rani thought. *And if they don't find her useful.*

The roar of the crowd grew louder as they reached the entrance and stepped into the bright sunlight. A giant mass of people were shouting and screaming at her, hurling all kinds of threats and obscenities; a row of armoured marines were keeping them from charging forward and lynching her, their armour glinting in the sunlight. Rani forced herself to stand tall and keep walking, shuffling up the steps to the gallows. A single noose hung down, waiting for her. She couldn't help thinking that she would have preferred to be shot.

A grim-faced man stood beside the noose, waiting for her. Rani held herself still as he measured it against her neck, then nodded to Colonel Stalker. The Colonel made a sign and the crowd fell silent. Rani felt a flicker of admiration, mixed with annoyance. Colonel Stalker had built a state of his own, too. The only real difference was that he had won the war.

"Admiral Rani Singh," Colonel Stalker said. "You have been found guilty of seventeen charges, ranging from taking power by force and launching an aggressive war to encouraging atrocities committed against both friendly and enemy civilians. It is the decision of the court that you will be executed for your crimes. Do you have anything you wish to say before we pass sentence?"

Rani hesitated, considering her words carefully. "Many years ago, it was made clear to me that the universe is red in tooth and claw," she said, simply. "Might makes right - practically, if not morally. Since that day, I worked hard to gain power so that I might protect myself from others. I did what I had to do to survive. That I lost..."

She shrugged. Colonel Stalker would understand, she suspected. The crowd, which was booing loudly, clearly did not. But then, that had always been the way. They'd cheered her when they'd thought she'd won a great victory, even while they'd hated her. They were weak. They didn't want to admit that she might be right. It would make them victims, permanently.

The hangman motioned her forward, then hung the noose around her neck. Rani felt cold, as if she'd passed beyond feeling. Death was behind her, waiting. The crowd fell silent, again, as someone rang a bell. Rani felt as though she should say something else, but nothing came to mind. She hadn't lied to them. She'd believed she needed power and she'd done everything necessary to take and *keep* power. How long would it be, she asked herself, before Colonel Stalker faced the same problem? Perhaps he was facing it already...

She dropped. Blackness.

"These are steep terms," Mouganthu said.

"Yes," Jasmine agreed. Colonel Stalker had dictated them, once the enemy fleet had been secured. She'd urged him to be harsher. Wolfbane was no longer in a good position to bargain. "But they're the best you're going to get."

She watched him scowl at the datapad. Wolfbane was a mess, thanks to the uprisings: the government had been gravely weakened, private armies were running large parts of the cities and *everyone* wanted a change. The corporations were still in control, for the moment, but no one expected that to last indefinitely. Mouganthu and the other directors had been weakened too. They might survive, if they started reforms, but she wouldn't care to bet on it. Their weapons had been knocked from their hands.

"You want us to surrender all our conquests," Mouganthu said. "And to refrain from rebuilding our mobile forces for the next ten years."

"Yes," Jasmine said. "But, at the same time, you don't have to be occupied, you don't have to pay reparations and…and you don't have to waste your resources trying to *keep* your conquests. You can concentrate on reforming your government and rebuilding your economy."

"Which isn't going to be easy," Mouganthu pointed out. "Half our workforce wants to decamp."

"A workforce consisting of conscripted immigrants," Jasmine countered. "Do you expect them to remain here?"

She shrugged. "You can offer to pay them better," she added. "You might get a few takers."

"Perhaps," Mouganthu said.

She didn't blame him for being leery, not really. Mouganthu and his fellows had been absolute masters of their corner of the universe for so long that they'd forgotten what it was like to compete. She had no doubt that removing the limitations on independent business would change Wolfbane, for better or worse. Mouganthu would adapt or his corporation would go the way of the dinosaurs. It wasn't as if he was in a bad position, either. He was the sole corporate director who was a genuine hero.

But he's still going to have to work on it, she thought wryly. *There won't be any more free lunches.*

Mouganthu keyed the datapad, signing his name. "There," he said. "It isn't *quite* an unconditional surrender, but it's pretty close."

"You have your independence," Jasmine said. "And you still have most of your industrial base. You're in a good position to dominate the sector. It isn't the end of the world."

She smiled, inwardly. There were people who'd argued that Wolfbane should be kicked - hard - when it was down. They'd urged Wolfbane to pay reparations to each and every occupied world, to surrender vast segments of their industrial base...even, perhaps, to give up control of everything outside its atmosphere. Colonel Stalker had argued against it, pointing out that Wolfbane's economy was a mess. They wouldn't be able to *pay* reparations, even at gunpoint. It would just make a resumption of the war inevitable, he'd said. And he'd carried the day.

"No, it isn't," Mouganthu agreed. "But it will not be easy, either."

"No," Jasmine said. "But worthwhile."

She took the datapad and rose. "Admiral Singh is gone," she said. "You can blame everything on her."

Mouganthu laughed. "I intend to," he said. "And we can bury everything with her too."

"So far, we've had over seventy *thousand* requests for uplift," Mandy said. Colonel Stalker nodded, curtly. "Roughly a third of those are conscripted immigrants, sir; the remainder are spacers who feel their talents will not be appreciated in the new Wolfbane."

"Or have something to hide," Colonel Stalker said. He shrugged. "Do we have enough lift capacity to take them all?"

"Barely," Mandy said. "Life support is going to be a pain in the ass. We've already commandeered half of the freighters in the system, just to help uplift everyone who wants to go. There will be others too, sir. Life in the new Wolfbane won't suit them."

"We will see," Colonel Stalker said. "And the enemy garrisons?"

"We heard back from a couple of systems," Mandy said. "They both surrendered without a fuss."

She smiled to herself. Admiral Singh had clearly not been inclined to promote officers who might be a threat to her. Her garrison commanders hadn't hesitated to surrender, when they'd learned the war was over. Mandy rather suspected the rest of the enemy systems would surrender too, save perhaps for a few squadrons. Rounding them all up - and repatriating the enemy soldiers to Wolfbane - would be a logistical nightmare.

But these are the problems of victory, she told herself, firmly. *The other side has it worse.*

"Very good," Colonel Stalker said. "Assign a squadron to remain within this system for the next three months, then prepare the remainder of the fleet to head home. We'll have to deal with the other problems later."

"Yes, sir," Mandy said.

She made a face. Avalon would have learned about the Battle of Titlark last week, if her calculations were correct. The council would know that Colonel Stalker had gambled, that he'd led the remainder of the task force to Wolfbane. And they'd say…they wouldn't know *what* to say. They'd be fretting until the courier boat reached Avalon, bearing the news of a great victory and the end of the war.

They won't be pleased the colonel ran off with the fleet, she thought. *But they'll be delighted that the war is over.*

"It was a bold plan, sir," she said. "And we won."

"We did," Colonel Stalker agreed. "And now we have to clean up after the war."

Mandy nodded. "We won," she said, again. "That's all that matters."

"I've been told you'll be staying here," Jasmine said, as she glanced into General Mark Haverford's office. "Are you sure?"

Mark nodded. "There's nothing for me on Avalon," he said. "Here, I can work to rebuild my homeworld."

"It will be difficult," Jasmine said. "Are you *sure*?"

"Yes," Mark said. "I choose to stay."

He didn't blame her for being sceptical. Wolfbane *was* in a mess. But the government *needed* a military commander with an unblemished - or at least reasonably clean - record and a genuinely good reputation. Defecting to the Commonwealth looked bad, but helping to overthrow Admiral Singh counteracted *that.* There were opportunities now for ambitious men, he knew. He had no intention of letting them pass.

"You might wind up being killed," Jasmine pointed out. "Or worse..."

"I know the risks," Mark assured her. "But what's my alternative? Staying on Avalon? I don't think there's anything for me there."

"Maybe not," Jasmine agreed. She shrugged. "I've been told that we'll be pulling out within the week. After that, you'll be on your own."

Mark winced, inwardly. The Commonwealth had handed over the orbital fortresses, but they'd flatly refused to return any of the captured starships. He didn't really blame them - it was what *he* would have done, if the situation had been reversed - yet it was a major problem he'd have to solve. Wolfbane was going to be vulnerable, even if her orbital defences had remained untouched. Sending out convoys without escorts would be asking for trouble. He had no doubt that pirates would come sneaking back into the sector now that Admiral Singh was dead.

And half the researchers want to go too, he thought, sourly. Professor Tobias Jameson - damn the man - and his staff had volunteered to go to Avalon. Their records had been destroyed, too. Recreating their work would take years, unless a copy turned up somewhere in the files. Admiral Singh had purged her private datacores before she'd been taken into custody. *That will put us years behind the Commonwealth.*

"I'll be fine," he said. "If nothing else, it *is* one hell of a challenge."

Jasmine smiled. "How true," she said.

She saluted, briskly. "Good luck," she said. "And I wish you the very best."

Mark nodded, returning the salute. He had no intention of allowing Wolfbane to collapse, let alone fall further behind the Commonwealth. Given time, the corporations could start to innovate again...and he'd be at the forefront of technological development. He had no intention of restarting the war, but he was damned if he would accept permanent subordination either. And he knew the corporations agreed with him on *that.*

He watched her go, then turned back to his work. There were thousands of little problems to handle, thousands of matters that demanded his personal attention…at least, until he managed to build a staff. And then…

His planet was a wreck. But his future seemed bright and full of promise.

She died well, Ed thought.

He'd seen hundreds of bandits and terrorists, or bullies and traitors, being marched to the scaffold and hung. They'd bragged of their willingness to face death, but when they'd seen the noose most of them had collapsed into snivelling puddles. They hadn't hesitated to send *others* to their deaths, yet when it came to dying themselves…Admiral Singh hadn't died poorly, he conceded. He'd give her that much, at least.

He sat in his cabin, mulling over her final words. The universe *was* red in tooth and claw - that much, he knew, was true. And might *did* make right…maybe not *right*, but it determined what *happened*. It didn't matter, in the final analysis, if it was a decision enforced by the local strongman or the police. The principle was the same. Might made right.

And yet, he knew there was something more. Strongmen ruled by dint of force alone. They lost their power when they lost their ability to project strength. Smarter strongmen set up institutions to give them some legitimacy, co-opting or suppressing other strongmen…yet, what of democracy? What *of* it, when the strong could subvert the entire process?

Ed had never been particularly loyal to *Earth*. It wasn't something he'd thought about, during his childhood. He'd been too focused on the fight for survival. And yet, he *was* loyal to the Marine Corps, to the *ideals* of Empire. He wasn't blind to their flaws - there was no such thing as a perfect system - but he was loyal. It was the institutions - and the institutional mindset - that mattered, not people. The system came first, granting legitimacy to those who played by the rules. Individual might meant nothing compared to the power of the state…

And so we have to keep people involved with the state, he mused. *Or the state will fly out of control.*

He understood Admiral Singh's problem, more than he cared to admit. She'd taken power by force. She had had no choice, but to use force to *keep* that power. Stepping down would prove lethal. But in a better society, people *wouldn't* seek revenge - or even to overturn the law - as long as they felt it had been handled fairly. And yet…how many people would believe it? Was Admiral Singh *right?* Was democracy just a veneer over barbarism?

The Empire fell because the people in power lost touch with the real world, he thought. He'd done everything in his power to make sure the Commonwealth never developed its own out-of-touch elite, but he knew that might not last. *Will we go the same way*?

He sighed. History told him that societies evolved. They changed… sometimes, they decayed. But the damage could be fixed, if people were willing to admit that there was a problem and do whatever it took to solve it. And then…

His wristcom bleeped. "Colonel," Mandy said. "We'll be departing in twenty minutes."

"Understood," Ed said. It was time to go home. Avalon *was* home now, to all intents and purposes. He never wanted to go back to Earth. "I'm on my way."

CHAPTER FORTY

"It has been my great honour to serve as your President," Gaby said. Her voice echoed around the council chamber. "And, for my last speech, I'd like to offer a little observation."

She paused, looking from face to face. "Right here, right now, we are having a peaceful transfer of power. Councillor Sampson won the greatest number of districts, making him the next President" - she paused as the audience began to clap - "and he will be inaugurated today. He will move into the official residence and start to grapple with the checks and balances worked into our government."

Ed nodded, slowly. Gaby had insisted on seeing out the rest of her term after the victory, although she'd come under intense pressure to step down after the Battle of Titlark. The councillors had not been amused that they'd been kept in the dark, although they would probably have overlooked it if Titlark had been a victory. He didn't blame them for fretting, not really. If he'd been defeated at Wolfbane, the Commonwealth might well have lost the war.

"The Empire did not handle transitions of power particularly well, if at all," she added. "A man in power *knew* he didn't dare lose it, if only because of the certainty of violent retribution from his victims. He'd abused his power badly, ensuring that his successors would do the same and *their* successors would continue the cycle. In the long term, the Grand Senate became full of people who were effectively aristocrats, completely isolated from the people they ruled and yet unwilling to change, because change would put their power at risk.

"We cannot afford to fall into the same trap. None of us can afford the development of a permanent political class, one that might - that *will* lose touch with reality. And a peaceful transfer of power is one of the keys to maintaining a *working* government."

She paused. "I was there when we hammered out the constitution," she said. "It was, in many ways, my first child. And now...we have to see how well it stands without me."

It will, Ed thought, as Gaby introduced President Sampson. *The public won't let it change too much. They've paid too high a price for their government.*

He sobered. He'd learnt a great deal of history over the past few decades, first from the Slaughterhouse OCS and then from Professor Caesius. It was never the first generation that threw away the fruits of victory. It was the second or the third, the one who had risen to maturity - and power - without understanding the price, without understanding why the system *had* to be maintained. He didn't want to let go, to let his child stand on its own two feet, yet he knew he had no choice. Remaining in control indefinitely would be just as bad as letting go too soon.

Afterwards, they met Jasmine and Emmanuel Alves outside the council chambers and went for lunch. "Colonel," Jasmine said. "Are you *really* going to take on the Badlands?"

"Someone has to," Ed said. He'd decided against naming the new Marine Training Centre after the Slaughterhouse. It would be something different, something *new*. A mixture, perhaps, of old *and* new. "It'll take at least a year or two to set up properly, then we'll be working out the bugs for years to come."

"And adding new technology and concepts," Jasmine agreed. She looked down at the table for a long moment. "Should I be thanking you for the promotion or cursing you?"

"A little of both, I think," Ed said. He'd nominated Jasmine to take over as the Commonwealth's senior uniformed officer. It wasn't a post she'd like, he knew, but she'd be good at it. He'd be worried about giving it to anyone who actually *wanted* it. "You'll be standing down in five years, if you last that long."

Jasmine pointed a finger at him. "You're leaving me with the task of organising the General Staff," she said, dryly. "*And* giving orders to people who used to outrank me."

"A common problem," Ed agreed. "But they'll all defer to your experience."

Gaby nodded in agreement. "You have a decent record," she said. "And you are a genuine war hero."

"Hah," Jasmine said.

Ed shot her an understanding look. The Commonwealth's military had always been an *ad hoc* organisation. The pressures of the war had made it impossible to conduct a proper reorganisation, let alone sort out the obligations each planet had to the alliance. Ed could easily see the network of treaties that made up the Commonwealth Charter splintering under the stresses and strains of peace. Only the grim awareness that hanging together was the only thing that would keep them from hanging separately would bind the Commonwealth together.

"Mandy will be on your side," he said. Mandy Caesius had taken over Home Fleet, allowing the former CO to take command of the border guard. "And others will be supporting you too."

"Just start churning out new marines," Jasmine said. She smiled, tiredly. "Mindy was complaining she wouldn't have a chance to go."

"She will, if she wants it," Ed said. "And so will the others."

"Too late for Meade," Jasmine said, quietly. "She handed in her resignation when we returned to Avalon. I think she's shipping out with the Trade Federation."

Ed winced. Meade - and the other Auxiliaries - had never quite got over the stigma of not being *quite* good enough to be marines. Some of them adapted well, some of them carried a chip on their shoulder for their entire career...and some of them just left. He silently wished Meade well, knowing there was nothing else he could do.

Jasmine looked at Gaby. "Are you *really* reopening your farm?"

"Yes," Gaby said. "It's quite some distance from Camelot."

"And quite close to the Badlands," Ed said, seriously. He looked at Douglas, sleeping in his buggy. "We'll see each other every night."

"I hope you do," Jasmine said. She glanced at Alves. "It's been a wild ride, hasn't it?"

Ed nodded, slowly. In some ways, it didn't *feel* like they'd only been on Avalon for seven years. Too much had changed, too fast. The Empire was gone and everything was still in flux. He dreaded to think of what might be happening closer to the core, where there were more industrial nodes, starships and military installations...and larger populations that needed to be fed. Earth was gone, if Admiral Singh's sources were to be believed. Who knew what had happened to the rest of the Core Worlds?

"Yeah," he said, finally. The Wolfbane War might be over, but the cynic in him knew that there were other wars to come. "It has."

He closed his eyes for a long moment, looking into the future. Avalon was booming and the rest of the Commonwealth wasn't far behind. Technology was advancing, slowly changing society as it filtered out of the labs and into the real world. A whole new universe was arising, like a phoenix, from the rubble of the old order. He'd helped build it, he'd helped shape it...now, it was on its own. And it would learn from the mistakes of the past. They would not be repeated.

We'll be making new mistakes instead, he thought.

"We should send a mission to the core," Jasmine said. "Find out what's going on before it stabs us in the back."

"That's something to discuss with President Sampson," Ed said. He *was* curious. The Commandant would still be alive, wouldn't he? Major-General Jeremy Damiani, Commandant of the Terran Marine Corps, had always struck him as too mean to die. And the Commandant *had* known that change was coming. He'd done everything in his power to prepare for the fall. "But he might not want to provoke trouble."

"He'll want to know the worst," Gaby said. "And if that means going and looking, he'll do it."

"Perhaps a covert recon mission," Jasmine said. She smiled. "The Trade Federation is already sending ships corewards, sir. Perhaps we could assist them."

"They may have destroyed themselves," Alves said. "There might be nothing left."

Ed shook his head. Earth was gone - and countless other worlds could be blasted from orbit - but he doubted the devastation had been *complete.* There were hundreds of thousands of asteroid settlements and small colonies that would probably have been left untouched by a civil war. But then, Avalon hadn't seen fleets of refugees fleeing the Core Worlds. God alone knew what was happening there.

Someone destroyed the Slaughterhouse, if the sources are to be believed, he mused. *Why?*

He sighed, inwardly. Admiral Singh wouldn't have been the *only* Imperial Navy officer with ambitions - and the wit to realise that the old order was starting to collapse. There would be others, nearer the core. And planetary governments, coming to think of it, who would see opportunity in chaos. No, there would be no peace. There would be war as the new leaders struggled to determine who would rebuild the new empire. Sooner or later, their wars would spread to Avalon.

A chill ran down his spine. "It's too much to hope for," he said. "We will find out what's happening there, sooner or later."

"Better we find out before they find us," Jasmine said. "We don't know who will win the struggle for the core."

Ed smiled. "No," he agreed. "And now *you* have to convince President Sampson to back a mission to the Core Worlds."

Jasmine nodded. "I will."

"Good luck," Gaby said. "Just remember to frame it in terms of how it will benefit the Commonwealth."

"We'll be heading out to the farm tonight, after dinner with Leo," Ed said. "Feel free to message me if you need advice, but…"

"Only if I *really* need advice," Jasmine said. Her lips quirked. They'd both been told that, back at the Slaughterhouse. "You'll probably hear from me, sir."

"We will see," Ed said.

He peered out the window, shaking his head in awe. Camelot seemed to have doubled in size - *again* - since the squadron had departed for Titlark and Wolfbane. The vast majority of the emigrants from Wolfbane had come straight to Avalon, some taking up jobs in the cities while others struggled to raise funds to return home. Avalon would have problems coping with such a large influx, he was sure. But there was land enough for everyone…

And a willingness to enforce the law, he thought. *We can hold the planet together.*

Jasmine finished her coffee. "I need to get back to the office," she said. "There's work to do."

"I know," Ed said. "Just remember to make sure that everyone rotates between a desk and active service."

"Definitely," Jasmine said. "Me as well, sir."

Ed nodded. "You as well."

He smiled. There was no danger of *Jasmine* forgetting the real world. She had too much experience to forget the practicalities. But she'd have to make sure the General Staff didn't run into problems. There was too great a chance of 'temporary' positions turning into permanent ones if she wasn't careful. Too many of the wrong type of officer fought to get behind a desk and stay there.

And it wouldn't be so bad if they just kept things running, he thought, sourly. *It's when they start issuing orders that we run into trouble.*

He wondered, suddenly, if *he* would ever return to the front lines. He'd written the rules carefully, very carefully. He wouldn't remain at the Badlands for more than two years, but afterwards? There was no way to know. The thought of retiring, of going to work on the farm and bring up his son, was tempting. And yet, he didn't want to leave the marines.

I'll find out, he thought. *Who knows what will happen next?*

Jasmine rose, saluting. "Thank you for everything, sir," she said. "*Semper Fi.*"

Ed returned the salute. "*Semper Fi!*"

The End

The Empire's Corps Will Return In:

THE PEN AND THE SWORD

Coming Soon!

AFTERWORD

"What this country needs is a short, victorious war to stem the tide of revolution."

-Vyacheslav von Plehve

"Enjoy the war while you can, because the peace will be terrible!"

- *Wehrmacht* joke, WW2

When I started drafting out the plot for *Wolf's Bane*, I came to a sad conclusion. This will be the last book (at least for the moment) focused on Colonel Edward Stalker and the Avalon Marines. The next set of books will return to the Core Worlds, picking up the story of Roland, Belinda, Glen and the remainder of the Terran Marines. Or at least that's the plan.

I hope you've enjoyed following the adventures of Stalker and his men. And if you liked this book - or *any* of my books - please leave a review.

One of the fundamental truths of human history is that wars are easy to start, but very hard to stop. (As the saying goes, it takes one to start a war and two to end it.) The delusion that a nation can fight a 'short victorious war' has damned countless nations to endless effusions of blood and treasure, if only because their target refuses to admit they have been beaten (if, of course, they *have* been beaten.) History is replete with stories of nations, kings and warlords who have charged into war, only to discover that achieving their aims isn't always enough to win the war.

Indeed, the key to winning a war - any war - is to convince the enemy that they have been beaten, that further defiance is useless. This is not as easy as it seems. The government - whatever form it takes - is often insulated from the effects of the war. It may be ruled by pragmatics smart enough to concede that the war is lost and should be abandoned until things look better, it may be pressured or overthrown by its population… or it may be fanatical (or desperate) enough to fight to the end. Calculating the exact degree of pressure necessary to convince a government to give up is not easy. Indeed, there are very few examples of limited, but decisive victory.

In 1939, for example, Adolf Hitler presented his demands to the Poles. On the surface, they appeared to be very limited. The Germans wanted control over the 'Polish Corridor' and very little else. They sounded reasonable enough - reasonable enough to make France and Britain reluctant to fight over the corridor - but they were actually lethal. German control over the Polish Corridor would have given them an unacceptable degree of control over Poland itself, as they would be in a position to cut off Polish trade through the Baltic whenever they felt like it. Even if Hitler had been a honourable man - and there was plenty of proof that he couldn't be trusted - the Poles had good reason to refuse. Their choice was simple. Fight in 1939 or fight in 1940, under far worse conditions.

Hitler believed that the Western Allies would not go to war. He was wrong. The war did not remain limited. Hitler was thus committed to an endless series of military campaigns, each one costly and yet undeceive. He could not drive either Britain or Russia (or later America) out of the war, therefore ensuring his eventual defeat.

At the same time, the Allies could not convince the Germans to give up *without* invading Germany and crushing the Nazis. There were no shortcuts to victory. (The insistence on unconditional surrender demoralised Germans who might otherwise have overthrown Hitler, as they would have caused chaos in the rear and perhaps shortened the war without any guarantee of better peace terms.) Hitler's utter refusal to contemplate defeat merely ensured the war would go on until he was removed from power and his government crushed.

In short, Hitler's 'short victorious war' sparked off a series of conflicts that continued until Germany was defeated. He underestimated his opponents and was thus unable to understand that he had forced them into a corner. They had to fight.

In 1982, the Argentinean Government invaded the Falkland Islands, calculating that Britain would grit its teeth and surrender. In doing so, they severely underestimated the British Government. Margaret Thatcher committed her country to recovering the islands. Worse, having assumed there wouldn't be war, the Argentinean Government made no real plans to defend the islands until it was far too late. Operating on a shoestring, the British were still able to outmatch the Argentineans and force them to surrender.

The British did have a number of advantages, it should be noted. But perhaps the single greatest advantage was that the war was fought for limited objectives. At no point did Thatcher intend to invade Argentina and overthrow the Junta, a task that would have been beyond Britain in any case. Britain's sole objective was to recover and secure the islands, ensuring that the Argentineans could not achieve *their* objectives. The combination of military defeat and popular outrage convinced the Junta to surrender, for now.

On one hand, Britain won a great victory. On the other, the victory did *not* convince Argentina that the Falklands were *definitely* British. The underlying causes of the war continue to bubble under the surface to the present day.

And that brings us to the War on Terror.

Invading Afghanistan - and later Iraq - was not necessarily a mistake. What *was* a mistake was going to war without a solid plan for overall victory *and* a willingness to pay the price necessary to win. Removing the Taliban from power and smashing Saddam's government was relatively straightforward, but it was not enough to reshape the region to make it impossible for terrorists and insurgents to operate. The US needed to build a new governing structure that would give the locals a stake in their country, thus limiting support for opposition forces. This was not done. Instead, the US smashed local governments without replacing them with anything acceptable to both the locals and the US. The net result was a power vacuum that allowed terrorism to thrive.

In order to win, one must *want* to win - and be willing to do whatever it takes *to* win. The image the US consistently presents is that it is *not* willing to pay any price, bear any burden, to eradicate the enemies of freedom and build a better world. In the Middle East, the US has managed the remarkable feat of being engaged for nearly five decades *without* establishing itself as a permanent power. The perception that the US is constantly on the verge of pulling out (and abandoning its local allies to their fate) undermines any US attempt to actually win the war. Its allies are constantly looking for escape routes and *not* committing themselves because they might be abandoned at any moment.

There is no easy path to victory. In the short run, we must show that we will not be cowed by terrorism. Because so many of our leaders *have* been cowed, either by the threat of terrorism, riots or being called racists, establishing this will not be easy. In the long run, we must work to weaken fanatical societies - and governments - and work to replace them with the rule of even-handed law. It is this, more than anything else, that will undermine our enemies and eventually discredit religious fundamentalism as a government.

History tells us that the only way to win is to either destroy the enemy or convince them to stop fighting. It does not matter that we do not *want* to fight. Our enemies are more than willing to fight - it only takes one to start a war - and we have to stand up to them. We have to convince our enemies that we *will* fight…

…Because the only alternative is surrender.

Christopher G. Nuttall
Edinburgh, 2017.